Steve Marr launches 1960 illegally up the East[...]
below. His year fast-tracks into the student prote[...]
and the all-white All Black trials. He and an anarchist prankster raid the visiting American nuclear submarine and the statue symbolising the British Empire and join in the Hastings Blossom Festival Riot. His appetite for sex, beer and rock 'n' roll swings from Eastbourne National Party to hippie star-gazer to left-wing lifestylers, sliding to backstreet abortion, the nascent drug culture and violent death. Never far away is an ex-cop minder with another agenda. Steve is at the shook-up start of the revolutionary sixties, shedding — for better and for worse — religious constraints and the cocoon of the welfare state.

Advance comments on this book:

'An entertaining, rollicking, visceral read for those who remember — and would rather forget — and those who are coming of age.'

Linda Niccol, award-winning screen and short fiction writer, and more recently, short film director.

'An existential blast from our pop culture past.'

Redmer Yska, author of *All Shook Up: The Flash Bodgie and the Rise of the New Zealand Teenager in the Fifties* and a new history of *Truth* newspaper.

'They say if you remember the sixties you weren't there. Well, McGill was, and he remembers it all—the names, the places, the events. Nostalgia has rarely been so entertaining.'

Roger Hall

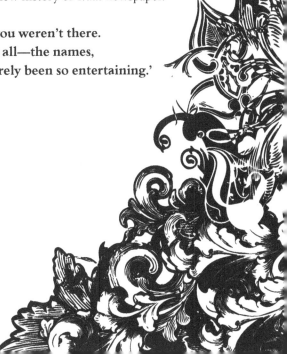

*Shaking* 1960

Dedicated to 1960 teacher trainees, especially
Merlene Cutten, painter,
David Mitchell, poet,
Peter Blizard, psychologist,
Mick 'Fox' Dennehy and his Phys-Ed crew;
our masters Pat Macaskill, Jack Shallcrass, et alia,
led by Liberal of Liberals Walter Scott;
those mighty left-wing extroverts Ian Forsyth and Ikar Lissienko.


'National Mum and Labour Dad'
                    James K. Baxter

'Against themselves men may be violent,
And their own lives or their own goods destroy …
And turn to weeping what was meant for joy.'
                    Dante Alighieri

'Him that I love, I wish to be free – even from me.'
                    Anne Spencer Morrow Lindbergh

Published by Silver Owl Press, 24 Aperahama St, Paekakariki 5034.
04 292 8226 / dkmcgill@xtra.co.nz / www.davidmcgill.co.nz

ISBN 978-0-9864519-2-8

Design and Typeset by Mission Hall Creative
Front and back cover photographs by Kate McGill

# Shaking 1960

David McGill

SILVER OWL PRESS

 **1**

'Hey, Elvis?'

I turned around and these two jokers with lopsided smirks stood with legs apart, thumbs hooked into the tops of black stovepipes seemingly glued to those absurd winklepickers. They were swaying about, and it wasn't just the wind, they were pissed. They were also at a loss, like many of the lads clustered around the climax of the Eastbourne Mardi Gras, the 22 teenage lasses parading in swimsuits. The 16-year-old Wellington blonde Elaine Miscall took the tiara, 40 guineas and a frock, my pick, Doreen Melville, 17, of Upper Hutt, was third, the shivering beauty queens were being covered up by swarming chaperones, the show was over. What next for two bodgie boys fit to burst?

I instinctively patted at my Brylcreemed quiff, which was not going to hold up in this wind. I squared the already too square padded shoulders of my green, tinsel-threaded long jacket which attracted the Elvis greeting, and stepped towards the greeters.

'Come on,' Liz said, tugging at my arm whilst clutching the silver alloy horse, the coconut, her glossy pink handbag and a stick of half-consumed candyfloss. It was too much to manage, even for a sporty lass. The wind lifted a corner of her cherry red and apple blossom white dress and at the same time teased her hairspray. She tried two opposing adjustments and the coconut dropped to the grass and rolled.

The smaller joker bent and picked it up.

'This yours?' he said, holding it out to her.

Liz eased to take it, he pulled it further away.

'Don't you want it?'

I fronted. 'Pick on girls, do you?'

'Not just girls,' he laughed. His mate laughed too.

'Mutt and Jeff?' I asked, looking from one to the other.

The tall guy presented a straggle of dirty blond hair and a lurid shirt the colour of cochineal, possibly intended to deflect attention from the livid neck patch of angry red pustules forming where others had gone before, a relief map detail of an intermittently active volcanic zone. His dead face was as spooky as a barn owl.

The short guy was all in black, his black leather jacket hooked by a finger over one shoulder of his too-tight black T-shirt. He was sporting a futile attempt to max his disadvantage with a greasy pompadour several tiers taller than mine. Marlon Brando's dwarf cousin, right down to the leer and fag at the lowest point of the curled lip. The T-shirt had the obligatory packet of fags tucked into the shoulder fold.

'Better still,' I proposed, 'the Two Stooges?'

'Steve,' Liz pleaded. 'Let it go.'

'Hey, Max?' the little guy said, nodding at the acrobats' pole. 'Reckon Elvis can climb?'

'Not if he's chicken, Gerry.'

Liz was staring hard at me. 'Forget it, Steve. Don't be stupid.'

'It's their gauntlet,' I said, eyeing the guy ropes that so far held the pole and its platform in place, if not steadily. Everybody knew the acrobats were not allowed to perform today, the wind so violent the radio announced NAC flights diverted to Paraparaumu. The acrobats might have been more miffed than relieved, given their exceptional skills. I had seen them on the first day, Colin and Clive, Australian father and son team. The father went first up the pole and on to the platform, the son followed him up like he was taking a stroll, climbed on his father and upended himself on his father's hands.

Today was different. No Ocker acrobatics. Eighty feet up, the platform was quivering and bucking about like a medieval catapult that had just released its iron ball. Time to put Elvis on the backburner and do my James Dean number. I did a quick sight check of the steel guy ropes and climbed over the thick white rope barrier.

'Pock, pockpockpock,' I chanted as I did hand-farting under my chicken-flapping arm, giving the two bodgies the old barnyard concerto. 'See you tuggers at the top.'

Liz was protesting as I jumped up on to the first ladder hold.

I took off, trying for the same effortless scamper of Ocker Junior. I heard more objections, male ones now. I ignored them, pausing about halfway to check on my challengers. Both had the saggy, off-white complexion of the Gear Meat Company sheep pelts I had several months of slinging around, which I reckoned put me in reasonable shape compared to them. They were on the first rungs, but not convincing. I headed for the top, blissfully aware of the increasing pitching about of the pole. I guess our policeman had a point about a ban on the acrobatics.

Hard to tell how puffed as opposed to wind-stressed I was when I slipped on to the platform. It was so turbulent, I couldn't hear myself think. I did feel good, especially when I peered below at the bodgies doing their banana peel tango.

Now the first faint second thoughts were intruding, that this was not such a great idea. I was trapped up here, there was nowhere to go. I'd done my Ed Hillary act, but there were no prizes for it, no knighthood when I descended. Dumb thing to do. Mum always said I was too impulsive for my own good.

I had a topside view of what awaited me as Constable Hogg pulled those two dorks sprawling off the base of the pole. It was like some kind of uneven all-in wrestling match, Hogg tussling with them surrounded by spectators crowding the rope barrier. Actually, it was more like one of those rodeo turns where a cowboy tackles a steer to the ground and hog-ties it, no pun intended. With the bodgies cuffed, Hogg was picking up the megaphone.

THIS IS YOUR FIRST AND LAST WARNING!

I heard Hogg distinctly. Obviously sound as well as heat rises. I looked about for an escape route. A parachute would have been handy. Nothing presented itself. Everybody was looking up at me. I had their undivided attention. It was what I wanted when I climbed the pole; now it was the last thing I welcomed. I needed divine intervention. Was it St Anthony you prayed to for losing yourself? He was the saint to go to for lost items. I had to do something, or it was going to be literally a case of a climb down and face the music and, worst of all, lose face in front of Liz. I could not face this. Face up, lose face, no face. I was getting antic, manic, mantic. Call me a frantic romantic.

I saw that the two bodgies were taking advantage of Hogg's sky watch and were attempting a tandem escape. Being cuffed together at a wrist apiece would not have stopped them, but some of the spectators had decided to do their civic duty and assist the law. Hogg dropped his mike and joined the mêlée. One of the bodgies was on the ground, I could see arms and boots flying about like one of the *Eagle* comic Terrible Twins sequences, PC 49's helmet toppling off his head as he hauled them back into the ring.

Now was my chance and I thanked St Anthony devoutly. I don't know why I hadn't thought of it first off, given how much I had admired Clive – or was it Colin? The young trapeze artist had flipped himself upright on the tower, bowed to the crowd, shaken dad's hand, then jumped into space. Some girl shrieked, many of us gasped. As we all gawped skyward, a pool of expectant salmon at crumb-feeding time, the junior acrobat caromed down the steel guy rope on a short hank of whatever, something metallic and designed for maximum presentation, sparks shearing off it like an oxyacetylene torch. Spectacular. It was better than Douglas Fairbanks in that pirate movie, when he slides down the sail on the handle of a Bowie knife. I might not be able to offer sparks, but I reckon I could replicate this gimmick for the punters below.

I shrugged off my Elvis jacket, wrapped it round the far guy rope and leaned out with both hands gripping the jacket. I threw back my head and delivered my best imitation of the radio Tarzan's ape call:

AHHH-EEE-YAHHHHH!

I launched myself over the rail and away into space, an informal version of the

Knocknagree Camp flying fox launch manoeuvre. For a few glorious seconds I was hurtling down the wire, but then the tearing of the jacket indicated I was about to find out what a freefall jump was going to feel like. I grabbed at the top of the jacket with one hand, trying to keep it on track, which caused me to sway and yaw like a P-class yacht in a Cook Strait southerly. I prayed frantically to any and all saints as I was wrenched this way and that, not at all a good copy of the descent through the air with the greatest of ease/that daring young man on the flying trapeze. I had to slap my other hand on to the top of the rapidly shredding jacket and endure the cloth burn, a secondary prayer that the fabric held and my hands did not make contact with the twisted wire rope.

I had no idea how far I had to go, what the impact would be, as I hurtled towards a blurred outline of tents. I could hear shrieking, which might have been spectators, or the wind, or me. My hands were on fire, but I was going too fast to know if they were being skinned or only enduring cloth burn. The shreds and tatters of my Elvis jacket lining were flicking me nastily about the eyes and ears like a ring of bullies whipping towels at the designated victim in the after-match shower. The roar of the elements was supplemented by blood and adrenaline mainstreaming around my skull.

The pain in my hands reached the level where all your nails have been removed with pliers and you beg to be allowed to tell the Nazi torturers everything. I flashed on Spencer Tracy in that mountain movie, holding the rope to save young brother Robert Wagner tumbling to his doom, the blood spurting through Spencer's hands, his face set in Mt Rushmore stone. No time for prayers, no time to resolve this, I was close to ignition, Fahrenheit 451 in the hands department.

The tents had to be a better potential option than hard grass. I let go of my sorry jacket and commended my body to its fate.

I bounced into glorious yielding fabric, somersaulting in discombobulated fashion like a circus clown on a trampoline, settling upside down into a collapsing tent, whence I tumbled hard on to grass. I was dazed and confused and waiting for a bolt of pain from a twisted or broken ankle or wrist. My first priority was to check my hands by the flickering light from tents and streetlights. My hands felt like the end of the first day at the Gear, after 13-hours of handling sheep pelts pickled in sulphuric acid. But they were only tender, I couldn't see any blood. God bless Elvis' tailor.

Slowly I eased to my feet, accepting helping hands, shaking my head as people asked if I was okay. Somebody was shouting to hold me.

A large young man reminiscent of that new Clutch Cargo cartoon character had pushed his way through the crowd around me. He sported a grey tweed jacket, underneath a blue shirt, dark trousers, clodhopper black O'B boots looming. Crew cut, eyes glinting like fragments of mica in a slab of granite, the oblong blunt structure of the proverbial brick shithouse. Just my luck, an off-duty cop happy to do his sworn duty.

'Impressive,' he said, grinning. 'Fun's over now, matey.'

He was overconfident, reaching out to take charge from my helpers. It was somewhat churlish, but I pulled on their helping hands until they were close, then I pushed them into Big Boy. I had time to note the grin evaporate before I was scooting around the collapsed tent, pushing apart the gathering onlookers.

'He went thataway!' I yelled, having seen enough Keystone Cops and other silent shorts to remember the invariable script accompanying the chase sequences, which seemed to be about all those crazy comedies had to offer. I couldn't help myself, I was pumping and fizzing like a shaken-up bottle of creaming soda.

People I passed looked baffled, as best I could judge in the darker areas behind the sideshows. I pelted for the trees, my yellow shirt unfortunately also containing glitter that would help identify my flight. It was some kind of nasty nylon fabric clinging in patches to my back and chest where my sweat was pooling.

Adrenaline was totally blotting out any sense. With a euphoric yelp, I sprinted away from all calls and commands, ducking through the tree line and doing my school gym vaulting horse act on the wooden fence. I enjoyed it so much I bounded across the road and repeated the fence ascent.

One foot landed on glass, going straight through into something squashy. Fortunately it was only a matter of a foot or 18 inches. I carefully stepped squelching out of the orbit of the broken frame, which looked by the light from an open back door to be an old window acting as some kind of cloche for what I would guess were marrows or squash. The exclamations of outrage accompanying the door opening were incoherent and possibly Italian, and the dark shape advancing was blocking the initial value of the light. I could see something being waved, at worst an axe, at best a broom. I didn't hang about, given that there were a number of people at the fence line offering aggressive advice.

'He's the one you want,' I shouted, pointing to his left, ducking around him, hurtling inside his house, slamming the door behind me.

Not such a good idea. Several naked bulbs of at least 150 watts apiece highlighted an old crone in masses of black clothes with a large black pan upraised, her expression leaving me in no doubt I was going to be whacked with it.

I was saved by the back door opening and more inchoate shouting. I ducked past her, just avoiding the pan smashing into the red rose-patterned wallpaper where I would have been if I had stayed put. I darted up the hallway, grabbed at the door handle and turned. It didn't open. I risked a glance back at the snowy-haired old chap inadvertently exposing himself as his pyjamas dropped in his attempt to push past his gabbling other half. I spotted the locking clip, pushed it with my thumb, the handle turned and I wrenched open the heavy door. I was through, pulling it back on its occupants, down a brick path between flower beds and out the gate and away like the scalded cat.

I scampered down the side street, virtually leapt in several seven-league strides across the beach road and through the informal pathway in the dunes. My best brown patent leather slip-ons filled with sand around and under my yellow socks as I scrabbled on a right vector off the path into the dunes and rampant marram grass.

I lay there panting and sweating and making hoarse sounds, not I guess unlike a cornered wild pig burrowing into a thicket. The mix of sand and mush in my left shoe was significantly unpleasant. On the bright side, the grass was high, the tickling bearable. If I didn't sneeze, I was home free. No sign of any pursuers. I could hear indignant voices from the coast road, but none of them were coming on to the beach.

I crawled through the dunes aiming for Rona Street, paused and sensed as much as heard, in counterpoint to the roaring wind and lapping waves, somebody moving down the pathway I had just vacated. I froze, blessing the wind whipping sand and marram grass around. Double back would be the smart move. I crabbed to the path, stood and saw a solid silhouette moving on to the beach. I crouched and returned to the road, stood and strolled calmly through the asphalt tennis courts as if not a care in the world, stoically telling myself to endure the discomfort of sand shifting between socks, squash and shoes.

I took the shrub-lined alley into the church grounds. There were still people out on the street. Some might recognise me. I needed cover.

There was a light coming through the side windows of the church. San Antonio Catholic church, which I reluctantly attended with my father, when I could not find an excuse he would accept. The church of Saint Anthony, bless his sandals, come to my rescue, so I would look more favourably on future visits to this sanctuary. I sat on the step, shook sand and gunk from my shoes, brushed at my socks, my neck rotating like a hungry owl. No pursuers. I tried the handle. It was open. I went in, shutting it quietly behind me.

The wind was still my friend, belting the small wooden church with all the abandon of a Christian Brother prodigally laying his leather strap into a classroom of kids. The noise masked the creaking of my progress from the hunched figure of the priest bent over the altar rail on his knees, muttering prayers no doubt intended for the salvation of his wayward parishioners. I marginally came into that category.

No lights on in the confessional. I carefully slipped into the penitent's booth and knelt with a blessed relief I had never known before in an imposed lifetime of confessing sins more of thought and word than any of the deeds I fantasised about.

 2

He pulled me out in a painful upper-arm grip, a finger across his smirk, a nod at the murmuring priest. I accepted his enforced invitation and him taking the lead, past the baptismal font and porch.

'Resourceful bloke, aren't you?'

I asked him what he wanted. I was assuming the worst, which was that I was under arrest for any number of misdemeanours. Like failing to stop when ordered by an officer of the law, wilful trespass on an area declared of danger to public safety, damage of festival structures and reckless disregard for the safety of the public. The collateral fallout would be my father's aggrieved lecture about my rash behaviour jeopardising any chance of me entering the profession he had chosen for me. Right now, I'd settle for PC Plod releasing my arm.

He obliged, without being asked, and offered me the remnants of my Elvis jacket. I took it carefully, keeping a weather eye on him while I planned to make another dash for it. Possession was nine-tenths of the law, and I could lie my way out of any repercussions.

He shook his head. 'Don't even think about it, Steve.'

I wasn't. I was wondering how he knew my name.

'I've seen you at Mass,' he explained. 'Down the back, with your father and the other late folk. Best not think about cutting a track.'

'Why not?' I growled, shrugging into my distressed jacket. The sleeves were more or less intact, but there were new vents in the sides and back through which the once pristine crimson lining fluttered like poorly stitched ribbons. The jacket did afford a modicum of protection from the wind, which was tossing the pohutukawas about, a loose branch thrashing around a streetlight. I didn't actually care why he thought I shouldn't, if you'll forgive the double negative, Brother Monahan. I didn't need to think through the implications of scarpering.

'Hello, father?' I said. The plod turned back to the presumed priestly source of my greeting at the entranceway of the church, long enough for me to take off. There was no shouting this time, and no pursuit. Fight was not a goer with this cop version of a Frankenstein creation, so flight was my better and indeed only option.

I forced myself to a walk, like everybody else on Muritai Road, the voices excitedly discussing the wee flurry of unplanned festival frolics. Nobody hailed me with any accusations about my role. The luck I had enjoyed at the fair was continuing. I guess nobody would have seen enough of me. It wasn't as if I was known locally, we'd only been here a matter of months. To boot, it was my first outing with the Elvis jacket.

Easy come, easy go, I thought as I turned into Makaro Street and casually peeled off the jacket and dropped it in the street bin. It would be my first point of denial, given it was the most obvious item witnesses would recall. The off-duty cop would need the jacket to make any case against its alleged owner.

Back on Marine Parade I stepped out, ignoring the discomfort of unliberated sand and squash remnants in one of my socks. I slipped in the side gate, noting the only light was coming from the sitting room facing the sea.

At the back door I accidentally stood on the silver horse, which succumbed to the flattened shape Tom is often reduced to in his endless attempts to catch Jerry. 'Jap Crap' was the term my war-defined father might have used for this feeble alloy. I bent to retrieve the battered beast and the coconut, entering as quietly as I could manage. I could hear the muffled squawking of some soprano pretending to be raped or strangled or stabbed, opera favouring extreme melodrama. I ducked down to my bedroom as the music paused.

The sitting room door opened. He had a sheaf of typed foolscap in his hands, held by one of those ginormous bulldog clips. He peered at me over his half-moons.

'Ah, son, there you are. Have you eaten? Your dinner's in the warmer.'

'Not to worry,' I mumbled, reaching for the bedroom doorhandle. 'We ate at the Mardi Gras.'

'What happened to your shirt?'

'Dunno. Nothing.'

'I see you won some, er, trinkets?'

'Yeah.' I could have mentioned 'Jap Crap', but I was too stuffed to bother winding him up.

'Your friend's mother rang.'

'Right oh. I'll just … be a tick.'

I shut the door. Hopefully his report would take priority over any inquisition. He always had questions, I always felt guilty, and this time I guess I had something to be guilty about.

He was tapping on the door.

'What?'

'Better ring her back.'

'I will.'

I dumped the horse and coconut on the floor, slumped down on my bed and waited. The soprano was protesting again. I opened my door carefully. No sign of him. I went down the hall to the wall phone, lifted the handle, got the dial tone and fingered 67712. The mother answered. I asked to speak to Liz. I was told she was not available.

'Can you leave her a message, Mrs Atkinson?'

'No, I don't think so. Don't ring again.' A pause. 'Thank you.'

'Did Liz say …?'

'Goodbye, Mr Marr.'

First the Elvis jacket, now Liz. I was striking out before I had got to first base. My earlier luck had ended. It was not to be my night.

I was on my way back down the hall when the phone rang. I grabbed it on the second ring.

'Liz?' I said, keeping a weather eye on the sitting room door. The soprano had not yet been executed.

'Is that her name?'

'Whadya want?'

'I've been chatting to Mr Hogg.'

The prick was dropping me in it. What else would I expect?

'Told him you got away.'

'Right,' I said.

'He was hoping I might know who you were.'

'Yeah?'

'Feel like a chat?'

'Do I have a choice?'

'Meet me outside. You'll hear me. Got another jacket?'

'Why?'

'Warmth.'

I looked up at my father. Shrugged. Told him I had to see a friend.

'Don't make it too late. Remember, church tomorrow.'

Back in my room I peeled off the shirt. Feeling shivery, I selected from my limited wardrobe my scarcely worn St Peters footy jersey and the black zip-up woollen jacket I'd bought off a joker at the Gear. Keans jeans and heavy woollen work socks to go with my battered old work boots completed my ensemble. I was getting used to this heavy-duty gear, ha ha. No more shivers. For now. The cop had something planned for me and it was not likely to be handing me a medal for my high slide and bunking off. Oh, shivers, as Mum used to say, when she meant, Oh, shit.

I was in the kitchen eating a burnt and greasy cold shoulder chop, when I heard the motorbike approaching. Bit hard not to, it was making one helluva racket outside the side gate, somebody revving it with total disregard for Katherine Mansfield's sedate seaside suburb.

The revs stopped, followed by a succession of spluttering gasps punctuated by loud explosions not unlike the day our school cadet unit was treated to some of the army engineer's bag of tricks. This had to be the mechanical equivalent of a serial farter with terminal emphysema. It duly died, just as I let myself out.

He was straddling the biggest motorbike I had seen. There was enough light to make out a duffel coat and his grin. He tossed his head behind him, then stood and jumped hard on the kick-start. The bike roared into life, responding to his throttling with a cacophony of harsh revving, several explosions and the dying wheezes of a severely distressed beast. He rose again, rammed the kick-start, revved furiously and this time kept the motor going. Again he tossed his head behind him. I climbed on the back, noting he had not changed out of his off-duty cop clobber.

He was jabbing with his foot, revving fit to wake the dead, yelling something I could not hear, then we surged forward, the front of the bike rising like a drag racer. I grabbed his duffel in time to avoid hurtling backwards off the bike. He got it back on two wheels and powered at the crossroad, again shouting something I couldn't hear.

I'd seen the newsreels of the Isle of Man races, the sidecar guy hanging horizontal a few inches from the road at a crazy speed. Our entire bike was heeled almost horizontal, and that included us, as he shot around the corner with the unnerving sound of the bike stand scraping the gutter inches beneath my feet. I clenched everything from and including breakfast entry to arsehole exit, praying the footrest would not emulate the stand. Then we were straightening up and roaring down the parade.

I released his coat and felt behind for the bar as he cranked up the gears, getting some reasonable speed. He had to downshift quick smart, without time for a wank, as Brissie boy Jelly Belly invariably said of any and all school prescriptions. This time I was prepared, and leaned with him, gripping the bar and tacking pretty well, if I say so myself. First time on the back of a motorbike, so far so good.

We did a shimmy through the side streets and flat tack out on to Muritai Road. The bus depot loomed ahead, a familiar sight from the times I'd been shaken awake by the driver after dropping off on the way back from another 15-hour Gear shift. The clown went straight through, hard on to the no-exit road, straight at the locked gate. This had to be some kind of test of my nerve. Okay, I was not going to blink.

He was not slowing, he was aiming at the gate. Shit oh dearie oh. I closed my eyes and again shut down all soft apertures.

We were bucking about on gravel, sliding sideways. I held on grimly, waiting for this lunatic to dump us both. I had to look. His arms were working the handlebars like he was riding an enraged bull by its horns, bouncing about on the seat, the rocks and sea looming. We swivelled and shook and he was changing gear and we were off along a track beside the sea, no street lights, only his weak headlamp and intermittent moonlight for guidance. The wind was buffeting the bike, every so often a shower of spray salting the experience. What was he trying to prove?

I knew this was the way to Pencarrow Lighthouse, but so what? Duane Eddy's *Forty Miles of Bad Road* came to mind.

Finally he juddered to a stop. He motioned for me to climb off. I did so, feeling as stiff as I did at the end of a day at the Gear. The bike was still turning over, with some revving from him, as he swung it round. He looked at me, grinning like a gargoyle. He was going to leave me here, I'd have to walk back, some kind of salutary lesson. No, he was getting off, holding the handlebars.

'Want to try it out?'

'Eh?'

'Come on. Character like you, it's got to be easy. Depress the clutch, see? Flick into gear with your toe. Rev her up, let out the clutch and you're away laughing.'

He was demonstrating as he walked the bike forward, bending to push the foot gear, letting out the hand clutch, jogging as he eased the throttle. He stopped, tapped it out of gear, said we'd swap places.

It looked possible, though I'd have preferred daylight and less wind for losing my driving virginity. I straddled the driver's seat, keeping one foot on the ground as I positioned my hands. He was up behind, waiting.

Okay, clutch in. The bike was screaming. I'd worked the throttle with my right hand instead of the clutch with my left. I let the throttle go and pulled in the clutch. By the weak back-lighting from the headlamp I got my foot under the gear lever and pushed up. It clicked in, I let out the clutch too fast and stalled. He'd kept his feet on the ground, which stopped the bike tipping over. He had the kick-start out.

Holding the bike, throttle open, I lifted myself and came down hard. The bike roared, the kick-start lived up to its ambiguous name by kicking back viciously into my leg. I lurched left, tipping the bike and both of us on to the gravel. The noise was that of 10,000 ruptured banshees, the smell a potent and not unpleasant mix of exhaust smoke and spilled oil and petrol, the wind whipping about and my mind in much the same random mode. I could feel his hand on mine, him yelling to let go. I relinquished my death grip on the throttle.

He bumped me aside and grabbed the bike, heaving it upright. He was looking my way, I couldn't see his expression, but he had kept the revs chattering. I got to my feet.

'Give's another go!' I shouted at him.

He nodded and I took charge of the handles, feeling the huge weight of the bike as I unsteadily climbed back on. He was up behind as I carefully declutched, engaged gear and revved a little as I let the clutch out. We jerked forward. Yo! We were moving.

I throttled up a bit more and we were bumping along. I pulled in the clutch, kicked the gear up and let the clutch out, throttling too hard and we lurched both sideways and forward, not unlike tacking in high wind. I could feel him tossed about behind me, his boots alternately carving gravel channels, which was some satisfaction. I eased the throttle, enjoying the sensation of being in a measure of control.

It was a slow ride back to the locked gate. I wasn't willing to go up another gear. Nor was I going to take whatever path he found between the gate and the rocks. I pulled in the clutch and bumped to a halt, my feet sliding through the loose gravel.

He whooped, shouted something about me up for it, and whacked me in the middle of the back, causing me to let go. The bike was going over again, but he got hold of it in time. He grunted he'd handle it now and we swapped. He revved up and jigged us round the gate and drove at a moderate speed back past the depot and down a deserted Muritai Road.

This time he went up to the village, left into Rimu Street, the Norfolk pines giant flanking sentries as he puttered past the shops and the cinema. He pulled up beside the old wharf. He switched off and pointed to the dunes beside the changing sheds.

I followed him out to the beach, where he sat down on a clump of marram grass.

'Look at that,' he said.

I joined him. The string of foreshore lights were a dull amber necklace, behind them the blurred lights of a hilly settlement marooned between a restless harbour and the black immensity of the turbulent night sky. There were occasional portals of clear space between scudding cloud, a gibbous moon and stars appearing and then gone behind fast-moving swirls, those ghost riders in the sky. The city looked vulnerable. One decent promised shake and it would slip into Cook Strait, never to be seen again.

'Thanks for the ride,' I said. 'What's next?'

He shook his head. 'Nothing.'

'You don't want something?'

He picked up a white driftwood twig, spread his left hand out on the sand, fingers apart. He jabbed the twig to the right of his thumb, then between thumb and forefinger, a jab back the free side of his thumb and between forefinger and middle finger, back outside the spread, on to next finger gap, back outside, between last two fingers. He started the cycle again with thumb and forefinger, a little faster working through the five gaps. His third cycle was faster again. On the fourth he jabbed a finger.

'Damn!'

He snapped the twig in half, tossed it away. He looked at me. 'Career interruptus.'

'Eh?'

'I tell Hogg, you get charged, no Teachers College.'

I repeated 'Eh?' like a retard. I couldn't figure why he had bothered to find out about me getting into Teachers College. It was scarcely of earth-quaking proportions in the scheme of police surveillance. Perhaps to my father, but I could care less. Still, the ride was odd. The whole blimmin day was odd. If I'd just not been such a show-off, if I'd taken Liz's advice, if, if, if, the story of my life. Spilt milk.

What did it matter why he was not dropping me in it? The main thing was he was not. Another crazy Doolan, not the first I'd met, not by a long chalk. Start with those loopy nuns and power-mad pisshead priests and the wankers at the back of the class at the convent, one of whom was yours truly. As for secondary school, don't let me get started.

Standing, he reached down, picked up a pipi shell and flicked it. Up it went like a tiny white kite, arcing on the wind until it disappeared.

'What was it like?'

'What?'

'Up there.'

'Fantastic.'

'Were you frightened?'

'I like heights. Maybe I was a bird in another life.'

This time he gave me the puzzled look.

'You're not going to tell Hogg?'

He stood there, contemplating the corrugated harbour chop. 'Nope.'

I couldn't figure what his game was.

'Aren't you obliged? Sworn or something?'

'I'm out of the cop shop.'

'Yeah?' I said uncertainly. 'Doesn't the oath …?"

I wasn't sure what I was trying to say. It was doctors took oaths. Cops swore something, like allegiance to Her Majesty. Let's face it, I didn't know what I was saying. A cop who was no longer a cop? So why did he dress like one?

'Dead end job, mate,' he grunted. 'Chasing clowns like you.'

'Why did you then, if you're no longer a cop?'

He looked at me. I couldn't see much, but I could see the grin. 'There's got to be more to life, Steve, than arresting drunks and petty thieves and the odd yahoo show-off. Wouldn't you say?'

I shrugged.

He stared out at the dark sea, one foot thumping into the sand. 'Look,' he growled. 'I tried the university of life. You know the spiel you get from the careers adviser, the majority of you lads are not cut out for tertiary education, there are many honourable jobs in the workplace, all labourers are worthy of their hire.'

'I didn't take much notice.'

He was nodding, a heel divoting sand. 'You get a visit from the police recruiter?'

My turn to shrug. We had, but I had been absent that day, due to an urgent appointment with a James Dean movie.

'The cops target the Catholic schools. Half the St Pats guys stuck their hands up. Half the First Fifteen, anyway. So I did. Dumb, eh?'

'I dunno,' I mumbled. 'We need cops,' I added feebly.

'Anyway, I'm out of it. Off to the real uni, try and prove to me mum I'm not a complete drongo. Might see you there, eh?'

'Eh?' I echoed gormlessly.

'A man's reach,' he said, leaning over to punch me hard on the upper arm, 'should exceed his grasp.'

I rocked back, rubbing my arm, protesting pathetically, 'That hurt.'

He was getting to his feet, pulling from under his coat some kind of a hook. I crabbed away, fearing he was not just a few kumara short of a hangi, he was also pathologically insane and aiming to dish out his own ex-cop idea of law enforcement. I cringed as he raised the hook above his head. He swivelled towards the sea, stood with his legs apart.

'No more fuckin rules!' he yelled, punching the shiny hook heavenwards. I saw the end of it glint against the black sky. I was readying to do a sideways scuttle if he swung my way, my life could depend on it.

No worries, he was only funny peculiar. The hook still aloft, he threw his head further back and delivered a barking mad 'Arrk! Arrk! Arrk!'

Was this his version of a Tarzan rebel jungle yell? It sounded more like the demented squawking of the seagull that always patrols closest to your al fresco fish and chips, its head down as it angrily caws at its agitated mates to keep back while it gets first dibs at any spare bits you might toss their way. Unpleasant, but harmless.

I still wasn't sure about this clown's intentions, so I was tensing to take off. No need. His crazy cries done, he swung round and headed back through the dunes. I got awkwardly to my feet.

'Hey? Hang on!'

He paused, but didn't turn.

'You know my name. What's yours?'

'Gull,' I think he said, and he was gone.

I stood there feeling stupid. What was all that about? Why give me a bike ride instead of what he was supposed to do, inform Hogg I was the third miscreant? And how come he thought he might see me at uni? I was off to Teachers College at my father's behest.

My problem was I had no idea what I wanted to do. Mum's death had numbed me, I'd got through School Cert and UE on automatic pilot, a zombie in an indolent seventh form, the student of the living dead. The other kids eventually laid off poking the borax when the victim didn't respond, the Christian Brothers forswore wasting their sarcasm on deaf ears. I was left to rot, which was fine with me.

The shift from Auckland seemed to suit Dad, so far it had not done a lot for me. I did know one thing for sure, I couldn't take manual labour at the Gear for much longer. The money was good but the job was mind-bogglingly boring and repetitive. I did not fancy a lifetime of manual labour, full stop. I understood why the guys kept pushing over each others' piles of pelts, why the slaughtermen let a sheep go, it was a break in the deadly routine. They got a laugh out of it, or a fight, anything to ease the drudgery.

Even so, when my father said he had organised an interview with the panel for Teachers College entry I had been appalled. Teaching! I loathed school. In my initial hostility I repeated the old mantra: Those who can, do; those who can't, teach. My father did not rise to that. He said I had to do something, I seemed to have some aptitude for English. I had a few weeks to decide. He had already made it clear he was not financing me through university, where he suspected I would treat it much the way I had school, something to be avoided wherever possible. I retreated to my room and put on Elvis' Golden Hits on the new turntable financed by my first Gear pay packet.

He left me to stew for a few weeks. I endured the Chinese water torture pace of Gear pelt stacking, with stacks of time, pun intended, to ponder my options. Could I bear manual labour to pay my way through varsity? Did I want to go anyway? I had no answers.

But solutions, like God allegedly, work in mysterious ways. I'd met Liz when she woke me up on the bus one night. The least I could do was walk her back the few streets to her house. We got talking, I answered her enquiry about whether I played tennis with a false affirmative. It had the desired effect, of trotting out with her, albeit too often for my taste, to the tennis club.

It was a Sunday afternoon, I was resting in the pavilion after another underwhelming display, given I loathed all organised sport, when one of Liz's tennis mates mentioned there were five girls for every boy at T Coll. Bingo! The old cartoon light bulb switched on like a halo of light and understanding. I thought, why not?

So I did the interview. And blew it. I cocked up a snaky question, answering Hemingway when the snowy-haired old geezer in charge said it was not the answer they wanted, some poet done it. I knew I was right and said so, argued that Hemingway did write *For Whom the Bell Tolls*. The panel exchanged looks, Old Snow turned his gimlet eyes back on me, repeated the poet done, which I came to know later was the poet Donne. At the time I thought I was better off avoiding such a peculiar fellow. I figured I'd just had my first and last lesson about answering back and had thus blown my chance at five girls for every boy.

But no, a week later I got a letter of acceptance. It was months afterwards, one of the other male entrants informed that they had so few male applicants for the sissy job of primary school teaching that you'd have to be a Purple People Eater with a voice like the Chipmunks for a male not to be accepted at Teachers College. I resisted the urge to say he pretty much qualified.

So, I was destined it seemed to become a teacher. I doubted at the time I'd see any more of this cop, or ex-cop. On second thoughts, he didn't deserve to be compared to a cartoon character. More like that heavy-duty Hollywood he-man Clark Gable. But still, one weird guy. I'm sure he said his name was Gull.

 **3**

Gull did see me at university, before classes had begun for the year. We were at the university sports ground with the Physical Education master Pat Shields lining us up for sprints. It was a spectacular blue sky day, not a whisper of the usual wind. We had had a morning in the Teachers College hall banging out rhythms on bongo drums with music master Tommy Young. I'd managed to chat to one large-bosomed lass over the bongos, and there was potential for rapport there. If not, there were two or three other girls well worth engaging. This arvo, we got to stretch the legs, but not in mixed company.

For some daft regulatory reason, girls and boys did not compete together, practice perhaps for the rule about a teacher not permitted within 18 inches of a pupil of the opposite sex. I would have been happy on handicap, giving some of the women a head start, not trying too hard to catch them. Instead, boys-only sprints, and the paucity of boys had been resolved by roping in some Asians here on the Colombo Plan scholarships, which my father went on about as a desirable bridge to something or other. One of the Asians was a sprint champ, so one could say we had an international competitive flavour added to the occasion.

There had been preliminary run-offs, the first four going through to the next round. I'd come in fourth in what you might call a canter. Eight of us to sprint the 50-yard dash down these white lines. The Phys-Ed lads and lasses were all baying for Fox, a dirty big joker lined up at the far side from me. The Asian champ, a skinny and intense kid, was positioned alongside Fox, hence the Phys-Ed team barracking for Fox, whom they had already announced more than once was going to be the next All Black winger.

'On your marks,' Pat called. We crouched, one foot braced for take-off, fingers spread on the turf for maximum thrust. I was used to this from St Peters. The running spikes sported by Fox and the Asian champ gave them an unfair advantage and me an incentive. I hadn't brought my spikes with me, had not thought I'd ever need them again.

'Get set.'

Everybody was tensed for the 'Go' call, but a red-haired guy next to me broke early. Fox went with him. Pat blew his whistle several times.

When we were settled again, Pat called for marks. I could see from the corner of my eye the red-head quivering. I was fine, nothing to lose, no starter's gun to scare the shit out of everybody.

'Go!'

I got a good start, red-head did not. The Asian and Fox were ahead of me, duelling it out with each other, casting glances at what they both assumed was their main opposition. A mistake. They were locked in what might have been a dead heat, but I darted past them at the last second. I could hear the booing from the Fox camp. Both the Asian and Fox were looking startled, like they had been finessed on a full house by a Royal flush – or is it the other way round? Anyway, lots of huffing and puffing, bent-over figures, not the popular outcome.

'A fluke,' I said, smiling. 'You jokers were too busy watching each other.'

'Fair enough,' Fox said, shaking my hand. 'Bit early in the season for me. You play rugby?'

I shook my head. 'Nah,' I said. 'Not into team games.'

'Just as well for me,' Fox said generously, before he was surrounded by the acolytes reassuring him that he'd peg me in the rematch, he was too fast not to. The Asian champ was engaged in his own language with his group. Pat was asking me something about what sport I liked, when I spotted this guy in a duffel coat watching from the rise. He looked familiar. Big guy like Fox, arguably bigger. It was the change of hair fooled me, or, rather, the fact it had grown out on top and around his face in a developing beard. Add in the camouflage change from cop neutral to the tailored chocolate pinstripe cords and leather boots that were a match for the dark brown duffel. It was Gull. He beckoned to me.

I asked Pat to excuse me and jogged to meet him.

'Glad I didn't try catching you,' he said, shaking hands, the grin splitting the red-brown moustache and the darker brown beard.

'I used to sprint,' I said.

'I can see that. Do any good?'

'Second in the Intercollegiates. I hate second. Gave up.'

He nodded. 'You beat Fox. I gave up on Marist St Pats when he arrived. Same reason as you.'

'How come you're here? Varsity hasn't started, has it?'

He tapped one side of his lopsided nose. 'Advance planning. You free for a beer?'

I wasn't, we had to play softball for an hour. He said he'd see me after it. Dead boring game. I got a home run, after Fox whacked the ball down the bank and all bases walked it. By then the Fox supporters were back in full admiring roar, my upsetting of the sprint expectation relegated to an aberration. I changed into the unofficial Training College male uniform of sweat shirt, cords, desert boots and mandatory duffel coat. Mine was a cakky colour a few shades lighter than the rough khaki uniforms of the school cadets. The toggles were plain wood. Gull, when I joined him, sported the fancy version, cashmere soft wool and toggles made from what looked like boars' teeth.

On the way down and across the park to the cable car stop, I asked how come he had the clever gear and he said he wanted to blend in with his fellow law students. Next I asked him what his name was. James Patrick Flynn, he had acquired the nickname Gull when he went to work on the wharf.

'How come?'

He pointed and we dashed for the descending cable car, both leaping on to the outside, side-on seats. Great view of the city and harbour, the big white Kelburn fountain in the foreground, and then we were in the first tunnel, the car swaying and screeching as the driver in the cab above our heads applied the big handbrakes for the next stop.

When the noise eased, he told me he'd taken a temporary job on the wharf after he left the Force. It didn't mean he stopped drinking with some of his former colleagues, and they called him 'Seagull', because that was the name for a casual wharf worker. Lots of students did the job.

'Cull to Gull?'

'Yeah, cop thing, *reductio ad absurdum* where I'm go …,' he said, his voice lost in the screeching seagull machinery and swaying and clattering, and we were in the next dark, noisy tunnel.

Gull led the way through the crowd in Cable Car Lane, out and right to Plimmers Steps, in the side entrance of Barretts. He got a jug from the barman and two glasses and we stood against a tall corner table. Gull poured.

'Down the hatch,' he said, tapping my glass. We both drained the first, he refilled, smacking his lips. It was just after four, so fairly empty before the after-work rush. There were a few dedicated drinkers nursing glasses and consulting *Best Bets*.

'Been here?' he asked.

I nodded.

'Encountered the boys in blue?'

I nodded again.

'You'll be right with me,' he said.

I'd been in once with a few of the few men in our English group and the Fox Phys-Ed team, most of them looking even more callow than I did. The cops made their ponderous entrance, a sergeant and a constable who was probably no older than us. We had briefed each other about standing our ground, drinking steadily, not showing nervousness. At the first Assembly we had been warned by the principal Walter Scott — the snowy-haired panel leader who caught me out with the poet Donne — that if we were caught drinking under-age in the pub and we were prosecuted, it meant instant dismissal from college. The Phys-Ed guys, who seemed invariably to know the important info, assured the post-Assembly crowd that old Scotty always went in to bat for his students and usually got the cops to lay off charging and ruining promising young careers. So what were we waiting for?

Barretts was first port of call on the first day, chosen because it was the nearest pub. Once we had downed a few glasses, we pretty much stopped being nervous, until the police sergeant and constable marched into our midst. They eyed us, we eyed our beers, I mentally offered up a prayer to the patron saint of lost causes. It worked. They proceeded through the side door.

'Cheers,' I said, gulping a little more of the old Dutch courage. 'Get the hook on the wharf?'

Gull grinned. 'You got it. This anarchist joker, Bill Dwyer, he carries one. He needed it, for protection.'

'I thought they carried bombs?'

Gull wasn't grinning. 'Dwyer got up a few noses. Union push didn't take kindly to his motions of no confidence in them.'

I had a notion what he was talking about. My father had these committee meetings with the National Party, he talked of passing motions. I'd asked if they suffered constipation. Dad didn't make jokes, and did not appreciate the level of mine. I figured Gull would, so I asked if the union was bound up in its own red tape. I got a grin out of him.

'Union no sense of humour?'

'Not a lot,' Gull said, draining his glass, passing me the empty jug. 'Root-faced bunch, could be improved with a bomb under them.'

I took the jug over to the bar, feeling the familiar cold band tightening around my skull, idly wondering what more surprises Gull would spring. Did he share Dwyer's views as well as his wool hook? Not exactly law-abiding sentiments. What was his game? Studying law, rejecting law enforcement? Gull was getting curiouser and curiouser. I plonked the jug down and said a trifle loudly: 'Fill her up.'

The barman, a middle-aged chap with a concave chest and a complexion that matched his grey cardigan, silently filled the jug. He slapped down my change and went back to his literary geegees.

As I filled Gull's glass, I asked him why he had the hook, had he needed protection too?

'Yep,' he said. 'How's teaching?'

'Apart from sprinting and softball? We pound bongo drums. Macaskill cracks puns like there's no tomorrow. He's our English master.'

'Sounds exciting.'

I shrugged. 'I might be doing varsity, like you thought. You're law full-time then?'

'What else?' he said, grinning again.

I wasn't grinning. The same sergeant, and a new sidekick, I think; last time I'd not spent much time looking at the cops. Last time there had been a scrum of patrons. This time there was nowhere to hide. The room had shrunk to its true bleak proportions, a rectangular box with a wooden floor and a bar, a few photos on the walls of footy players and racehorses, otherwise no graces and nowhere near enough people insulation. There was no safety with no crowd. The cops were coming straight at us. Talking of root-faced, the sergeant met that description to the Mt Rushmore degree. He eyed me up and down.

'Sarge.'

'Gull,' he acknowledged, not taking his eyes off me. The Phys-Ed crowd's wisdom was to keep chugging. I picked up my glass, spilling some, my eyes locked on the sergeant's as if hypnotised. I managed a sip, which went down the wrong way, causing me to splutter. Gull bashed me on the back, saying he couldn't take me anywhere. The sergeant gave him a curt nod and walked out, his constable aiming to give me the evil eye as he marched after him. I gulped beer, clearing the pathway.

'Not to worry,' Gull winked. 'Reckon that young cop was under-age too.'

'Guess I still get to teach.'

'Guess you do.'

'I appreciate you – y'know — knowing them.'

'No charge. I wouldn't have asked you for a beer if I didn't think you could handle it.'

'I'm not sure I did.'

'She's jake. Drink up.'

I could feel my stomach beginning to do the old Hauraki Gulf polka. 'I've had enough for now.'

'Nah. One for the road. Then we'll catch a feed, eh? I'm so hungry I could eat the arse out of a low-flying duck.'

By the time I'd drunk my share of the next jug, my stomach and head were moving outside the Gulf into stormy weather.

'Come on,' he said. 'Time to eat. Speaking of duck, we can try the old Peking variety – though it might be cat, eh?'

He might have winked, I couldn't be sure. I reeled after him, out the front and up Willis Street. A glance in the bookshop window and I was seeing double Penguins, two *Daring Young Man on the Flying Trapeze*, two *On the Road*, two *Women in Love*. I started to say that I thought Macaskill's list of 100 best books included these, but the rising tide of beer suds caused me to clamp my mouth shut and stagger after Gull.

We crossed the road past the George and the billiard saloon and into the Nanking.

The place was as forlorn as you get with old wooden floor and off-white walls. Apart from the flickering neon restaurant sign, the only decorations were a few fly-spotted Chinese lanterns dangling inside the window. It was as empty of patronage as my belly, if you don't count the liquid swirling around. I blinked from the excessive lighting of half a dozen naked bulbs. We had a choice of any of the small tables with bright red, oily tablecloths. The wooden chairs were painted a sickly hospital green, bad enough to cause a stomach spasm. Gull motioned to the nearest table, scraping out a chair.

Gull called out loudly for two chicken 'flied lice' to the rapidly advancing little Chinese man smiling blankly and wiping his hands down a greasy black apron.

'I'll fix this,' Gull said. 'Seeing as I got you pissy-eyed. Have some bread while you're waiting.'

Gull lifted two of the slices of white bread off the stacked plate, shook the bottle of soy sauce over them. He handed the basic sandwich to me.

'You need the salt as well,' he said. I wasn't arguing. The black-stained bread looked like it had been rescued from a grease trap, but it was delicious. I liked the soy sauce so much I doused the chicken fried rice the instant it was deposited by the scurrying waiter.

It was better than two helpings of hangi. And the bread was manna from heaven. We polished off one plateful and Gull ordered another by holding up the empty side plate. Our waiter disappeared with it and was back in a flash with the other half of the sliced loaf. There was enough fatty residue rimming the bowl to scrape the bread around it. Dad might have had mixed feelings, concerned at my table manners, proud that I was fulfilling his philosophy of 'Waste not, want not.'

By now I was feeling as full as a Catholic school. I said it was the first decent meal I'd had in ages, cooking at home was pathetic. Gull looked interested, asked if we did it ourselves and if so, why didn't we get a home help? I shrugged, not having an answer to hand. The subject had never come up, Dad handled things, or tried to. Best meal of the week was invariably Friday, when we got fish and chips.

'Think about it,' Gull said as he snapped his fingers. Our waiter was there, quick as a genie. Gull ordered coffee. His wish was the waiter's command. The coffees arrived, the Brissie Boy's subordinate clause best left unsaid, the contents of the thick white railway cups had a gelatinous, milky look. I shook half the sugar dispenser into mine as a barrier to tasting the brew and made the mistake of gulping, the scalding mix burning a new pathway down my gullet. Gull was banging my back again as I coughed and spluttered and waited out the fire in my belly.

'Should've warned you,' he said, grinning, not the least contrite. 'Tell us about teaching. What are the lecturers like?'

'They call them masters,' I gurgled.

'Any radicals?'

I must have looked puzzled. 'You know, like you get at uni? Lefties, spouting revolution.'

I had to think about that. At least the searing milk and coffee essence had sharpened my focus somewhat. 'Does free love count?'

Gull nodded.

'This English master Anton Vogt. They say he's into free love. I couldn't say. All I've heard him do is spout poetry at full volume.'

'I thought they were pretty political up there?'

'I suppose. You could say Shallcrass is.'

Gull leaned forward, carefully sipping his coffee. 'How's that?'

'He played us this Canadian record. He said it was a satire about this ranting and raving senator in the States, Mac somebody.'

'McCarthy.'

'That's the one. You know about him?'

'Catholic. Weeds out the Commies in positions of power. Hollywood even.'

'Yeah? Too late for James Dean, eh?'

'Come again?'

'Dead rebel.'

'Right. This Shallcrass bird, didn't like Senator McCarthy?'

I shrugged. 'He just played the record. Told us to make our own judgments. It reminded me of Tom Lehrer, without the laughs.'

'Right oh. So what other masters you got?'

'Nutty music guy, the one who likes bongo drums. A few education masters, as you'd expect. There's a German woman teaches pottery. She's in another area from me. I've heard it said this geography master is an atheist. Or was it a socialist? But he's in the furthest area. I saw him at Assembly, wears a mustard cardigan. I reckon some of the students have more to say about politics. At least, the one who runs a coffee bar.'

'You know which one?'

'Symposium. What's with all the questions?'

Gull grinned. 'Idle curiosity. Man, those Chinks do a good feed. We need to walk it off. Go a few frames next door?'

I agreed, not ready to confess I'd only played half a dozen times. Gull left a shilling in the saucer, scraped the chair and went over to the till.

'Good tucker, mate,' he said to the smiling waiter, who nodded vigorously as Gull paid him.

We entered the St George billiard saloon, half an acre of full-size green baize tables occupied by shadowy figures bending beneath the low, wide tin shades that lit up the green baize like a miniature footy field under floodlights. The players did a lot of aiming, stepping back and grunting, bending and whacking balls into pockets. We had to wait for a free table. I began hiccupping and Gull pointed to the Gents. I got there in time, got rid of most of the excellent meal, but did return somewhat less at sea.

Not enough. When it came to our turn my focus was not good, I was seeing shading on the balls. Gull broke big time, scattering red and coloured balls all over the cloth. I lined up the cue ball on a red sitting on the lip of a pocket. Whack. It smashed in. One to me. The pink was on. I made an effort at steadying my vision, rammed the cue at my white, and missed. I heard a laugh behind me, not from Gull. I aimed again, and the cue ploughed a chalky furrow all the way to the cush.

A sharp prod in my back. I wheeled as best I could to the sight of the back end of a cue raised high in the hands of the guy behind the counter.

'Out.'

Gull shrugged. We left.

'Bike's on The Terrrace,' he said. 'You up for a stroll?'

A stiff stroll, up Boulcott Street to the Church Street steps. To the left of us St Mary of the Angels church, an undulating grey and white edifice, one of the better examples of the favourite Kiwi building material, concrete. Gull was striding ahead. He started taking the steps three at a time.

I gazed up at the challenge of what was now a vertical stroll. It was not a good idea, my head was spinning. I gasped warm air, shook my head and set off after him. There are landings where you can pause. He didn't, I did. The bike was revving when I finally ascended the north face of the Eiger, not as fit as I thought I was.

Gull was wearing traffic cop gloves. He handed me a helmet, which I promptly dropped. He dumped it on my head, told me to hang on, and roared down The Terrace. It was good advice, he took the turn before Parliament at an obtuse angle, swung completely on to the opposing angle, a noisy, gear-changing charge down Thorndon Quay and on to the Hutt Road. I kept waiting for the siren. The traffic cops wouldn't know him, he could hardly pull the cop brotherhood with them, given they were a law unto themselves. This heavy old splutterer would not outrace Triumphs or BSAs, so if we were spotted, we were dog tucker.

We weren't. Gull negotiated the Petone foreshore with no concession to the speed limits or slumbering citizens. I had my own problems, but one was not a full stomach, or I'd have lost it. My thumping head I could do nothing about, but I could hold on, which was important as he started to do Isle of Man swerves around the eastern bays the local bus company advertised as 'The Finest Marine Drive in the World'.

I'd never really assessed it on my trips to and from the Gear, I was either half-asleep for the early morning start or fully asleep on the way back. This time my attention was totally concentrated on staying on the bike as he did a noisy waltz through every sharp corner and a noisier surge around every brief bay crescent. On a night with a clear head I could have enjoyed it.

He clattered to a stop outside my place.

'Fantabulous,' I muttered, tumbling off the bike. He had a gloved finger pointing at my head. It took a few brain circuits to get it. I handed over the helmet and staggered inside. I was into my room before any soprano got to shrieking, and collapsed without the precautionary tall glass of water.

Somebody was attempting to break the door down.

'Rise and shine,' my father called out. 'Haven't you got classes?'

The daylight through the open blinds was murderous. Even with a hand over my eyes, the light was penetrating into the farthest recesses of my tormented skull. I had the mother and father of a headache, my throat was as dry as a wooden god, I had the shivers and no doubt eventually the shits. And he was active again with the sledgehammer pounding on the door.

'Are you awake?'

'Yeth,' I croaked. 'I'm just getting up.'

I had to get up to get some water out of me, and then into and over me. It was too difficult. I could hear the Rover turn over, the garage door shutting. Next thing there were shrill sounds probing my inner ear with the persistence of a disturbed wasp hive. I reared up. The phone. I got to it as it stopped, so I went to ablute. I was under a blessed shower when it started ringing again. I grabbed a towel and lurched down the hall. Mrs Dellapiccolo identified herself and asked when I was coming.

'What for?'

She reminded me I had an appointment to do a child study of her daughter Donna. Oh blessed, merciful Jesus, I didn't have to catch a bus into college. I told her I would be there in two ticks, if she could just remind me of the address.

The idea, so Junior Education master Jim Lundy told us, was to observe and write up notes on the child's play. There wasn't much to observe. The little pre-schooler was too shy to even look at me, let alone speak, despite being urged to by both parents. There was also my reluctance to speak much myself, given that they likely would have heard of the ancient Italian couple whose garden had been vandalised and house invaded by some hooligan. So I stayed discreetly at the edge of the garden, watching Donna roam around her father, who was mixing cement. Mrs D served the most fantastically strong black coffee and chocolate wheaten biscuits, which did wonders for my aching head.

Writing up my slender notes brought back the headache. I gave up and dozed. I woke with a head full of kapok. I headed down to the beach for a dip, and then joined the 20 or so folk pulling in the long net. It was hard work, the net must have been several hundred yards or so, and there was a lot of shouting in Italian and grunting in English, and some lingo that was Double Dutch to me, more exotic than in Katherine Mansfield's day.

I kept my head down and initially declined one of the incredible numbers of fish hauled in. The Italian guy was insistent, so I accepted one. It wasn't Friday and anyway I had no idea what to do with it. Sailing was the closest I got to live fish. I put it in the fridge, washed my hands and got out the push bike, I needed something to eat.

At the Rimu Street dairy I bought a custard pie. I was sitting on the bike scoffing it, trying to ignore the slight odour of fish on my fingers, when I spotted Liz jogging down the other side of the street. Sand shoes, pink shorts, grey T-shirt, her bob also bouncing. So was my heart. She looked fantastic. Even so, I was glad I had not bumped into her, relieved she had not seen me. Or pretended she hadn't. I stuffed the last portion of pie in my mouth and set off in the other direction, feeling a bit sorry for myself.

There was a tap on the front door. I was on my bed, half-reading *East of Eden*, half-dozing, wondering when the book was going to get to the James Dean character and his brothel visit. I opened the door on to a striking blonde, middle-aged woman with bright orange lipstick wearing a crisp sky-blue print dress and holding towards me, in floral green and blue pot mitts, what looked like a yellow casserole. It was not immediately apparent, for most of it was draped in a folded apron with an image part visible of tomatoes, celery, carrots and other salad stuff. All these primary colours made my head spin, and her heavy perfume didn't help either.

'Hi-de-hi,' she said in a cheery voice. 'You must be Steve.'

I said hello, not sure if she was offering me the pot.

'I'm Irene,' she said. 'Your new cook.'

'Pardon?'

'Aren't you going to ask me in? I don't bite.'

'Dad sent you, right?'

'Exactly. I hope you don't mind. I thought he would be home by now.'

'He's often late.'

'I see. So, if you can lead the way to the kitchen, I'll do the rest.'

I showed her the fish, said I'd been given it. She said she'd handle that, but tonight it would be steak and kidney pie. I saw now what the apron was for, as she put the pot down on the formica bench and lifted the apron carefully. Underneath was pastry shaped around a funnel, a ceramic beak poking through.

'The meat and veg I did in the pressure cooker,' she said. 'All we need is to get this stove up to speed.'

She pulled the apron over her head, asking me would I be a gentleman and tie it behind. I did so, noting the apron was a bit small for her ample front.

'Thank you, kind sir,' she said, spinning on her party heels and patting my cheek, releasing a cloud of that sickly perfume. Mum never wore perfume when she was cooking.

'Okey-dokey,' she said, rubbing her hands together. 'Stove time.'

She bent over to examine the opened oven. I looked away.

'Clean enough. Right then, on high for now. I'll check your cupboards while I'm waiting. A cuppa? Or are you like my son, prefer coffee?'

I said I wasn't really thirsty and had to get on with my study. She said that would be fine and not to worry, she would locate what she needed. Did I mind the radio on? I said I didn't. She switched on the little muddy green bakelite and tuned to 2ZB. Thank God I guess for small mercies, she wasn't looking for warblers on the YC. I excused myself and returned to Steinbeck. She was singing along to Perry Como smooching *Catch a Falling Star* as I closed the bedroom door.

The tapping woke me. Steinbeck was a good soporific, I guess, especially if you've seen the film and there's no sign of it in the first few hundred pages.

'Stephen? Are you decent?'

'Eh?'

She had the door open. I started off the bed, embarrassed to be caught asleep, then even more embarrassed she might think I was being indecent with myself.

'What?'

'I'm off. Pie's done, in the oven on low. I did some jam boats with the leftover pastry. They're cooling under a tea towel. The pot on the stove has broccoli. Just switch it to high, five minutes. Hope you like it, dear.'

'Yeah,' I mumbled, not sure about being called 'dear'. 'Um, do you … should I tell my father?'

'All taken care of. See you tomorrow then?'

Thankfully the door shut. I slumped back, thinking was I going to have to put up with my home invaded every day from now on? This was my penance for invading the Italian couples' home. Stuff her and her perfumed pastry. I started reading again. The story seemed to be picking up, at last. I put on *Hound Dog*, for company.

When the door opened, I thought she was back. It was Dad. I had to ask him to hang on, while I lifted off *Don't Be Cruel*, still my No 1 Elvis.

As usual, he wanted to know if I had eaten, now that there was this delicious home cooking on offer. I can hear guilt at 40 paces, having been well versed by a lifetime of nuns and priests going on about it. Oddly, it made me feel sorry for him. So I lied and said I was waiting for him to get home. A white lie. He looked absurdly pleased.

'You shouldn't have,' he said, checking his Timex. 'But nice you did. I'll just have a quick wash.'

It must have been months since we had shared a meal. Kind of odd, sitting at Mum's end of the table, even though it wasn't our table. This was way shinier, with carved legs, and twice the distance from end to end. Everything was twice as big, twice as plush. A *Citizen Kane* of a dinner table.

Dad in an old striped shirt. He had the table laid, best silver, white cloth, glasses of orange juice. He had even lit a candle, which only reminded me of church, of my disastrous year as an altar boy.

'Thought this might be nice,' he said, using pot mitts to lift the slightly singed pie out of the oven. 'Smells tip top. I should've employed a cook ages ago. What do you think?'

He set the pie on the breadboard in the centre of the table. My saliva glands were doing the talking. 'Yeah,' I admitted, sitting down. 'You want to have that broccoli stuff?'

I pointed to the stove.

'Ah,' he said.

'Forget it.'

He nodded, motioning me to help myself. I took the big spoon and dived in. Meaty smells engulfed me. I took a large helping. Dad was smiling.

Steak and kidney and mushrooms, carrots and onions, and whatever made the gravy deliriously delicious. It was so good I had another serving. I hadn't realised how hungry I was. And Dad was not far behind.

I got up and put the pastry boats on a plate and offered him one. He shook his head, said he couldn't fit them in, but I should go ahead. I did. Plum jam. Yum. I had three. I could hardly move.

'So we keep her on?'

I had to agree with that. Man, talk about pork out at the puha factory.

'So how's teaching?'

I told him I had done child observation of a local girl, but there was not a lot to observe. He said he was sure the teaching staff would tell me what to look for.

As we did the dishes, he said he hoped I didn't mind Irene coming in to cook. Not if she keeps making pies like that, I replied. I did mind, but I could see he was trying. It could be he felt guilty saying he wouldn't support me. And it wasn't like he couldn't afford it, all the overtime he was clocking up at the bank. At least, I assumed he got overtime. Dad never discussed his job. Not with me. And never politics, unless you count the odd agreement with an editorial attacking the Labour government, and that was only since Mum passed on. She voted Labour, he was National. He was already in the local National Party scene, dining with Dan Riddiford, the local MP. I'd seen Old Dan dozing at the back of the church, his Groucho eyebrows wriggling like a bevy of black caterpillars.

'Great bunch of masters at Training College,' I said as I put the dinner plates away.

Dad was sponging out the sink. He stopped, looking at me.

'Yes,' he said, frowning. 'I'm sure they know their onions.'

'There's a Lit Club. Short for Literary Club. Thought I might join.'

He gave the sink another circling with the cloth. 'Sounds worthwhile. If it doesn't interfere with your studies.'

'They want everybody to join something. Sport, pottery, that sort of thing.'

He wrung out the cloth, folded it over the back of the hot tap. 'You take after your mother. I mean, you like literary stuff.'

'Long as it's not too melodramatic.'

He gave me a glance. He knew what I was referring to. He let it go. We hadn't argued much since Mum died. My days of belittling opera were long gone. His days of scorning Elvis were buried in the same back cupboard.

'So where did you find this Irene woman?'

'Mrs Flynn?'

'Eh?'

'Mrs Flynn,' he repeated. 'Very nice lady. I met her at the Riddiford soirée. She does occasional catering. She happened to ring up and ask if I had need of a cook.'

I felt myself flushing. 'Does she have a son?'

'Yes. In the police, I understand. Why?'

'What's his name?'

'I didn't ask. Does it really matter?'

'Did she say why she thought you wanted a cook?'

'No. I don't see that it matters. I'm sure you would be the first to agree I can't cook for … well, toffee. I believe you may have alluded to that — a few hundred times.'

I could see he was trying to make light of it, wanting me to accept the arrangement.

'Surely getting the cook is what counts. You liked the pie, didn't you?'

'Yeah,' I said.

'Good. That's settled then. Let's look forward to what she prepares for us tomorrow. Don't wait for me if you're hungry.'

'Fine,' I said. 'I have to get on with some homework.'

'Good night, son.'

I muttered a good night and retreated to my room. What was bloody Gull playing at?

**4**

O n the bus in next morning I hardly took in 'The Finest Marine Drive in the World'. I was continuing my night-time questioning of Gull's motives. Was he compounding the Good Samaritan number, first saving me from my foolishness, now saving me from Dad's dire cooking? How would he know about it? Did I go on about it that much in the café? How embarrassing, blabbing to a virtual stranger. Had I said more about our family? God, I'd have to watch the piss intake, Red Band was stronger than it tasted.

Was it all out of the goodness of his heart? Did he believe in Boy Scout good deeds? Or some Catholic thing, St Paul saying the greatest of all virtues was charity. Was he a do-gooder? A Catholic who practised what the priests preached, do unto others as you'd have them do unto you? Well, I hadn't done anything for him. I couldn't say I'd ever encountered such selflessness? Or was he being a stickybeak? To what end? None of it made sense. I should just be grateful. We needed better home cooking.

I arrived at Teachers College with no answers to what Gull might be up to. One thing you can say for the place, there are plenty of distractions. First up, the Literary Club, dominated by Vogt delivering poems like a demagogue. New chap in the Lit Club, just arrived at the college, beatnikish sort of joker in navy-blue jersey and green trou, and wooden clogs, for Pete's sake! The jersey without anything underneath made me feel itchy just looking at it. He had a straggle of light-brown hair tied in a pony tail so tight it made his eyes pop behind glasses as thick as Coke bottle bottoms. There was an earring the size of a curtain ring in his right lobe. You wouldn't want to play a team sport with that thing dangling.

He was a Pom with the weirdly memorable name of Jasper Porteous. He talked quietly, not posh, more hayseed drawl, like Ron and Eff on that radio show *Take It From Here*. This could be the reason he was attracting most of the girls, including Melissa, who looks like a pop singer with her long hair and bright floaty clothes. Perhaps it was the earring, along with the name and clogs, endowing him with exotic appeal, piratical even. It couldn't be the goggle eyes behind rimless specs or the absurd little tuft on the end of his chin which just invited a decent tug. It could simply be another male to ever so slightly tilt the uneven ratio of five girls to every boy.

Macaskill cracked plenty of funnies about *The Horse's Mouth*, enough for me to want to race out and read the book before I caught the movie with Alec Guinness as the artist. Jasper would fit the artist image, but he hadn't chosen the Glen, where they did pottery and *papier mâché* and art with a guy with half his face blasted by some terrible rash, or even shrapnel.

In the afternoon we had folk dancing in the hall and I managed to grab Melissa for a few whirls. Her patchouli perfume made me think of exotic dancers, Arabian Nights belly dancers. The sequence of shimmering, jingling silver and gold bangles up one arm and exotic rings on just about every finger added to the effect. At the end of one sequence I asked her if she had bells on her toes, like the nursery rhyme about rings on her fingers. She laughed and said that was for me to find out, then I was holding her ringed fingers at arms' length as we swung in giddy circles. I could go a lot more of this sort of teacher training.

The dancing put me in a good mood that lasted most of the way back on the bus, until I remembered what awaited me. As I opened the door I could hear two voices, a deep male and a high female singing *I Was Born Under a Wandering Star*. There was a fishy smell.

'Hi-de-hi,' she said, turning down the radio as I entered the kitchen. She was overdressed again in a floral frock, an apron over it, hair as stiff as a crayfish pot. 'I've done a fish fidget pie with apples and potato slices. I see you cleaned up the beer and beef number. Coffee? I've made some afghans, if you would like?'

I tried to ignore the way she put on the dog voice-wise, I did ignore her questions and her nodding at the plate of biscuits on the table. I couldn't ignore her perfume competing with the fish. 'Gull tell you we needed a cook?'

She put a hand up to check her do. 'I don't follow? Gull?'

'Isn't he your son? James?'

She was frowning. I could see beads of sweat breaking through her peachy makeup. It was stifling, so why didn't she open a window?

'James is my ex. You mean Paddy?'

'He calls himself Gull.'

She patted her hands on her apron. 'Well, I don't know what you mean, I'm sure. Your father mentioned his problem with cooking. I offered.'

I stayed in the doorway. 'So your son never said anything about us needing a cook?'

She looked flustered. 'I really couldn't say. He might have. How is this important?'

'It's important to me,' I snarled. 'And I don't like fish in a pie.'

'I see,' she said. 'Perhaps it's best if I go.'

She was pulling at the back of her apron. It must have knotted. She didn't ask me to untie it. Instead, she gave up, wheeled round and made for the door. She turned, her mouth quivering. 'I'll speak to your father.'

I was in my bedroom relating to the James Dean character when the phone rang.

I thought about not answering, but it kept on ringing. I gave it every chance to stop, meandering down the hall. It was Gull. 'Don't hang up.'

'Why not?' I growled.

'The accused deserves a chance to plead. Not guilty.'

'Eh?'

'I never spoke to mum about cooking.'

Okay, so what? 'How come you said nothing to me? You must have known she was coming round.'

'What, that a capital offence? As it happens, I have only just heard. From mum. I told her I'd clear the air, eh?'

'My father's business, not mine.'

'You want to talk about it with him, this issue you have?'

My first impulse was to deny I had an issue. That was dumb. I did have an issue with her intruding.

'Think about it, Steve. Ring us back, we're in the phone book.'

I told him I would — now I knew who they were. He hung up without responding to my feeble dig. I knew I was being childish. I should ring back and apologise, eat humble pie. Not fish pie.

Instead of ringing, I turned the radio up full bore, *Mr Blue* by the Fleetwoods. Lever Hit Parade. I got out the bike for a twilight ride through Eastbourne, out to the bus depot, through the gate and on to a good old rock and rolling down the fast-darkening gravel road. I didn't want to think, I wanted to be shaken. *Whole Lotta Shakin Goin On.*

It didn't stop the din inside my head. What possessed me to be so shitty? I should ring her. I will. It's not her fault. It's not Dad's fault. It is my fault. *Mea culpa, mea culpa, mea maxima culpa.* Through my fault, through my fault, through my most grievous fault. Not a mortal sin, but a pathetic sort of venial misdemeanour. Fuck, fuck, double fuck.

I cycled slowly back. Dad was at the table, glumly shovelling in fish pie. He lifted a hand in greeting. He looked dead tired. Too many money worries, of other folks' making.

'Anybody ring?' I asked carefully.

He looked up, his eyes bloodshot. He shook his head. 'Were you expecting somebody?'

I shrugged. 'You like the pie?'

He gave a weak smile. 'I gather you don't. We'll have to draw up a food list. Likes and dislikes. Shall we do that?'

'Sure,' I said, taking Mum's seat. 'I'd better check out this pie. It was my idea, really.'

I told him about giving her the fish yesterday. He looked almost pleased, I suppose at me offering her something. I'd have to ring her. First, I scooped up a portion of the odd-looking pie. It was nowhere near as bad as I feared. In fact, it was quite tasty. She really could cook. I said there was no need to make a list, just tell her no tripe or pig's trotters or chokos. In fact, I added, I could ring her now.

That surprised him. So I was being just a teensy-weensy bit hypocritical, but the white lie worked, he also looked relieved. End justifies the means, wasn't that what the Jesuits said?

While Dad put away the left-over pie and cleaned up, I looked up their number. I had my line rehearsed, but it was Gull who answered. I blurted out the pie was great, unable to stop myself. He told me I should tell his mother. She came on, an understandably rather formal greeting. I told her I was sorry I came in grumpy, the pie was really scrumptious, which was an exaggeration, but I had to make the effort. She thanked me, a thaw in her voice, suggested we could perhaps then get together at the weekend, work out the kind of food we liked. I said that would be fine, I'd tell my father. She said to ring back with a time. I promised to, hanging up with a silent vow not to bare my fishy fangs ever again. It wasn't the last vow I broke.

That Sunday evening, the Flynns were round to share her roast, what Dad called high tea. Nothing wrong with the roast leg of lamb, the roast potato, kumara, pumpkin, onion, parsnip, you name it. The peas, the mint sauce, the incredible thick, black gravy she made. All of it served on our best Crown Lynn plates, which extended to Dad bringing out the gravy boat and the big platter, plus a bottle of red wine that tasted like cork shavings and burnt blackcurrant jam.

My mistake was gulping a glass. I gagged on the cork silt and went into a paroxysm of coughing and had to lurch from the table, my ears incandescent, expecting to hear Gull say, 'You can't take him anywhere.' I returned sheepishly to the table, saying I was fine.

'Never mind, dear,' she said. 'You'll get used to it.'

'I'll never get used to it,' I growled, bristling at what I felt was her patronising tone, and then realised how vehement I was. Nothing was said, nobody looked at me. On the contrary, everybody was looking away from everybody else.

'I mean,' I said feebly, 'it brings back my altar boy days.'

Nobody responded. Even I could tell how dopey that sounded.

'Not to worry,' Dad finally said, clearly meaning the exact opposite.

Up until then the evening had been okay, if a trifle stiff, like Dad's new collar. Dad had been valiantly asking polite questions from the moment they arrived. They were still coming in the door when he asked them if they wanted Dry Fly or a cream sherry. I was coping with the cloying perfume as he followed up with some asinine question about whether they had any trouble with the gate. She was carrying a tureen held away from her as if it might contain live katipos, Gull in behind with an oven tray laden up under cover of several tea towels. I assume Dad meant getting the food through the gate. It was a change to hear him nervous.

I could see why. Irene was in a black dress that might as well have been a corset, it barely contained her considerable assets. Her hair was shellacked into a petrified blonde nest, her lipstick was the dirty orange of the South African/Suid-Afrika sixpenny stamp. Dad was assuring her he had the oven on 425 as per instructions, but would she like to check? She was laughing loudly, said she would love a sweet sherry, but first things first, the roast should go straight in the oven.

Even I knew a roast was an hour and a half away from serving, which meant they had plenty of time to polish off both sweet and dry sherries. Gull accepted the sweet sherry too, to my surprise. Dad already knew I was not into wine in any shape or form, a hangover, ha ha, from my days of sampling, when the priest was not looking, the appalling altar wine. I had a beer.

Irene and her son sat on our rust-coloured moquette settee, his grey Donegal tweed jacket adding to the hairy effect of his advancing beard and quite a contrast with his fashion plate mother.

'Cheers,' Dad said, raising the little sherry glass.

'Bottoms up,' Irene said, leaning over to clink his glass, then mine. I looked away, managing to avoid spilling any of my beer.

Dad passed around the side plates ringed in gold I hadn't seen out in several years. On each plate was a stiff white serviette I had never seen before. We tried one of Irene's cheese straws.

'Grouse, Mums,' Gull said, reaching for another.

'Indeed they are,' Dad said, nibbling one end.

A melt-in-your-mouth finger of cheese and paprika pastry. I too had another.

'Glad you like them,' Irene cooed. 'Do try the *vol au vents*.'

We did, gobbling the little oyster and mushroom pastries, murmuring appreciation.

'Truly, the way to a man's heart,' Dad said.

'Oath,' Gull said, winking at me. I did not wink back.

Dad topped up the sherries, asking Gull if he would return to police or be a lawyer.

'Jury's out,' he replied.

'The police encourage degrees now, I understand?' Dad persisted.

'Yep. Move with the times.'

'You must be proud of your lad,' he said to Irene.

'Ditto you,' she said, putting down her empty glass on the side table. She put a hand over it as Dad went to refill. 'I'll check progress. You boys tuck in. And don't forget the food list.'

Dad stood with her, assuring her he had pencil and pad at the ready. He hardly took his eyes off her. As it was rare for him to not wear his glasses, a less charitable person than me might say he was perving. I wondered if Gull noticed, or cared.

With her gone, Dad asked Gull what his father did, a blunt question coming from Dad under normal circumstances, which clearly these were not. Gull shrugged, said last he'd heard he was in Oz mining at Broken Hill. Dad quickly apologised. Gull said no problem, he'd cleared off years before.

There was a bit of a silence after that.

Dad picked up the pad and pencil, ruled down the middle, headings 'Likes' and 'Dislikes'. He liked lists, was always putting up grocery items on the blackboard by the fridge. He used to make entire spreads on the school year, all the holidays and excursions planned. He was disappointed I wouldn't play cricket. He used to, and loved that absurd job of keeping track of every single ball bowled and run scored and batsman out and wickets taken. He kept the graphs in a binder, looked like some mad trigonometry exercise that had no conclusion. He loved orderly activities. A tidy mind, he liked to say, means a tidy life. There was nothing tidy about Mum's illness.

I realised Dad was trying to move on from his unfortunate question, so I repeated my dislikes, said he could put just about anything in for likes, no need to do a Noah's Ark roll call. Got a laugh out of Dad as well as Gull. If they'd asked me for general dislikes, I would have said that unfamiliar perfume topped my list, except I would not have said it. I was trying to keep my dislike side of the ledger to myself.

Irene returned, with added layers of peachy cheek powder and that egregious orange lipstick. She leant down and picked up the list, at risk of bursting out of her semi-constraints, said cheerily she should never have left it to the men, we had no idea. She started running through the food alphabet, checking with me first and then Dad on meats, fish, puddings, biscuits, jams, jellies, you name it, she mentioned it. Half the things I had never heard of, but it was no problem rating things like rump steak, mixed grills, mince pies, golden syrup pudding, trifle, anything sweet or savoury in a pie, anything with almond icing, anything with coconut in it.

I'd have to say by the time she had got through the third sherry, her chest was inflating further, if that was possible; hopefully it was only with the culinary possibilities. Dad watched her like Eddie Fisher did with Elizabeth Taylor in every magazine photo of the happy couple, he couldn't believe his luck. I preferred Eddie's previous wife, Debbie Reynolds. Correction, I lusted after her. You'd have to be mad after seeing her playing blue-jeaned Tammy to prefer the little porky pouter pigeon Liz Taylor.

Dad had volumes of cricket bios and tour accounts. Gull had been flicking glances at that section of the library. Dad actually noticed. He asked him to help himself. Gull did, and was soon absorbed in something about Bodyline. Perhaps he was uncomfortable about the question from Dad, wanted a distraction.

Irene saw what he was looking at, started gabbling about how Paddy was such a good bowler and it was a crime he had not made the First XI, that priest had it in for him. Gull looked up, eyes narrowed, said the other guys must have been better, several had played for Wellington. Dad chipped in with his preference for slow bowling, said there were fewer wanting to do that, at least in his day. Irene said something pathetic about that not being long ago.

She asked if there were any cookbooks that had been favourites. Dad glanced at me, said it was pretty much Edmonds, nothing she would bother with. She insisted there was nothing wrong with Edmonds, the sales proved it was the nation's favourite. I was thinking I didn't want to hear anymore of this and I'd have to get out of the room. Fortunately, she left. I was even relieved Dad went with her. I didn't want him to see me glaring.

Gull put the book aside, told me he never bothered with cricket since he'd left school. Asked me what I was reading. I told him about *East of Eden*. He said he'd seen the film. We got on to talking about *Blackboard Jungle* and this led on to *The Black Cat*, an old horror film. From there it was the entire canon of Peter Cushing and Christopher Lee and *Dracula*, a book he had read. We were well into horror movies, me over a second beer, when we were called to the table.

It was then I made the mistake of gulping the wine Gull poured into the glass beside me. I'd heard you shouldn't mix grain and grape. If I hadn't had my defences lowered by two beers, I probably would not have. But I did. I said I would never get used to wine. It was the way I said it that was the problem, snapping back at her no doubt well-meaning comment.

I couldn't take it back. I had to sit through a pear tart with whipped cream that lodged in my gullet and made conversation impossible. Not that the others did much better.

Coffee was declined. By the time Dad had seen them out, I was in my bedroom with the door shut. He didn't knock. I could hear him cleaning up. I should have helped, but I couldn't face it.

In the following weeks Irene was not there when I got in, which I made sure became later and later. I didn't say anything, nor did Dad. We dutifully said grace: 'Bless us Oh Lord for these thy gifts which of thy bounty we are about to receive, through Christ Our Lord, Amen.' We dutifully ate the gifts Dad paid Irene Flynn for, but I doubt I enjoyed them any more than his burnt chop offerings. I would have been happier if we had stayed with the old status quo. But that is not the way the world goes round. Anyway, big change was coming. With Gull, it already had.

 **5**

G ull surprised me in the Mung Café.

'Steve-oh.'

I peered through the cigarette fug.

'You going to introduce us?'

His grin was barely visible, but that went for just about everything in the Mung. The décor is black on black, black walls and ceiling, black lampshades with of course black tassels, slinky/silvery/silhouette paintings of tall, slender ladies on black velvet, black fishing nets dangling, even the glass buoys painted black. About the only area that is not consciously black is the food, and even then the hot waffles and toasted sandwiches sometimes come a little blackened round the edges, not that anybody complains. Beatniks don't complain about bourgeois things like how your food is served. Coffee, man, like *café negro*, like that is black joe, no teat-sucking, cow-cocky crap in your java, right?

This was the beatnik haunt of the second year Teachers College poets, painters, performers and posturers. I was there because of Melissa Davies, who was there because of them. She was doodling on a black napkin, drawing with a little brush that came in a bottle of white nail varnish. With a few dabs she captured the earnest faces of our intense scrum crouched over two tables pushed together. We looked ghostly against the flickering light of the black candles in black wicker wine bottles.

If I was a superstitious kind of Catholic, I guess I would be crossing myself. This was like the blackout for Good Friday Mass, where the statues and crucifix are all shrouded in black, the priest wears a black chasuble. Come to think of it, it was likely the black-clad proprietor got his candles from Catholic Supplies round the corner. Most of the patrons were into the black theme, the boys in fisherman's knit jerseys and black cords, the girls in black tops and black skirts, tights and boots.

Melissa was not, her red outfit matching her long floaty red hair she was always flicking off her face, which was a mass of freckles. She didn't bother with lipstick, but she didn't need it, she had pouty lips and a snub nose and the most incredible green eyes I've ever seen. In a word, Melissa was exceptional.

Gull was another kind of exception in his brown combo, though in this light it was dark enough to pass muster. His toothy grin reminded me of a Black and White Minstrel get-up, a flash of white in the middle of a dark rampant forest of facial growth, the kind of hirsute statement I associated with the Wolfman.

Not that the others were noticing. All eyes were on Gull's companion, a tall, thin woman in a tight black skirt and high-necked black turtleneck sweater which emphasised the parts that were not skinny, while her height got an unnecessary boost from high heels. If she'd been wearing a shiny, low-cut dress she could have stepped straight off the wall art. The way the prematurely bald proprietor was hovering like Peter Lorre, you might think he was eager to hire her as a living prop.

'You can introduce the doll,' Don said, peering from under the brim of his black beret, leering through aquarium-strength glasses opaque as toadstools.

We were all guilty of peering, if not leering. She had eyes the size of Satsuma plums, a face as pale as a Pre-Raphaelite portrait, her rough cropped platinum hair only adding to her allure. The wide-eyed way she took us all in I thought you could put her in a penguin suit and celluloid bib and she could double for Audrey Hepburn in the posters for *The Nun's Story*. Only seconds ago Don had been in his Jack Kerouac stride, reckoning you had to experience everything before you could write about anything. He was proposing to let the old fruitcake Unity actor seduce him, for the sake of his future art. Now he was looking at and no doubt for a more direct experience.

'Ignore him,' Frank smirked at her. 'Want to see my etchings?'

She directed the wide-eyed look at Frank, then Don. 'You boys couldn't afford me,' she said in a husky voice. Not a real nun, more a pretend nun. There was something arch in the way she spoke. Cancel the nun connection, make her a classy version of those blank-faced Hutt Valley widgies.

'She's jake-a-bon,' Frank salivated, standing and offering her a seat. 'We never pay for it.'

'Clair might change your mind.'

Clair flicked Gull a look. 'Clair makes up her own mind,' she said, easing on to the bentwood chair Frank was holding at the ready. Like most of the chairs in this establishment, it both bent and wobbled, but Clair perched without problem. High heels are not supposed to be good for balance, but Clair made a mockery of that theory.

Melissa held out her hand and introduced herself. 'Can I draw you?'

Clair smiled. 'Sure,' she said, pulling a pack of Matinée out of her pocket. Don, Frank and Jaffa had their American Zippo flamethrowers open and flaring, the air acrid with the smell of kerosene. Clair tapped out a fag and eased it between her glossy plum-red lips, her hand circling Frank's lighter. Frank spread around his triumphant grin.

I did the introductions as initially requested. I'm not sure how interested the three Second Year jokers were in the niceties, but they took the opportunity presented to shake Clair's hand. Gull returned the favour, all three wincing, even Jaffa, a big bloke who did a lot of tramping and scrub-cutting and such outdoor stuff and presumably got his nickname from his flaming orange hair. Jaffa said he knew Gull, had played against him. Gull checked he was Number Eight in Petone Seconds, got the nod, said they ought to celebrate then, he'd order coffee all round.

The coffee had to be sought. The mere mention of rugby had provoked the proprietor to toss his gleaming head and flounce away. You could put your hand up, but the waiters might choose not to see. The noise from all the opinions flying and the noodling drone of some modern jazz LP meant you'd have to do a sheepdog whistle to cut through the atmosphere, and that wouldn't elicit coffee with this disdainful crew.

I joined Gull at the counter. I wanted to check out how come he was in every coffee bar I visited. It could be coincidence, but I wanted to ask.

'Groovy lady,' I said, employing a word the jazz aficionados here used about anything they liked.

He shrugged. 'Just good friends.'

'Where'd you meet her?'

He laughed. 'Around. Why? You want some of that action?'

I said I was with Melissa. He nodded. Melissa was busy drawing Clair indolently smoking. I had in fact picked up this all-purpose term of approval 'groovy' from Melissa, who got it from the poets at Teachers College, who got it from the jazz freaks. I knew nothing about poetry and loathed jazz, but I knew what I liked, which was her.

It was obvious at the Lit Club that she was an artist who was into poets, so I started trying to write poetry. This of course required hanging out with the top poets. Don had already been published in *Landfall*. When the famous poet James K. Baxter came to talk to the Lit Club, Don talked to him as if they were on the same level. For all I knew, they were. I hadn't taken much notice, being diverted by Melissa drawing James K while he raved about Catholicism, something I had had a lifetime too much of.

I had aimed to get to know Melissa better. Accidentally on purpose, I got alongside her in the tiresome two hours filling in those endless forms to register at Vic. She enrolled for English and French and Latin Reading Knowledge, the latter two half-units, and by a curious coincidence, so did I. To be fair, I had done Latin and French at school and they hadn't seemed too difficult. After this testing time just getting accepted for these subjects, I asked her if she felt like a break somewhere. She suggested the cable car down to the Rendezvous coffee bar at the end of Cable Car Lane, sitting upstairs above Lambton Quay.

Melissa ordered heavenly Napoleon cakes to go with the black coffee. As usual, she was in shades of red, a red jersey, a brown skirt with red flecks in it that looked like it was made from felt, short enough to reveal red tights sheeting into high red boots. She was flicking hair and doodling with a piece of red chalk on a white paper napkin, drawing a couple at the far end of the coffee bar. The guy had his back to us and it was a little while before I realised it was Gull. He might have seen us come in, his position offering a view of everybody passing below. He was totally concentrating on his companion, who was, I now knew, Clair. I didn't disturb them, there didn't seem any point in intruding.

A few days later I was in the Picasso coffee bar with Judy and I saw him stroll past, again he didn't see me. That weekend I met up late with one of the Phys-Ed lads, Toby Burton, who wanted someone with him to check out the Mexicalli coffee lounge, where he'd heard you could pick up prostitutes. I left him trying his best and took off to catch the late bus. As I left, I thought I saw Gull.

I had seen him deep in conversation with a gaunt character in the Symposium coffee bar just down the road from the Mung. It was run by one of the guys at Teachers College, with his wife, and was the place to go for meaningful political conversations. It looked like Gull was into that all right. I was with Jasper when we went in, Jasper pointing out that he knew the guy Gull was chatting to, Bill Dwyer.

I asked Jasper if that was the anarchist. Jasper shrugged, said yes, so what, he was one himself. I shouldn't have asked him if he had a bomb in his duffel coat, Jasper is another who does not seem to have a sense of humour. Typical caricature, he sneered. If I wanted to know about anarchists, fine. If I wanted to be an idiot, forget it. I assured him I was interested. I got one of his blurred but hard looks. He tends to be censorious in class, never laughs at Macaskill's puns. I tried to retrieve things, asking him how he applied anarchy in New Zealand.

'You'll have to wait and see,' he said, getting up abruptly and leaving. I know he regarded me as a lightweight. Indeed, I'd been surprised he bothered to ask me down for a coffee. But, truth to tell, he was right, I was not interested in anarchy. I was interested in Melissa, and that meant poetry and … groan … jazz. After Jasper took off, I looked around, no sign of Gull or Dwyer. I wondered if they shared wool hook stories, which goes to prove how lightweight I was.

Gull appearing at every coffee bar I went to seemed to me deserving of enquiry. I asked him.

'I like coffee,' he said. 'Come on, he's bringing it now.'

Back at our tables, Clair had shifted around next to Melissa. The poets and painter were able and willing to stare at both of them. Melissa had finished the drawing on the napkin and was offering it to Clair.

'Yeah?' she said in her throaty Eartha Kitt purr. 'It's a groove. Let me pay you for it.'

Melissa shook her hair out of her eyes. 'My pleasure. Steve, you want to see that dance?'

I did. When Melissa told me on the way to the English lecture about her creative dancing, I'd blurted I loved creative dancing. It was news to me, not having seen any and having no idea what it was, but I wasn't going to admit that or my image of Melissa dancing the dance of the seven see-through veils.

Clair was asking what sort of dancing. Melissa said it was free form, usually jazz, but she was practising a primitive fire movement to the 'Sabre Dance' music by Khachaturian for the college concert. She was on her feet, her red hessian shoulder satchel in place.

'Can I come?' Clair asked, staring hard at Melissa. 'I can give you a lift. Him too.' She nodded at me without looking my way.

'Neat,' Melissa said, checking Gull. He shrugged.

'Catch up with you prancers later,' he said, seemingly unconcerned.

'We'll come too,' Frank said.

'Sorry, my place is too small. When I get into rehearsals at college, okay?'

Frank could hardly object. Nor could I. The looks I was getting from Frank and his fellow Second Years suggested I didn't know my place, which was that of a First Year, a rung below them.

Outside I knew my place, climbing over into the crawlspace behind the bucket seats. It was no problem, the black fabric roof was down. It offered something to lean against, while I held on to the backs of the bucket seats and looked about at shops and pubs closing, at the office workers buttoning up their gaberdines and piling on to trams screeching and rocking by on their controlled iron rails. All these folk wanted to do was get home, get their feet up, have their meat and three veg and hokey-pokey ice cream on the tinned Wattie's peaches. Their day was over. Ours was just beginning, the street lights coming on, the darkening sky clear and full of promise.

Clair's sports car was white, cute, and a little battered around the edges. I asked what it was. Clair said MGA. The rest of what she said was drowned by the exhaust revving. She shot out into traffic with first gear screaming, drowning out some angry tooting behind us, the car bucking about, a shriek of excitement from Melissa, me clawing on grimly to the seat backs. Clair was no better at driving than me.

At the lights we shuddered to a stop, the exhaust rumbling dyspeptically. I couldn't help but notice Clair scissoring off her high heels, alternate flashes of stocking-tops. Stilettos had to cause her jerky driving. Now she was in her black nylons, she should have more control. Even so, as Melissa pointed towards The Terrace, I braced myself. I'm glad I did. The lights changed and we reared off, screaming in first across town and up that incredibly steep end of Vivian Street, no discernible improvement in Clair's driving.

She flung the car right on to The Terrace without looking, graunching gears, cutting across the stately path of an old Model A, provoking a comical horn protest. Melissa's hair flicked about, keeping her busy, while I concentrated on not becoming airborne. The roof up would have been a good idea, it would anchor me and offer protection from the battering I was getting perched above the windscreen, really no better than being on a motorbike. The way Clair changed gear it might as well be a motorbike.

We rumbled up hill, round Salamanca Road and below the ancient brick Hunter building with the peaked roofs and mullioned windows that convey the very essence of academe. We took the chicane in a series of jerks and gear change screeches and lurched up the parade past the brutally new Easterfield Building where I had sourced above the entranceway the full quote from Browning which Gull had partly used: 'Ah, but a man's reach should exceed his grasp, or what's a heaven for?' If my grasp faltered, I guess I would find out soonest.

Clair didn't bother with the higher gears, which was, from my point of view, a good thing. It was more screech and jerk around the opposing chicane into Glasgow Street and up on to Kelburn Parade, Melissa yelling directions, down Rimu Road to a shuddering, spluttering halt, a final threat to send me airborne as Clair banged the offside front tyre into the kerb. I shakily slid off the side of the car, in no condition to appreciate Clair fingering on her high heels. Melissa led the way through a creaky iron gate, up deep, damp concrete steps and round the back. By the time we had got up the rickety wooden fire escape ramp to her flat, I had ironed out most of the wobble in my legs.

Melissa was not fibbing about no space for the Second Years, there was scarcely enough of it to swing the little black kitten meowing piteously when she shoved open the stuck door. Melissa captured the hissing creature, cuddling it quiet as she invited us in. It seemed to me the place was basically an attic extension on to the upper terrace level, partitioned initially into a tiny kitchen whence Melissa directed us into a marginally bigger room.

Clair sat down on the rather large bed which accounted for possibly half the available space, bouncing to test its resistance. 'Nice,' she said.

Melissa switched on the central paper beehive shrouded in a shiny red scarf. It added little to the indirect lighting from the street filtering through half-drawn heavy green velvet drapes. The walls had been painted almost the same dark green as the curtains. It was like being inside a compressed version of Hongi's Track, green, green everywhere, nor any a light to see. There was actually just enough light for me to note a desk in the far corner, no bigger than those we had at primary school. In fact, it might well have come from a school. It was not easy to tell, it was covered in curled thick sheets of paper which had to be her sketching.

'Take a seat,' Melissa said. 'I'll feed Nigel. Won't be a tick.'

I pulled out the only alternative to the bed, a metal tube chair tucked into the desk, turning it to face Clair. The scooped wooden seat shifted a little as I sat.

'Love your nudies,' Clair trilled.

I followed her gaze. Two large framed paintings took up half the opposing wall. I had to peer to make them out, reclining nudes with voluptuous bodies and angular, chiselled faces not unlike Clair's.

'Modigliani,' Melissa called out. 'My fave.'

Underneath them was a small table hosting a turntable, a stack of LPs leaning against its thin legs. To one side a homemade bookcase of planks of wood supported by bricks, full of mostly red Penguins on the top row, larger hardback books beneath. I got up for a closer look. Clair did too, except she was fronting up to the nudes. I was interested to see what LPs Melissa had. I crouched and made out Monk, Coltrane and Davis, enough to figure it was end-to-end jazz.

'You okay with green tea?'

'Should go well,' Clair said, 'with my contribution.'

'Okay,' Melissa said. 'I'll put the pot on.'

Clair laughed, said that was her line. Melissa disappeared again. There was the smell of gas, a match lit and a whoosh. Clair was back on the bed, rummaging in her tiny black handbag. She carefully removed a tobacco tin. She opened the lid and looked at me.

'Helps everybody relax,' she drawled.

'Roll-your-owns?'

'You could say that.'

I didn't say I didn't smoke. Melissa was coming in with a tray with a teapot and three mugs. She nodded at the desk, asked me to put the papers on the floor. I did so, getting unfamiliar whiffs from the tea, which smelled smoky sweet, or it was the cigarette Clair was lighting. She took a drag and handed it to Melissa.

'You tried these?'

Melissa nodded, taking a pull and handing it to me. When in Rome, I figured, taking a careful puff.

'That's wasting it,' Clair said. 'Have a decent go. Hold it in.'

I looked at Melissa, who was doing just that, and grinned encouragement. I did, coughing and dropping the fag. Clair practically levitated across the room, up there with our spectacular Teachers College halfback Barry Cull in the middle of a dive pass.

'Hey, careful,' she cautioned me, capturing the cigarette, cradling it as attentively as Melissa had her kitten. She examined it, puffed its lit end to life. 'No harm done.'

Clair took another judicious draw and passed the small end to Melissa, who turned her head sideways to maximise intake.

'It's a reefer, right?'

Clair laughed. 'Read that in a book?'

I flushed, thankful for the low light. I thought I was showing my worldly knowledge. She made it sound like all I knew was out of books, which was mostly true, but nonetheless not something I wanted to be made obvious.

Melissa poured and handed us each a mug. I took a swallow and brought it back up, burning my lower lip. I quickly covered my mouth and coughed again to smother my clumsiness. At least I managed not to spill any, again grateful for the low light. Melissa was talking about this painter Modigliani and neither of them seemed to notice what a dork they had in the room. Another cigarette was being passed and this time I took a lungful and held it, determined not to cough. I handed the fag back to Clair and sipped the brew that I could only compare to our Waitakere camp experiment with boiled tea-tree leaves.

'Better not have anymore,' Melissa said as she handed me the reefer. 'Not if I want to remember my moves.'

Clair smiled, leaning against the wall. 'No need for us to worry about that.'

Melissa handed me an LP, asked me to put it on when she gave the signal. She pulled the curtains closed, reducing the ambient light to about the level of a schoolmate's dark room for developing his Box Brownie shots. Melissa rolled up the exotic carpet, disappeared behind one of the curtains, which I had not noticed screened some kind of an ad hoc wardrobe. In a surprisingly short time she called out to switch on. My first attempt the needle skidded off the side of the record, with a vinyl threatening protest. I mumbled an apology and focused on doing better.

The room exploded with this incredibly fast sawing of strings, such that I feared I had not only turned the music up too loud but put it on 45 instead of 33 rpm. Before I could check, Melissa had leapt from behind the curtains in this skintight leotard outfit like those ballet lasses wore at the Mardi Gras. The difference was that they were somehow demure. Melissa was anything but, as she began to dart and writhe, her arms going ceiling-wards. Her legs swivelling, she flung herself on to the ground, writhing and undulating in snake-like movements. Not that I had ever seen a snake, but I did feel mesmerised, as allegedly a rabbit does when the snake fixes it with its beady eyes.

There was no sign of Melissa's eyes, just her hair-fall moving in swirling counterpoint to her limbs accelerating to keep pace with the wild, pagan rhythms. I couldn't credit how the music could get any faster, or that Melissa could match it. This was not the floaty, slow peeling of muslin layers I had envisaged, this was way more visceral and exciting and throat-choking sexy.

The music took a breather and Melissa slowed to its gurgling wind instruments, then percussion kicked in and the strings again as the music took off into a ferocious final lick. Melissa was up to it, leaping literally in amazing bounds around the confined space, using every available inch with astonishing dexterity. I found I needed all my concentration just to follow her three-dimensional and totally controlled frenzy.

The music crashed to a halt, and with it Melissa slammed to the floor, lying in a crushed heap. I was about to rush and assist with her injuries, but Clair was clapping and Melissa rose like a phoenix from the floor, flicking hair out of her eyes as she bowed to each of us in turn. Her eyes were lit up like glow-worms in her pale face, her mouth was open, her chest was heaving, she looked astonishingly sexy.

Obviously Clair thought so too, for she had slipped off the bed and was embracing Melissa the way I wanted to. Melissa accepted her embrace and was pulled into a full-mouth kiss. She laughed as she eased away, asking me what I thought.

'Fantastic,' I said, hoping she meant the dance and not its aftermath. I wasn't sure how I felt about Clair doing what I wanted to. I had mixed feelings about Melissa grabbing me. I felt overdressed and overextended when her body swelled against mine, embarrassed at my obvious excitement but not wanting to let go. It was Melissa who released, suggesting I might like to remove the hissing needle before it cut a hole in the record. I stumbled over to it, trying to shield my discomfort. Couldn't take me anywhere.

I was down on one knee, lifting the needle arm into its socket, praying the limited light concealed my condition.

'I can see you liked it,' Clair laughed.

Melissa giggled, and I heard myself giggling too.

'Why don't you get some of that gear off?' Clair suggested. She was showing the way, her skirt already detached. She was pulling her skivvy over her head. I looked up at Melissa. She giggled again.

'It is hot in here. Go on.'

I used a hand on my knee to push myself upright, not looking at Clair laughing as she flung her bra across the room. I then had to look away from Melissa, who was peeling her body stocking off her shoulders, no bra underneath. I was peripherally aware of Clair's stockings and knickers dropping to the floor, mainly because I didn't know which way to look and was trying most directions.

'Don't be a piker,' Melissa laughed. 'Remember what Don said about experiences.'

Clair was giving me two helping hands, hauling off my duffel coat from behind, reaching around to undo my belt. Melissa joined in, lifting my jersey over my head, at which point my desert boots encountered each other and I fell backwards, knocking myself and Clair on to the bed.

'Sorry,' I gasped, feeling stupid with my pants around my ankles, wishing they would stop giggling.

'I can't reach,' I whined, my words taking ages to emerge, 'my … blimmin boots.'

They were now in fits behind me on the bed as I tried to stand and toppled over on to the floor, which achieved one previously desired result, my rajah was bumped into submission. I looked up at Clair writhing on top of Melissa like a Modigliani nude rudely come to life. I tried to stand and my head started spinning, and then my stomach began to heave.

'Sorry,' I mumbled, my hand to my mouth. 'Bath … room?'

Melissa managed to say it was the other side of the door before they went into paroxysms of laughter, from which they subsided into giggling and then murmuring. I crawled and scrambled across the floor, pulled myself up by the chair, my stomach in spasms. Holding my trou, I stumbled and bumped against the wall and curtains, reeled through into the kitchen, where I tripped over the kitten's basket, provoking a hissing from a small, arched shape. I couldn't contain myself and I heaved up coffee and waffles all over my bare chest and hands and cords. I grabbed the door handle with one hand, my trousers half-falling. It would not open. I fumbled with my free hand and found the key, twisted the lock and wrenched the door open.

'Steve?' Melissa was calling out as I lurched on to the ramp, my pants falling. I used the wooden rail to steady myself, casting a quick look back at the house, relieved they were not coming after me. I took off in a shambling run like I was tied to somebody else in one of those three-legged races, my head revolving at the same speed as that mad sabre music, my stomach engaged in its own uneven counterpoint. I lumbered down the tall steps and out into the street, praying to whichever saint rescued the desperately embarrassed.

I reeled up the footpath, my only aim to put distance between me and my idiocy, managing to belt my pants over the mess I had made, my stomach protesting at contact with my own vomit. I stumbled on, working to do up the damn fly buttons, shaking my hands, flicking muck off my chest, wiping my hands on the sides of the cords rather than putting my filthy fingers in my pocket for a hankie. I was relieved there was nobody around to see my shame.

Wrong. A motorbike started up. Fit to wake the dead. Its light exposed me. I ducked over to the nearest gate and was fiddling with the latch as the bike pulled up alongside me.

'Want a lift?'

I saw his grin.

'Come on,' he said. 'You can't break in there.'

I gave up, turned and came over to the gutter.

'Jesus,' he objected. 'On second thoughts.'

He didn't take off, instead kicked out his stand and climbed off. He pulled off his jacket and threw it at me. I dropped it.

'I don't want to know,' he said. 'Just get on.'

I picked up the jacket and put it on over my bare skin. I was beginning to recognise through the floaty head fug that I had little choice, it was cold, and I was in no condition to catch a bus, particularly when I had left my wallet in my duffel coat.

'Sorry,' I said, as I climbed on the back of his bike.

'Get it cleaned,' was all he said, before he took off. I felt terrible, my stomach protesting, my head aching, my body shivering. I managed to find the spare key under the pot, grateful Dad was not home.

I collapsed on the bed, my head revolving like a Catherine Wheel.

I woke with a jolt, some terrible whistling sound was in the house. My heart thumped as I reared out of bed, my head splitting, my throat dry as a dead bear's bum. I smelled like a septic tank overflow. Stiffly I eased to my feet, cracked the door, realising Dad was home and playing his Devil's tune again. I crept to the bathroom and used the glass I kept my toothbrush in to quench my thirst. It cracked against the tap as I plonked it underneath for a refill. I needed a shower and so did the clothes, but I settled for more water intake and getting back down the hall without any pesky questions.

I had to reassure Dad that it was something I ate that caused the stink and my sneezing established I had caught a cold. He was off at some meeting when I hand-washed my boots and cords and Gull's leather jacket, and naturally, that was when I began to question what he was doing lurking outside Melissa's house.

When he rang, he had a perfectly good explanation, he was worried about what Clair might get up to. Anticipating my next question, he said obviously he asked my companions at the coffee bar where Melissa lived. Clair's car was outside, *quod erat demonstrandum*.

He didn't have to spell out his Latin knowledge. QED would have done. But, I managed to thank him for the lift and that – letting the 'that' stand for his heroic rescue work in the face of my pathetic and offensive behaviour. I promised I would have his jacket properly cleaned.

There were more immediate problems. I had to avoid Melissa ringing to get me to pick up my clothes.

The solution was simple, albeit cowardly, but I was sneezing and feeling totally grotty in the head. I left Dad a note and went back to bed, drawing the blind.

Dad was excessively cheery, I thought, as he brought in a glass of water and two

Aspros. Irene, he informed me, was bringing around soup for the invalid.

The tapping on the door woke me. Irene was cooing about chicken noodle and where would she put it down. I was embarrassingly aware of the condition of my bedroom. My bedside table was piled with books and lecture notes, with a spill-over zone around the base. Clothes occupied the surface of the chest of drawers and surrounds. There was not a lot of room, and not much light, the blind still down. I pretended to sleep, inhaling the odours not unlike rugby changing rooms as I recall them from my playing days, before Mum got ill.

I heard the slight susurration of nylon rubbing nylon. She said she was leaving the tray on the floor, and there were several phone messages.

The moment she closed the door the aromas of hot food replaced all else. I flung back the covers, cracked the blind and slid the sash window up a notch. The tray had a white linen cloth on it, and on that was a bowl of steaming soup with chopped green bits on its surface, on one side salt and pepper shakers, on the other two thick slices of wholemeal, butter soaking into the uneven texture of homemade bread.

After demolishing the soup and bread, I checked the tiny notes, ripped out of a perforated pad, pink and blue flowers decorating the top of each sheet. I could smell her perfume on them. Melissa rang twice, and Patrick wanted me to call him.

I checked the coast was clear and tiptoed to the bathroom, locking myself in and getting under a hot and then cold shower. Just like the coaches always said, water is the magic cure. I came out almost a new man.

When I emerged into the kitchen, tray in front of me, Dad called out was I feeling any better. I grunted a yes as I heard his paper flicked out and folded, which masked a remark about the remarkable recovery rate of the young.

In the sitting room Dad was in his high-backed, big-buttoned brown leather chair next to the floor-to-ceiling bookcase, his chair angled so the natural light from behind him illuminated his newspaper; it was a dark room without the two bowl chandeliers ablaze in the panelled ceiling. Dad liked to relax weekends in this twilight zone.

Right now there were several strips of sunlight streaming through the mullioned windows on to the easy chair in the corner, bands of light like the representation of grace coming down from heaven on to the upturned face of Saint Catherine of Siena in the Standard Three and Four classroom at Kohi convent. Dust motes danced like Disney devils above the rumpled mustard brown velveteen surface. That was where old Roger (as in Roger the Dodger) slept away his last years, passing on soon after Mum. Dad never replaced the cat, but he did keep the chair, and in its original condition, which included the tufting ripped comprehensively down the side Roger made his scratching post.

I went across and sank into the old chair, tilting it with eyes closed until the sun was in my face. Mum loved this chair, spent increasing amounts of time in it towards the end, Roger usually on her lap. Dad would be there as he was now, reading the papers in his armchair. Towards the end he openly ruminated over the political stances of the *Herald* and the *Auckland Star*, no longer bothering to mute or modify his political opinions.

'Damned freezing workers,' he was muttering. 'They want a 24 per cent wage increase. Between them and the government's welfare handouts …'

I dozed off, his ranting about the workers a stuck record. If he ever wanted my penny's worth, I reckoned 24 per cent was nowhere near enough to compensate for the mind-boggling boredom of stacking pelts and cutting throats 15 hours a day. The government couldn't be that bad for business, he'd been on the other day about the share price up 27 per cent in the last year and business profits 10 per cent above the previous Christmas. Like Mum used to say, without Mickey Savage and Walter Nash the workers would never have seen a brass razoo from the export boom in wool and meat.

The snap of the newspaper woke me.

'Hah! Old Lee's got it spot on. Labour fund welfare out of private enterprise to the limit of what they gouge out of the producers. Taxing to the limit.'

Dad smacked the paper. Most unlike him. I opened my eyes.

'Listen to this, son. John A Lee, erstwhile minister in the First Labour Government.'

'I know who he is,' I said, tilting the chair upright, pulling the information out of the memory bank Mum left to me. 'Savage sacked him.'

'Well, Lee is on the right track here. I quote: *The people will endure no more. People are not likely to give a political mandate to Socialism again for many years. People who would vote to acquire a bank in 1935 will not vote to let Nash and Nordmeyer acquire a State pie-cart. Hah!*' He delivered another smack of approval.

'Socialism,' he declared, 'is finished.'

'Not in Russia and Cuba.'

He peered at me over his half-moons. 'Look at the mess they're in.'

I stood up to get the sun out of my eyes. 'At least Labour is not warmongering.'

'What's that supposed to mean?'

'They don't force you into the army.'

Dad removed his glasses, pointing them at me. 'That sort of attitude would have finished us in 1942, son. You wouldn't have minded being a slave labourer in the Nippon Empire?'

'I didn't say that. Labour was in charge in the war.'

'It was a coalition government of unity, actually.'

I shrugged. 'What's it matter what I think? I can die for my country but I'm not allowed to drink in its pubs or vote.'

'I've been hearing some worrying things about some of your lecturers. Free this and free that. Including the man in charge.'

'What? I can't work out for myself I'm cannon fodder with no civil rights?'

Dad slumped back in his chair. 'Let's not argue, son.'

'Like with Mum?'

He was massaging his eyes. He looked at me. 'We both miss her.'

'Yeah,' I said. 'I'd better get on with my study.'

Dad stood up. He looked hesitant, but he was putting out a hand. I sneezed, grabbing for my hankie as the second sneeze arrived. I retreated behind the hankie, not sure what he intended.

'Son?' he called.

I stopped at the door.

'You got those messages Irene took?'

'Yeah,' I said, leaving.

I put on the freezing works jacket, zipping it up, enclosing myself in worker solidarity as I went sneezing into the street, heading for the uncomplicated safety of the sea. As usual the breeze went up a few notches as I emerged on to the open beach. Stray bits of marram grass were skidding along the foreshore, seagulls wheeled about the wharf area, no doubt after a share of any fish caught. Gull was right about one thing, the sea was where freedom lay.

I was alone heading away up the beach, just the way I wanted it, the northerly whipping across the side of my head, the waves coursing in. The sea was the same monochromatic grey as the sky, except where the sun intermittently burst forth, splintering across the water and catching the corner of my eye, probing at my headache and tickling my sinuses.

I heard a distant scatter of applause from a game of cricket on the same ground where I had done my dubious acrobatics. I could have been playing tennis with Liz if I'd not acted the giddy goat. Not to worry, I didn't really want to spend my spare time playing tennis and being polite. I could have been with Melissa if I'd not made an oaf of myself. The problem there, I didn't want to share Melissa with that weird woman. Was I just too square to cope with a new experience? What did I want? If only I'd not shown off. If only I'd been more restrained in sucking on that reefer? If only Mum hadn't got cancer.

If I had a motorbike like Gull's, I'd head off out of here. The impediment was it would take a year and a day on the teacher trainee salary to get one. Where would I go anyway? I really wanted to see Melissa, I had to get back my boots, if only to get out of these sand shoes, which were living up to their name, filling with sand.

I picked up a pipi shell and tried Gull's flick that sent it soaring into the free air. My shell fell into the sand. Feeble. I probably couldn't even, as Elvis sang, catch a rabbit. And he sure ain't, as Elvis concluded, a friend of mine. I walked alone and lonely, pondering the ifs and buts between sneezing sequences. All I knew for certain was that I wanted to be free, free as I was on the trapeze pole, free as I was flying down the wire, free as Gull leaping in the air. Freedom — or flight?

 **6**

Sunday was indoors of necessity, the cold running its course, doses of Aspro and hot lemon drinks, the lemons courtesy of Irene. One more perfumed note, my sweatshirt and duffel coat could be picked up at Training College reception, she hoped I was feeling better.

Monday I got into varsity in time for a back-row seat at the English lecture. I didn't see Melissa among the 500 scribblers interpreting the Scots accent and trenchant opinions expressed by Professor Gordon about his own course book on English prose technique.

I picked up my gear from reception. Inside the shopping bag the clothes were folded, on top a cute drawing in ink on white paper of a duffel-coated figure running away. I shrugged off my Gear jacket, put on the duffel and ducked into the cloakroom to leave the Gear coat and sweatshirt in my skinny tin locker. I took another look at the card. Melissa had written a message inside, 'Hope to see you soonest'. Signed 'Meow', with a paw mark.

In the crowded caff there was some fast, rhythmic drumming and yells of appreciation coming from the centre of a group in the corner next to the street windows. Surely Tommy Young had not taken his bongos to smoko? I moved carefully through the Phys-Ed scrum scoffing Anzac biscuits and the English section sipping mugs of tea or coffee, looking out for Melissa. As I captured a cup of milky Greggs, the drumming accelerated to a sudden stop, followed by cries of 'Too much' and 'Mighty' and the like. A smiling Don was holding up a bongo drum set in several directions to acknowledge some cool drumming Tommy Young had not taught us, more your Gene Krupa going ape.

'Hey, Dead Cat!' he called out to me.

The others were nodding at that, even if not all of them got it, a reference to the first poem read at the Lit Club, about a dead cat. I flashed on Melissa's paw mark.

'Yeah, Dead Cat,' Frank followed up. 'Over here, man.'

I edged over, unsure I wanted their attention. Frank was banging my back, Don saying to make room, Dead Cat has a story for us. I took a seat and looked around the expectant faces.

Frank was snapping his fingers. 'Two hot diggety chicks, man. Tell all.'

My ears were flaring. 'Nothing happened,' I muttered, wishing I'd taken a sickie.

Jaffa craned forward. 'Pull the other tit, Dead Cat.'

'Honest,' I protested.

'Christ on a bicycle,' Don scoffed. 'You expect us to believe that?'

'It's true,' I mumbled. 'I wasn't well.'

'What happened?' Frank persisted. 'When you got there?'

'I don't think it's really any of your business.'

Jaffa was on his feet, his hands supporting him as he leaned across the table. 'We decide if it's our business.'

'You're not being fair to Mel.'

'Mel?' Jaffa mocked.

I cringed, unable to credit I had just called her 'Mel' to these oafs. I was saved by the buzzer, signalling the end of the break. Chairs were scraping, students moving out of the caff. Don pointed a finger gun at me: 'You're not off the hook, Dead Cat.'

None of us were off the hook with Assembly, where the entire college had to endure the ravings of a crackpot Professor Page from the university advocating electronic music as the only viable music for the *weltanschaung* of a twentieth century riven by *sturm und drang*. One of the Phys-Ed crowd down the back caused ripples of laughter when he said in a loud stage whisper he didn't know 'electric' music was in German. Scotty swept his Biblical frown across the back rows until all was quiet for our guest speaker. Not that the mad professor seemed to notice, he continued to stride back and forth across the stage, barking out his message with the kind of Messianic zeal I can remember from the agitated Redemptorist missionary priest doing a guest sermon at St Peters.

I had learned from years of boring parish sermons to make myself an habitué of the back row, where one can sidle out of church during the ringing of the communion bell, or sooner, like during the sermon, if you think you can manage it undetected. I was off while the desultory clapping was accompanying a pleased looking prof who had finally, like one of Dad's operas, come to an end.

The rest of the week I perfected my last in/first out from lectures and was grateful to be on section at Brooklyn school, where singing nursery rhymes with Primer One was a pleasant enough way to spend one's time. I didn't bother with the college caff or the Lit Club the rest of the week, and I went from the cable car straight to the library, bypassing the coffee bars. I studied the set poet Yeats, but found myself having to reread lines my eyes had glazed over. I knew a reckoning was coming and it was only my puerile side-stepping Catholic guilt shame that was delaying the inevitable.

Jasper offered a diversion to suit my fatalistic mood. I called in to the Symposium, where I figured I was least likely to encounter Melissa. Jasper was the only person

I recognised, and only just. He was crouched over coffee in the darkest corner and I might have missed him if I had not been intrigued by what he was wearing. He looked like a caricature of a bomb plotter in a houndstooth deerstalker hat pulled low over his face, with a matching coat reaching to the floor. Its attached cape was turned up as if he was drawing attention to his disguise.

'My dear Holmes,' I said. 'You've come into funds?'

He looked up, the dead-fish stare magnified by his lenses. 'St V de P,' he said in funereal voice.

'Eh?'

'You're a Mickey Doo, aren't you?'

I nodded, getting it. St Vincent de Paul second-hand shop in Newtown. Don mentioned he had got an exotic black coat from there, some deceased judge's, he was told.

'Discards of the consumerist society, brother. Planned obsolescence. Check Vance Packard.'

'Vance who?'

'The hidden persuaders, man. Cost you a coffee.'

I purchased two coffees and endured a rant about the guy exposing all these evil American marketeers out to make us buy more, ditch last year's model and get a brand new car, fridge, washing machine, whatever. Selwyn Toogood gave them away every week on his radio show. I personally couldn't see much wrong with that. Fat chance anyway in New Zealand, with old Wally Nash blocking any purchases from the United States. I didn't say I would settle for a car, full stop, and all the new records Elvis could produce. Jasper, I could guarantee, would not be into Elvis. Instead I told him his outfit was grouse.

'Practical,' he snapped. 'No knowing how long those union clowns will be chatting Nash.'

I had to show my ignorance again, asking what it was all about. He said I could see for myself, outside Parliament, where a 'No Maoris, No Tour' group was gathering. I was not this time totally ignorant of what he was referring to, given coverage was all over the *Herald* and *Star* last year. There had been a student march on Parliament to protest the exclusion of Maoris from the All Blacks to tour South Africa, and some kind of public committee had been formed to change the government's indifferent mind.

'Why not?' I said to his retreating figure.

Jasper strode head up and coat swirling through the Friday crowds with almost regal indifference, although 'regal' would not be a word he would rate. He'd already jeered at a newspaper headline: *Princess Margaret engaged to Court Photographer.*

'Monarchy,' he snarled, 'is the way they keep everybody in line.'

He didn't pause for debate or even comment. I had no chance to ask who this mysterious 'they' were, but I suppose he meant the Big Brother state.

It had been cloudy all day. As I followed Jasper's serene progress down Lambton Quay, the northerly began to intensify, lifting the corners of his coat, exposing the incongruity of his black cords and desert boots. We crossed to the Cenotaph, rain spitting into our faces. It had as little effect on Jasper's advance as the swaying tram, screeching brakes to avoid flattening him. I could see the angry face of the driver, then the flinging about of passengers holding on for dear life to the overhead straps as the tram slammed and swayed across the Quay like an interisland ferry entering Cook Strait.

The big iron gates of Parliament were wide open, allowing the procession up the curved path of groups of duffel wearers with hoods up against the rain, the lecturers identified among the students by the better quality of duffel, à la Gull's. Indeed, I saw the distinctive green of the notoriously left-wing geography professor Keith Buchanan, and I was pretty sure from behind I spotted some of our masters, including Macaskill, Shallcrass, Fox and Vogt. There were a few business suits and gaberdines pulling their hats lower, a number of them Maori. A third group I could identify in the short black or blue coats like the one I got from the Gear, these last with no head covering, heads as high as Jasper's, seemingly oblivious to the rain as they marched to a reckoning.

The various groups sidled together at the base of the steep sequence of steps up to Parliament, flanked by several contingents of police.

'State goons,' Jasper said as I bumped up against him.

I looked around for Bill Dwyer and his wool hook. No sign of him.

'Any of your anarchist mates here?'

'No mates of mine,' he said, jerking his head towards the duffel coat clutch. 'You can see them any Tuesday outside the Student Union waffling away. Ruddy armchair revolutionaries.'

'At least they're here,' I protested.

'Forelock tugging lot.'

A bulky business type with heavy black-framed glasses had ascended a few steps and faced us.

'My friends,' he announced in a fine, rounded voice of the kind I am sure Jasper would regard as ruling class. 'My friends, a delegation of us will shortly ask our leaders behind us here …'

He was interrupted by boos from the duffel coats. One of the workingman jackets was more explicit. 'Farkin' wankers!' he bellowed, eliciting cheers from his colleagues.

'Yes,' agreed the speaker. 'Walter has already told us that a rugby tour of South Africa is not his problem and not a subject he could talk about. We are here to challenge that.'

Applause and cheers.

A smaller man with a weatherbeaten face and a long, straggly beard moved up alongside the speaker. 'Bloody oath!' he boomed. 'Wally's comments are a requiem at the burial of the concept of racial equality in New Zealand.'

Applause, sheepdog whistles, roars of approval, shouts of 'Good on yer, brother.'

The main speaker had his hands up for quiet. 'Thank you, Bernard,' he continued. 'You are absolutely correct. Like Pontius Pilate, Walter Nash has washed his hands of the Maori. He says he cannot see a way of sending Maoris without incidents and troubles. Well, we can give him a solution. Don't send them any players.'

Shouts of agreement.

'Bet ya boots, eh?' some working jacket chortled.

'Bloody Nash,' his mate said. 'Can't tell his arse from his elbow.'

'Yeah. Neither for nor against the 51 lockout.'

'Fence sitter.'

'Prick.'

'That is why,' the speaker was saying, his voice rising to cut through the crowd comments, 'we formed the Citizens' All Black Tour Association. To remind our political leaders of their duty to announce – in unequivocal terms – the attitude of this country to racial segregation. It is a matter of our national honour.'

'Blatherer,' Jasper grunted.

'Remember what Corbett said: *Sport without morality no longer deserves the name.*'

'Tory wanker.'

'What's their problem?'

The boots commentator turned to me. 'Bloody Nat, that's what.'

'Who? This guy?'

'Nah, he's a surgeon.'

'Another of the ruling class.'

'Shut up.'

'Friends,' the speaker appealed. 'Since our town hall meeting, thousands have joined with distinguished All Black George Nepia, distinguished New Zealand cricket captain Walter Hadlee, distinguished New Zealand writer Ngaio Marsh ...'

'Fuck distinguished,' Jasper growled.

'... in calling on our leaders to abandon their gross and indefensible racial discrimination. Not one pakeha politician has uttered one word of public condemnation of this act.'

His words were interrupted by a guttural cry to one side, followed by slapping of cloth. The group of – *pace* Jasper's feelings about the word — distinguished Maori gentlemen were doing a haka, led by a man in a dog collar. The stage was ceded. Nobody can resist a haka. Despite the rain, it was performed with gaberdines unbuttoned and swirling like pakeha piupius. The men were twice or three times the age of most All Blacks, but its collective power might even warm the cynical cockles of Jasper's heart.

When it had ended, the Maori men formed up alongside the surgeon and some of the working class and business gents.

'We will now, friends,' the surgeon said solemnly, 'proceed with our deputation. We will request that our prime minister use his mana to cancel the tour and stop radio censorship.'

'Fat ruddy chance,' Jasper snorted as the men proceeded up the steps to general encouragement and voices urging them to 'Give it to Walter' and 'Don't come back without a cancellation'.

We stood about in a wet huddle. Jasper reckoned it was a waste of time, going in on bended knee tugging your forelock. The powerful, he said, never give up anything.

I asked him why in that case was he here.

He shrugged. 'Know your enemies,' he said mysteriously.

'Then what?'

'Put a bomb under them.'

One of the workers overheard. 'You're right there, mate. It's the only answer.'

It was not a long meeting. The surgeon came out to tell us he got the same hollow response from the prime minister.

Boos, jeers.

The Acting Leader of the Opposition Jack Marshall, he said, refused to accept any moral responsibility and accused us protesters of doing more harm than good.

Lots of boos and jeers.

'Those who care about race relations,' the surgeon said, 'will feel bitterly disappointed and Maoris will feel let down and humiliated. Thank you for coming. The fight is only just beginning. Don't forget to get as many signatures as you can.'

As the crowd started to disperse I saw a young man appear from the side of the steps with a camera and flash. I was watching him position himself when a figure bumped me to one side.

'Gull,' I said, startled as his large shape masked the flash going off behind him.

'Who's your mate?'

Jasper had gone. I told Gull I thought he would know one of Bill Dwyer's lot. He said he didn't, and offered me a lift home. I wasn't going to get much wetter, but it was a lot more appealing than slumping across the road to wait for a bus.

Gull insisted I take the only helmet, reckoned the goggles were all he needed. Coming down the overbridge on to Petone foreshore he failed to spot the lurking traffic cop, probably because his goggles were coated with rain. Lights and siren overtook us, a gloved hand waving us to a stop just past my former employer the Gear Meat Company. The northerly blew its appalling stink up our noses as Gull stopped, swung off, leaving me to grab the handlebars as he moved to meet the stormtrooper in his bagged-out trou tucked into glistening boots. Gull had a brief chat, showed the officer something, the officer waved him on. As he got back on the bike, he said he was glad he held on to his warrant card.

It was a relief when Melissa ambushed me scurrying out of Orsman's baffling lecture on language families. I had pushed the swing door and she was standing in front of me in the corridor in an inside-out sheepskin coat with a wool-fringed hood. My eyes were drawn to a single ruby-coloured stone the size of a pullet egg dangling on a thin gold chain around her neck. I looked up at her quickly. She took my breath away. I felt weak in her presence.

'Ah, Melissa,' I said feebly, trying pathetically to look over her head, as if I had some pressing meeting. I didn't. I had run out of running. I stood there, my temperature rising.

'I'm not dangerous,' she said. 'Come on, let's go have a coffee.'

She took my arm and I meekly went with her. On the way to the cable car I tried to apologise. She tugged at my duffel and said it was she who should apologise, she didn't realise I was unwell. I started to say I was not used to marijuana, but she told me to hush, first time could be tricky and anyway it was really strong bhang.

We took the outside wooden seats. She laughed as the cable car lurched off and grabbed hold of me. You couldn't hear yourself speak let alone think with the noise, an enforced breathing space which allowed me to calm down.

It was only a temporary calm. In the Rendezvous, her rings glinting and bangles jiggling inspired me to explain the origins of bells on toes. I gulped black coffee and started gabbling about the hidden political meaning of the nursery rhyme I had looked up: 'Riding a cock horse to Banbury Cross. It's about Queen Elizabeth — the first one. She'd gone to see the Cross at Banbury and her carriage broke a wheel and she transferred to this cock horse.'

Quick glance at Melissa, me flushing. I felt compelled to continue. 'See, the townsfolk decorated the horse with ribbons and bells and minstrels sang to her, because it was the fashion to attach bells to pointed toes. On shoes?'

Melissa was smiling as she forked in Napoleon cake. I wasn't sure I was making sense.

'You know, pointy-toed, like winklepickers?' I paused. I said I must be sounding as hyper as that music professor.

'Weird, eh?' she said.

'Like me.'

'Nah. You're trying to find out if I have bells on my toes.'

'Guilty as charged,' I said, starting to relax. 'I do know what you have got – a flake of pastry on the side of your mouth.' She quickly dabbed, on the wrong side. I reached out with the edge of the paper napkin and flicked it off.

'You want to go to the Grand Orientation Ball?'

'You do?'

'I'm asking you, dummy. Do you want to come with me?'

'Do I what!' I said too emphatically. 'Actually, I mean, I would.'

She giggled, bringing to mind the reefer fiasco. Undoubtedly my face reflected the unease in my stomach.

'Hey!' she said, taking my hand. 'I'm not into — you know – girls.' She shrugged. 'I thought you were for experiences. Kerouac stuff. Like Don talking about sleeping with that old actor. Hey, you're not into men, are you?'

'No way!'

'Just kidding. I know you're not.' She waved her hand vaguely. 'At the time it seemed like fun. Let's face it, I dunno what I'm trying to say.'

I squeezed her hand. 'I don't know either.'

'We didn't do anything ...'

I squeezed harder. 'I'll get us tickets, eh?'

She laughed. 'I've got them already. It was just a matter of ...'

'Getting hold of me.'

I made the point concrete by taking both her hands, as I pulled her gently into a long kiss.

'Excuse me?'

It was the waitress, wanting our cups. This time our giggling was in synch.

'I loved the card,' I said. 'You are so talented.'

We were kissing again, until the waitress coughed.

'So are you,' she said. 'Neat poem about the dead cat.'

'Thanks.' My problem was now diminished to how I handled those second year jokers wanting the bad oil. Stuff them.

She was frowning. 'Anything wrong?'

I looked at the little furrow across her gorgeous face. 'Not on your nelly,' I said, kissing her. 'Whatever your nelly is.'

'Whatever you like.'

We were deliberately late for the ball. This was only partly because neither of us liked the corny old dances such as the Gay Gordon and the Foxtrot. Nor was it because of any reservations by either of us about the Second Years making off-colour remarks, because they didn't deign to attend this first year hooley. It was mostly because we wanted to snog. And we did, until Melissa finally told me to go play with the kitten in the kitchen while she got dressed.

I flicked a biro this way and that in front of Nigel, who found it endlessly fascinating. I didn't. What I did find fascinating was Melissa in a close-fitting dark green dress made of something semi-transparent and rustic like cheesecloth, barely supported (pun intended) in the upper area. The dress and the bare feet would have gone well on Maid Marian in Sherwood Forest. They went very well on Melissa. It took us a little while longer before she got her inside-out sheepskin coat on and we headed along Upland Road to the ball.

The Assembly hall was transformed from the regimented rows listening to the drone of Prof Page into a pulsating floor of writhing couples lit by the flickering flashes of the revolving ball in the ceiling and the shaded red lights around the sides. The professor and Scotty and other stuffed shirts were replaced by a band of sweaty young guys on guitars and drums belting out *At the Hop*.

Melissa dragged me into the writhing, twisting mass, ducking under a guy's arm as he twirled his partner on the end of his extended fingers, her dress ballooning out as she swung this way and that, her legs bare all the way to knickers flashing, inspiring male yells and chortles of appreciation. I got hauled round a couple doing the locked hands above the heads as they arced in opposing circles. Then we were into it, bopping and jiving, Melissa at the end of my hand, bangles sliding up and down her arm, letting go as she spun, me catching her other hand to flick her the other way, then both hands as we bumped to the left, bumped to the right, and hugged tight as the band thrashed to a stop.

'Dead Cat!'

It was the runty Phys-Ed joker, legs apart, eyes somewhat glazed. Obviously Don's nickname for me had got around.

'Give's a go, eh? No need to hog her.'

I looked at Melissa. She shrugged.

'Good on yer,' he slurred, lurching against Melissa. 'Baz or Jeff'll give you a snort.'

I looked at the tight group. No sign of Fox.

'Where's your leader?'

Jeff, the tall, dark and handsome one, curled his lip and said if I meant Fox, he was in training for the trials — if I knew what they were.

'No idea,' I lied, knowing he meant the All Black selection trials.

There were calls from the crowd for *Daddy Cool, Hound Dog, Tutti Frutti.* I put my hands round my mouth and yelled *Jailhouse Rock.* Instead the band launched into another all-time fave, *Rave On,* which obviously was to the liking of the crowd, judging by the yippees and howls and somebody barking approval, with more skipping on to the floor from the sidelines.

A show-off couple had commandeered the front area with frantic frugging and whirling clearing a space around them, which gave him the chance to fling her up over his head, lower body bared, *exsultate jubilate* from the group behind me. He swung her down through his legs and he leapt around to capture her and continue jiving, without losing the beat. I checked Melissa, who had her hands full holding up her stumbling partner.

'Stump's a bit pissy-eyed,' a voice drawled as I was nudged hard in the kidneys. I swung round. Jeff was poking a brown paper parcel into my stomach.

'This'll get you goin,' he said, looking back at his group. 'Don't make it obvious.'

I took a swig, gasping at the raw kerosene effect.

'What is that?' I managed, as he snatched the bottle and held it behind him.

'Vat 69, sissy,' he sneered. 'Sorts the men from the boys.'

The Buddy Holly number was over and the band was into '*Wop bop a lop bop,*' the start of *Tutti Frutti* drowned out by collective cheers. Jeff pushed past me. 'My turn.'

I was still swallowing as he pulled Stump aside and swept Melissa into a smooth embrace and then out with his hand, twirling her and lifting her skirt a little, her bare feet visible as she pirouetted on his hand steer.

'Hey, Dead Cat?' Stump burped as he lurched against me. 'Your sheila naked all the way?'

I pushed him hard in the chest, telling him to piss off. Somebody belted me from behind, causing me to stumble.

'Pick on someone your own size,' the Phys-Ed hulk said, thumping his hands into my chest.

'Take it easy, Hooks,' one of his mates cautioned, hauling him back. 'There're still some of the masters here. Save your energy for your turn.'

Hooks joined in the group chortles. There were six of them, hunting as a pack.

'Can't you jokers get your own partners?' I said, nodding at the row of girls sitting along the wall.

'We like yours,' one of them said, which set off another round of group nudges and sniggers.

'Looks like she don't mind.'

I swung round. Melissa and Jeff were getting into the fancy moves up front alongside the show-boaters. The area had cleared to let both couples do their expanding moves.

'Oh rooty!' one of the clowns behind me yelled as Jeff swung Melissa under his legs and then out. I could see he was aiming to get her upside down, but she deftly spun out of his grasp, landing on her feet, bangles shaking like wind chimes.

'Hello, Stephen.'

Liz Atkinson was standing there with an uncertain smile. She was dressed to bop in a blue flower-patterned party frock and those American knee-length white socks and flat shoes.

'What are you doing here?'

'Pat asked me.'

I had the same question for Gull, but he got in first.

'Thought I'd take up the invite,' he said, grinning through his trimmed beard. He was in a white shirt and jeans. 'It was on the student noticeboard.'

I said I hadn't seen it. Did I care? The band was into *Love Potion No 9*. There was no sign of Melissa up the front, then I saw her pushing past several of the Phys-Ed team.

She took my hand. 'Shall we go?'

Gull had his hand out. 'Last dance?'

'Sorry,' she said, tugging on my hand.

I was happy to go, away from the vulgar grunts, arm pumping and loud mock protests from the Phys-Ed camp. Liz looked puzzled, but Gull was impassive. Odd he'd turn up at a Training College ball.

As we collected our coats, Melissa said the girl with my big friend seemed to know me. I said she was just a local Eastbourne girl. She was simply that to me now, an acquaintance, somebody from another life. I had got a surprise seeing her there, but not any agitation in the heart department. I was more surprised to see her with Gull, she'd never mentioned him and he didn't fit the tennis crowd, but there was no reason they wouldn't know each other.

 **7**

We walked back along Upland Road holding hands, our coats on our free arms. 'Disorientation ball, eh?'

I looked at her. 'You weren't.'

'Jeff fancies himself.'

'I fancy you.'

'I'm sick of those apes.'

'Sport dorks to a man.'

Melissa snorted. 'I'd say to a boy.'

'Totally right.'

She squeezed my hand. 'Come on, race you.'

She was off, holding her dress up and disappearing fast. I wasn't going to let her get away, though I did not need to actually beat her. In fact, I doubt I could, the slip-ons were not great for speed, irreparably stretched from their Eastbourne outing. I put on the puffing and leaned against the concrete wall as she pushed the gate open. She batted at my arm, saying I was putting her on, she knew I could run, that's what the Phys-Ed guys had against me.

Nigel made his requirements obvious with more meow volume than you'd expect from a tiny black kitten. He got the cuddling until he was purring and then a saucer of milk. We left him to it.

'No need for the dancing this time?' she asked rhetorically as she pulled the curtains half-closed.

'No way,' I agreed. 'I can't match Jeff on the dance floor.'

'We're not on the dance floor,' she said.

We were embracing and kissing. She put a hand on my chest. I could feel my heart pulsing against it. She gently pushed me on to the bed, which accelerated my heart rate, before she pushed away. My heart lurched.

'It's okay,' she said softly. 'I won't be a minute.'

She switched off the overhead light and in the sudden darkness glided like a ghost across to the small table. I peered anxiously to see what she was doing. With the curtains almost closed it was difficult to see. She had the drawer open and was taking out what looked like the tapers you use to light candles on the altar. She placed these brown straws in a small holder, something like Mum used to hold flowers upright inside a vase. She struck a match and placed it at the head of a taper. It flared and then fizzled into a thin stream of pungent smoke winding towards the ceiling. It was not quite the incense I knew as an altar boy from spooning it on to the hot charcoal at the base of the censer, more exotic, and like her perfume made me think of Arabian Nights magic.

Next she lit a candle, a large object the size of a can of Wattie's peaches. It shed enough light to make an upright dark blue glass cat figurine seem as if it was hovering like ectoplasm just above the surface of the table. The alien smoke curled to the ceiling. I felt uneasy, as if we might be dabbling in something occult.

She was next to me on the bed. 'Venus is aspecting Mars,' she said, giggling as she took my hand.

'Is that good?'

'Oh yes,' she said, turning my hand palm up towards the light. 'Try and relax, Steve,' she said, her forefinger tracing the lines across my hand. Fat chance of relaxing. She was generating tingles like little electric shocks, straight into the centre of my heart. Relaxation was not an option. I was ready to jump out of my skin.

'Yeah,' she said, nodding approval. 'That's a groove. Romantic head line. Oh-oh.'

'What?'

'I can't.'

'No, please, don't hold back.'

'Hmm.' She had moved to my little finger. 'Mercury.'

She lifted my pinkie between thumb and forefinger with no difficulty, there was no resistance, like the person attached to it. I hardly dared breathe. She brushed her lips across the tip. It was a jolt. I couldn't believe the effect. She leaned down and put her mouth over it. A swarm of blood prickled all over me, out of all proportion to the contact. I couldn't help but jerk involuntarily.

'Sorry,' I said, quickly feeling for her hand. 'You have to tell me.'

'Sincere.'

'Is that all?'

'Nooo. Sensual. Your heart line's really artistic, romantic.'

'You're just saying that to be nice. Anything you're not saying?'

'Let's see, you're very sentimental, idealistic.'

'Is that bad?'

She laughed. 'That's what I can feel. I must do your horoscope. All I need is your date of birth, and time.'

'Now?'

She nibbled my ear. 'No,' she whispered thickly. 'Oh Steve, I can't wait.'

We flung off our clothes, mine taking longer to shed. Our hands were all over each other. I was almost bursting and Melissa was hot and wet.

'I want you,' she said. 'Do you have a condom?'

I stopped moving. 'No,' I said feebly, turning away from her, not trusting myself to say anything else. I wasn't sure what to say. Catholics don't believe in tampering with nature, we practise the rhythm method of birth control. I wasn't sure what the rhythm method was. I had not faced this situation. I didn't know what to do.

'It's okay,' she said. 'My period's due. Come on.'

She pulled me against her. I had gone limp. I felt hot and sweaty and yet cold.

'I'll have to warm you up,' she said, sliding down my body, her bangles scraping across my stomach.

She soon brought my temperature back up, and then she wriggled under me and guided me inside her. It was like a furnace. I could hardly credit the intensity of heat. We were both moving faster.

'Pull out,' she gasped. 'Don't stay inside me.'

We moved faster and I could feel myself building. At the last second, I heaved out of her and spilled myself over her stomach. She had her arms around me. I slowly slid down and kissed her breasts, sucking one nipple and then the other. She was moaning and murmuring not to stop. I slid further, smelling my sharp rankness on her.

'Yes,' she said, as I slid down into her mound and kissed and licked and buried my face in her.

'There, there,' she urged, pushing my head into her, urging me to suck just there, yes, there, more, more, her breathing accelerating until finally she yelled and her back arched and bucked and she shuddered and her legs clamped my head in a vice-like grip. She released me, laughing, her bangles dancing up and down her arm.

'Groovy,' she said.

'No bells on your toes.'

'Now you notice.'

We lay in each other's arms. She suggested we could get under the blanket and we did. Soon after I was on top of her and inside her and the heat was, if anything, more intense. I was possessing and possessed. I thrust into her again and again, she moving to meet me, and then I was ejaculating in a sequence of spasms deep into her.

'I love you,' I moaned, then yelled in alarm as she flung me out of bed.

'Jesus!' she squealed. 'I told you not to.'

She clambered over my exposed body and rushed through to the bathroom. I heard the shower turn on.

God! How could I? What had I done? She said it was okay. No, she said she was almost going to have her period. Why hadn't I just pulled out like the first time? Because I wanted to be one with her.

Feeling totally stupid, I scooped up my clothes and took off, this time knocking the cat's saucer flying as I pulled open the door and fled like a thief into the night, my ears roaring with shame and disgust.

There was no motorbike starting up, but the MTA or whatever was parked outside, the roof up. A burning point appeared inside, then smoke, the door opening.

'Steve?'

I crouched in the dubious protection of the concrete trench, keenly aware what a naked and pathetic spectacle I was.

Clair came towards me, laughing. I couldn't see what was funny.

'Why are you here?'

'Same reason as you, by the look of it. Not a good time to call, I guess.'

I had no answer to that. I pulled on my green Elvis pants and the slip-ons sans socks I had left behind. She opened the creaky gate as I slipped on the yellow shirt and shrugged into my duffel. She was looking amused as she eyed me through a haze of pungent smoke, not a reefer, it was long and looked black. Not a cigarillo. Smelled like dung burning. I felt like someone off the turnips, like a scarecrow kitted out in the kind of colours that would scare off any but the boldest bird. She was undoubtedly bold, standing with her hands on her hips in a purple jumpsuit so tight the only way out of it would have to be the fat zip running from chest to navel, a large silver ring to help download it.

'Let's ride,' she said. 'Has to be better than standing out in this.'

The drizzle was unpleasant, but I hesitated. I had not at this stage developed any options, given it was way past the last bus home and I was in a state of post-priapic despair. I cursed my own lack of planning. I just wanted to be out of here. I could get her to drop me off and hitch on the Hutt Road.

She shrugged, which must have tested the holding strength of the zip. 'Suit yourself,' she said, swivelling and high-heeling to her car, flicking her fag into the gutter.

What the hell. I got in.

'Jesus wept,' she exclaimed, cranking down her window, lighting another of her own brand of pong. 'You need a bath, hombre.'

Hombre?

'I guess,' I muttered, bracing myself as she crunched gear and jerked up the hill. Her driving was showing no improvement. She screeched and bucked down the parade on to The Terrace, down and into the city. I was all fingers and thumbs, it was not easy working the shirt buttons into place, all the time reminding me how intimately they had been involved only minutes ago. I wrenched the toggles closed over my sweaty chest and a heart that I swear had shrivelled up. The echo of Melissa's words identifying the sentimental, idealistic, romantic, artistic, it was now mocking, angry, rejecting. I slumped against the door. There were a lot of other adjectives I deserved. Stupid, self-indulgent, irresponsible, insensitive, plain doltishly dumb.

All was quiet, not a drunk or cop to be seen. Just as well, for Clair's car, or at least her driving of it, had to be an attention gainer. Gloomy streetlights and poor visibility were bad enough for her to get the wipers slapping. Last year a Sydney beauty queen was asked when she returned home what she thought of New Zealand and she said she didn't know, it was closed.

I was too dispirited to ask where we were going. At Courtenay Place she swung left past the yacht club into Oriental Bay, then up a side street that was as steep as they come. It looked like we were not going to make it when her foot slipped, but she stabbed back on the accelerator and the car hiccupped around a bend and up another and arguably an even steeper street. She flung the car left into an overgrown driveway and skidded along it to a stop.

Clair got out, telling me to follow her as she ascended a wide set of steps to a porch entranceway flanked by a square bay window on the left and to the right a bull-nosed veranda disappearing into dense shrubbery. The light from a subdued red overhead light glinted on panes of coloured glass either side of a gleaming varnished door with a huge brass knocker. She ignored that, pressing a small button to the side.

There was some delay, during which I noted a small eyehole flicker above the knocker. Finally the door opened and internal lighting revealed some kind of butler in a white penguin suit with a pink bow tie and a luxuriant stack of swept-back, silvery-white hair.

'Clair, my dear,' he said softly, his hands clasped in front of him, small black eyes giving me the once over.

'I know, Harold,' she said apologetically. 'It is late. This kid's in the poop.'

He acknowledged with a dignified inclination of his head, stepping back and inviting us in. Clair led the way down a dimly-lit hallway of dark red carpet, black lower walls of pressed tin, above a dividing wooden rail a thick flock wallpaper of a dusty pink *fleur-de-lis* design. She opened a heavy wooden door. I followed her into an enormous sitting room with several sets of chesterfield suites of a wine-red colour matching the tall sets of curtains surrounding several bay windows. Clair climbed a few carpeted steps to a bar, where she slipped on to one of the high stools next to the counter. Cut-glass mirrors reflected the backs of the line of liquor bottles arrayed behind, with glasses on a cloth-covered tray.

Harold eased around me to take up a position behind the bar, his plump pink features expectant. I stood in the doorway, taking in more details. The brass urns with arching palms, a side table supporting an ebony carving of an elephant, its tusks and trunk raised. Across the other side of the room I could make out another such elephant triumphant. The lighting was low, filtered through large red lampshades balanced on dark metal nudes.

Aromatic incense rather more pungent than the stuff used in High Mass curled lazily around the room, along with the anodyne music of one of those innocuous orchestras of syrupy strings, Frank Chacksfield or Mantovani or Andre Kostelanetz, often played on the afternoon request session Mum had been addicted to.

The music was at odds with the art on the walls, featuring oil paintings of large nude women of the Italian traditional school in heavy gold frames. Not like Melissa's Modigliani ladies with their sharp angles, unlike Melissa ... the image of her under me was so powerful I gasped. God, she had accepted me, and I had abused her trust.

I blinked and shook my head. I thought I was hallucinating on a white hand hovering in the air beside the high-backed sofa. I blinked again to clear my vision. It was still there, revealing a white cuff and gold links as it reached out and claimed a thick glass off the elaborately carved wooden surface of an exotic coffee table. Another, darker hand with bangles wriggling at the wrist curled over the hand with the drink, arresting its progress, long red nails curling into a clamp. The cuffed hand relinquished the drink, but not without some muffled protest.

The controlling hand waved towards the bar, then from the sofa rose the rest of a resplendent figure the equal of the oil paintings, except for the crimson satin dress and an astonishing array of both piled and cascading black hair. Everything about this lady was extravagant, her dress barely containing curves Mae West would have died for, the kind of embonpoint that would have Groucho Marx spinning in lascivious circles. Her enormous black eyes were enclosed to a gravity-defying degree by mascara heavy lashes, such that they brought to mind those old lidded telephone exchange sockets which flicked up to announce a caller. The large red lips parted like the slow-motion opening of a luscious tropical bloom.

'Darling,' she gurgled, looking me over, her arms jangling with twice Melissa's layers of bangles all the way to her elbows, 'isn't it past your bedtime?'

'Miranda,' Harold cautioned. 'Don't be naughty.'

Miranda flicked out her hair with one hand. 'I am always naughty. Which cradle did you snatch him from, Clair?'

Clair was not required to answer. A dishevelled older man, a professional judging by the thick, chalky pin-stripes of his dark suit, staggered to his feet, his tie askew, his waistcoat unbuttoned. He embraced Miranda in a bear hug, his shape more akin to that of an overweight but excessively clean pig, his face and wobbling neck only a few shades lighter than Miranda's dress.

'You're with me,' he squealed indignantly, toppling both of them back into the sofa.
'Call him a cab,' Clair said tersely. 'But I'll use the phone first.'

Harold brought a black phone from beneath the bar, seemingly unconcerned
at the wrestling match taking place on the sofa. He beckoned me to come in. I was
reluctant. I felt like a fish out of water. A river fish, that didn't fancy the ocean. I
wasn't totally green, this was some kind of brothel. Harold was coming towards me.
He was harmless enough and if he didn't care about the grunting and commotion
coming from the couch, why should I?

My concerns were with Melissa. I wasn't drunk, there was no excuse. I was out
of my skull with lust, I suppose. I couldn't think straight. Was there anything I could
do to make up with her? In a word, no. I had not wanted to think about condoms,
and it was not from any conscious Catholic objections, more the subconscious,
superstitious, ignorant, bog-Irish Catholic side catching me out. I hadn't thought
about the repercussions, I hadn't thought, full stop. I had been overwhelmed by the
moment, the cardinal sin of lust. Now I was in a place where you paid for it.

'It's not the end of the world,' Harold said, patting my arm. 'Come and sit down.'

He took my arm and steered me away from Miranda and her eager client to the
bar. Clair was crouched over the phone, speaking insistently. She slammed it down
and pulled out her cigarettes. Harold held a thin gold lighter offering her a sedate
blue flame. She inhaled, blowing out smoke, eyeing me.

'Don't worry,' I said. 'I'll take off.'

There was an angry exclamation from the couch, a loud slap and a yell of pain.
Miranda was advancing, smoothing her dress around her ample hips, eyes flashing.

'Give us the phone,' she snapped.

Harold did as bid, and excused himself. He went over to the couch and leant
over the client, speaking too quietly for me to detect anything other than a certain
firmness in his tone. Miranda ordered a taxi, Clair released more noxious fumes from
her long black cigarette. I was getting the picture, she didn't enjoy babysitting me.

I was heading for the door when Harold caught my arm. 'Let's go into the parlour,'
he said. 'We can have a cup of tea. That usually calms things down.'

I smiled back at him. Mum always used to say the same thing, a cup of Choysa
the answer to any problem.

Harold told the two ladies of the tea party and ushered us through the door the
far side of the bar. It was a kitchen nook. He indicated chairs at a small round table
covered in a pink gingham tablecloth with a bowl of yellow daisies in its centre.
Miranda sighed and took a seat, I took one opposite her. Clair remained standing,
puffing noxious smoke. Harold poured water at the sink into a kettle, put it on, asked
us to give him a moment as he stepped daintily out the door on glossy white patent

leather slippers.

'Huh!' Clair grunted. 'About time Murphy was banned.'

Miranda pouted. 'He pays top pound.'

Clair gave her a sharp look. 'Then why are you here?'

'Fuck a duck!' Miranda squawked, her voice dramatically out of the purr register into fishwife mode. 'You know what he gets like, the vicious old bugger. Pinching my fanny adams.'

Clair pulled a face. 'He doesn't touch mine, sister. It's your fat arse he wants.'

The red claws were being unsheathed, but a distraction appeared in the doorway. An anxious looking man with a thin white face and a thin black moustache was tucking his white shirt into his charcoal grey trousers, sharp little watery blue eyes swivelling in every direction.

'I heard someone shout,' he said accusingly. 'There a problem?'

'Nothing you need worry about,' Clair said. 'Just silly old Murph.'

Harold appeared behind him. 'All is well, Gus. Ticketyboo.'

Gus did another eye check around the room, paused on Miranda, nodded curtly and retreated.

'Freak,' Miranda growled.

I glanced at Clair.

'Vice Squad,' she sneered.

'Comes for Sister Immaculata's attentions,' Miranda said suggestively. 'Can't get enough of it.'

The phone rang. Harold went out, returned and said it was for Clair. He had the creepily calm manner of a retired religious brother wandering the quad, safe in the knowledge he would never again have to face another class of unruly lads. He pulled a small gingham apron that matched the tablecloth off a hook behind the door, put it on and got a brown ceramic teapot and delicate pink teacups rimmed in gold out of the cupboard. He was precise about pouring hot water in the teapot before he got out a tin tea caddy. While he made tea he told Miranda that Sir Michael promised to behave himself in future and had left a double surety by way of making amends.

'Promises, promises,' she sighed heavily. 'That's all I ever hear.'

'There we are,' Harold said. 'A cuppa soothes the fevered brow.'

'Sounds like a quote,' I suggested.

'Not quite,' he said, raising an eyebrow as we heard Clair's voice rise into shrill. 'But let's hope I'm proved right.'

'Silly cow,' Miranda growled. 'What's she doing with you?'

I shrugged. 'Giving me a lift.'

'Sounds like she's giving Gull the hurry-up.'

'Ah, yes,' Harold nodded, sitting down and removing the beaded muslin cover off the milk jug. 'Milk first, yes? I thought Gull might be in the mix.'

'God!' Miranda scoffed. 'Don't know what she sees in him. Sneaky cop.'

'Gull has his good points,' Harold mildly protested as he poured. 'Don't you agree, young man?'

'I suppose,' I said noncommittally. I wasn't really sure what Gull's points were, good or bad.

The phone was slammed down once more.

Miranda let out an unladylike snort of derision. 'She's not called Clair de Lune for nothing. That is one loony tune.'

'Now, Miranda,' Harold objected a little more firmly. 'You know how Clair feels about him.'

'She's in the wrong job then,' Miranda muttered.

Harold got up without comment and glided out of the room. Miranda flipped her hair, sighed heavily. 'That girl will not learn.'

We sipped our tea. Harold returned, said Clair had gone to lie down.

'Not unusual,' Miranda sniggered.

Harold gave her a chiding look. 'The path of true love, Miranda.'

'Definitely a quote there,' I said.

Harold smiled benignly. 'A top up?'

We both accepted. Harold and Mum were right, tea did help. Miranda also excused herself. Harold put the dishes in the sink, declining my offer to help. He said they could wait upon the morrow.

He invited me back into the empty bar. He collected a bottle of VSOP Martell I was acquainted with from Dad's modest liquor cabinet and two brandy balloons and directed me to a seat on the set of sofas opposite where Sir Michael had been a pest.

'A bedtime snifter,' he said, pouring two generous measures. 'Good for the tummy.'

I accepted the balloon.

'Stephen, yes? I take it you were in need of some assistance?'

I sipped the potent liquid, the fumes alone enough to clear a pathway through my sinuses and fill my chest with a sense of warm wellbeing. I told him that I too had bungled the path of true love.

'Enough said, dear boy. It's not something I have encountered myself in a very long time. But I still have vestigial memories.'

I asked him what he knew about Gull. He shrugged. 'A complex cove,' he said, dipping his nose into his balloon. 'He should make a better lawyer than some of those who frequent my little establishment.'

I frowned, not sure how to phrase it.

'Go on, dear boy. Speak, as they say, or forever hold your peace.'

I glanced at him, momentarily thinking he had made a Macaskill-esque pun on 'piece'. He looked calmly avuncular.

'Gull keeps cropping up,' I said slowly, unsure what I had in mind. 'Keeps turning up wherever I am.'

'Is that a bad thing?'

I shrugged.

'I see,' he said, swirling the balloon, looking at me. 'If it's any help, I trust him. But then, I'm not one of his lady friends.'

The buzzer went. Harold excused himself. He brought Gull in.

'Sorry about the delay,' he said. 'I promised Mrs A I'd get Liz back before the witching hour.'

Harold fetched him a cognac and joined us.

'Stephen,' he said, 'is puzzled about you.'

Gull grinned. 'Okay, fair enough. Cards on the table. I promised your father I'd look out for you.'

'Eh?!'

Gull's grin widened. 'Your little escapade at the Mardi Gras, as a for instance. He worries about you.'

I felt a flood of resentment. 'He's got no right to interfere.'

'Has helped, yes?'

'How'd he know about the trapeze thing? You tell him?'

'No, Liz did. Indirectly. He rang her mother, that's where it came from.'

Harold coughed quietly. 'Perhaps your father has your best interests …'

'At heart,' I finished the sentence. 'I know what it is. He's worried I'm going to shame him. Name in the paper, or worse, in *Truth*. Horror show.'

'You know, Gull said slowly, 'he's in line for a big job come election?'

'No,' I grunted. 'He doesn't confide in me.'

'Ask him.'

It struck me how weird this was, sitting in this nancy man's brothel talking about my father with a guy who'd snatched my old girlfriend. The thing they didn't realise was that none of it mattered. The only thing that did was Melissa, and I definitely could not get any assistance from anybody on that score.

'If you're here as my bodyguard,' I said, standing up, 'let's go.'

Both of them stood. Gull thanked him for his usual discretion. Harold patted his shoulder and suggested nothing would be solved without a good night's sleep. I accepted his handshake. He might be full of platitudes and half-quotes, but he was the sanest person of this crazy day. I thanked him for his hospitality.

'Anytime, dear boy,' he said, as he opened the door. Eartha was purring from an invisible speaker *'bees do it, even educated fleas …'* The door closed softly.

On the way down the steps I said I supposed Liz was just another good friend. Gull turned, said for what it was worth, yes, she was an old family friend.

'Did you get her to pick me up?'

He shook his head. 'Come on,' he said. 'It's been a long night.'

It was silent, except for the noise of his bike and the wind roaring in my ears. He dropped me home. I managed to mutter thanks. He might think I was upset at his dissimulation and that of my father setting him to spy on me. In fact, I wasn't. There was only one thing on my mind, and body, and I knew I had stuffed up royally, unforgivably, unconscionably. I crept into bed, aching for Melissa, dreading my next encounter with her, dreading the news she might have to impart, that she never wanted to see me again.

 **8**

The next time I saw Melissa, she was walking ahead of me up Kowhai Road, with Jeff. I retreated back to college. This was the other side of the love coin, in that I felt the sensations of being electrocuted, my blood prickling, my heart beating so fast I thought I was going to collapse. Same symptoms, opposite diagnosis. This time it was not heavenly euphoria, it was hell with bells on. I slumped on to the concrete steps, my stomach in an advanced state of distress akin to severe seasickness.

'Hey, Dead Cat.'

I ignored Stump.

'Your sheila dumped you, eh?'

'Fuck off,' I muttered, refusing to look up.

He might have said something else, I didn't hear. I flashed on Jeff's swagger, cock of the walk, King Shit. A hand rested on my duffel, I pulled away.

'Hey, man. We haven't seen you at the Lit Club lately.'

I shrugged.

Don sat down on the steps beside me. 'You got any new poems for the mag?'

'Nah.'

'Don't fret it, man.'

He pumped a soft fist into my shoulder and left me to it. Now I knew for sure why she was avoiding me. I had not seen her at lectures or in the caff. I had checked the coffee bars, even the library. No sign of her. I had been around to her flat every day and left notes to call me. Nothing. I had gone down to the Glen to see if I could spot her in the art and craft classes. I was frantic. I had been in to reception to see if the secretary had any record of her being ill. No record. Then I came out of college and there she was, green jacket, green skirt; different outfit, different companion. That runt Stump merely confirmed what I feared – Melissa had not only rejected me, she had taken up with a Visigoth, a good way to ram home my careless, culpable approach to love, demonstrate there were consequences.

I walked slowly along Upland Road, took the path beside the cable car to the Botanic Gardens. I stumbled down the steep path, mooched across the rose garden pruned back to stumps, down Tinakori Road and Bowen Street, past the stark white Cenotaph with the bronze rider on his rearing horse. I wandered to the back of the empty Eastbourne bus, sat staring out the window at nothing until it filled with chattering schoolkids, the young louts swarming and barging against me on the back seat, punching each other and shouting crude, jocular remarks towards the girls congregated in the relative safety of the front seats. It was a relief when the bus lurched and shuddered off on its journey round the harbour to a place I was supposed to call home.

There were rich meaty smells coming from the oven, but it was too early to eat. I grabbed three ginger biscuits and retreated to my room to read more of Yeats. He waffled on about fanciful love objects, like silver apples of the moon and golden apples of the sun and bean-rows and salley gardens with snow-white feet. I came to the line about being young and foolish and not agreeing with his love telling him to take it easy. This was too close to the bone. Poetry was no different from pop music, all about love lost and love betrayed.

I slung the collected poems on the floor and went for a walk along the beach. It didn't help. All week I had been doing the same thing, wondering what Melissa was doing a bus ride away across the harbour. Now I knew. I flicked a few pipi shells, unable to achieve the lift Gull had got.

On my way back I saw Liz running up Rimu Street past the flickering light of the television set in the window of the electrical shop where I'd bought my turntable and Elvis records. I was about as interested in her as folk now were in what the owner boasted in the paper was the country's first working television set she was jogging past.

Nobody gawping outside the window tonight. The footpath had been crowded early evening for days with people including, I confess, myself, all come to marvel at the first transmissions from Australia. The images were so poor the novelty soon wore off. The status of having allegedly the first television in the country didn't survive the ghostly, flickering black and white shapes. They were no competition for the technicolour travelogues and movies across the road at the Royal picture theatre, with the added advantage of its adjacent milk bar where they did a mighty double-malt.

*The Dumb Onion* and *The Evening Ghost* were reporting the squabbles in Parliament about where the first local television station would be sited and Wellington was not first choice, too many hills in the way. That couldn't apply to this flat little sand dune village. Flat was the operative word. I was flat. Liz loping along the street staying in shape for tennis was no longer any attraction to me. Love or lust or infatuation or just plain ego-puffery from going out with a pretty local lass, whatever it was, or combination thereof, like television it was no longer an attraction. To me Liz and Yeats and life generally had faded to a dull monochrome like the television set in the shop window.

After too much steak and kidney pudding and apricot upside-down cake eaten alone, I retreated to my bedroom. Ignoring the lead ball lodged in my stomach, I picked up Yeats again. No disrespect to Ireland's finest, I soon dozed off with those lines of his about being young and foolish on repeat, ruing for the umpteenth time my churlish behaviour.

I craved sight of Melissa, I dreaded meeting her. One day in this conflicted state I snuck into Assembly at the last minute and hovered at the back. This geezer Rewi Alley, a Commie, talked to us about how he had missed cups of tea in China, which seemed odd. He reminded me of one of Nevile Lodge's cartoons of the ordinary Kiwi bloke, pear-shaped and bland and bald, but he put the boot in to our smug society. He reckoned we were full of quarter-acre apathy, our newspapers reflecting our self-satisfied reliance on Britain and kowtowing to the Queen. He denounced our paranoia about the Red Scare and the Yellow Peril, said we were complicit through our military pacts with American imperialism in Korea. He rated the Maori collective way of working, said the rest of us were only collective for ten minutes a day, between ten-to-six and six o'clock closing.   This won him an ironic cheer from the Phys-Ed crowd near me. Then he said we were apathetic and our youth needed a challenge.

'We could challenge Ardmore to a beer tournament,' one of the Phys-Ed wags suggested, achieving collective agreement among his fellows.

'Prunes.'

It was Jasper. 'Rewi's right,' he sneered. 'Those pissheads will be cannon fodder in the next imperialist war.'

I could have pointed out to Jasper that was not exactly what Rewi had said, if I could have cared. He was just like James K. Baxter delivering to the Lit Club his new poem about Calvary Street, full of loathing for sterile middle-class New Zealand. I guess, as Buddy Holly said, it doesn't matter anymore. The only thing that came to mind was the random thought that Rewi would have enjoyed that collective haka on Parliament steps, even the collectivity, albeit briefly, of us protesters.

I did care about the reports coming in that the South African police had fired on unarmed and peaceful black protesters at somewhere called Sharpeville. The whole college was buzzing with the news. The newspaper comment was full of crap about the police not being ordered to fire, as if that excused the apartheid government of complicity in the murder of 67 innocent men, women and children, with hundreds injured. There was almost a grieving hush about the place, except for indignant gatherings in the caff, the hopeful saying Nash had to change, there was no way we could condone a trip by our national team to support this murderous regime.

We were wrong. Nash continued to sit on his fence. Leopards, someone said, do not change their spots. Nash was no leopard anyway, more a timid old neutered tomcat. Mum must be turning in her grave. The party she supported because it cared about people and invented the welfare state to prove it should have come down to this milksop leadership. Even Dad seemed muted about these events, not that he had any interest in sport, muttering one evening that sport and politics did not mix.

The assassination attempt on the South African leader Verwoerd was unfortunately unsuccessful. Like Hitler and Stalin, evil leaders seem to lead charmed lives. God not looking again. As usual, no comment from the Pope. Or the Anglican hierarchy. Only some Anglican priest at Sharpeville stood up to this murderous regime. Incredibly there was no denunciation from our leaders on either side. It was business as usual in the land of rugby, racing and beer, sport going ahead. With the exception of the Phys-Ed gang, it made everybody sick. Baxter was right about middle NZ, but it was made remote by the storm inside my head.

I was sick with longing for Melissa. I avoided her all day, and all night I thought of nothing else. What a mess I had made of things. I craved her, she was my heaven, but I existed in a hellish limbo of unrequited lust, Limbo supposedly the place where you are forever denied sight of the One. I wandered the beach at night and wrote poems about lost love. When I closed my eyes, I could smell her perfume, I could feel her hair tickling my nostrils.

One evening I worked late at the library and just missed the 8.30 bus. While I was waiting at the bus stop across from the Cenotaph a drunk shambled up to me. 'I'm a no-hoper,' he said. 'Yer couldn't help a fellow out, could yer?'

I said I couldn't, and felt guilty all the way home on the bus. I had a few shillings in my pocket. I knew he would spend it on booze if I had given it to him. He was full of self-pity, and so was I. Was this where self-pity ended up? There but for the grace of God go I. Really, I should go to church, pray for myself, ask the only mother left in my life, Mary the Mother of God, to intercede for me, show me why I should be bothered. I didn't. I wallowed.

For weeks I went through the motions, going to lectures, only saying something when the tutors and masters required it. I did the required reading of Dr Spock on childcare, but it might as well have been in Bantu for all I absorbed. I didn't bother with the Friday dances, in case I saw Melissa with Jeff. I read *Bleak House*, which was anything but, and *To the Lighthouse*, which totally was. I read Yeats and walked the beach, occasionally flicking shells, with none of Gull's success.

A week on section at Te Aro School was a relief, it meant no chance of accidentally bumping into Melissa. I went with one of the other students to see a fantasy Italian film called *Miracle in Milan*. Janet knew all about the director De Sica, said he was a neo-realist. I would have said he was unreal, angels and umbrellas from heaven. Not my thing. A few days later I went on my own to see *Rear Window*. Much more like it.

One afternoon after class Maggie Salter grabbed hold of me and asked me if I'd like to join her male ballet. I said I'd think about it. Maggie had been a ballet dancer. One look at her and you could tell, she was so light on her feet, wore these black tops and skirts like she was ready at any time to dance, big calves, hair tied back in a tight bun, a cross between Margot Fonteyn and Audrey Hepburn. It was nice to be asked.

Macaskill put us on to this New Zealand book *A Gun in My Hand*, about some joker wanting to shoot somebody at a rugby match. The character not groovy like, say, Holden in *Catcher*, but I liked the language. It was our language, not this stuffy English prose analysis we had to do at varsity, commenting on sentence structure and literary devices by long-dead Europeans. This was real. I started writing a story about the drunk I met at the bus stop.

Maggie asked me to come to a ballet rehearsal. I figured it was something to do. We met in this empty room in the Student Union building. Maggie was in delectable raspberry and black slacks and her usual tight-fitting black jersey. There were only three other students there. She told us we needed more and we should recruit our mates. It was going to be a lot of fun. She was going to teach us how to dance the correct steps.

She started us off pretending to be swans. She showed us the way and we lumbered around the room, waving our arms, tiptoeing on desert boots, about as balletic as a bevy of baby elephants. We were pathetic but she was forgiving, saying we would improve. She got us in a descending line from beanpole Ron, me, Jeremy to little Morry. She said we needed to recruit a big bloke, they always got the laughs in the tutu. We glanced at each other. Tutu? Strewth.

Afterwards I went back to Jeremy's place for tea. His sister Shelley was stroppy, but it was nice to sit down with an ordinary family and have middle-loin chops and three veg, followed by golden syrup pudding. I could fully understand why he was on the porky side, this sort of tucker every night. Afterwards we played 'Snap', Shelley to the fore, until it was time for me to catch the last bus.

Next day I came down the steps from the Massey House coffee gallery with Jeremy and Gull was there, grinning.

'You avoiding me, cobber?'

I denied I was and introduced him to Jeremy. He suggested we go back up for another coffee, he'd pay. I had a hot chocolate. Jeremy is a friendly cove, asked Gull what he did. As usual, Gull was not very forthcoming, merely observing he was struggling with first year law.

'You know,' Jeremy said, 'you're the kind of shape Maggie is after.'

Gull looked a bit nonplussed. I explained we were recruiting for the Extrav's male ballet. Gull said it sounded fun, he'd check it out. I warned him it meant giving up his Sunday. He shrugged, asked what time, said he'd pick me up. I thought but didn't say it would make it easy for him to keep an eye on me, but on the plus side I didn't have to wait for a bus. At least he had not engineered this, it had been Jeremy's doing.

On Sunday we arrived at one. Maggie was clearly delighted with Gull's appearance. She clapped her hands, told Gull he would bring the right kind of gravitas as one of the cygnets. We were in footy jerseys and shorts and bare feet, thumping around the wooden floor, not exactly flying through the air with the greatest of ease. Maggie was a slave driver. We repeated these incredibly difficult leaps and pirouettes, arms in the air *à la* Margot Fonteyn not, both feet in the air trying to make like Gene Kelly, bending and stretching in ways I had not thought possible.

I don't know whether Gull took offence at the gravitas crack, but he started to act up, and he was hilarious. Whenever Maggie turned her back to demonstrate the correct posture and sequence of steps, he would do a far-out imitation of her, duck-waddling with his feet pointed out and at the same time throwing his arms skywards and kicking up his feet. An Aberdeen Angus bull could not have been much clumsier. She didn't know why we were all in fits until she caught his clowning in the long mirror.

'Perfect,' she said, eyes sparkling. 'We'll work that into the show.'

The moment her back was turned to resume her demonstration, he went one better, posing side-on in his undersized jersey and pulsing his stomach in and out in time to her 'one, two, three' calls. It was as if he had a rugby bladder in his belly which he could inflate and deflate at will. It was hysterically funny. Maggie pirouetted, clapped her hands sharply, said he was just what the doctor ordered, but she didn't want the rest of us getting ideas, one deranged spastic was all there was room for in her male ballet. And, she said, directing an imperious glare his way, he still had to learn all the classical moves. She would choreograph his interludes later.

Maggie produced corned beef and pickle sandwiches and a thermos of tea so we could work through. She played Tchaikovsky's *Swan Lake* on her portable turntable, on repeat for the tripping bit where the little swans are tiptoeing in line. We did it again and again. By seven I could hardly move. Gull had behaved himself, no more duck-waddling leaps, no more of the tummy turn. Maggie told us we were coming along, in a month's time we would be up to scratch. She got, take note Mr Rewi Alley, a collective groan.

'Not to worry,' she said. 'You've got the Easter break. Keep practising the moves, or you'll regret it next rehearsal. That's when practice gets serious with our two new leads.'

The good thing about all this intense physical exercise was that I slept like a log. It blocked out any brooding over Melissa. Mostly.

Melissa had given me a second chance. I was telling her that it was actually the way Catholics preferred, the rhythm method, as we came together. This time she was holding me fast, whispering it didn't matter because we both wore green. We moved in perfect rhythm, faster and faster, wilder and wilder, silver apples spilling and golden apples bursting in explosions of light. At which apocalyptic moment my heart I swear banged hard against my ribs, jolted by the pounding on the cathedral floor of Archbishop Liston's mace, or whatever he called it. We were caught *in flagrante*, the bishop in his mitred hat like a chess piece come to life. He was pointing his mace at us, denouncing me as anathema, not fit for the holy sacrament of Confirmation, for I had wilfully committed the Cardinal Sin of Lust and would be damned to hellfire for all eternity.

'Get your hand off it!' Gull warned as the door was flung open. I reared off my stomach, and then fell back, almost sobbing with relief that I was fully clothed.

'Come on,' he said. 'I have a modest proposal for you, your father willing.'

He said I had five minutes and then he was going to come back and drag me from my bed. My first reaction was to tell him to stuff his proposal. I had fallen asleep in a bad mood, glumly contemplating the Easter break, starting tomorrow with surely the most ironically named day of the year. My second reaction was to get out of the pathetic reality of my room. I'd managed to avoid Dad in the main, by working at the library until late, when we were not rehearsing. He was increasingly home later and later anyway. When I did see him we exchanged greetings and I retreated to my bedroom, pleading study demands. But now we had the prospect of all of Easter with each other. Having Gull there should make conversation easier, and my first reaction had been ill-judged. I rearranged myself as best I could and joined them in the sitting room.

Dad nodded and sipped his vile sherry as Gull explained that Mr Atkinson had made his yacht available for an Easter break, subject to certain provisos. Gull held a finger for each proviso. One, he himself was nothing flash as a yachtie and Mr Atkinson required a skilled hand at the helm. Two, I was skilled, and if Mr Atkinson received endorsement from my father to this effect, they could take the yacht. Three, Gull was in charge of maintaining proper arrangements and ensuring people were back for their respective Sunday services. There were five confirmed to come, but none of them had handled a yacht this size before. What did I think?

Well, truth be told, I had never been in charge of a big, crewed yacht. I had only ever been a hired hand. I may have given Dad the wrong impression about this. Before I could qualify my alleged experience, Dad held up his hand.

'You've been pushing yourself hard lately, Steve. A break would do you the world.'

I was still processing this heaven-sent opportunity to avoid been stuck here thinking about Melissa. Gull possibly took my slow response for indifference. He asked me when I had last been on a yacht. I told him too long, last Guy Fawkes, when I got an offer I couldn't refuse, taking a ride on one of these new British catamarans out on the Gulf, actually getting to helm it. That was a blast. You wouldn't believe how fast they can go. I asked him what sort of yacht.

Gull stroked his beard. 'Ah, I think she's a 40-footer. A double-ender, if that means anything?'

Not much actually, but yachting was yachting, and it was the perfect way to get me through the oppressive Easter break. I was still jangling from my dream. I did not fancy lurking in my bedroom fantasising about my stuffed relationship with Melissa. There were of course plenty of options for the religious minded, like the Easter vigil and the Mass of the Resurrection. Unless you are into the religious thing, Good Friday has to be the worst day of the year for doom and gloom, with empty streets, shut shops and weeping and gnashing of teeth in a church entirely shrouded in black. By the end of it I'd want to slit my throat.

I didn't expect Easter Saturday or Sunday to be any better. There was plenty of secular activity on, if you had someone to go with. I didn't fancy going on my own to *Some Like It Hot*, my first choice movie, or, at a pinch, *Carry On Teaching*, though the occupation was off-putting, teaching had not been a bundle of laughs so far. Basically considered, there was no resurrection for me from the sackcloth and ashes. Like Dives, the rich man in hell, I craved relief, and knew none was forthcoming. Now I'd been thrown a lifeline.

I muttered I might as well, which sounded more surly than I had intended.

'That's the ticket,' Dad said, clearly relieved I had not completely shut down.

They arrived late next morning, when we were back from the dire Good Friday Mass and I was almost weepingly grateful I was not going to be marooned at home on this *dies irae, dies illa*.

The car was one of those new roofless Aussie coupé versions of the Triumph Herald, something I only knew about because of an article I read in a *Pix* magazine at the barber, after of course checking out the titties in Witchetty's Tribe. It was duck-egg blue in patches where it was not comprehensively camouflaged with mud, as if driven around a milking shed on a wet day.

Gull was cramped up in one of these absurdly small back seats you get in cars originating from Pongolia. He wore a light blue shirt under a navy-blue windcheater, his beard was trim. Sporting a rumpled captain's cap with its brim at a rakish angle, he could be taken for a naval officer on shore leave – or a cop on a nautical holiday. Liz was in a Smoko-pink tracksuit top and short white shorts and barefoot in the passenger bucket seat. The driver was a languid blonde in an old shirt, so my tatty blue and yellow St Peter's footy jersey did have company.

'Donna, Gilly and Hippo couldn't make it,' Liz said brightly. 'This is Heather Anderson. Heather's just dying to ride waves.'

'Not a lot of waves around Martinborough,' Heather drawled, dangling her hand over the door. She had a slight crease at one corner of a long, thin mouth, the faintest of mocking smiles. Her head was cocked to one side, her straight straw hair falling over one eye, the other the deep blue sea colour of one of my once-prized bonza marbles.

I took her hand carefully, and encountered the unrelenting grip of a top sail grinder, though her fingers were long and slender. She held the grip until we had more or less equalised pressure, involuntary in the first instance on my part, and I suppose ultimately rather ungallant.

'You going to open the door?'

'I thought we were sailing?'

She hurled the door open, requiring me to step back smartly. 'I'm sure Liz won't mind if I have a quick look-see,' she said, unfolding to my height. 'Eh, Liz? Have to see where the comer lives.'

Comer? She couldn't mean me. That left Dad. Liz was saying something, but I was distracted by the white singlet that – operative word — barely reached Heather's midriff under the unbuttoned red-check shirt knotted in front above the waist. Below her plimsoll line, so to speak, mermaid-like she was encased in a tight cream sheath not unlike the supple texture of those Gear Meat Company skins. These had to be riding britches, tucked into mid-calf boots the colour of raspberry toffee.

I laughed. 'We're riding waves, not horses.'

She strode imperiously through rather than past me. My eyes snagged on the lateral shifting of her ample buttocks, the way one of those ceiling nudes by a Renaissance Italian master might move if enclosed in a sheep pelt and animated by a lascivious Disney. She swivelled at the gate quick enough to catch my gaze at half-mast.

'Then I'll have to get my gear off, won't I?'

Without waiting for a reply, she ducked inside.

Gull was doing a finger corkscrew to his head.

'Don't mind Heather,' Liz said breezily. 'She is *such* a show-off.'

'How come you know a riding gal from Martinborough?'

'Queen Mags. She was riding when I called, obviously didn't change. She's actually a good sport.'

'And a quizzy one. I'd better see how Dad's coping.'

They were in the sitting room. Heather was perched on the edge of the settee. Dad with glasses dangling from one hand was standing looking somewhat startled. He was used to young women as tea and scone makers, and this one seemed to be predicting the political outcome of the November election.

'Tizard's another we'll get,' she was saying. 'This new man Muldoon, used to be Jack's batman or something in the war.'

'Yes,' he said. 'We must hope so. Ah, Stephen, Heather's been giving me ...'

'Nice to meet you, Mr Marr,' she said, standing and offering her hand. I felt sorry for him before he winced. 'See you at Irene's soirée.'

'Yes,' he said as she turned, grabbed my arm and swung us about. 'Have a good day.'

Heather pulled us to a halt. 'Too right,' she said, tacking us both round to face him. 'Box of fluffy ducks, eh, Steve?'

I could only murmur agreement, but I was thinking of Gull's finger twirl suggestion. Clearly she was stark, raving, bonkers.

On the way out I asked her what this do at Irene's was all about. Dad had no reason to mention it to me. Even if he'd wanted to, he'd scarcely had the opportunity.

She flicked her hair to one side, a lazy eye revealed. It didn't stop her looking directly at me as she said I could be her escort come Sunday, unless I had something better to do. I had no plans, but I said I doubted my father would want me at a National Party bash.

'Apolitical, are we?'

I shrugged. 'No vote, why should I care?'

'Black budgets affect everybody. You want more of that?'

The toot from the car let me off the hook.

Heather did her own door-opening. I clambered in the back with Gull.

'Straight ahead?' she said to Liz, her answer lost in the revving. She shot on to Muritai Road, Liz pointing, Heather's hair flying about. As she adjusted the rear view mirror, she caught my eye and winked with her good one.

I asked Gull what this Sunday lunch thing was.

'Brunch,' he said. 'You're coming, aren't you, Heather?'

'Too ruddy right I am,' she said, glancing at me. 'Steve's talked me into it.'

'Great,' Liz said. 'You're a brick, Steve. It won't be all olds now.'

Heather socked her arm. 'Spoken like a Young Nat.'

Gull snorted. Obviously he was amused by it all.

I was feeling trapped, and not just from the tight squeeze. It seemed I was being dragooned into National Party socialising. I was regretting now that I agreed to go sailing, but when I had said yes I had not known it was with the National Party. It wasn't that it was the worst thing in the world, but it was light years away from where I wanted to be. That slick bugger Jeff was there. The only good thing was I got to do some sailing. I had a few days to get out of this lunch. It didn't seem like Gull's thing either, but for him it was probably all to do with Liz. I could accidentally head us out into the Strait and keep going, get into the Marlborough Sounds and get lost. Apart from a few folk walking their dogs, Days Bay beach was deserted. No kids with ice creams, no beach balls being bounced about, no pock of tennis balls and sharp exclamations from the lawn tennis courts behind the macrocarpas. Not even the dairy open. Your typical Good Friday. My first look at the yacht Gull pointed to I was impressed. Good looking cruiser, white with a red trim. We pulled life jackets out of the boot and put them on.

Gull and I were dressed to get wet in khaki shorts, me with the perfect casual beach footwear, jandals that should have been invented yonks ago, him in old sandshoes. We pushed the dinghy into the water and invited the girls to take the back seat. Liz was looking hesitant despite being better dressed for it. Heather stomped into the shallows, indifferent to the impact on her boots, and climbed aboard. Liz held her hand out for Gull to assist. I pushed off and motioned for Gull to climb in. The dinghy was rocking too much as he tried to settle his considerable bulk in one rowing position. I held it steady and slipped aboard.

We went round in circles as Gull missed the water completely with several heavy thrusts of his oar, the second effort removing the oar and attached rowlock from his grasp. He lunged for and managed to retrieve them, in the process almost capsizing us. Heather was enjoying it, Liz was looking embarrassed. I told him to climb over me into the front. I balanced the dinghy as he got around me in clumsy stages, then I took the oars and pulled away. There was scarcely a tickle of a northerly on my neck, which made progress easy. Heather was saying to Liz it must be exciting out in the Strait in rough weather. Liz said she didn't know, she had only been on the *Bountiful* a few times, out to Somes and Ward. I was clearly marooned among landlubbers.

They proved the point as I manoeuvred sideways to the stern of the yacht. Always step out of the centre of a dingy. I was too late to tell Gull, who thought bounding off the gunwale was the best way to get aboard. I caught the stern line in time to hold us against the boat with minimum agitation, but not without a yell of alarm from Liz and a yip of excitement from Heather. Both were clinging hard to the sides of the shaking dinghy. I told them to join me in the middle and climb the little metal boat ladder Gull should have used.

All aboard and dinghy secured, I suggested they take it easy while I got us underway. Liz had retreated to the relative safety of the seats at the back, Gull joining her. Heather hovered, wanting to know what I was doing, what she could hold. I figured she was better clear of the boom, so I told her she could steer, back in the company of the others. The main thing, I said, was to turn the opposite way from the direction you intended.

'Aye, aye, skipper,' she said, clomping along the deck, using the boom to steady herself.

I was going to need eyes in the back of my head, or I'd have man and women overboard. I checked the sky, scuddy cloud but only 10 or so knots of norwester. Nothing much to go wrong. I got busy with a double reef on the mainsail, up anchor, feeling the tug as we started to drift. I quickly corrected Heather, who had of course turned the wrong way and we were sliding towards the wharf. Like backing a trailer, I suggested. She got it and we were off, sails fluttering and filling.

Liz was pressed into Gull, who had his arm around her. I joined them, telling Heather I'd take over.

'Men want all the fun,' she said, but she relinquished the wheel. I got an emphatic thigh bump from her, an eyebrow arch when I looked at her. 'Just kidding.'

'We'll go out to Ward for starters,' I suggested.

'Got halfway as a kid,' Gull said. 'There was a wooden boom to the island in the war, it was a dare to walk it.'

'What was it for?' I asked. 'It wouldn't have stopped a warship?'

'To do with submarine defences, I think.'

'Must have been some boom,' I said. 'Has to be a good four miles out there.'

'Something like that.'

'You're having us on, Pat,' Liz objected. 'You'd have been really young.'

'Too young,' he agreed. 'I chickened out.'

Heather leaned across, pressing against me. 'Can't see you as a chook, Patrick.'

'Reckon,' I said. 'More a rooster, I'd say.'

'I'll bet,' Heather laughed, steadying herself with a hand on my thigh as she craned around me. 'Cock of the walk?'

'Rooster yesterday,' Gull joked. 'Feather duster today.'

'Dipstick,' Liz chided him.

In about the time it would take to tie two bowlines, we had zigzagged with minimal trimming across into the lee of the island. It was safer to keep them *in situ*, Heather with her hands off me and on the wheel, while I dropped sail and anchor. Liz I noticed as I returned to the stern was the colour of the canvas. But the sun was out and we were rocking gently and she should be able to relax now. Heather had other ideas.

'Who's for a dip?'

'No, ta.' Liz said, shivering.

'You're nuts,' Gull said. 'It'll be freezing.'

'Chicken,' she scoffed as she pulled off her boots. 'What about you, Steve? Up for it?'

She didn't wait for an answer, headed up to the bow, peeling and depositing clothes as she went.

'Blimmin heck,' Liz objected as Heather wriggled vigorously out of her riding britches, adopted a provocative tiptoe pose beside the bowsprit, and dived in.

'She's a goer,' I said, shaking my head as she powered towards shore, flashes of white bum and flailing limbs, an albino dolphin with a malfunctioning compass, heading for rocks.

'Don't look at me,' Gull said, as Liz nuzzled against him. 'I'm chicken, remember.'

'Me too,' I said. 'I'd better get her gear. You coming?'

Liz made severe sideways movements into Gull's chest.

'You go on,' Gull said.

Heather was hunched up and shivering on the stony beach when I scraped the dinghy's keel.

'Gr-great,' she said, standing and catching the towel I tossed her.

I dragged the dinghy half out of the water and held her clothes high on my chest, partly to avoid looking at her sawing her towel across her body.

'Dump the clothes,' she said, tossing the towel back at me. 'You wanna rub me dry?'

The towel wound around my head as I put her clothes down.

'That was not a request, skipper.'

She was hauling on her britches as I held the towel out in front of me. She got her sheep pelt pants up and flicked her hair.

'Rub my back,' she snapped, sitting down and grabbing a boot.

I tentatively did as I was told, kneeling behind her and rubbing the towel across her shoulders.

Harder,' she said, tugging at the boot, her breasts wobbling. 'Judas Priest! Put some elbow grease into it, you pussy-wuss.'

I did, as she got the second boot on with a lot of wriggling and heaving, then sank back hard against me, knocking us on our backs, her on top.

'Go easier in front,' she said, trapping me on the small stones. I slid the towel out and very carefully patted at her frontage.

'Nice,' she said. 'Very nice.'

I could only agree. Some of me was agreeing rather more than I would have expected, given how awkward it was trying to dab her dry without lingering, whilst trying to ignore the extreme countervailing discomfort of sharp stones rolling and digging into my back like some natural version of those beds of nails fakirs lie on.

She put me out of my confused misery by rolling over on top of me, stroking my centre of khaki gravity and laughing.

'You can knock that idea on the head,' she said, continuing to do the exact opposite. If she continued, I'd be coming to a head. She stopped, leaving me in yet another altered state of misery.

'I'm freezing,' she said, pushing off me in a most distressing manner. 'If you'd brought me some decent clothes, I might have been persuaded to stay.'

I could see how cold she was, my efforts at rubbing her dry generating a pink tinge to the swarming goosebumps and areas of erectile tissue. I shook my head to try and clear my mind, forcing myself to look away as she put on the undersized singlet and shirt, this time buttoning up. Cockteaser was the word that came to mind. Of course, I could always have not responded. Once again I was acting on a whim without a prayer. I got awkwardly to my feet, not helped by Heather employing that eyebrow arch as she observed the epicentre of my discomfort.

It didn't get any better on the row back to have her sprawled over the back seat, legs apart, that half smile on her face. I concentrated on rowing, finding some odd relief in having my back to the yacht. I prayed we would have been too far from Gull and Liz for them to have seen anything.

Heather used my shoulder as balance to climb on to the boat ladder. She ignored Gull's hand offer to help. He said Liz was lying down below, she was not well, we should get back. Fine with me. There was no joy in playing nursemaid to these non-sailors. Well, not in regard to sailing. I don't know why Liz wanted to come out if four flat miles of harbour made her ill. I had a fair idea of Heather's plans, but remained somewhat dazed and confused about my own.

There was an undertow of guilt, as if I was being unfaithful to Melissa. I consciously chided myself for such retrograde Catholic conscience, given she had dumped me for the egregious Jeff. How could she go with one of those sporty philistines, when she agreed with me how odious they were? Was I any better, any less of a hypocrite, happy to be plucked by a Young Nat raver?

I couldn't answer that. I didn't want to answer it. I didn't want to think about it, just experience it. I was in a lather of unrequited lust. Melissa had got me going and I didn't want to stop. I wanted to get it on with Heather, to hell with the next day. All I could see in front of me were those bobbling breasts and her sumptuous hips in those tight cream riding pants. If I had to mix with Young and Old Nats, it was not a price too far. Why should I care, when I didn't have a vote?

 **9**

S aturday was supposed to be when the Lenten fast ended. For me the fast endured throughout a fallow day. Nobody rang me. I couldn't exactly ring Liz and ask where Heather was. It was obvious there was no more sailing. Gull was possibly helping his mother get ready for the brunch tomorrow, more likely consoling Liz.

I checked the movies in the paper. *Sapphire* was on at the Prince Edward, Woburn. I'd heard some good comment about it as some sort of breakthrough drama about race relations when a black girl is murdered in London. It seemed a bit irrelevant when I'd read in the same paper of the South African Security Branch raiding the offices of the local non-racial sports association and confiscating a sympathetic letter from the former English runner Chris Chattaway, now an MP, while the English star batsman the Reverend David Sheppard was refusing to go on the English cricket tour of South Africa. Sport and politics were mixed in Mother Britain, but not in the uptight little dominion of New Zealand.

I was eating my brunch, toast with Vegemite, wishing you could get Bovo down here, when I heard Dad's motor. He ducked in to get something from his study, said he was off to a meeting, have a good day's sailing, glad I was coming tomorrow. I didn't need to say anything, he was gone. He was in his three-piece and collar and tie, which was not usual at the weekend, even for him.

I put on *Jailhouse Rock* extra loud and tried to read John Donne, but was depressed by the opening lines wondering what he and his beloved did before they loved. My question was what did you do after you had loved and been rejected? Donne joined Yeats on the floor.

I checked out a book of Beat poets Don had loaned me. Corso asked whether he should be married and be good, or astound the girl next door in a velvet suit and faustus hood? I had no answer to that. I moved on to Ferlinghetti. He wanted someone to come lie with him all night and be his love. So did I. Ginsberg asked if the Catholic church would find Christ on Jupiter. I had no answer there. His talk of moons and planets reminded me of Melissa. At least Elvis delivered his maudlin lines with brio and beat. Beaten by the so-called Beat poets, the book joined the senior poets on the floor.

A letter fell out. I knew instantly what the thrice-folded thin sheets contained. It was Mum's last letter to me, written from hospital. 'Guess you are busy with your exams,' she wrote in her beautiful script, always with the Parker fountain pen Dad had given her. 'Have been thinking of you.' My eyes blurred.

I blinked. The Beat poets lay open at a poem headed 'One Thousand Fearful Words for Castro'. I must have read her letter a thousand times, all 100 or so words. The upright, elegant lines were collapsing as she ended with 'All my loving, dear. Mum x'. I initially kept the letter in my wallet. I had not remembered using it as a bookmark. I put it back in my wallet and closed the unintended host. If I had returned the book to Don unopened, I would not have seen the letter again.

I went for a walk along the beach and kept going, through the gate and on the gravel road all the way to Pencarrow Lighthouse. Nobody about and nothing to say, not even to myself. My mind was what our Latin teacher Brother Calixtus called a *tabula rasa*, as blank of content as the stones I stumbled over. I picked up and tossed a few select pieces the size of Melissa's ruby jewel. I aimed to get them over the rocks and into the sea, and failed. I mildly regretted I didn't have a shanghai with me, I could guarantee that would propel them far into the ocean. St Paul said when he was a child he acted like a child, and when he became a man he put away childish things. I'd put away my shanghai, but I was still throwing stones. Pathetic. I lay with my head against a rock, my face to the sun.

The cold breeze woke me. I shivered, not having worn a jacket. The sun had set, leaving its poker work on my forehead. I got up, stretched and trudged home.

It was dark when I got back, famished and thinking about fish and chips, hoping Irene hadn't had time to cater for us. I would have missed the note if I hadn't stood on it and the Sellotape caught on the sole of my Roman sandal. It must have fallen off the door. I bent and retrieved it. Not one of Irene's perfumed missives. It was a larger sheet, folded over, one end with the serrations from being ripped out of a spiral ring notebook. When I switched on the hall light I recognised Liz's handwriting. They had rung earlier and called round to see if I wanted to go into Petone to see *Some Like It Hot*.

Bugger! Why had I not stayed put? Why had I not come back earlier? I had wasted the day and now I had wiped out the night. I really, really wanted to see Marilyn Monroe in that dress.

There might be time to catch a bus in, join them at the State theatre. I checked all my pockets. No change. I poked about in the kitchen, hoping Dad might have left a ten bob note lying about. He hadn't, which was no surprise. The lights of his car pulling up. The grandfather in the hall was striking seven. Too late.

Dad got one thing right, he came in cradling what my nose, mouth and eyes identified as a feed of fish and chips.

'Wasn't sure you'd be here,' he said, as he used one hand to loosen his tie.

'You're a mind reader,' I gasped through a mouthful of erupting saliva.

He smiled and said he was glad to oblige, setting the pack on the kitchen table. He went one better and opened a warm DB and poured two glasses, asking me how the sailing went. I said it was neat, my nose tickling as it encountered the frothy head. I took a swig of the yeasty brew as he unfolded the still warm and somewhat soggy newspaper.

'No need for knives and forks, eh?'

I nodded as we dived in and demolished the lot. Both of us burped and simultaneously said 'Snap', a game we hadn't played since Mum had been diagnosed with cancer. We wiped our fingers on the edges of the paper, Dad rolled it up and took it into the sitting room and stuffed it straight in the grate.

'Another beer?' he asked as he undid the buttons on his waistcoat.

I said I wouldn't object. He was full of surprises today. I asked him if he'd won the Golden Kiwi.

'In a manner of speaking,' he said, patting his tummy. 'All things being equal. That was fantastic.'

'Not going off Irene's cuisine?'

'Not a bit of it. I'm looking forward to tomorrow. It'll be nice to have you along, son.'

I laughed as he poured even worse the second time, beer surging over the table. It was nice to have a beer with the old man. I could count on one hand the times we had. He got the dishcloth and wiped the underside of the glass and handed it to me.

'Cheers,' I said, raising a glass that was mostly froth.

'I need more practice,' he said.

'What's the celebration?'

He sipped his beer. 'Shouldn't be counting any chickens.'

'Come on,' I said. 'I'm family. I'm not going to spill the beans.'

He frowned. 'It's not that. Well, I've been offered a top job. Depending.'

'On the election?'

'Quite. I suppose Patrick told you, did he?'

I confessed he did. We finished the beer and Dad asked me what plans I had for the evening. I told him I didn't have any, except I wanted to finish the set English.

'Very commendable,' he said as he filled the kettle. 'But it is Easter Saturday. What are Patrick and the girls up to?'

'Movies,' I mumbled, then lied for no good reason that I could have gone, but I was a bit behind on study.

'I know the feeling,' he said. 'Tea?'

I declined, thanked him for the beer and f and c, and excused myself.

I didn't bother with the potted history of the best English prose. Instead, I put on *Heartbreak Hotel*. Not too loud, not wanting to compete with the storm music starting up on the Columbus radiogram, and picked up a Saint paperback I'd got second-hand. After all, it was Easter Saturday and the fasting was supposed to be over. Unfortunately, it only took a few pages to realise I had read it. The story was too flimsy to warrant a rerun looking for the scene where she lets the satin nightgown slip to the floor. I picked up Yeats, attempted to concentrate, but reading about breast lying upon breast conjured up a full-blown image of Heather's erect nipples on the Ward Island beach. Once again I let Yeats fall to the floor, switched off the lights and abandoned myself to pictures of Heather. It had not been my day, but the night had been worse, definitely a downer.

Tapping on the door caused me to rear guiltily off my stomach.
  'What is it?' I growled.
  'Phone,' he said. 'She insists on speaking to you.'
  'Coming,' I said, which was damn near true.
  I staggered out to the hall and picked up the phone.
  'Hello?'
  *'I wanna be loved by you, da diddly diddly doo, boop boop de doo.'*
  'Is that who I think it is?'
  'You think?' Heather snapped out of high-pitched, girly singsong.
  'I've been thinking of you.'
  'Better. How much?'
  I checked the door to the sitting room was shut. 'I could show you.'
  'You didn't tell me what you thought of my Marilyn.'
  'I love anything to do with the divine Miss M.'
  'So it's all about her, is it?'
  'I didn't mean that. My offer remains open.'
  'Save it for later.'
  'Promise?'
  'You missed a great movie. Where were you?'
  'I went for a walk. Unfortunately.'
  'All is not lost. See you tomorrow, tiger.'
  'Can't I see you now?'
  'You're an eager beaver.'
  'I can vouch for that.'
  'Meet you outside in five.'
  I put the phone down and waddled back to my bedroom. It was not easy getting

into my Elvis pants, but needs must. I blessed the frenzied male and female vocal exchanges coming from the sitting room, they masked my exit. I wore the slip-ons, misshapen from the evening I ran away from Gull. Outside I virtually ran on the spot, like a cat on a hot tin roof, like that strange rocket poem of Ginsberg's, ready to go up like a Roman Fountain or an Emerald Fire the moment my wick was lit. I was damn near choking with mind-blinding lust.

There was no sign of her or the car. Where the hell was she? Headlights flashed a few doors down. She was parked on the wrong side of the road. I came up on the driver's side, enough light from the far streetlamp to see that she was in a loose fawn-coloured dress pulled up over her bare legs and tucked between.

'Like what you see?'

I let my eyes do the talking.

'You going to stand there all night perving?'

'Do you want to come inside?'

'Slow down, cowpoke. How about a romantic ride in the moonlight? Climb aboard.'

I did as I was told. I was putty in her hands.

As she pulled out, my putty instantly hardened as her hand strayed off the gear stick and brushed across my Elvis trou. Just as well I wasn't driving, we'd be all over the road, or off it. She accidentally on purpose continued to brush back and forth across my strides, each time pressing a little harder.

'Didn't I tell you to slow down?'

I didn't dare reply. I couldn't. I was frozen stiff, rigid and quivering, a mouse cornered by a cat patting the victim before she pounces. If she kept up this cock-teasing a few more times, I wouldn't be responsible for my own action. She returned in the nick of time to the gear lever, changing up and increasing speed down the parade.

As we merged at the end of Eastbourne, she did a quick, smooth double-declutch down-change, her thighs scissoring, and swung back on to Muritai Road.

'Fair dos,' she said, pulling my hand across between her legs.

She had no pants on. As she put in the clutch, her thighs opened. As quickly they closed, second gear engaged, her thighs clamped on my fingers. She was sopping wet.

'Don't stop,' she insisted, double-declutching and engaging again as she sped up. 'Faster,' she said urgently, the car picking up speed as we passed the dairy and post office, street and shop lights on and blessedly not a soul visibly home. Our roles might now be reversed, but I was as much a prisoner as I was before, unable to withdraw, unable to proceed, caught on the horn of my own lust, all in a lather with nowhere to go.

'Yes,' she urged, the car beginning to jerk and cross the centre line. 'Yes. Yesss! Fuck!'

She got the car back under control, changing down, cursing again.

'What?' I said, alarmed I had hurt her in some way, done something I shouldn't have. 'What is it?'

'My bloody contacts,' she growled, patting my unresolved problem, laughing throatily. 'One or other usually goes when I come.'

She was smoothing her hands over her dress, crouching and peering, no overhead light to help.

'In the glove box,' she said. 'Get me the torch.'

I did, but she couldn't locate the missing lens. I opened the door and got out, crouching to help her search the mats, banging heads.

'Just leave it,' she said. 'I'll manage with one for now. Remind me where you live again.'

I asked her if she was sure about driving. She said I'd find out, if I'd tell her which direction. I did. She managed fine, not that there was far to go in this handful of asphalt patch-overs of a sand strip. She coasted the last few yards to a stop, pulled on the hand brake and leaned across.

'Kiss, kiss.'

We kissed, as best you can twisted sideways in bucket seats with a metal shaft diagonally separating your endeavours. She settled for giving my bottom lip a sharp nip.

'Ow!'

'Pussy-wuss,' she laughed, punching me in the stomach. 'Come on, let's see what you're really made of.' She fluffed up her dress, threw her door open and climbed out. I followed, as if I had any choice. She opened the gate and bowed me through, snuffling with laughter as I stumbled against her, pushing me away, pinching my bum and propelling me forward. I didn't need the encouragement.

At the door I fumbled to find the key, fumbled getting it in the lock. The door creaked loudly, which was of no concern, Dad's ecstatic squawkers were building to a climax. That set her giggling. She grabbed my hand and I led her down the darkened hallway.

I had scarcely got the bedroom door open when her dress was rising over her head. My jacket and sweater took too long to remove, me even more fingers and thumbs than usual. She was on the bed watching with the aid of the ambient streetlight as I hopped about, one leg caught. Finally I heaved the damn strides off, pulling one leg inside out.

'Don't worry,' she said, the two male and one female next door blotting her out as they rose to glass-shattering levels of competing distress.

'Sorry?' I said, pushing my pants under the bed. 'You said?'

'Come here, you dork.' Her hands and legs were spread.

I sank on to her magnificent body.

'Don't need anything,' she hissed as she lifted her bottom and me with it, settling and guiding me inside.

'You sure?' I said as we began to move in the same direction as the music.

'Shut up!'

I did, and we did, sooner than the prolonged vocal orgasms next door. She eased me off her and we lay gasping like beached fish, eyes blankly contemplating the flickering shadow hands of the pukapuka leaves on the dark ceiling, our ears under assault. Music can be the food of love, but not the infernal bellowing through the wall.

'Bloody hell,' she said as Mephistopheles did his last, long, angry whistle. 'What is your father listening to?'

'The Devil is the detail,' I said. 'Some French opera. He can't get enough of it.'

She laughed as she grabbed my equipment. 'I could say the same for you.'

To my amazement, she was right. Dad's music was done, but we were not.

We did come to a rude pause when there was a tap on the door.

'What?'

'You all right, son?'

'Yeth,' I managed as she jabbed me sharply in the side, causing me to thrust hard and her to yelp and bury her head in the pillow, stifling her laughter.

'Night, son,' he said.

'Garggh,' I said, or something to that effect.

We waited a beat, and then were at it full-bore, like All Blacks and stewardesses aiming for the mile-high club.

It was as we soared into that erotic stratosphere, our bodies in a slippery, pounding frenzy, that I nuzzled into her neck. As she shouted and I erupted, I moaned the name 'Melissa'. This time I was heaved like a bull that has missed its aim, spurting into space, landing awkwardly and painfully on the floor.

'Who the fuck is Melissa?'

I got up carefully, dreading an injury.

'Sorry,' I said, inadvertently emitting a coarse chuckle. 'Slip of the tongue.'

I was belted back to the floor by the pillow, which she used to rain down a fusillade of blows, beating me in my toddler-like scuttle backwards, until the far wall below the window cornered me. I know it was no laughing matter, more the nervous conjunction of my second *coitus interruptus excitatum ad solum fundamentum*. I wanted to explain that it was like some people get at a funeral service, inappropriate laughter. I couldn't of course say it was the second time I had been chucked out of the pleasure pit on to the floor. It didn't matter I got no words out, she allowed no time for explanation.

'You utter prick!' Whack. 'Fantasising.' Whack. 'About some fucking…' Whack. 'Other.' Whack. 'Woman!' Whack. 'Who is she? Who's the scrubber?'

'Nobody,' I said feebly. 'Just a friend.'

'Fuck you!' she yelled, tossing the pillow at me and grabbing her dress. She stumbled over either Yeats or the Beat poets, cursed and kicked them away, wrenched open the door, slamming it hard. That shook the house. The noise she made slamming the front door really shook the house. I waited for the sound of shattered glass falling to the floor.

I scrambled to my feet, rushed out into the hall as the light came on in Dad's bedroom. Dad peered out the door in his pyjamas.

'What's happening?'

'Ahh, I think I was sleepwalking. I had a bad dream.'

I could not have been a pleasant sight, crouched over and stark bollocky.

'I thought I heard somebody?'

'I must have been talking in my sleep.'

He looked dubiously at me. God knows what he thought, but there was not much left to the imagination. I shrank and covered my nethers, retreating. 'I'm okay now,' I said. 'Honest.'

I darted into my room and shut the door. Thankfully, he didn't pursue me with any further questions. I had no answers.

# 10

The rapping on the door woke me from a dead sleep, my heart hammering.
'Come on, son. Early Mass. We're being picked up at ten. Bathroom's free.'

I groaned, eyed the window, thought about bolting. But where? And then what?
Heather's scornful word came back like a burp: 'Pussy-wuss.' I had to go, face the
music for a change. With any luck there'd be plenty of booze.

Back in my bedroom, I smoothed down my crumpled green trousers, trying to
flick off the dust burrs sticking like dags, the result of months of sweeping the carpet
dust under the bed and failing to get the vacuum cleaner into gear. It looked like I'd
slept in my strides, instead of on top of them. They'd have to do, I couldn't wear my
cords, they were in a worse state, and jeans were not remotely acceptable. I tucked in
my one decent white shirt, patted down my damp hair, spat and wiped my slip-ons.

Dad was waiting with the front door held open.

'Happy Easter, son,' he said, nodding at the hall table, on which rested an egg
shape wrapped in yellow cellophane and tied with a yellow ribbon. 'Go on, open it.'

Mum used to leave a little basket on the kitchen table on Easter Sunday, three
hardboiled eggs she had painted bright yellow with pretty pink flowers around the
midriff. I got to choose first.

I opened the wrapping. It was not a real egg, it was made of hard white icing sugar,
little purple rosettes stuck around its circumference. Not bad. Edible too. I asked
him where he'd found it. He said Irene had got us one each. I put it back on the hall
table and pushed past him. It was a silent walk to the church.

When Dad went up to take Communion, I left.

I was in my bedroom with the door shut, still stewing over her getting us Easter
eggs, when there was a toot outside, followed by a tap on the door.

'Here's our ride. You ready?'

The Triumph was idling when I finally appeared. Dad was in a sharp brown suit
I hadn't seen before, standing by the passenger door. As I got nearer I could smell
her enticingly sharp perfume. She had her hair pulled behind and held by a large
tortoise-shell clamp, revealing most of her shoulders. She wore a plain black dress
that somehow stayed up in front. It was not tucked in between her legs.

'Good morning, Stephen,' she said coolly. 'Get in the back, would you.'

I did, noting Dad had achieved a shine on both his jaw line and his Oxfords which our school cadet drill instructor might have admired, not something our polishing of boots and brass buttons ever attracted. I could smell Dad's Old Spice as I eased into my back seat possie, noting a drop of blood from a shaving nick on his cream silk shirt collar. Heather's pearl earrings jiggled as she drove off. I wished now I'd made more of an effort. I felt like a Salvation Army hostel deadbeat relative being taken out for an Easter treat by a family constrained to make a charitable gesture. I could imagine Jasper mocking the bourgeoisie who occasionally felt a duty to remember the outcasts. Of course, in my case I could have spent more money on clothes when I had some coin, but Elvis and Duane were priorities.

I had the time to ponder, as an ignored passenger. Heather congratulated Dad, he thanked her and said it could be premature, Labour might yet pull another rabbit out of the hat.

'Huh,' she jeered. 'The public won't fall for that bribe a second time. They've had three years of misery to think about those misers. They'll not trust that push again.'

'We must hope,' Dad said in his usual mild fashion.

I trailed behind them into the Flynn's villa at the top of Kowhai Street, Heather with her arm linked in Dad's, as tall as him in her black high heels. I could not help notice the sway of her hips.

All the chatter was coming from the deck looking out over the bay. Gull was doing a butler act at the door, welcoming us inside, this time dressed up like a naval officer on shore leave in a smart double-breasted reefer jacket with glittering silver buttons, a blue tie decorated with crowns and anchors, cream shirt and cream flannels and patent creamy yellow shoes.

He shook Dad's hand, Heather patted his beard as she passed him. I had a glimpse of her dress sliding sideways.

'Yo, Steve-oh.'

'Aye, aye, cap'n,' I said, making an effort to snap into party mode. 'Ever thought of acting?'

'Life is an act,' he said. 'Glad you made it, you dog.' He biffed me on the shoulder with the side of his fist. 'See how the other voting half lives, eh?'

'National Mum and Labour Dad?'

'Come again?'

'A line this poet came out with at T. Coll. You haven't waxed your mo.'

'No time,' he grinned. He leaned close. 'Come inside, shagnasty.'

This time I blushed. Liz or Heather or both must have said more than they should.

Liz was the first person I saw, her back to me carrying a tray of drinks. She had her hair piled up and clipped behind, pearl earrings, a black dress, with a white linen bow at the back, sheer black nylons and black high heels. This must be the uniform of the

Young National comer, to retool Heather's word for Dad. Liz must have sensed my eyes on her, she turned, full champagne flutes tinkling. She wore a small, scalloped white linen apron. Her eyes were heavy with mascara, which had smudged a little, and might have explained why they were red-rimmed.

'Hello,' she said tightly. 'Would you like a drink?'

'You feeling better?' I said, as I took a glass.

'Clearly you are,' she said nastily, turning away with more clinking as she took the tray towards the chat.

'Stephen!' Irene grabbed my hand. 'You got the Easter egg?'

'Yeah, thanks,' I managed.

'Soo pleased you could come,' she cooed. 'You must meet some of our people. Tell them all about teaching.'

She too had her hair up and wore a plain black dress, which was obviously *de rigueur*. In her case there was a frilly white band across front and back, which looked to me like it was a cover for something bulky, a misplaced bandolier. She brought me into a living room that was wall-to-wall gold carpet matching thickly embossed gold wallpaper. No question it clashed as much as Irene's orange lipstick with the hefty red and white striped chairs and sofa occupied by older women with blue rinses and lots of pearls around their shrivelled necks. They were tucking in to savouries and small sandwiches. Standing around them were middle-aged folk talking animatedly, mostly women at this end where a white-clothed buffet table was piled with more plates of cakes and scones. Men held forth near a baby grand piano at the other end of the room.

I wasn't paying Irene attention and missed her name for a red-faced old geezer in a smelly Harris tweed jacket and yellow tie, matching yellow buck teeth and nicotine fingers shoved my way. There was a rotted compost tinge to the comb-over of what strands of white hair he had left.

'Sven, you say?' he said, his fleshy, mottled hand enclosing mine and pulling me into range of his tobacco breath. 'Foreign name, eh?'

'No, Dicky,' Irene said, her voice raised. 'Stephen. Joseph's son.'

'Joseph?' he said, his eyes watering. 'Don't think I know him.'

'Joseph Marr. Our banker.'

'Yes, yes, I know,' he grumbled, pumping my hand. 'Reason we're all here.'

'Dicky's in China,' Irene explained mysteriously.

'Delft,' he said, still clamping my hand. 'Doulton. Only bring in the best, subject to the blithering licences from the damned socialists.'

'I see,' I said, finally getting out of his grasp. I took a quick gulp of the fizz, I needed it.

Irene had moved on, her son coming to my rescue. 'Dicky grizzling, is he?'

'Huh,' Dicky growled. 'Too many blasted import controls.'

'You do all right, Dicky. You'll excuse us, we have to circulate.'

As Gull led the way through the braying crush, I recognised Dan Riddiford from church, and a few other faces looked familiar. I hastily looked away from Mrs Atkinson's glare. Dad was in their midst, being questioned by one of them.

I followed Gull through the open French doors on to the deck. At the far end Heather had a very tall, balding man bending to catch what she was saying, in his mouth a smoking pipe pointing directly at her. I grabbed Gull's arm. He grinned, said he thought I'd want to be with my new friend.

I told him she looked like she was coping. 'How do you, with all this?' I asked for something to distract him as well as me, draining the champagne, beginning to feel the first welcome signs of the anaesthetic buzz.

'It's Mum's thing,' he said. 'And your dad, obviously.'

'Not yours?'

'Nah,' he said. 'But needs must, eh? Sorry about the sailing yesterday. Liz cancelled it. Still, worked out for you, by all accounts.'

'What did?'

He nodded at Heather. 'Getting to know our putative first female prime minister.'

'You're kidding.'

'I kid you not. If batty old Mabel can get into Cabinet, why shouldn't somebody with all the right qualities get to the top of the slippery pole?'

'Mabel?'

'Mabel Howard. You must have heard of her – the old duck waving outsized women's bloomers in Parliament.'

'What for?'

'Something to do with wanting standard sizes.'

'Same size for everybody? That would be New Zealand. When was that?'

'Dunno. Six or so years ago.'

'I was still at primary school.'

'They have newspapers in Auckland. Anyway, my point is this, you stick with Heather, you could be the country's first consort. You know, Prince Albert?'

'I don't think so.'

'She's got money, determination, passion, clues. She comes from a political dynasty. Her grandfather was the moneybags for the Liberals.'

'I never realised,' I said, managing to stop myself adding a sarcastic rider that he was making quite a fist of National Party cheerleading for somebody who claimed this was his mum's thing.

'Yep, she talks and breathes politics. Won all the debates at Queen Margarets and in the nationals. She's a natural. And another thing, she gets on like a house on fire with your father's generation, all the old dyed-in-the-wool, blue-ribbon brigade. Look at her.'

The guy was nodding in agreement with her. I felt a twinge of jealousy. How crass.

'She's worth knowing.'

'Piss off.'

'Another drink?'

I could only say yes.

As he disappeared back inside, I shifted to the far edge of the deck, looking down on the village. From up here among this dense green native bush that stretched high and wide behind, the sand strip village looked like one decent king tide would wash it out into Cook Strait. When it spawned Katherine Mansfield, it must have been even smaller. She left in order to express herself, get away from her banker father and his mates.

'Irene's acres.'

I turned. A solid, middle-aged woman in a teal blue jacket and skirt and the obligatory pearls was holding two flutes, one directed at me.

'Patrick asked me to give you this.'

'Thanks.'

She nodded at the view below. 'We call it Irene's acres. She must've handled half the real estate deals down there.'

'I was thinking how small it is.'

'Street level is another matter. Those would be the most valuable quarter acres in the country.'

'What about Remuera?'

She sipped her drink, her eyes assessing. 'Do you miss Auckland?'

'Not especially.'

She thrust out a hand. 'Muriel Witherspoon.'

Several rings pressed hard into my palm. Strong grips seemed to be a feature of the National Party ladies. I introduced myself.

'Yes, we know about you,' she said, emphasising her knowledge with a tightening of her grip.

I let mine go limp and managed to extricate my throbbing hand, not looking at the stigmata rising across the insides of my middle fingers.

'Because of my father, you mean?'

Her mouth rippled a little, a parody of a smile. 'Not entirely, Stephen. This as you say is a small town. We heard the rumours.'

I tried to look baffled, tried not to look guilty, tried not to think which if not all my local transgressions had been noted. There were now crinkles around her disconcertingly direct eyes. They didn't seem particularly friendly.

'We hear quite a lot at the surgery.'

'You're a doctor?'

'For my sins. Yes, I delivered Elizabeth among a few dozen others. I'm very fond of my babies.'

'Liz?' I said faintly. 'Liz Atkinson.'

She acknowledged this with a slight but brusque inclination. I hoped she was not the only doctor in town, her manner was more Sister Mary Discipline than Florence Nightingale. She smiled possibly, certainly she bared her teeth, exposing a crooked set of chompers that looked in dire need of a dental appointment.

'I was thinking Burt Lancaster. You're more that pretty boy Curtis.'

This time I was baffled. The way she said 'pretty boy' with utter disdain, I adjusted my view of her faux smile to the fang-baring of a predator. Was it just me, or did she have this brutal bedside manner with everybody?

'You didn't see that movie *Trapeze*?'

I flushed, which caused her smile to erupt into a cawing I might have expected from some creature in the bush behind me. She tilted her glass mockingly at me and went back inside. I had been put in my place, and it was at the bottom of the doctor's patient list. No matter, I wouldn't have wanted to be seen by her if I'd broken both ankles in my little trapeze landing. I rubbed at the enflamed stigmata, wishing I had found some excuse not to come, looking for outdoor steps in order to get out of here. Surely Liz hadn't confided in her? Did Dad know? Bloody dragon. Doctors were supposed to heal, not inflict injury.

I got a jab in the side so severe I very nearly toppled over the railing.

'Show time, Stevey.'

Heather swept past me without a second glance, into the polite applause.

The tall, bent gent was eyeing me with sceptical pop-eyes. 'Speeches,' he reminded me, poking the wet end of his pipe indoors.

I said I would be there in a tick. He shambled past me, I drained my bubbly, looking along the deck in the hope of seeing an abandoned glass with some bubbly left. No such luck.

A droning but penetrating voice like an amplified oboe was informing the gathering that Joseph Marr was going to be a driving force in the new deal for this country, once the electorate had done their duty and a National Government was returned. I hardly needed to move to hear him.

He paused for more polite clapping and 'Hear, Hear' calls.

'We welcome Joseph into our electorate. The most enlightened if I may say in the country.'

More murmurs of approval.

'We know that we will be returned, we know that the country will return the National Party to power we would never have lorst – were it not for the shamefully dishonest bribe the Labour Party put to the electorate as a last-ditch grab for power. It may have worked, but at what cost to our country? Eh? We all know the answer to that. This country has not been marking time, no! It has been going backwards. As the Governor of the Reserve Bank Mr Fussel – with whom we anticipate Joseph will soon be working — has recently said, New Zealand is enjoying greater financial and economic equilibrium than at any time since the Second World War. The stage is set for expansion. The potential spending power of the country is higher in 1960 than it has ever been before. Our perspicacious leader, Mr Holyoake, has been saying consistently and clearly for several years that our economy is sound. What has the Labour Government done? It has continually talked depression, adopted panic measures, and very nearly talked and indeed taxed us into a serious slump.'

The speaker had to pause to allow polite concert hall clapping and supportive noises.

'Thank you, thank you, my friends. I know I am speaking to the converted. Let me simply say – before I hand over to Joseph for the facts and figures – that this Labour Government has become the laughing stock of the world with its foreign policy. Due to its leader's indecision and vacillation – one has to wonder, my friends, how the good people of Lower Hutt can bring themselves to vote for this man clearly in his dotage, unable to release any controls for fear of what, I don't know – success, perhaps?'

There were loud guffaws and the shrill cawing of my recent deck companion, clapping and cheers and hoots of derision. It reminded me of the school's behaviour when the opposing captain attempted to speak at the after-match presentations.

'Thank you for your insight. As I was saying, the notorious indecision of the government in regard to failing to appoint a United Kingdom high commissioner and an ambassador to the United States has made the country look utterly foolish in the international community. That will change, I promise you. Now, without further ado, here is our next Deputy Governor to tell you some of the facts. You already know the reality – come November we will return to power and turn the tired old tramp steamer Labour has made of us into a thrusting ocean liner ploughing full steam ahead into a new era of prosperity for our country. The people will endure no more of the Labour policy of taxing to the limit and stifling all private enterprise!'

'Hip, hip, hoorah!' somebody shouted, joined by many in the assembly for several repetitions.

'No! No! Please, my friends. Let us hear from Mr Marr.'

The tempo returned to gloved clapping. I edged inside, never having heard Dad speak in public.

He cleared his throat, looked around at those present, nodded at me. 'Thank you, Dan. That was most kind of you. I hope I can live up to your advance notices. I will do my level best. As Dan has told you, I am a facts and figures man, a backroom chap. The last financial year Labour borrowed £45 million pounds when exports were at £273 million, the second highest on record. This was a madness.'

'Hear, hear.' I took advantage of the hubbub to snaffle a full glass of bubbly off the end of the buffet table and drain half of it.

Dad's voice had been subdued, but he lifted the level.

'The year 58–59 our export receipts were 1.6 less than the record year. At the very least the government should have shown restrained optimism. Instead, it imposed drastic restrictions and controls and increased taxes.'

Groans and boos. And a good swallow of bubbly for me. Time to grab another full glass.

'We believe the task of government is to set the field for vigorous, healthy, individual enterprise. We will have a policy of expansion. I can reveal that without fear, for I know it will not for now be divulged outside this room. The policy will be an expansion by maximum energy of individual enterprise and maximum freedom through the elimination of socialist-type controls ...'

Cheers from the audience, glugging from me. I seemed to have polished off another glass. This stuff was like lolly water.

'... which have plagued enterprises over the last two and a bit years. With this unhappy chapter in our political career closed, we can look forward again in the destiny that was fulfilled by the National Government of 1949 to 1957. The formula was simple – encourage and handle record development and expansion in every field. Let us have this maximum expansion of industry by free bank advances and capital issues, avoiding credit squeezes, retaining only enough import controls to allow industry to spurt enormously.'

'Bravo!' somebody yelled. There was much clapping and cheering, subsiding to approving sounds and some back-slapping. I could see another glass of bubbly but it was just out of reach. I moved towards it.

'Very naice, didn't you think?'

I looked down at the nearest little old lady, who was looking up at me through thick lenses set in those butterfly-shaped frames, little sparkles of diamond studs at the edges. I blinked.

'My father,' I managed before hiccupping. I turned away, aware of the tightening band around my head. I was near enough to capture another glass, stumbling against the sofa and hiccupping loudly.

'Pardon,' I said to the blurred butterfly glasses, not sure if it was her or me or both of us not seeing straight.

I hiccupped yet again, and received a bash in the back which shot the remaining bubbly over the little old lady.

'Whoops,' Gull said, nudging me aside, whipping out a hankie and dabbing at the poor old dame's damp sapphire silk dress, her hands fluttering helplessly, her companions tutting and giving me dagger looks from behind their butterfly frames.

'There we are, Mrs Pawson,' Gull said. 'Better now?'

He left her and turned to me. 'Better ease up,' he hissed. 'It's not a piss-up.'

I raised my hands to the surrender position, palms out, thereby framing Irene pulling Dad to one side, whispering in his ear and kissing him on the cheek. I jerked back, as if my own cheek had been prodded by a sizzling steam iron. I felt choked with rage and resentment. How dare she! I couldn't take anymore. I had to get out of here. I ignored whatever Gull was saying, my ears blocked by the clamour inside my head, my eyes unfocused as I bumped and barged past people, indifferent to protests and an indignant suggestion I look where I was going. The front door was thankfully open. I stumbled outside.

A dizzy spell hit me and I grabbed the rail to avoid collapsing. I held on tightly and took deep breaths, feeling like I wanted to be sick. I glanced around. To my relief Gull was not coming after me. I shook my head and set off, half-jogging down the steep street, fighting waves of dizziness and nausea. I was determined I was not going to be sick.

At home I got under a shower, blasting my head with hot and then cold water, shivering and heaving but avoiding being ill. I wasn't used to bubbly, let alone in the middle of the day. I did not want to get used to Irene Flynn embracing my father.

I located my old training shoes under my bed, dusted them off, changed into sweater and shorts, and set out on a run along the beach.

Grey sea and sky suited my mood. I welcomed the northerly whipping into my face as I jogged around the headland and into Days Bay. A stitch in my right side was something else to battle. I kept going into the next bay, and the next, the stitch staying with me like a penance. I deserved to be punished for getting pissed. I forced myself to keep going, ignoring cars tooting, bloody Sunday drivers.

At Lowry Bay I was bent over. I was not going to give up. I shuffled around to Point Howard and sank down in the protective shadow of the outcrop. Hunger was nipping at my stomach like a trapped mouse. Let it nip. I was getting shivery, that was fine. Any more miseries to inflict, God?

By the time I got back home I really needed sustenance. There was none. Irene was catering *chez lui* – or should that be *elle*? Whatever. I found a stale crust, a piece of dried-out cheese and a tin of sardines. Fortunately I liked all three, washed down with several glasses of water.

No sign of Dad. I belched sardines, had more water. My head was pounding, so I changed into another sweater and jacket and wandered down to the beach. When I was a kid I would have resorted to shanghai practice. Not an option. I flicked shells, unable to achieve Gull's flight.

The headache was worse. I shambled home, pulled the blind and lay down.

The phone woke me. I ignored it. Then it started up again, and kept ringing until I conceded defeat and answered. It was Dad, asking me how I was. I said I was reading. He was not going to get back until late, he suggested I get fish and chips again, he'd recompense me. I said that was fine with me, just what I felt like. He hung up. I was relieved he had not said anything about my behaviour at Irene's. Hopefully he had not noticed, being the man of the moment.

The fish shop was closed. I checked out the top cupboard and located a rusty tin of pilchards in tomato sauce. Grouse. I scoffed the lot.

My head was still playing up, so I returned to bed, put *(Let Me Be) Your Teddy Bear* on low and dozed.

 **11**

Irene and Christopher Lee were lurking in the darkness, and I was praying for daylight. I was trying to stay quiet, making my breathing as silent as possible, hoping they would not spot me. I could hear the scratching of their black bat wings getting louder, I was sure the window was closed, but perhaps I had forgotten to shut it. I could feel the panic tightening in my chest, I could scarcely breathe. The sound at the window intensified to a tattoo of tapping. I did not dare move while it was still dark. I could feel sweat pooling in my neck, creating an insane urge to scratch, but that would be fatal, if they heard.

I sat up, realising it was dark, and behind the blind somebody was tapping on the pane. I tried to breathe, my head thumping. My name was being called in an urgent whisper. *Don't Be Cruel* was on continuous scratch, the turntable arm having failed to lift. The bloody Collaro Conquest was supposed to be the best on the market, certainly the most expensive. I lifted the arm and set it in its socket, then edged over to the window.

'Stephen?'

I pulled up the blind. It was Liz, looking frantic. It was almost dark outside, but there was enough light to see that she had been crying. I fingered the two metal hooks and raised the sash window. She was still in her black frock, minus the apron, and she had been drinking.

'Aren't you gonna ask a girl in?'

She was managing that herself, one leg flung over the sill, and then she tumbled on top of me.

'Whoops. Shorry.'

I helped us both up. She clung to me, shaking I suppose from cold. I asked her if she was okay, which was redundant, but I couldn't think what else to say.

'Nobody wants me.'

I knew that complaint, I had made it myself more than once. I helped her to the bed, where she rolled over on her back.

'D'ju want me?'

I started to say that she wasn't herself. She laughed coarsely.

'You had her, didn' you? Go on, admit it.'

I sat down on the bed next to her. My head was splitting, I felt dry and nauseous.

I did not need this.

'Where's Gull? Paddy?'

'Pad-trick. Hah!'

She lurched over the side of the bed, spewing.

'Oh God,' she wailed. 'God, I'm so ...'

I told her it was okay, which it wasn't, the smell was appalling. She was shaking and sobbing. I told her I would get something to clean up and rushed to the bathroom. I couldn't use Dad's flannel. There was nothing else there. I switched on lights and hunted around the kitchen, finding under the sink a bucket with a tin of Ajax and the pink gloves Irene used. Picking the gloves up, I felt another surge of anger. Who did she think she was?

With the gloves tossed aside, I filled the bucket with hot water, took in the dishcloth and Ajax.

'No light,' Liz pleaded. She had a hand up to ward off the threat, like it was me who was a vampire.

'Okay,' I said, kneeling and sprinkling Ajax.

'Steve?'

'Be quiet.' I squeezed water on the vomit and began mopping it up, wishing I had put on the gloves. I did the best I could, took out the bucket and emptied it, washed my hands and found some old newspaper. When I got back Liz was in my bed.

'I was cold,' she said plaintively.

I put the paper over the wet area.

'Will you hold me?'

She might not be able to see my look of disgust, but she sensed it. She flung the blanket aside, pushed me away and stumbled out the door. I stood there, indecisive. I had to get her to go. I suppose I would have to take her back home myself. But how would I explain her being with me? Her mother would go ape. God knows what her father would do.

I heard the toilet flush. God, what had I done to deserve this?

I was still standing there when she returned.

'Not very romantic,' she said. 'Why didn't you ring me?' she added, a non-sequitur that was accusing and somewhat belligerent.

I had not formulated a reply as she eased around me, naked. She climbed under the blanket, pulled it up to her chin.

'Well?'

'Crikey,' I said. 'You're with Paddy.'

'Wrong.'

'Eh?'

'He's not interested. Shays – says he doesn't rob cradles. You didn't hesitate, with her.'

'Look. I'm sorry if I offended you. You can't stay here, Liz.'

She pulled the blanket over her head, sobbing and shaking.

I sat on the edge of the bed. She had to leave. The place stank. She should not be here. God, if Dad came home now.

The blanket was flung off. 'You never rang back,' she accused. 'Then the moment she skinny dips.'

I avoided looking at her.

'Don't fancy me?'

This time I did look, as her defiant expression crumbled.

'Please?' she said. 'Can't you put on an act?'

I started to object, she pulled the blanket over her again. 'I'm not going,' she mumbled.

There was a pounding at the front door, a male voice yelling to open up. More pounding.

Oh God!' she said, flinging off the blanket, grabbing her dress. 'He mustn't catch me.'

She went back the way she came in, while I went to answer the door.

Mr and Mrs Atkinson stood there quivering with rage.

'Where is she?' Mrs Atkinson screeched.

Her husband didn't wait for an answer, pushing past me.

'Where's your father?' she demanded.

I told her he was not home. Mr Atkinson was switching on lights and opening doors.

'This your bedroom?' he yelled at me. Without waiting for a reply, he flung it open, then reeled back. I couldn't blame him. He retreated, snarling it was a disgusting cesspit. I would have agreed with that, but not with his wife delivering a sucker jab into my kidneys the equal of Heather's rabbit punch, further evidence that National women packed a punch. I tried to draw some consolation from their likely belief that their precious daughter could never have created or even wished to be in the same room as that stomach challenging smell.

'Elizabeth said she was coming here,' she spat.

I stepped back out of range of any further possibility of assault from her, only to be grabbed by her husband. One hand on my arm, a finger shaking under my nose, he sprayed saliva over me as he assured me that if he found a hint of me near his daughter again he would lay charges.

'Damn you, boy! She's only just 16!'

He glared at me and finally let go.

'Come on, Arthur,' she said. 'We'll speak to his father later.'

His finger wagged under my nose again. 'That's a promise, boy.'

They left and I went looking for something to get rid of the smell in my bedroom. I found a full bottle of Airwick that had never been used, pulled up the impregnated pad and sprinkled it on the offensive area. It seemed to improve things, or at least offer a competing pong. I checked outside the window, thankful Liz had had the nous to scarper. I left the window up and the Airwick open on the sill.

I was in the sitting room listening to the request session when Dad got in. I muted the sound and told him his speech was pretty impressive. I wasn't going to get into any more conflict if I could avoid it. He thanked me, said I had disappeared early, typically as tentative as me about raising any potentially touchy subject. I knew he would not mention the Easter eggs again. I shrugged, said I had reading to finish. He said he appreciated me coming, even if he had a fair idea I would not be voting for his views.

'No vote, Dad, remember?'

I sat on my bed and sulked. I couldn't articulate how I felt about Irene kissing him, I wasn't sure myself why I was so incensed. We had not found a way of really talking, something I always could with Mum. I figured if I was out of the way when Atkinson rang, he might not disturb me. There was no case – well, no proof — to answer, for once, so I could get righteous if I had to. In the event, there was no phone call that night.

It was a pure fluke I looked out the window before closing it. There were her high heels, all the proof the Atkinson parents would have needed if they had checked outside, instead of standing on their dignity by coming to the front door. It was probably inappropriate to thank St Anthony for this find, so I chalked it up to plain, uncomplicated luck. A very lucky escape.

Liz waylaid me next morning as I got off the Eastbourne bus by the Wellington railway station. She was in her Queen Margaret uniform, which made me cringe. Not because of the uniform as such, but because she was a schoolgirl. God knows what would have happened if she'd been caught in my bed by her parents. I imagine he'd be looking for a horsewhip. The court case would be reported in *Truth*, carnal knowledge, jailbait, shame, for me and for Dad. We'd have to move back to Auckland, after I got out of jail. Or would it be Borstal? End of his top job, but also the end of Irene.

It was no comfort that none of this happened. Liz was still chasing me. I told her I couldn't talk to her. She grabbed my arm, ignoring the exclamations of encouragement or chastisement from her companions.

'You go, girl,' one of them urged her.

'I have to talk to you, Steve.'

I figured it was best to get out of range of the growing group of noisy schoolgirls hoping no doubt for some street theatre. I pulled free of her grasp, hissing at her to move away from the shouts of glee and derision. I took the lead, directly away from her school, up Lambton Quay. She followed as I crossed diagonally, accelerating across the iron rails ahead of the dingalinging trams that enjoyed right of way over all other forms of transport, even pedestrians. There had been a case of an elderly woman in Willis Street who was struck by a tram and had her leg broken. The magistrate ticked her off for putting herself in the path of the tram's right of way.

Roy Parsons was open. I ducked inside and up the stairs to the coffee gallery. I waited for Liz, pointed past the suits and scruffs guzzling coffee and those bowls of incredible goulash and rice. She headed to the farthest, darkest end, ignoring the heads turning as her satchel swung free on its long straps. I too ignored the disapproving looks the suits cast my way, all they saw was a ratbag student leading a schoolgirl astray. I ordered two black from the dumpy old lady behind the counter.

'Okay?' I said as she spilled several sugar sachets into her brew.

She looked up at me, red-eyed. 'Sorry,' she said.

I asked what exactly she was sorry for. She sniffed, sipped the scalding coffee, shook her head.

'I just wanted Pat to notice me.'

'Eh? Funny way to go about it.'

She peered into her steaming cup, as if the answer could be conjured out of coffee. 'You don't understand.'

'Huh,' I grunted. 'You're right about that.'

'Please listen,' she said, a hand on my duffel sleeve. 'I knew Heather was coming over. I hardly know her.'

'Fooled me.'

She shook her head. 'She was years ahead. The star, school dux, competitive jumper, and a legend for her extracurricular activities. You don't want to hear all this.'

I did actually, and said so.

She sipped more coffee. 'Anyway, I knew she was coming to Mrs Flynn's do. She knows the Riddifords. All of them have farms over there.'

'So?'

'So I suppose.'

'What?'

'I was hoping something, when we got out on the yacht.'

'You mean I was some kind of bait? What if Heather didn't fancy me?'

She shook her head. I could see the tears brimming. She sniffed. 'Sorry. I don't know what I thought. Just that Pat might …' She pulled a hankie out of her skirt, dabbed at her eyes.

'So Gull – Patrick, he put you up to checking me out on the bus?'

She nodded miserably.

'What about last night? In my bed. What was that about?'

She blew her nose, looked at me. 'He told me I just had a schoolgirl crush and not to be … childish.'

The anguish in that word more or less told me everything.

'So why turn up at my place?'

'Heather said …'

'Yeah?'

'She said you were a slut.'

I didn't know what to say to that. Bloody cheek coming from her. I knew what provoked it.

'Did she say why?'

She wouldn't look at me. She nodded. 'Yes,' she said softly. 'She said you used some other woman's name when … you know?'

Was this an example of the irrational 'female logic' Dad often observed in Mum? 'And that's why you came over last night?'

She was shaking her head from side to side, tears streaming.

'Young lady?'

I looked up. One of the bulkier suits was standing over us, glaring at me.

'We're jake,' I said.

His face was almost scarlet, probably not helped by the tight collar around his neck jowls, his outrage heightening his colour. 'Doesn't look jake to me,' he said, his jaw jutting as he bumped the table, my untouched coffee spilling.

'Look,' I said, pushing my chair back and standing. 'We're having a private conversation here.'

'Not a very nice one, by the look of it,' he jeered, crowding against me. 'The young lady should be at school.'

'I'm fine,' Liz protested. 'We're just going.'

She got up, but Beefy was not getting out of our way. I didn't want to push him, but it looked like the only way we would get out of this narrow space.

'You mind?'

'Yeah,' he said. 'I do. What's your name?'

'Oi? Whatsa wrong here?'

It was the little old lady from behind the counter. She was prodding Beefy, who turned angrily.

'I'll handle this,' he growled.

'Not your court, Ol-iver. I look after this. This my son's plice. Missy, you not well?'

Liz grabbed my arm, said we just wanted to leave but this man here was stopping us.

The little lady reached up and tapped Big Oliver on the chest. 'This not your plice, Oliver. You leave them alone.'

Oliver was getting redder. 'Mrs S, this is not my doing. This lout is upsetting the schoolgirl.'

'So, when are you the policeman, uh? You leave them alone. Come on, you keeds, you want to go, you go.'

Liz thanked her as she gave Oliver some of his own medicine, pushing him into the wall. He looked like he was going to burst a foofoo valve, but we didn't wait to see if he did.

Out on the footpath Liz was actually laughing. 'What my mum would call a pickle. Sorry again.'

I told her I still didn't quite get it with Patrick and the yacht and Heather and me.

'Nor do I,' she said. 'Can we leave it at that? I've got to get to school.'

I accepted her handshake, and watched as she took off down the Quay. I had not had the heart to tell her where she left her high heels. I'd drop them over the Atkinson fence and leave the family to sort out the why of that. What was it Shakespeare said, something about the tangled web we weave, when first we practice to deceive? Whatever her web was, it was broken. It was strange being the recipient of a drunken offer from somebody who had been jilted. Love's old sweet song is not always sweet. Whoever wrote that love is for the very young did not get it right with Liz. Well, Gull didn't want love with her. Was that what her seasickness was all about?

Whatever, I now knew I had been a patsy. At least it had not got out of hand last night, possibly thanks to her being too ill to be appealing. What I did not understand was what was motivating Gull.

 **12**

Maggie sprang several surprises. There were three new recruits waiting beside her when Gull and I entered the rehearsal room.

'You know each other,' she said to me as I gawped at Jasper doing a pretty good imitation of a stick insect in a bilious green bodysuit. He gave me the dead-fish stare. She introduced the other two. The tall, willowy chap was Randolph Maclehose, his chestnut hair masking one side of his face, making me wonder if he had Heather's wobbly eye problem. He was also in tights, but red and revealing, with a short pink girly jacket made of what looked like the fringes you get on either end of rugs.

'Randy,' he corrected Maggie with a hip dip. 'By name and by nature.'

His short, chunky companion smacked his hand. Bosco Watts was his name. He had little hair left on top, it had prematurely migrated to his chest, a dense black thatch sprouting out of a tight electric-blue shirt like a burst horsehair mattress. His matching tights at least concealed the content if not the shape of his equipment.

'Wasn't Bosco a saint?' I asked him.

'Oooh,' he simpered, 'I'm no saint.' This time Randy did the smacking.

'You were at the protest,' Jasper said, his disconcerting stare directed at Gull.

'Uh huh,' Gull agreed in his minimalist fashion.

'Jasper,' Maggie said brightly, 'is a very good mover. I saw him doing his exercises on Kelburn Park. What do you call it?'

'*T'ai chi,*' he said, spelling it for us ignoramuses.

'That's a martial arts thing,' Ron said in an accusing voice.

'Wrong,' Jasper sneered. 'It's peaceful exercise, for those of us who don't do conventional sports.'

Maggie clapped her hands. 'Yes, now Bosco and Randy are the leads I promised.'

'Which one's the ballerina?' Morry piped up.

Randy tossed his angled fringe out of his face, establishing there was nothing wrong with either eye. I had not seen mascara and blusher on a man before, but perhaps he was in character. 'I would have thought,' he pouted, 'that was obvious to the meanest intelligence.'

Before Morry or anybody else could challenge that, Maggie clapped hands, told us we were in for a busy afternoon. There were now three dances to learn, Swan Lake, Balinese and Milkmaids. We would go down later to Kelburn Hall, where the full Extrav cast was rehearsing, so we could see where our dances fitted in.

She put us through several hours non-stop on the new dances, ignoring Bosco and Randy pleading to be allowed to practise their dying swan. Morry said in a loud whisper that would prove which was the ballerina. The Balinese dance required us to assume a whole new set of contortions, hands pointing out, fingers curling, knees bent. The Milkmaids dance was more like skipping sideways in unison, which we were far from achieving. Maggie was right about Jasper. He looked odd but he moved fluidly and picked up the moves almost as well as Randy, who had to have had classical training. I couldn't say the same for Bosco, but Randy guided him through it all with a close grip, confirming Bosco was the ballerina.

Kelburn Hall was chaotic. Dozens of people were talking at the same time, some to themselves, reading from cyclostyled sheets. Some kind of jazz orchestra was busy exchanging notes on piano, saxophones, trombone and drums. A tiny, sandy-haired fellow as near as I have seen to a dwarf was alternating between a group of about a dozen men and a dozen women, eliciting chants. A serious fellow in striped shirt with no collar and slicked-down black hair was issuing instructions to a group dominated by the biggest woman I had ever seen. Maggie told us to wait by the door and went over to this group. The solemn gent pointed without looking her way towards a woman crouched in a chair to one side, spectacles on a string round her neck, making notes in an open ring-binder.

Maggie conferred, the note-taker pointed to a stack of paper beside her. Maggie crouched and helped herself. She distributed stapled sheets to some of us and said we could share a look at the script, but we were not to chatter. Jasper had hold of one and was already snorting. It was the synopsis page. He had a finger on the solicitors for Phil's football company, Benjamin Doone and Philip McCracken.

As he flicked the pages I gathered the hero Phil Andrews was a stony-broke winger intent on organising professional football, with trade unionists trying to take it over and Wal, as in Walter Nash, out to nationalise the exercise. Wal goes to Bali and then Russia, cue two of our dances.

'What does a farmhand do at Cadbury's?' the big lady bellowed, getting everybody's attention.

Pause, the serious fellow with a hand up, then down.

'Milk chocolates,' somebody said, causing a group chortle.

Jasper was snorting again.

I read F.P. Hoffa telling Phil his men were violating basic union principles. Phil asks if he means that they work.

Jasper had turned the page, a song about trusting the union and the Court of so-called Arbitration used by the union to encourage inflation. His page-turning was too fast for me to take in much, but I did pick up Wal's sidekick, if that is the right word, was Mabel Howard. It looked like a lot of fun, plenty of jokes and songs.

There was a break. Maggie introduced us to Bill and Terry. Bill the serious one told us we were fail-safe, the male ballet always got the biggest laughs, so don't fail. He allowed a twitch of a smile, so we knew he was kidding, then he was off with Terry to confer with the band. Maggie took us to meet two women in cardigans, Janice and Amanda, who would be doing our make-up and costumes.

On the way to the bike Gull wanted to know about Jasper. I could only confirm he said he was an anarchist and I had no idea why he wanted to be a teacher or, for that matter, a male ballet dancer. I couldn't have given much of an answer to either question for myself, let alone this odd bod.

Thursday after Assembly Jasper asked me if I was going to the All Black trials at Athletic Park. I was startled and said I thought he wasn't into conventional sports. I knew the Phys-Ed contingent would be there en masse, with Fox and Barry Cull both in with a good chance of making the tour. Jasper surely would be boycotting the trials, if he had ever been interested in the first place.

'You satisfied with standing around outside Parliament?'

'Of course not.'

'Some are taking it to the turf.'

'Yeah?' I said, starting to get it.

'You in?'

I said I was. Making fun of Nash was one thing, but it was disgusting that as our leader he refused to cancel the tour when some of his own party were advocating it, along with the Federation of Labour. It was outrageous that we put up with the South African Rugby Board president Craven saying it would be too dangerous to allow Maoris to tour because the non-whites in South Africa were so backward and primitive. I suppose I also had a personal angle, with the Phys-Ed guys so gung-ho about touring. I had not seen Melissa with Jeff again, but the mere thought burned Gear sheep pelt acid in my stomach. In fact, I had not seen Melissa for several weeks, but as I was avoiding the Lit Club and my university attendance was restricted to the male ballet, it was hardly surprising.

This was my first visit to Athletic Park. At first sight it was not much different from the newsreels, a grey impression of tens of thousands of men in gaberdine raincoats and big hats surrounding a rectangle of murky turf. Close up it was somewhat daunting to be swept along in the crowd of grimly purposeful men and excitable boys pushing to get through the turnstiles, where you had to fork out what I thought way too much for what was only a talent-spotting exercise.

People spread like herds of uncontrolled sheep round the perimeters of the field, a sweating, eager rabble, many smoking and all gabbling about who should make it and who wouldn't have a dog's show. It was not easy staying in touch with Jasper as he pushed ahead, oblivious to objections. Several times I copped a push in the back as I darted after him, along with rude advice to pull my head in. Seeing people scoffing steaming pies had my mouth streaming. I tried to concentrate, reminding myself why we were here.

Jasper had a possie almost within touching distance of the corner flag at the northern end furthest from the entry gates, and as it happened not far from the Phys-Ed gang. He said the plan was to wait until half-time and run out on to the field and stage a sit-down. He indicated the half-way line, where the first five was preparing to kick off. The rest of what he was saying was obliterated by the collective roar around the ground as the game got underway.

I have to confess I was swept up in the mass excitement. I strained my eyes but couldn't spot Fox or Cull. They all looked much the same to me, except for different bumblebee bands on the opposing jerseys, and the forwards twice the size of the backs.

As the game settled down to a kicking duel, the crowd got restive and abusive of the kickers and the ref. Every time there was a forward surge, there would be shouts of encouragement to get stuck in. I thought of that book *A Gun in My Hand*, the guy in the rugby crowd with a gun. We were not by any stretch intent on such violence, but I could guess those around us might well feel inclined to some when we invaded the sacred turf. At least it was a fine day, so it wouldn't be slippery underfoot if I had to run for it.

The whistle blew, the teams were ambling off the field.

'Come on,' Jasper said, ducking under the barrier and doing his spindleshanks stride, head up, as if he was out for a stroll. I followed him, ignoring someone shouting out you weren't allowed on the pitch, somebody else saying they couldn't do any worse than the rubbish so far. Nobody initially came after us, as we crossed to the kick-off spot, a dozen or so joining us, including three women.

As we herded together and sat down on the pitch, police started to jog towards us from different parts of the ground. Comments from the crowd encouraged the police to 'arrest the bloody student stirrers', but none sounded particularly hostile. I still felt nervous as I sat on the surprisingly uneven turf, divots and clods and patches more thick mud than grass, with myriad puncture marks from the pounding and ploughing up of all those determined studs to so little effect. Jasper was saying something to the guy with the Stalin moustache about resisting the fascists. A banner was being unfurled and held out: 'No Bloody South African Apartheid for New Zealand'. The crude red lettering dribbled like blood.

There were no more police than protesters. When they started grabbing people roughly by the arms and hauling them to their feet, a woman shouted 'You're hurting me, you pig'. The policeman was hauled off her by his neck, his helmet flying. Jasper grabbed one of the sticks the banner was attached to and yelled out to charge. The duffel coat on the other end responded, and they ran towards the left touchline, banner held up, several policemen in pursuit.

I was yanked backwards by my duffel hood. I spun awkwardly, stumbling into the cop and both of us falling over. I was up first and off, running away at a diagonal from the cops overhauling Jasper and the other guy with the banner. Some in the crowd were yelling encouragement to go faster, like it was some kind of race. I suppose it offered more incident than the All Black wannabes provided.

The good thing was that the cops were not dressed for running, held back by their heavy clothes, thick raincoats, those daft helmets and of course their big boots. It was no problem for me to dodge around one of them coming at me, jink sideways to avoid a flying tackle that left the cop sprawled on the turf. I could hear the cheering and laughter as I sprinted towards the far end of the main stand, where I noticed the gates were part open.

As I darted into the crowd, I was caught again by my hood, slamming me into several spectators, causing us all to stumble. I wrenched free and elbowed my way ahead, ignoring objections. I was through the crush and taking off when I was ankle-tapped.

'Hold the bugger,' somebody said. Several did. I was nabbed.

'I'll take charge,' Gull said, his grip inside my right shoulder too emphatic for the two beefy but obliging young men, and way too strong for my comfort. They were looking uncertain, but the handcuffs he produced did the trick.

'Move aside,' Gull ordered them. 'Crowd control.'

The young men stepped away, used no doubt to accepting orders from authority figures.

'Move it,' Gull said, ensuring I did.

We left behind a crowd who seemed generally to be enjoying the fracas, judging by the calls to put him down and go get them. 'Student wanker,' an excited, pissy-eyed member of the gaberdine brigade said as we passed. 'Draft them in the army,' another suggested.

Outside the park Gull let go his grip. 'You're lucky. There aren't going to be any arrests with this government. There will be a few stiff reminders. Cops don't like being made fools of.'

'We don't have the right to protest?'

'Idiots,' he said, stuffing his handcuffs in his jacket pocket.

'Glad you had those,' I said.

'Bike's over there,' he growled, crossing in front of the line of stationary trams.

I followed him, relieved not to be experiencing whatever procedures Jasper and the rest were subject to under the stands at the hands of the discountenanced police. Once again Gull to the rescue. He deserved a bonus from Dad for his efforts.

When he dropped me off I asked him if Jasper was now on his list to keep an eye on.

'Jasper,' he said, 'craves trouble.'

He revved and shot away, economical as always with his words.

It was apparent next Saturday afternoon that Jasper had found what Gull claimed he craved. One of his lens was starred and the frame on that side held together with several sticking plaster strips. A wider plaster was employed over his left temple and he sported a bandage just above it encircling his head.

'*T'ai chi* go wrong?' Ron enquired in his sepulchral voice.

'Something like that,' Jasper said, squinting with his good eye, though good is hardly the right word for it.

'Martial artist, eh?' Morry chortled.

Maggie gave us all a sharp look and asked Jasper if he was sure he should be extending himself.

He waved away her concern. 'Superficial. Shall we get on with it?'

Maggie did just that, meticulously taking us through our Balinese paces. After several hours it wasn't just Jasper who looked stuffed.

Gull dropped me at the bus stop, he had people to see.

Once home I went for a jog to Pencarrow and back. Nothing much else to do, and by the end of it most of the stiffness from the unnatural Balinese postures had been shaken loose.

Sunday we did a three-hour session on all three dances. On the way downtown afterwards there were thousands of people lining the waterfront. I assumed it was some sort of performance, like a free Howard Morrison Quartet concert, Selwyn offering punters money or the bag containing either a washing machine or a toothbrush. I mentioned it to Dad and he said it was the capital welcoming the brand new American nuclear submarine into harbour on a goodwill visit, the first ever by a nuclear sub to New Zealand. Hadn't I seen the reports of it on its way down from Auckland?

I confessed I had not, told him I had been too preoccupied with this play we were doing. Actually, this was an anticipatory if not disingenuous remark. I had to spend the evening reading *Hedda Gabler*, I'd been cast as the dull academic Jorgen Tesman in Macaskill's play-reading. It proved to be total Nordic gloom, up there with the doom-laden Swedish film about the devil playing chess with one of his inevitable victims. Jorgen's wife Hedda and her lover both commit suicide. Perfect Sunday night reading.

I have no doubt it provoked the nightmare about Liz getting preggers and me about to strangle myself with Jasper's bloody head bandage. Dad woke me in time to prevent any serious loss of breath from the sheet wound round my neck. He told me he would make an appointment for me to see a doctor.

Monday I felt like death warmed up, Dad proving his point about a visit to a doctor, but possibly ideal for playing this pathetic academic. After that interminable experience, I forced myself along to Maggie's third rehearsal in a row. No Ron or Gull there. We did an hour on all three dances, Maggie urging us to encourage the absentees to make the effort, we were nowhere near up to speed as a group. I wasn't up to speed, full stop.

I was actually in desperate need of a coffee or three. I joined Jasper, thankfully minus his Frankenstein monster headscarf, at the Symposium. People were full-on discussing the nuclear sub visit. I had to thank my father for even knowing about it, thus spared any possible humiliation from Jasper.

Jasper was deep in a denunciatory conversation with an older Pom, judging by his accent. Jasper called him Ben, but no introduction, that was too bourgeois conventional and anyway I didn't count for much. Both were exchanging similar views about the arrogant coercive superstate surpassing itself by parading the weapon capable of annihilating the planet.

'Real-life version of *On the Beach*, eh?'

Both looked at me as if I had crawled out of a septic tank.

'I mean,' I faltered, 'if there was an accident or something.'

'Capitalistic crap,' Ben scoffed.

Jasper sniggered. 'Hollow-wood frightens the masses.'

Ben turned back to Jasper. 'This has to be the most conformist country in the world.'

Jasper put out a hand to shake Ben's. 'Conformist is what they call egalitarian. Jack as good as his master. Pull the other one, it's got bells on. Kiwis've hoodwinked themselves. Didn't they get it in the world wars, they're cannon fodder, peasant pawns of the ruling classes in dear old Muvver England. Welfare state's sucked the soul out of the place.'

Pommie pricks. 'Why don't you do something about it?'

This time I had their attention.

'Like what?' Ben said. 'You got something in mind?'

'A protest?'

Jasper was nodding, a nasty grin on his face. 'You see that carton of fireworks at the rehearsal hall?'

I had to admit I had not.

'The Yank captain reckons his sub is the first that can fire a missile. Well, what about firing a few of our own at them?'

'Ya,' Ben chortled. 'While their friggin' crew is marching in the warmongering Anzac Parade.'

'Could be fun,' Jasper agreed, his eyes like poached eggs under cracked glass spectacles. 'Fuck up those smug bastards. Might even score a lucky strike, straight down an open hatch. That'd shake them up.'

'Pop a few poppies,' Ben cackled. 'Nice one, Jas.'

Jasper said he'd extract some rockets tomorrow. I was the local, I could scout out a good firing possie. I said I'd have a go.

'Needle noddle noo, Jim,' Jasper said in a fair imitation of a Goon. There was some humour lurking after all behind that blank fish face.

I crawled on to the 8.15 bus, wondering what I had let myself in for. It wasn't as if we were going to do any real damage, just make a statement that not everybody fell at the feet of these nuclear warriors. One of the masters at Teachers College had quoted the old English protester Bertrand Russell challenging the feeling that individuals were impotent against governments. Russell advocated civil disobedience, surely a necessary as well as noble cause when we had the Americans already mistaking the moon and flights of geese for Russian missiles. Sooner or later some trigger-happy American military clown was going to press the button that ended it for all of us. Perhaps a little protest might lead to bigger ones, until finally governments could not ignore the will of the people. I don't know if Jasper and Ben cared about the will of the people, but I thought this might be a start. And it had started as my idea.

I struggled through Irene's beetroot soup. I passed on her disgusting cold pancakes full of fishy muck and smeared in sour cream, which Dad told me were called blinis, a Russian delicacy, as was the *boeuf stroganoff*. The beef and plenty of rice I did enjoy, which pleased him. He said Irene was experimenting with different cuisines.

I resisted the impulse to suggest this could signal to some of the Nats, like that buck-toothed Dicky, that she was showing culinary sympathy for the nasty Commie Russkies. Instead, I asked if that made us guinea pigs. He laughed, supposed it did. I told him all I needed now to come right was a decent night's sleep.

It was not an option sleeping with a conscience, used to feeling guilt courtesy of Catholic conditioning, arguing with itself that a citizen had every right to practise civil disobedience in the cause of trying to save humanity. The end justifies the means. Wasn't it St Ignatius who coined that phrase? I know his Jesuits were often provocative to the Pope, but that was all the more reason to go with them, they were the intellectual conscience of the church. Damn it, if I could, I would.

# 13

I was up at dawn, but only because I couldn't sleep, not for the poppy-flaunting Anzac Day service from Dad's lot, standing to attention by memorials to their fallen comrades. The way they carried on, most of them wanted us to go out and get a taste of the war they were lucky to survive. In the next war, there would be no survivors.

I got out the map of Wellington streets Dad had acquired when we arrived. I checked the Clyde Quay area, where the nuclear sub was berthed, all 350 feet of it, according to an absurd article in the paper which compared the captain of USS *Halibut* to Hornblower. Pathetic. Hornblower was not only a fictional character, he fired cannon balls, for Pete's sake. No Hornblower ever had the capacity to launch five Regulus missiles, each pretty much guaranteed to destroy the North Island of New Zealand.

I put the radio on for company while I studied the map. A brigadier was reinforcing my misgivings, saying New Zealand must seek peace from a position of strength. The visit of this nuclear submarine served to remind us that we lean heavily on the US for our defence, a defence that saved us at the Battle of the Coral Sea. Well, it wouldn't save us this time. The RSA was living in the past and ensuring there would be no future, by boasting about New Zealand ordering two Whitby anti-submarine frigates. Hadn't the guy read the article about the sub's incredible fire power? The Russkies had their nuke subs. Us deploying anti-sub frigates would be like sending out white mice in walnut half-shells to confront a great grey shark.

The roof of the Herd Street Post Office looked to me the perfect place to rain down a few rockets on the sub. Guy Fawkes rockets would be no more threatening than tossing three blind mice at a hungry cat, but symbolically we would be the Peter Sellers' *The Mouse that Roared*, and look at the impact of that.

The arrangement was to meet outside the Symposium at nine, as the coffee bar would be closed, like most of the shops on the only day of the year to rival Good Friday for shut-down. No bus until eight. I got to the Symposium a few minutes after nine, it was five-to when I jogged past the Pigeon Park clock. No sign of Jasper. He turned up ages later, by which time my sweat had cooled to a soggy state inside my well-named sweat shirt. Of course I could not complain, having been the initial time-lapse culprit.

He said tersely that Ben had other fish to fry, and he had the rockets back at his flat. He about-turned, no discourse deemed necessary with his tardy factotum, and briskly led the way. We walked against the tide of sightseers come to look at this monster grey shark, two storeys high according to the newspaper.

He had a small room off The Terrace that smelled of dodgy fish and too many spices. The single gas ring hosted a wok with a lid on it, the most likely source of the exotic pong. There were piles of paperback books leaning against each other for support in one corner, next to a small desk not unlike Melissa's, which provoked a little stab in my stomach. The other side of the bed and a lamp stand there was a curtained rod, below which trousers and shoes spilled. No bourgeois consumer trappings here.

I looked through the dirty glass of the single sash window. If cleaned, it would offer a superb bird's eye view of the harbour. He reached under the unmade bed and pulled out a cardboard box. He extracted a paper bag of rockets. As he rattled a box of Vesta matches, he finally broke his silence, asking I thought sarcastically if I had identified a command view of the enemy. I told him about the Herd Street Post Office, which had a flat roof overlooking the wharf and the sub. He asked if I had recce'd. I confessed I had not, but I blurted out that they never closed, telegrams and such had to be taken care of. He relaxed, so I must have got that right.

He frowned, muttered to himself, tugged the curtain aside and extracted a large coil of rope. With no explanation, he told me I carried the bag of fireworks and the milk bottles.

'Like this?' I said incredulously. 'Kind of telegraphing our intentions entering a P&T office with rockets and bottles?' He did not respond to a pun Macaskill might have approved. He returned to his curtain possie and pulled out a duffel bag, tossed it at me. I put in the bag of rockets and the eight pint bottles.

'You alert the newspapers?'

Another black mark against me, designed to put me in my place. I confessed I had not.

'No point in the exercise without an audience. If the papers are shut down, Press Association will have a duty journo, should be a photographer on call. I'll borrow the priest's on the way.'

We walked down Church Street steps, Jasper with enough rope slung around one shoulder to rappel all the way to Boulcott Street. We entered the familiar precincts of the castellated concrete neo-cathedral of St Mary of the Angels. Jasper dropped the coil of rope at my feet and told me to wait. He disappeared inside the side door entrance. I looked about, feeling like an idiot with my suspicious baggage. Finally he returned, said he had got through. He recovered his coil and set off, leaving his dodgy disciple to follow in his prancing footsteps.

Manners Street and Wakefield Street were closed. As we reached the windy Taranaki Street corner we could see at its top the marching contingent I assumed were the crew of the *Halibut* heading for the succession of dull thuds which marked the War Memorial mid-morning proceedings. People were getting off trams and trolley buses and heading in the same direction as us.

The crowd moved to a wharf view of the sub. We stopped outside the fluted copper columns that curved all the way up the imposing corner entrance of the Herd Street Post Office building. The big metal doors were shut. Without pause, Jasper stepped up and twisted the handle. It turned and he leaned against it, pushing it open. I don't know what he had in mind if confronted by somebody. Was he going to say he had plans to throw a lifeline to the sub? So what did I say about the rockets, that they were distress flares?

There was nobody lurking in the foyer, no caretaker or staffer on double-time, not even a receptionist. He sprang up the stairs, and I followed. It was a fair slog for six or so floors. Amazingly we were able to go to the top, and push open a door on to the flat tarsealed roof. Jasper waved me through and eased the door shut.

The view was stupendous, and it included the sleek hulk of the sub not more than a shanghai stone's range below. The day was cloudy and cool, the weather overhead toning in with the colour of the sub and the water lapping around it. Anzac Day was a traditionally grey affair, but at least it was not raining. The northerly was brisk in our faces.

People lined the wharf either side of the behemoth, pointing at sailors moving about on its superstructure, which included the kind of conning tower I had seen John Mills and a few other actors jump down, slamming the hatch shut and shouting 'Dive! Dive! Dive!' No machine gun mounted on the fo'c'sle, so we would be safe from direct attack if spotted.

Jasper had moved to the far side, unravelling some of his rope and hitching it to the metal rail. He pulled it tight to test it and then beckoned me to him. He took the bag, removed and positioned the eight bottles next to the long metal rail facing the sub. He set a rocket in each bottle, adjusting their positions for what he gauged was the right lobbing angle.

'You've done some climbing then?'

He ignored my question, pulling out the wax matches as a siren screamed in the distance. It was coming quickly. I could see no fire. There must have been an accident. Then I saw the flashing red bonnet light on the black Holden police car pulling up below where we had just entered the building. Another siren indicated another police car. Jasper trotted across the roof to assess the situation. He was quickly back and crouched beside the bottles.

'Never trust a journo,' he said. He struck matches and the rockets one by one ignited, flaring up and out over the water. I looked down at the sub, where there was no movement now on its superstructure. No klaxon sounding and the sub diving.

No need, the rockets wobbled into the sky and landed harmlessly in the water.

Jasper was peering down the back of the building. He tipped the rope over the edge and disappeared. I rushed to the rope and followed suit. It was not exactly abseiling but it was easy enough, and I had caught up to him by the time he hit the ground and took off. We had got around the corner of the shack when we saw the first police appear. They were too late. We had enough cover to dart across to the hard and drop down and scurry along it towards the Port Nicholson clubrooms, up the steps to the street.

Jasper caught me at the top and slowed me to a stroll around to Oriental Bay. As we passed the salt water baths another cop car sirened past. Nobody stopped us. Jasper retained the bounce in his stride, not disappointed at the failure of our little exercise.

'Queen Vic next,' he said. 'This time the press will notice.'

He offered no explanation, suggested I get myself an ice cream, abruptly heading off towards the fire station and the Embassy Theatre. And that was that for my first foray into anarchist agitation. Not with a bang but a whimper, to quote that bank clerk turned poet, another of Don's recommendations. No need of Gull this time, I had got away with it without his help, admittedly courtesy of Jasper's forward planning.

There was nothing in the papers about our little escapade, which was to be expected, but still disappointing. You like to see effort rewarded, to quote the sports master at St Peters. It was difficult after the excitement of our roof-top attack on the world's newest and most potent killing machine to settle down to child study and catch-up from all the lectures and assignments I had missed or neglected. I couldn't wait to hear what Jasper had in mind for Queen Victoria.

Over the next few days I forced myself to do study at the library after Teachers College. Dad and I both got back late most nights. He had flagged away the doctor appointment, thank goodness. He remained preoccupied with the financial loss to the country from workers imposing an overtime ban which reduced freezing works to a quarter of the present kill, because the Arbitration Court would not give them 24 per cent. I had no interest now I was out of the Gear work force. The only things that caught my eye in the paper were that Sabrina claimed the bust thing was finished and she needed a new gimmick, and that the police had made another raid on the opium dens in Haining Street.

I did care about the tour going ahead. I signed the 'No Maoris, No Tour' petition, like just about everybody at Teachers College. I imagine the exceptions were the Phys-Ed guys, who were in a surly mood because both Fox and Cull were robbed of places in the touring side by has-beens and never-beens. They could be heard repeating their resentful mantra loudly and bitterly more than once before and after Assembly.

At Thursday Assembly Vogt announced he was resigning because he couldn't walk down Lambton Quay singing. In the caff afterwards I heard Don confide to Frank it was a symbolic remark. I would have hoped so. Nobody actually would stop anybody singing in the street, though they might seek to commit them for it.

Jasper has this unnerving way of appearing behind me, just out of my peripheral vision, waiting. I had put down my cup on the caff counter.

'Quantocks,' he said, dodging my startled turn.

'Eh?'

He had new glasses, heavy black frames. His stare hadn't changed.

'You asked about climbing?'

'Quantocks?' I remembered my question, but had no idea what he was on about.

'Look it up,' he said, and was gone before I could question him about Queen Vic.

When Gull collected me on the Saturday, he switched off the bike and gave me a hard look.

'Know anything about rockets fired at our American visitor?'

I did my best to look blank. 'You mean that nuclear sub?'

He straddled his bike, feet on the ground, and stared me down.

'A prank. A stupid one. There could still be repercussions.'

I put on the helmet. 'What makes you think I'd know anything?'

'Our anarchist friend. Sort of thing I'd expect from him. I heard there were two seen in the vicinity.'

'Dunno,' I said.

He kick-started and scarcely gave me time to get on the back before he took off.

Outside the rehearsal room he said he was not able to make it, and to give Maggie his apologies. She was not pleased. Jasper maintained standards with his dancing, and his inscrutable manner.

In a break Randy pranced over to where us straights were comparing sore points. 'Where's the hunk?' he asked me. I said I had no idea, I wasn't his keeper.

'Oh,' he said, batting his mascara thick lashes. 'I thought you were an item.'

I looked at Jeremy and Ron. 'You've got to be joking.'

Bosco had an arm tucked in Randy's. 'We've seen the looks he gives you.'

'You jokers are mad,' I said. 'Gull – Paddy's got girls all over him.'

'I wouldn't mind him all over me,' Bosco giggled, spinning smartly to avoid Randy's backhander.

'Poofs,' Morry sneered.

'You should try it,' Randy said, running his long pink tongue slowly around his lips. 'Courtenay Place jakes if you're interested.'

Morry's face was a picture of disgust. 'You're unnatural,' he spat, turning away.

'So why are you wearing dresses then?' Randy laughed. 'Come on, my little sugar plum fairy, we've got moves to practise.'

As they pranced off I growled that they were ghastly little pricks.

'Only one of them,' Ron said lugubriously.

'Forget about them,' Jeremy suggested. 'They like winding us up.'

'Queer as clockwork oranges,' Jasper proposed.

The next week we had exams, English at varsity and child development at Training College. Maggie had acquired buckets for us milkmaids and we had fittings for our costumes, which were not ready in time for the Procesh. So no male ballet in the floats through Wellington the next day, which was also the day of the big 'No Maoris, No Tour' protest.

Jasper had a bucket idea of another kind, if I was on for another small protest which involved the symbol of global British oppression. He wouldn't say anymore, I had to join him if I wanted to know what. I was bunking over in a sleeping bag on Jeremy's sitting-room sofa, having explained to Dad that the rehearsals were getting later and later and if Gull was not around, I'd stay in town. All I had to do was meet Jasper at the corner of Courtenay Place at 4am.

Jeremy's parents are so obliging, they provided an alarm clock, no questions asked. Shelley had none of her parents' discretion, demanding to know what I could possibly be doing at that hour. I told her loftily it was *T'ai chi*, and that shut her up.

I got little sleep, the broken springs on the couch ensuring that. Mrs Shelton left out a bowl of Weet-Bix and a banana. They were life-restorers, but not enough to stop me yawning and shuffling to the dawn rendezvous. I don't know how those old diggers did it, getting up at this ungodly hour to stand to attention in front of some imperial reminder of their colonial cannon fodder status.

Jasper was there in his Sherlock garb, holding a large paint bucket with its lid still on. Yawning he set off up Cambridge Terrace, swinging the bucket by its wire handle. About 100 yards up in the centre of the boulevard was a huge and much larger than life bronze statue of Queen Victoria, the most famous dumpy old matron the world has known. God knows what she was doing in this insignificant arterial route staring at passing traffic.

A gutter-cleaning truck surged out of a side street. Jasper kept walking. He crossed to the statue. I joined him. We gazed up the solid granite pedestal at the doughty silhouette draped in bronze robes, holding something like a bishop's mitre in one hand, a baby angel in the other, her grim features surmounted by a crown without jewels perched at what struck me as a rakish angle. The entire edifice had to be four times my height. It was a big ask if he was planning to crown her anew. The problem was going to be getting over the layers of granite overhang. Still, where there was a will.

'New coat of paint for the old duck?'

His glasses were opaque in this light, but I knew well the dead stare behind them. He turned his attention to the bucket, pulling a screwdriver out of the folds of a robe as voluminous as his intended victim. He prised off the lid.

'Straddle the plinth,' he said.

I did so. He rested the bucket of dark paint on the ground and monkeyed up my back. He positioned himself on my shoulders, his desert boots digging in. A chill dawn wind was cutting up the wide road and into the half of me exposed to it. I shivered and began wobbling, the position not easy to maintain.

'Damn!' he said. 'Stand still. I can't get a grip.'

'Whoops,' I said, stumbling and cracking a knee against the unforgiving stone. Jasper gave up and descended, using my back as his ramp.

'We'll swap over,' he said. 'You're a bit taller.'

'A ladder would have been handy.' Dead stare. 'Okay, okay.'

He crouched, I got on his shoulders and he eased upright. I could reach the overhang but, like him, I could not get a grip on the damp, angled surface. Behind me I could hear the heavy rattle of a tram in the distance.

'Fuck it,' he said, tipping me sideways. I landed painfully on the stone steps. 'Stay on all fours, will you.'

He had hefted the bucket and got on my back. He started swinging the bucket, tensed and leapt upwards with a grunt. He landed a crippling thump on my lower back, which staged him to the ground. I could smell the noxious contents and observe them trickling down the sides of the plinth. It was light enough to see that the colour was blood, and it had only got as far as the bottom of her robes.

Jasper was cursing and telling me to move round the other side, there was time for another go. The tram was approaching from the Basin Reserve, getting louder and louder. My lower back protested as I tottered round to the other side. He jumped on my back and heaved the can skywards.

'Better,' he said. 'There's still some left.'

He flung it up at her head and scored a bullseye, the can hooked for a moment on her crown, paint streaking her features as the can bounced in bloody stages to the ground.

Jasper pointed to the far side from the tram that was nearly upon us. We sheltered behind the plinth as it rattled past, the driver not noticing or not caring.

I asked him about the newspapers. He said he'd take care of that, but now we should split.

He darted down the side street behind Courtenay Place. I gave the besmirched old statue one more glance. It had hardly seemed worth the effort. Would anybody care?

I headed down to the pie-cart, but it was closed. Next I tried the Green Parrot.

Closed. There was some traffic around, a few delivery vans. I mooched through town imagining the hot bread, pies, sausage rolls, trays of cream buns. If only one of those vans would stop and leave its back open, I'd be in like a robber's dog. Dawn painting of old metal ladies was hungry work. A cup of black coffee was an absolute priority, or I'd need toothpicks to keep my eyes open.

Trams and buses were making appearances, in Willis Street the butcher was open, the greengrocer was just opening. It was hot pastry I craved, but the KKK and the cake shop on the other side of Manners Street were still shut.

The cable car was my best bet. I went up the lane. A bundle of *The Dominion* was lying there for the taking. I left a coin and grabbed one. No coffee.

I proceeded on down Lambton Quay, finally a milk bar open. No greeting from the squalid guy with wet hair parted in the middle and a dirty white tunic behind the counter making sandwiches. I ordered a coffee and sat in one of those red vinyl leather booths with the little juke boxes. Plenty of Elvis, Buddy Holly, Cliff Richard, but I had no spare coins for that.

The Zip was hissing up to an ear-shattering whistle. He dumped in front of me a cup and saucer of the Railway variety for thickness and plainness. The milky coffee was a match, that ghastly stuff with chicory in it. Some of it was already in the saucer. I spooned in eight heaped teaspoons, noting with satisfaction the proprietor watching me. I took a sip and jerked back, spilling scalding brew over my duffel coat. I saw his face twitch.

I concentrated on the paper, reading things I would never bother with normally. Somebody called Hundertwasser had resigned because his wavy line painting was banned from state schools in Hamburg. Sir Donald Wolfit was here to show us colonials how Shakespeare should be performed. The 78 rpm record was declared dead, except in Ghana and Scotland, and the latter only wanted them because of a lack of electricity. Brigitte Bardot had to leave home in a dark wig because she was so famous. Okay, I might have read that.

Other people began to come in. Now I could smell pies, as he packed the warmer. The way he grabbed my cup, the grubby state of his clothes and hands, I thought it safer to get out of here.

I wandered down to the Railway pie-cart, thinking about that incredibly cheap plate of a meat pie swimming in a sort of pea gravy, but the pie-cart was shuttered. Inside the station the first rush of bureaucrats charged heads-down swinging briefcases, brollies and gaberdines, and a few schoolkids who must have some kind of pre-school activity they really rated. I could have bought flowers or an orange or a chocolate bar. I didn't. The caff was open, but it looked no more likely to have decent coffee than the milk bar I'd already tried.

On the way back the coffee gallery above Parsons Bookshop was open. No suits here yet. The old lady recognised me and gave me a big smile and asked if I'd like a leetle pastie with it, for nothing, left from yesterday. I did. It was cold, but delicious, a baby pie full of bacon, egg and mushroom. I was starting to feel human. I stared mindlessly at the lurid nudes on the walls, distorted in shape and colour, like Picasso had got to work on Modigliani. All thoughts eventually returned to Melissa.

At Assembly Scotty warned us to think carefully about the implications of going on an illegal march with no police permit issued for it. With a poker face the equal of Jasper he then said that he would meet up with fellow marchers on the corner of Glasgow Street and Kelburn Parade. The hall erupted in cheers, even some of the Phys-Ed guys, who would not be seen dead marching against the All Blacks. It was probably a way of expressing their displeasure at Fox and Cull missing selection.

The light-hearted Extrav Procession was nearing its end by the Public Library when I got there, having found a quiet corner of the near empty Hunter library and had a doze. The best float was about 'No Maoris, No Tour', with whites crowded behind barbed wire, a trooper holding a Ku Klux Klan cross, burnt-cork Negroes in chains being flogged by storm troopers. A big bird on a bike was 'Walter's Go-Anywhere Machine'. Eddus Hillarious and Low George were in search of the Abominable Snowman, a reference to Sir Ed saying recently in the newspaper there was something to the Yeti stories. An elaborate but not particularly interesting float was Auckland Harbour Bridge being painted before it rusted away. There were others about the atom bomb, the Olympics, the Nelson Railway.

A cocktail party for the departing All Blacks was the reason for the serious protest outside Parliament. There were thousands of us at the Bowen Street entrance, but the All Blacks sneaked in by another route. There was a storm of booing and singing of the Maori Battalion March to Victory song. I held one of the banners handed out for 'No Maoris, No Tour'. There were dozens of them, the best I saw would have gone well in the Procesh, 'I'm All White, Jack', a play on the current Peter Sellers movie *I'm All Right, Jack*, about trade union intransigence. Another banner reminded our MPs 'Only One Race – the Human Race'.

The Federation of Labour was at the forefront of this demo, with its leader telling us the tour was a shame and a blot on New Zealand condoning South African apartheid and his organisation had always said there should be no tour without Maori. Speaking of whom, a telegram was read out from the famous Maori and New Zealand All Black fullback George Nepia asking the protesters to let him know if they needed a fullback. That got a roar of laughter and cheers. It was announced that over 150,000 had signed the petition. The FOL guy led his deputation in to see Acting Prime

Minister Skinner, Walter of course swanning about overseas. There was nothing for the rest of us to do but disperse.

The newspaper photo caption next day claimed there were 1000 at the demo. I would have said at least double that. The All Black manager Tom Pearce got plenty of coverage with his claptrap about it being incumbent on every loyal New Zealander to get wholeheartedly behind the team. What a load of bullshit. The loyal New Zealanders were the 150,000 who signed the petition objecting to this dishonourable tour, those who marched against it, those students who rushed the tarmac waving fists at the TEAL Electra airliner as it took off. No mention of that in our free press.

I was beginning to see where Jasper, and the other anarchic British imports Ben and Bill Dwyer, were coming from. They all had the lean and hungry look. I'd said as much to Jasper and he'd taken me literally, caustically observed there wasn't a lot of food around Britain after the government had spent its money on a nuclear sub fleet. I said we'd sent over food parcels to help them out. He shrugged, said the parcels never got to Wigan.

My point had been lost. What of course I had meant was a compliment, the lean and hungry look, but I didn't pursue it when I realised I had got my Shakespearean characters confused. I had not meant Cassius the assassinator, but the apparently mad Hamlet denouncing the corrupt system. Another literary comparison more suitable perhaps would be Jasper and the other British anarchists akin to the turbulent priest one of the King Henrys complained of. I don't remember which Henry, but I know the priest was Thomas à Becket. The anarchists looked more and more like the sane inmates of an asylum run by lunatics called New Zealand. Well, perhaps not lunatics, more somnolent old socialists like Nash or indifferent capitalist swine, my father, of course, excepted.

That's the trouble with not paying full attention at school, I'd ended up mixing my quotable metaphors. If I'd pulled a Hamlet quote, suggested his mates could tell a hawk from a handsaw, I might have got my point across. There was a lesson here, shelve the half-baked quotes.

As for our attempt to freshen up the old queen, it took a lot of searching to find a small paragraph noting the council cleaning department had swiftly removed red paint tossed over the statue. A council spokesman imagined it was some sort of student prank, but not a very good one. Council cleaners reported seeing two men in the area in the early hours. The police were making enquiries. If they bore fruit, I didn't fancy their chances of getting much out of Jasper. My own enquiry got the stare and the bizarre remark that one day the fat lady would perform. I don't imagine he meant Margot, the huge lady who played Mabel Howard in Carry on Phil, she proved to be the most potent performer for presence and panache.

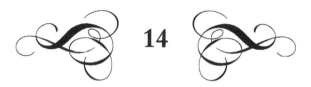

Dad woke me to take a phone call at 1.15am. The woman he said was most insistent. Being Dad, he didn't warn me she was also pissed. Clair called me a total shit in several different ways, and once in a French phrase that was not in our varsity syllabus.

When the phone was dropped, it was Harold who picked up, apologising for Clair's language. He said in his orotund fashion that the sweet lady had become increasingly distressed over the course of several snifters at the state of some damsel of mutual acquaintance. Do drop by, young fellow, he added, and bade me goodnight. The only lass we both knew was Melissa, whom I had not, regrettably, laid eyes on for weeks.

On the way from the cable car late the next morning I veered down into Rimu Road, feeling a few flutters of concern. I wanted to see her, but I was apprehensive about the reception. As I neared her address I slowed down. What if she wouldn't see me? What if she abused me? I had to tell her I did care for her. She might not be in. I dithered outside, looking up at the concrete steps where I had crouched naked clutching my clothes as Clair smoked that black cigarette. Sobranie, I think they are called. Russian. Did Irene serve them with her blinis? Were they now regarded as Commie ciggies? Odd the thoughts when you're stalling.

A stout lady with glasses swinging from a chain round her neck clumped past in brown District Nurse shoes and the heaviest green tweed jacket and skirt, giving me the once-over. Taller and younger and definitely not tiddly, otherwise she was not unlike Frances who took us for French Reading Knowledge. She paused several houses along, lifting her glasses to peer at me. I waved and opened the gate.

I climbed slowly up the creaking ramp, tapped on the rippled glass door. I heard a faint meow. A promising sign. I hesitated, tapped once more. Now there was somebody behind the glass. The door opened a crack. Melissa was in a faded green flannelette nightie, her hair dishevelled, her face the colour of yellow chalk. I could smell her perfume. She looked infinitely desirable.

'Stephen,' she said slowly, rubbing a hand across her face, bangles jiggling. 'What do you want?'

I wanted to embrace her, hold her tightly, bury my face in her hair. I said I had heard she was not well. The kitten took the opportunity to get out, and proceed to rub against my legs. Melissa looked at me. Even her gorgeous green eyes had a yellow cast, not that it mattered one iota. If anything, she was more beautiful, a sad Cinderella Madonna, that palely loitering lady in a poem I had otherwise forgotten. I stammered that I wanted to see her, I thought of her all the time. She continued to look at me. I couldn't read her expression.

'Please?' I said. 'Can I see you?'

'No,' she said, starting to close the door.

I put my hand on the handle, asked if there was anything she needed, anything I could do.

'No.'

'What about Nigel?'

The door opened. She allowed herself a faint smile as she bent down and collected her kitten.

'Sorry, Stephen, I have nothing to say to you.'

The door closed. There was nothing to do but retreat. I dithered again at the gate, thinking about a note I could leave her. I caught the movement of the curtain several houses away, where the large lady resided. I left, feeling utterly foolish, but if anything more in thrall than ever. I had to see her, but it was impossible if she would not agree. Would anything change her mind? I should have brought flowers.

Maggie blew my head off for being late. I told her I had slept in. No sign of Gull. We did a solid workout on the three dances and Maggie said it was beginning to shape up. She asked me to give Patrick the hurry-up, otherwise he would be dropped. Bosco wanted to know if I'd had a tiff with Big Boy, Morry wanted to know if he would like a bunch of fives, Maggie suggested we stop being silly, there would be plenty of opportunity for that the next day, when we wore the costumes in a run-through of the entire show. Jeremy offered to put me up, but I used the excuse I had to locate Gull. I was in no mood to put up with Shelley's pestiferous questions and I was not up to eating the poultices they provided.

It was Gull who rang me, to say he would pick me up in the morning. He warned me about extracurricular activities with Jasper and hung up before I could respond. I had nothing to say about Jasper. I had everything to say about Melissa, but nobody to say it to.

The Balinese costumes were the strangest, with pagoda-like headdresses, bras and sarongs. The milkmaid outfits were the polka-dot dresses you never see anymore, with puffed sleeves and cotton bonnets. The Swan Lake outfits were satin dresses with leftover bits on our heads. We were barefoot, except for Bosco the prima ballerina. The greasy make-up, with blusher and heavy black round the eyes, made us look quite girly, again Bosco the exception, his hairy chest and legs worthy of a werewolf. We got rounds of applause every time we appeared, and Gull was the star with his tummy tom-tom.

Most of the time we stood around in the wings while the principals cracked funnies and the chorus sang ditties based on popular musicals. Bosco and Randy were unable to keep still they were so excited. I guess everybody was getting into the mood of it, except me. I went through the motions. Even so, it was a helluva workout.

Climbing on the back of Gull's motorbike proved just what a workout it had been. It was almost too much for my screaming muscles, especially the hamstrings, which All Blacks backs always seem to be pulling. Mine felt like they had been stripped out of their sockets and tied up as tight as those three-string flax whips we used to weave.

Despite the cold, I actually dozed off on the bike, woken as he braked and accelerated around a Morrie Minor on to the Petone parade. The stench of the Gear meatworks was reliably appalling. The bright moon burnished the blood dark sea surrounding its outfall.

I was in a dead sleep when Dad shook me awake. 'Another one of your girlfriends,' he complained. 'She won't take no for an answer.'

It was Melissa. She wanted to meet me in the morning. I found it hard to think straight. I was like Bosco in the wings, shaking with excitement. I suggested the coffee gallery above Roy Parsons.

That was the end of my dead sleep. I reran the brief conversation again and again, looking for clues in her voice. She had been flat but insistent. Was she going to let me visit her? Had she forgiven me? Would she let me embrace her? I wanted to kiss her so hard we would stick like glue because, as Elvis sang it, I'm stuck on you.

It was dark when I woke, heart pounding, one arm flopping from blocked circulation, my fingers on the cusp of locking up from those extreme Balinese reverse stretches. I threw myself out of bed, causing both hamstrings to seize in a crippling cramp. I bit my lip to stop screaming. I couldn't think of a way to ease the comprehensive knotting. I was too stiff to touch my toes with my good hand. I rolled around on the floor, flexing my toes backwards, hitting my dead arm against the side of the bed. Blood prickling started in the arm, but the legs were excruciating. I massaged the backs of my thighs as best I could, and finally the cramping eased.

I tottered to the bathroom and gulped mouthfuls of water. Had I slept in? What time did we say? God, I wasn't sure. Hang on, the place wasn't open until eight. I checked the grandfather in the hall, it was 4.30. I couldn't go back to bed. I went for a run, through the damp dawn, mist hanging over the harbour to one side of Ward Island. KM wrote about the local sheep heavy with dew, but they are long gone, and now the human equivalent rise and shine, to use Dad's phrase, for another day at the office. I filled my lungs with the sharp air. A new day dawning for me. Hi ho, hi ho, it's off to Melissa I go.

She was not waiting in the bookshop. I bounded up the curved stairs. The pinstripe types were having coffee and cake. The same one who had confronted me with Liz, the red-faced fat guy, was leaning over a woman. It was Melissa. She was telling him she was waiting for somebody. When he saw me, he did a double take, glowered at me from under his salt and pepper eyebrow sprouts and lumbered past.

'What'd he want?'

She shrugged, looking like she needed a St John's blanket and one of Mrs Shelton's major meals. 'Hello, Stephen.'

I handed her the single red rose wrapped in cellophane I'd got at the station, asking her what she would like. She thanked me for the rose, putting it down on the table, asked for pineapple juice. The old lady didn't have that, but she did have orange juice. Nodding at Melissa, she said she could make a 'noice hot chocolarta'. I checked with Melissa, who said orange juice was fine.

As she sipped at the juice, I asked her what was wrong.

'I'm pregnant.'

My hand jerked, coffee spilling across the varnished surface, my foot colliding with the table's central leg as I lurched to stop the coffee reaching her, scooping it towards me with my hand. She had the orange juice held up in her hand, like a freeze-frame shot in one of those odd Cocteau movies. I seemed momentarily frozen too, except my brain was banging about like a pinball machine in an earthquake. Did she mean it was my fault? That one time? One-and-a-half. What about Jeff? Were there others?

The old lady was wiping the table, saying not to worry, she would bring more drink, this table no good. Melissa was telling her we had bumped the table, she need not go to any trouble.

'No trouble, no trouble.'

'Sorry,' I said, when the old lady had left. 'Are you sure?'

She put the juice down and looked steadily at me. 'Sure I'm pregnant? Sure it's you?'

I didn't know what to say. I flushed. 'I wasn't suggesting. I mean ...'

'It doesn't matter,' she said. 'I haven't slept with anybody else.'

'I saw you with Jeff. I thought.'

'Christ, Steve.'

I felt a twinge of triumph. She had not after all ditched me for him, it meant she cared, and if she did, then — I wasn't sure what. The old lady was back with a tray with coffee and juice, a small vase full of water and a plate of little pies.

'No, no,' she said to Melissa as she placed the rose in the vase. 'No charge. You eat.'

We both thanked her. Melissa picked up a pie. 'I've had this craving for pineapple burgers.'

I started to get up. 'I could get you one at the pie-cart, if they're open.'

'This is fine,' she said, taking a bite.

I didn't even feel like coffee. I felt like being sick. 'I'm sorry. I had no idea.'

'You wouldn't, would you?'

Was she being sarcastic? I had run off. But I had returned, left her notes.

'Oh, don't look like that.'

'I did try and contact you.'

She picked up another pie. 'Didn't realise how hungry I was. Eating for two, eh?'

I concentrated on sipping coffee.

'Look, Stephen. I have to make a decision.'

This time I did look at her.

'You look like you want to take off – again.'

I assured her I didn't. 'It's just, well, a shock.'

'You didn't know that's what happened?'

'Of course.'

'Didn't they teach you about sex at your school?'

There had been one biology lesson. Brother Mathews had been scarlet throughout his identification of the different parts of the diagram he put up on the blackboard. The loud questions like 'What's a penis for?' and 'Is that a typical pussy, Brother?' had been drowned in explosions of laughter.

'Funny, was it?'

'Not really. More like pathetic. We had one lesson.'

'Doolans for you. Surely your father taught you the facts of life?'

'Dad's reticent.'

'What about your mum?'

I didn't say anything.

'What? She too embarrassed to tell you the facts of life? Stephen? Look at me.'

I couldn't. My eyes were full of tears. Her hand gripped my arm.

'Stephen? I'm sorry. What is it about your mum?'

I told her she was dead. Then I burst into tears, I couldn't help it, I was sobbing like a total sook. I mumbled 'sorry'. All I ever seemed to do is confess my stupid failings. She was pressing something in my hand. It was a handkerchief about as big as the front pocket of my white shirt. That made me snort, which did at least shake me out of it. I dabbed at my eyes, drawing in a few breaths to calm myself.

'I'll get you another,' I said.

'Don't be daft. We rushed things, didn't we? I hardly know a thing about you.'

'Not much to know. I know I want you.'

She sat back in her seat. I glanced around, embarrassed people would have seen me crying. Nobody was looking, except for porker. Why didn't he mind his own beeswax? Melissa was finishing the last pie.

'Go on,' she said. 'Tell me about yourself. That's basically why I rang you, actually. Before I make up my mind.'

'About what?'

'Keeping it. Or not.'

'You mean the baby. Our baby?'

'Your baby?'

'But you can't!'

Porker was standing above us. 'Is he bothering you, miss?'

'Oi! Oi! Oi!' The old lady was pushing him away, a replay of the last time. Except he wagged a sausage finger at me, said he hoped to see me one day in his courtroom.

'You know him?'

I shook my head. Silly old bugger. I tried to get my thoughts in order. I couldn't talk about murder. That's what the Church called it, murder of the unborn child. A mortal sin. Did I believe it was?

'Against your religion, is it? But not the bit before. And don't say sorry again.'

I promised I wouldn't. I asked if she minded me asking where she would get it done.

She said Clair knew this old lady in Karori who fixed things. The problem was it cost a lot of money. And before I asked, she was not going back to that pig in Willis Street. Now she was crying. Just as well the courtroom porker had moved on, he'd be making a citizen's arrest. She waved my hand away.

'Bloody men,' she said. 'Only one thing on your minds.'

There was no way I could challenge that. I waited until she calmed.

'The doctor,' she said, sighing. 'He confirmed the test. Then he told me it was important to understand how to …' She stopped, taking a breath. 'Manipulate myself.'

I was flushing again, with indignation. 'Did you report him?'

'Who to? Who would believe me over him? At least I didn't pay the pig.'

We sat for a bit, both staring at the table. I said it was Clair who told me she was not well, which was not quite how Clair had behaved. She looked disappointed. I was obviously one more man who let her down, I had only contacted her after a woman friend had informed me she was ill. I asked her what she was going to do. She said she had not yet decided. I took that as a hopeful sign, though I wasn't clear what I was being hopeful about, except that it meant a reprieve for our child. I asked her if she'd told her parents.

She didn't reply at first. 'They're dead,' she said. 'Happened when I was a kid. My relations brought me up.'

'What?'

She looked at me, tears glistening again. 'My uncle kept coming into my room. Auntie knew he was.'

'God,' I said, stunned. 'Melissa.'

She reached out her hands and I took them. She asked if I would see her home.

All the way back she held my hand in a grip that made our hands sweat, but there was no question of letting go. Not on my part, not on hers. It required a little bit of twisting to position ourselves sideways on the outside seats of the cable car, for our ascent into heaven. That is what it was for me, a dream state, euphoric, ecstatic. There was nothing in the poetry I had read that dealt with this, unless you count those bits in the *Song of Songs*, probably the nearest to the way I felt. I wanted to shout out a hallelujah on the way along Upland Road. What had Baxter written, something about 'Upon the upland road/Ride easy, stranger?' I was. I had, in the twinkling of a hand-hold, been transformed from banishment to bliss, straight from Limbo to the Pearly Gates.

The prolonged period after I ran off, the loneliness, the craving for her, craving on a level above mere cravings like Gull identified in Jasper for trouble, all that eternity cast into outer darkness had been extinguished in a flash. I thought randomly of Jack Lemmon putting out street lights in *Bell, Book and Candle*. I was on a higher plane than such mundane matters as assisting Jasper poke the borax at the authorities. Such pranks were puerile. Love is all there is, it makes the world go round. The practical considerations of a bun in the oven were consigned to a locked cupboard and I had thrown away the key.

I don't remember what we talked about. I remember cuddling Nigel briefly, then comprehensively cuddling Melissa for an eternity.

We woke up starving. It was one in the afternoon by her little travelling clock. Starving for love, in the first instance. We resumed what began moments after the door was shut on Nigel. We were initially insatiable. There was no holding back, no need to. I flooded myself inside her, she held me there long after I had valid means of supporting myself. We laughed and then we couldn't stop laughing. The sun was making every effort to breach the curtains, but it was unsuccessful. Donne popped into my head. Something about a busy old fool, unruly Sunne, with an extra 'ne'.

'Why dost thou thus,' I quoted to Melissa, 'through curtains call on us? Must to thy motions lovers seasons run? Sawcy pedantique wretch …'

I could recall one further line: 'If her eyes have not blinded thine.'

I gazed into her pools of green love and gasped at her beauty. I groaned and smothered myself in her red tresses. I was possessed.

Finally she pushed me out of bed. 'Didn't you say something about starving?'

'Not pineapple burgers again?'

She tossed the pillow at me. 'Some of Alan's f and c would be delish.'

I clambered to my feet and bowed deeply. 'Your wish, fair maiden, is my command.'

'Better put on some clothes this time.'

'Why?'

'Don't want to frighten the locals. Miss Mango, for instance.'

'Mango? Not the tweed duck down the road.'

She laughed out loud, a splendid sight. Recovering the pillow, she placed it behind her head and stretched in a similarly abandoned sprawl to my favourite among her Modiglianis. 'It's a name like mango. Give me your DOB and time before you go. Need any money?'

'Do you have any?'

'Enough for a can of pet food. Could you get that too, the money's in a dish on the bench.'

I did my extravagant bow, thinking all that Balinese stretching had improved my suppleness in more than one direction. I giggled and addressed my legs: 'No more cramps, please. They could make things awkward.'

'Talking to yourself,' she said, pushing her magnificent hair out of her eyes. 'First sign of madness.'

I gazed down at her. 'I am mad for you.'

Then I was in her arms again, and that delayed the purchase of cat food and fish and chips until the more conventional hour for such consumption. Nigel had been making increasingly urgent noises for some time, such that Melissa said if I didn't go, she would have to. Reluctantly I forced myself to get dressed and get the tucker.

Afterwards, I stroked her belly, put my ear to it, asked if she'd eaten enough. She asked me how I knew it was a she. At which moment she had to rush for the loo.

When she had returned I said seriously, she had to change her doctor, go for the 'she' variety to match our baby. She waved airily. 'Another day, another decision.'

**15**

The fog of love cloaked reality for the next several weeks. I am not even sure how long it was. We were scarcely out of each other's sight the entire time. As far as Dad was concerned, I was staying at the Sheltons. As far as I was concerned, I resided in the Elysian Fields. This was my Mid-Autumn Night's Dream. Puck had placed a magic blindfold round my eyes. I could only see love.

We walked to Training College, we walked back to her flat at lunchtime. Sometimes we did not emerge again. I did walk down to rehearsals. I only half-heard what others said. In the caff Stump might have asked me some sneery question about whether I was scoring. I don't recall if I answered. At the Lit Club Don read out his new poems, but I couldn't say what I thought of them, I was thinking about Melissa. I don't even know if I noticed Vogt was no longer there declaiming his love poems; Melissa was my love, I only had poems for her. I don't remember what she said about them, I was too full of my own.

At rehearsals Maggie sometimes had to repeat something I had not registered. I know Gull and Jasper and the rest of the guys were there, we pranced better and better, Maggie said so. I waved to Miss Mango when I saw her, but she never waved back.

My real life was inside the green walls of Melissa's bedsit. We lived in and around the bed, Nigel sometimes managing to make his presence felt by getting under the blanket and nibbling or cuffing our feet. Melissa spread out the Tarot cards and murmured to herself. She worked on astrological charts. She read out one report with great satisfaction, given I was Sagittarius and she was Aries:

'Sagittarius will be drawn to Aries' intensity and wild side. Both love to play with fire and neither will mind using flattery to get sex. They get along great as friends and lovers and a mutually strong attraction can and will lead to a long-term love relationship. A love of the good life and lots of laughter will be experienced together. Children and animals will be involved in this relationship. Both have met someone who matches their stamina, in and out of the bedroom. Sex could be explosive and will be a reason to keep coming back to one another. They are a powerful combination and friends will maintain that each of them have met the right person. There is such a thing called love.'

In my pre-love period, whenever that was, I might have said sarcastically that the report predicted pretty much every facet of life and love, so it was bound to be correct. In my present state it was merely confirming what was self-evident. I was content to say it wasn't telling me anything I didn't know, careful to keep off the subject of children.

I was, she informed me, half man, half horse. I responded that she might be right, I loved sprinting.

In bed as well, she said, dodging my cuff.

'Sagittarians aim to overcome basic instincts,' she read, to which of course I objected.

Continuing on, she insisted, 'They did so by aiming their thoughts into the divine realm of the heavens.'

I claimed there was no difference, I was in heaven.

She said this was typical of my star sign, an optimist whatever the context. I was always questioning, questioning.

That, I reckoned, I could live with.

She raised a finger. However, I could get very sullen if I felt restricted.

I agreed I could not argue with that.

She said this impulsive side meant I burned whatever fuel was available without forethought, relying on intuition.

I didn't say so, but I thought this was veering into gobbledegook.

My planet was Jupiter, largest in the solar system.

Uh huh, so?

It meant I looked for opportunities larger than life.

Like?

She shrugged. Overindulgence?

Never! You cannot get enough of a good thing. Come here.

Later she summed up my characteristics as undying optimism with a tendency to gloss over problems and avoid difficult situations. I pleaded guilty. I didn't want to think about our growing problem.

What about us? I asked.

That took her longer research. Right now the love planet Venus was entering nurturing Cancer, so it was a time to be cosy at home with the one you love.

I gave that a loud endorsement.

But, she added later, you have to get out of the house to stimulate your senses.

I declared that nonsense. She stimulated my senses to an intergalactic degree.

Cut back on excesses, she said, laughing, and that will help build the life you want.

Out of the question, I said, reaching for her.

Later I began fingering her rings, asked her to tell me about them, what they meant to her. She told me the index finger was blue topaz, for relationships and sharing. I said already that was my favourite. She suggested I hold my half-horses. I asked her did I have to wait till Banbury Cross? Idiot, she said. The middle finger was coral, the finger of Saturn. That, she said, is where I should have a ring, a rose quartz, to reflect a sense of right and wrong, self-analysis, justice, conscience, all my Doolan hang-ups.

I didn't want to go there, so I stroked the green stone on her ring finger. That she said represented creativity, love of beauty. I told her I'd prefer one of them. She laughed and said I'd end up worse than her. 'Impossible,' I said, shaking her little finger: 'And this little piggy?' That was a moonstone, representing intuition. I said I'd have to have one of those too. The thumb? A garnet, for self-worth, for the cosmos. I told her she was my cosmos, my milky way. One track mind, she objected. I said I was prepared to pull back then to a mere solar system, she was the sun around which I revolved, day and night.

Later again, hours, days, weeks, whenever, she said nice things about us having a depth of sharing and intimacy.

I said by way of contribution that it was her sympathy and understanding that helped me cope with the guilt I was raised to feel. She drew the sarcasm out of me as you would a bee sting with a bluebag.

She said it proved yet again I was inclined to the fanciful, but she liked it.

She confessed that she was prone to feeling left out and unloved, which I said I intended to do everything to banish. She said she could get a feeling of being smothered, to which I had no immediate answer. Eventually I said she must tell me if she felt like that. She said she got restless at times. I said I hoped she directed it my way. She laughed, a trifle nervously, I thought.

Oh well, you could go on forever with this sort of swapping of feelings and failings. I didn't mind, so long as we went on and on. I told her about the medieval sense of being in thrall, pretty sure she had missed the Orsman lecture which was the source of my knowledge. I shouldn't have been so gushy. At the time I let it all hang out. I could not hold back anything. I confided and let my imagination roam and I soared into the emerald beyond.

I couldn't wait to get back, from rehearsal, from Teachers College, from school sections, from varsity, from my occasional trips home for underwear and a sweat shirt. Melissa had use of the clothesline belonging to her landlords, the retired university couple who occupied the large ground floor residence. I did not feel right about hanging out my underdungers on their line.

Dad and I were mostly communicating by notes, our paths rarely crossing. We did meet up when I was home to play Tchaikovsky's *Swan Lake*. The music as played by the band at rehearsals or on Maggie's turntable had seemed to me at first on a par with those request session numbers, Strauss waltzes and Mantovani strings. The music began to creep and seep into me. When I passed the new World Record Club shop on the way to the Central Library, I saw *Swan Lake* was a free record if you joined up, no commitments. You could return the records they sent you thereafter, so long as you bought a few by end of year. I signed up and headed home clutching a prettier ballerina than any of us. I couldn't take it to Melissa because she did not have a player.

The story on the back of the LP was the usual silly fairytale about a swan which occasionally becomes a princess when the prince is about, her fate determined by a wicked sorcerer. This was on a par with Dad's operas for daft storyline. The music had much more to it than the prancing bit we did. There were Spanish and Neapolitan dances and fanfares and grand ballroom waltzes.

Dad put his head in the door, said he was impressed, suggested I play it on the sitting-room system. We sat there for both sides. Then I told him I had to get the late bus back in for the final fittings. 'Don't overdo it,' he said.

A torrent of World Record Club offerings and communications over the next few weeks included Grieg and Mozart piano concertos and Handel's Messiah. I had to look up Grieg in the library. '*Peer Gynt*' I had vaguely heard of, more folk fairytale stuff. As for Handel, I'd had enough of him from our music teacher. I returned LPs, given the pathetic Teachers College stipend did not run to much more than beer and bus money and of course, gifts for Melissa. She had introduced me to Webster's art shop in Manners Street, where one week I got her a small Modigliani she did not have, another time a book on Renoir, whom she also admired.

She was so incredibly grateful, it was ridiculous. I said it was only fair, look what she had done for me. I had the wonderful painting she created for me on my bedroom wall, a clown with a flower in his hand, upside down the blue madonna witch. She had said I could put it whichever way up I felt, but she must have known it would be clown up, all yellow and red, the gloomy witch upside down forever. As she leafed lovingly through the rotund Renoir ladies, she protested that one little apprentice painting was nothing compared to this. I said it was a mere token compared to what she had given me, and I didn't just mean the love of my life.

'Silly,' she said, swiping at me. I grabbed her hand and traced the lines in her palm, said she was my head and my heart and my life and more.

'Sounds like more than enough,' she laughed. 'You are a hopeless romantic.'

I objected. Everybody was romantic, that was what made the world go round since whenever, since Romeo appeared below Juliet's balcony. Almost every pop song was about love. I paused. So she didn't bother with pop music. I regrouped mentally. First, I said emphatically, I was a hopeful romantic, hopeless was not in my vocabulary, as she had so astutely divined. I got an approving nod. Secondly, it was not mere romance.

'No?' Her emerald eyes enlarged like those of some imaginary half-cat, half-human jungle creature out of the amazing Douanier-Rousseau, another artist she had introduced me to. I dived deep into her gorgeous orbs. 'Drink to me only with thine eyes,' I said fervently, 'and I will ask for more.'

'Original,' she laughed.

'You want original,' I said, mock-accusing, closing my eyes and pressing my lips against her soft lips.

'You,' I repeated, allowing my eyes to open slowly. 'You opened my eyes to the ravishing world of great artists. All these incredible painters like Van Gogh, Rembrandt, Modigliani, Renoir, Picasso, Matisse, Gauguin. And pottery, which I previously thought of as crockery.'

'Stupe,' she said, smiling me into momentary silence. 'I think the masters at college might dispute my influence.'

'You,' I resumed, 'you took me on the eye-opening tour of the Glen's wonderful pots you make under the tutelage – yes? — of Doreen Blumhardt. The amazing abstract paintings by Paul Olds, who guides your fair painting hand.' I lifted her hand and kissed every line in her palm, then every planetary ring on every finger.

'I confess,' I said earnestly, 'you, and only you, changed my mind about the arrogant view we had of the Glen as the play pen where the kindergarten stuff was done. You know, junior school between the politics and prose of Kowhai Road and the Ngaio Road poets.'

'Oh,' she said archly. 'I always thought you were in the land of the lunkos, we were the enlightened.'

'You were right,' I conceded, down on one knee, my hands extended upwards towards my angel. 'But now I have truly seen the light.'

Everywhere we went, we held hands, we embraced, we enjoyed those kisses sweeter than wine Jimmie Rodgers sings about. Come to think of it, I didn't sink a beer the entire time. It never occurred to me. Others went off to the pub after rehearsal, I went back to Melissa.

Over these golden autumn weeks we did so much together. We walked hand-in-hand to lectures. In class I sent her silly love notes while Prof Gordon rabbited on about Johnsonese sentences and the stream of consciousness prose and such. In French Reading Knowledge old Frances had been so passionate about the Camus novel *L'Etranger* that we decided to read it to each other. Melissa was much better at French than me, but I did not find it too difficult and we agreed there was a lot lost in the translation. Ovid defeated us. Mrs Kephas did not have the same engagement with the Latin poet and nor did we, the erotic aspects escaped us. We had to go to

Donne for that, taking turns reading his red-hot poems. 'For every houre thou wilt spare mee now' she read. My turn: 'For Godsake hold your tongue, and let me love …' She did.

We were back in the Lit Club and its downtown extension, the black-clad Mung coffee bar. I was writing poems at a rate of knots and I tried out a few of them, feeble impressionistic stuff about dream ladies and moody waters, Melissa and Eastbourne via Donne and Yeats. It was almost an entry requirement. Don would critique my efforts, encouraging me to drop the abstract in favour of the concrete, why not use 'money' instead of 'mammon'?

There was this jazz wannabe Mike always lurking. He wore black-on-black and sunglasses everywhere, including the dark recesses of the Mung, as if that was so hip. He was always clicking his fingers and humming and doing imaginary drum sets on the table with his fingers or teaspoons. That was okay. What was not was that he was always whispering to Melissa while we read and critiqued, and that got on my wick.

I have no doubt it was his idea we all go to the Dave Brubeck Quartet concert at the town hall. Even though we went Dutch, it was still expensive. Melissa was so keen and I admitted to her I had quite enjoyed the repetitive hit *Take Five*. I had no idea that Dave and his group were going to extend the three-minute 45 into half an hour of what Mike calls jamming, which to me is like a stuck record. Afterwards Mike was finger clicking big time, going on about Joe and Gerry as if they were buddies. Melissa loved it, so I was happy for her. For me, if there was music in hell, to realign Oscar Wilde, it would be jazz.

The Monde Marie was a much better show for my money, which only involved spending enough to nurse our single cups of coffee for almost an hour. It was Frank's idea we check out this small corner café behind the Embassy. Mike wasn't so sure, said it was full of squares, man. Great, he didn't come. It was packed to the gunnels with mostly young folk, a good few of them with their own guitars. Gingham tablecloths with candles dripping down the sides of bottles, the fishing net décor like the Mung. It was almost impossible to get a table, the moment one was free, there would be a dive for it. The buxom middle-aged woman running the place was dishevelled of hair and manner as she shouted at people to wait their turn and others to buy another coffee or leave.

All the time the folkies were strumming and singing and often the crowd joined in. They might be fairly square with jackets, collars and ties and coiffed hair and frocks, but the atmosphere was party time. Some of the songs I knew, like *On Top of Old Smokey* and *Goodnight, Irene*, and participating in the singalong made us feel part of the scene. A guy did an amusing send-up of the *Goodnight, Irene* tune, local words about how boring and uniform state houses were, except for one where they kept fowls in the garage. It gave a new meaning to Irene Flynn and her housing acres. There was a bitter song about the blood red roses on the battlefield against the Germans, sung to that sea shanty *Blow the Man Down*. There was a tramping song that mentioned Lambton Quay, which one group knew the words of.

The pick of the performers for me was this slightly skew-whiff older chap in a tie and tweed jacket who seemed to be trying to force his springy hair into a side parting, a losing cause. When he introduced his songs he pronounced in a cross between a plum and a lisp. It disappeared when he strummed and sang dinkum Kiwi songs about Taumarunui on the Main Trunk Line and she'll be right. His one about puppies in apple boxes and pipis in sacks on some old express train was spot on. Then he sang a plaintive song about a rainbird in a tea-tree, during which you could hear a pin drop. It was beautiful.

It was a fantastic night, and only ended because I had run out of money to buy more coffee. As we left a lanky rough-as-guts joker was reeling in to the place. I heard somebody say he looked like that deer culler Barry Crump, who wrote this dinky-di local novel *A Good Keen Man*. I knew about it from all the publicity, but it was not on Mascaskill's list, so it had to wait until I ploughed through his Hot 100.

We strolled back hand-in-hand, past the Sallies playing their blaring brass band music at Pigeon Park, their audience mostly collapsed drunks. I said it was a pity the Salvation Army didn't play secular music as well as the *Onward, Christian Soldiers* stuff. This remark I extended into a bit of a rave, partly pumped up by the performances we had just seen, but also by way of diverting any thoughts of a pineapple burger from the pie-cart, given I was out of funds. The Sallies, I opined — as they say in Westerns — were more or less the only other street life around, unless you count furtive figures skulking to side and back doors of pubs to purchase after-hours grog.

I wouldn't count Sir Donald Bulfit as live theatre. I added, I thought rather wittily, he was part of the moribund succession of British thespians coming out here for a last stage gasp.

Melissa indulged me with a chuckle, before reminding me where I got that remark, courtesy of the Bruce Mason review in the paper, including the nickname Bulfit, cause for great amusement around the college. She said it was unfortunate it cost Mason his job. I suggested that was a good thing, he could now concentrate on his magnificent live show, *The End of the Golden Weather*. Everybody had been gobsmacked when he performed something like 40 parts in Assembly.

Man, I said reverently, was he live.

Melissa said his Firpo was an astonishing creation. I said you could say that again, and his recreation of childhood Christmas in Takapuna is as vivid as it gets; I know, I was that childhood. I was in I guess a dippy mood. The childhood remark she may not have got because she didn't have a radio or even a transistor and thus did not follow the charts. It was a variation on Wink Martindale's recent hit about the deck of cards which ends with what became a catchphrase: 'I know, son. I was that soldier.'

I summed up like I was finishing a varsity essay. Between Bruce Mason, Barry Crump, the Taumarunui balladeer, *A Gun in My Hand*, oh yes, and new novels *The God Boy* and *A Gap in the Spectrum,* I grandly if not bombastically declared New Zealand didn't need Mother Britain holding our cultural hand anymore. I left out the minor detail that I had not yet read the new novels.

Melissa tolerated my verbal diarrhoea, and it steered us well past the pie-cart. Fortunately she had done one of her amazing wok-ups before we left, pork and cabbage and onions and carrots and spices, along with her preferred brown rice. I loved her cooking, especially rice with meat; Mum had only served milky rice with fruit. Melissa's cooking was as good as the old lady's goulash on rice at Roy Parsons' coffee gallery, and that was the best, the old *ne plus ultra*. It didn't stop at Melissa's cooking. It didn't stop anywhere. I loved everything about her.

We remained in high spirits on the way across town, singing snatches we could remember of the Monde Marie songs, vowing to go back. I said it would be a great place for that Howard Morrison Quartet hit *The Battle of the Waikato*. Melissa didn't know it.

When I started suggesting names for the baby, like Sara, Samantha, Katrina, Desdemona, the star predictors were wrong, it was Melissa who became sullen. She said there was no way of knowing if it was a girl or a boy. I was dumb enough to let my guard down and revert to my unnecessarily sarcastic ways, suggesting she consult her charts or throw a few cards or consult chicken entrails. Yep, she was right about my inclination to overindulgence, as in sarcasm. She went quiet. I said sorry. She said it was okay.

On the cable car I mentioned apropos of the blood red roses that there would be no battlefields in future, just wastelands. My brain must have addled. Melissa said it was no world to bring a baby into. I knew that, I'd said it often enough, there was no point bringing a baby into a world that was going to blow up. The problem I had overlooked was that we were bringing a baby into this world.

We had a quiet walk along Upland Road, me cursing myself. This time both of us were sullen, until she blurted out we couldn't even afford coffee, how could we possibly afford a baby? I said there was our salary, quickly correcting that to my salary, which of course I didn't need to say was utterly pathetic. I mumbled there was the child benefit and Plunket nurses. She said the flat took most of her pay, so how did I expect to feed three on six pounds a week?

Another period of silent walking, hand no longer in hand. Then she blurted she wasn't having her child brought up a Catholic, with all their stupid rules. I couldn't blame her, but I couldn't say I wouldn't. I didn't know what to do. I was double sullen. I was struck down by *Love Potion No 9*, but deep inside me fissures were fracturing my heart. I would not consciously admit what Freud and Co would have spotted in a consulting second, our relationship was doomed.

I did not know what I believed in anymore, but I knew I could not face rejecting my upbringing as if it was meaningless. Was it fair to a child to bring her or him up with no religion, no set of beliefs? I didn't want to think about a child brought up according to star signs, which struck me as tantamount to superstition. We might as well go back to worshipping trees.

The biggest problem was I had nobody to confide in. I couldn't talk to Dad about this. I couldn't talk to him about anything much. Yes, there was *Swan Lake*, though it didn't seem to extend to my dancing to it, he was unable to get to our opening. That, a small, residually cunning part of my brain said, was a good thing, at least there was no chance the Sheltons would blow the gaffe on me not staying with them. Even that was pathetic. So what if Dad knew? Was he going to lock me in my bedroom and throw away the key? My only confidant was Melissa, but we couldn't talk about the most important thing in our lives, the child that was being created from both of us. From her perspective and mine, we were different versions of Shakespeare's star-crossed lovers.

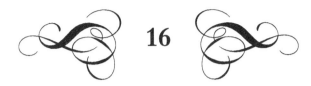

# 16

The dress rehearsal night of *Carry On Phil* was a disaster. For starters, we sat around shivering in our silly milkmaid costumes from 6pm. The Grand Opera House is not grand below. We were consigned to a dank dungeon with flaking white plaster walls, a rundown version of the Gear's chiller rooms where the animal carcasses hung on meat hooks. The bare bulbs blazing overhead augment smaller opaque bulbs lining the sides and tops of the huge mirrors running along one wall. No matter where you look you are blinded by the light.

The only happy chappies were Amanda and Janice, they could see every crease and furrow and surface they apply their greasy sticks and paints and powders to. We had to sit and bear it. By the time we got the call to go on at 9pm, we were close to being chilled carcasses.

Our condition was an excuse for our milkmaids managing to milk only a few hesitant titters, then for our Balinese effort to be met with stony silence. We knew our *Swan Lake* was about as impressive as scrum practice in a sawdust gym, us cygnets lumbering and flailing around, while Bosco misjudged his leap into Randy's arms and bowled both of them. It didn't help that the invited audience thought this deliberate and clapped madly, until the director killed the music and then turned on the invitees with something similar in mind.

Maggie's postmortem was upbeat. She said a bad dress rehearsal was always good luck for opening night. It did nothing to interrupt Bosco and Randy maintaining their post-performance sulk. She said nobody expected or even wanted a male ballet to perform like the film that had just opened of the Royal Ballet's *Swan Lake*, with Margot Fonteyn dancing the dying swan. Morry's loud stage whisper that Bosco's swan was already dead had the unintended consequence of Randy rushing to console Bosco, and they were finally able to kiss and make up.

The dress rehearsal set the tone for a miserable night with Melissa. I got back very late from the Opera House, the cable car long stopped and I had to walk. When I crept in she was asleep, or pretending to be. I was too overwrought to settle, so I eased myself out of bed and went for a night walk along Upland Road. When I returned I tried to make spoons, but she shrugged me away, muttering she was not feeling well. I asked if there was anything I could do. She said I'd done that already. The ultimate passion killer.

Some time in the night I was woken by her being sick in the bathroom. This time when she got back to bed she let me hold her until she slipped into sleep. She didn't say a word. I pressed against her, my face in her hair, trying to blot out my fears.

On Opening Night, Maggie was rushing around the dressing room like a flea in a fit. We were all nervous, but Randy and Bosco were flicking about like fantails in a garden shed. The tension was broken by Amanda appearing with a huge bunch of blue and yellow flowers crinkling in a cellophane wrapping. Some of us already had telegrams opened on the make-up bench, mine from Dad reading, 'Good luck for a successful show'.

'Oooh!' Bosco squealed. 'Who's the lucky one then?'

Amanda read out the name on the attached card: Mr Patrick Flynn.

'Stephen,' Randy said mock-petulant, one hand on his jutting hip. 'You shouldn't have.'

'Pansy,' Morry sneered.

Gull said the flowers were from his mother. Ron suggested he pull the other tit, Randy added something about sucking and got a push from Bosco, I heard Jasper mutter 'Mummy's Boy'. None of this was very nice, but the dressing room tension was eased.

We could hear the band striking up. Maggie announced we had five minutes before we assembled upstairs, Amanda and Janice fussed with a last chance to retouch make-up. Now we were eager to get on, the applause signalling the curtain had come up on the opening scene of Kuripuku Bay, where out-of-work Phil the Football Star is inspired by a Walter Nash speech about equal pay for less work to start professional football.

Melissa was the only person in the packed house I cared about. Not that I could spot her, as we pranced out on to stage to thunderous applause and piercing wolf-whistles. The show flew past in a blur of music and movement. Maggie's prediction proved right about opening night, our Balinese went well, the milkmaids got a good round of clapping, and we got a huge ovation for our prancing cygnets, Gull's tummy pulsing bringing the house down. There were shouts for an encore, but we were hustled off so the show could wind up to that rousing finale where the entire cast is on stage singing our hearts out.

As we peeled off our satin dresses, Maggie was a different sort of demented flea, rushing about hugging everyone and telling us we had done her proud. I had to pass on the party, to get Melissa back home. She was waiting outside the theatre. I smelled her perfume before I saw her. She looked stunning with her hair piled up, emerald teardrop earrings and a matching necklace of thick glass beads, framed by the woolly fringe of her sheepskin coat. She wore the long green dress from Sherwood Forest.

She gave me a hug and said it was good fun and she loved my swan. That had me prancing on air all the way to the cable car. I asked her would she like to see the real dying swan dance, I could get us tickets for Fonteyn in the Royal Ballet. She agreed.

We saw the matinée session the next day. It was my first proper ballet, after spending all those weeks actually learning the same steps. It was breathtakingly beautiful. I loved the music, and that included the other major work, Stravinsky's *The Firebird*. Melissa preferred that, said it reminded her of the Sabre Dance. She also liked Michael Soames, Margot's partner, especially in the rather drippy third ballet, *Ondine*. Afterwards we both had pineapple burgers, my first experience of fried pineapple ring instead of beetroot on the beef patty, and I told her I could get used to this combo. We returned along Upland Road hand-in-hand.

The male ballet performance the next night was the best yet and I went along to the party at the Little Theatre. Randy and Bosco did an impromptu repeat of their star turn, to pissy-eyed applause. No sign of Gull or Jasper, but most of the huge cast were there, including a stunning brunette member of the chorus who undulated around the stage like that sexy new Italian actress, Sophia Loren, in *Boy on a Dolphin*. Of course, the brunette wasn't emerging from water in a see-through shirt, but the way she writhed on stage had a similar impact. Naturally she was in major demand for dances. I had a few beers and was heading off early when I literally bumped into her. She bumped me back, saying she'd seen me dancing on stage, how come I wasn't dancing now? I said I had to meet somebody.

'Steve, right? You doing the hula hoop tomorrow?'

I said I had not heard about it. She suggested there was one way to find out, come to the caff late afternoon. She waved as one of her more persistent admirers whirled her away, calling over her shoulder, 'Jenny's the name, if you're game'.

Melissa was putting away her Tarot cards and astrology stuff when I returned. She asked me how it went and I said the best, and I'd dropped in on the party afterwards. She said she could tell.

'I didn't overindulge, if that's what you mean.'

'No,' she said. 'I didn't mean that.'

I don't know why I bit back at her. It pretty much guaranteed a quiet night, me turned away so she wouldn't have to put up with the beer fumes.

In the morning I told her there was some kind of hula hoop activity at varsity, would she like to check it out? She said okay as she cut thick wholemeal slices for her lunch. She preferred to make her own fillings, today she was boiling eggs. When we were at college we usually met for lunch in the caff, but today she was working on a painting and said she would see me at Latin.

After Mrs K took us through a relatively comprehensible passage from one of Cicero's Senate speeches, we walked down to see what the hula hoop action was. It had already begun, judging by the crowd cheering and clapping. From what was being said I gathered this was another stunt to see how many you could cram into a hoop, a follow-up to the students in a phone box. Photographs were being taken, the crowd parting on the resplendent figure of one, our Margot as in Mabel Howard, occupying a single hula hoop, but only just.

It took a little time to extricate her, and now they were calling for people to get into it. The big guy from our Extrav cast built like a wrestler was acting the ringmaster, shouting, 'Roll up! Roll up! We have a challenge, citizens! We must defeat the puny Otago-ite effort, a paltry baker's dozen! Your uni needs your pathetic figures, the punier the better, we want you inside the hoop. Come on now, don't be shy, boys and girls. Step up and drop yourselves in it!'

Students were shying from what looked less than appealing. The bamboo hula hoop did not have much give in it.

The MC was now castigating the crowd as a bunch of lily-livered fairies, demanding to know where the real sand-kicking shaggers were now they were needed. Nobody was meeting his eye. He switched to pleading, reminding us that we couldn't let a South Island shit shower take the prize by default.

There was a huge cheer as the hoop was lifted up by a young lady in a white T-shirt and red skirt. She began twirling the hoop, undulating her hips and flaring out her skirt, her dark hair flying. It was Jenny. She had her hands outstretched in different directions. She caught my eye.

'Steve!'

I looked away.

'Come on, Steve. You're skinny enough.'

Several were urging me to join in. 'Don't be a piker,' one fellow suggested. 'Look at what you get.'

I looked at Melissa. 'Well? She obviously knows you. Why don't you?'

I shook my head. Thankfully there were others accepting Jenny's hands to get into a tight space with her. Melissa shrugged and walked away from the chanting, laughing crowd. I went after her. We walked silently up Glasgow Street.

'It's only a bit of fun,' I said.

She flicked a glance at me. 'Sure.'

We walked along Upland Road and into Rimu Road. At the gate she stopped. 'Look, Steve, if you don't mind?'

'What?' My stomach was informing me exactly what she meant, well ahead of my brain.

She turned to look directly at me. 'I did say I get ...'

'Restless? Am I too full-on?'

She shook her head. 'It's not you. Would you mind?'

I turned away so she didn't see tears starting. I took off, feeling awkward, foolish.

'Hey!' she called.

I swung around.

'See you tomorrow.'

I nodded, not trusting myself to speak. She pulled open the gate and disappeared into the concrete trench. I felt the tears prickling. I wasn't sure what had happened. Had she rejected me? She said she would see me tomorrow. What a fool I was suggesting the bloody hula hoop gathering. As usual I had not thought of repercussions.

It was a blurred ride down to Lambton Quay, and it didn't get any better. If only I could have rung her, explained there was nothing between me and Jenny, she was one of the cast I saw every night, that was it, full stop, end of story. I loved Melissa. So why did I have to check the hula hoop scene? What was I expecting? Why ask Melissa along? I had questions, but no answers.

At home I put on *Swan Lake*, but it only deepened my gloom, so I took it off and went for a long jog down to Pencarrow, trying to shut out shrieking akin to seagulls descending on a spilled parcel of fish and chips. The racket was in my head, and it did not subside.

The smell from the oven was enticing. The lid lifted, the casserole released mouth-watering smells. It looked like baked beans. Great. I heaped a plate and shovelled in a forkful, then spat it back out. The bloody beans were laced with gunpowder. Chilli? Or paprika. Put in by the tablespoon load. What bloody experiment was this? Maximum Mexican? I drank several glasses of water and went down to the milk bar for a double malted. I left with a big bar of Cadbury's dairy milk and walked the beach, scoffing the lot.

Feeling ill, I caught the bus in for the evening performance. Jenny informed me while we waited in the wings that they got 23 in the hoop, they were going to claim a world record. She added she was sure there was room for one more, before she sashayed on to stage to wolf-whistles from the cheap seats.

Melissa was okay, but said she still felt a bit off-colour. She said it came and went, no need to concern myself, she would come right. When I turned away, she snuggled into me. Neither of us said anything.

The writing was on the wall. I waited for the inevitable and it came, the last night of Extrav. Melissa told me she could not keep the baby, it was not fair to either of us. I couldn't tell her what lousy timing it was, that would sound like I was self-centred.

Instead I asked her how she could afford it.

She sighed. 'I can't. I borrowed the £100.'

'Not from your uncle?'

She shook her head.

'Who then?'

'Clair. So you don't have worry about it, okay.'

I did worry. I couldn't stop myself snapping at her that I had every cause to worry about the murder of my unborn child.

'I don't see it that way,' she said softly.

'So how do you see it then?'

'It was … an accident.'

No, it was my fault. I couldn't bring myself to say it. I stood side-on to her, not knowing what I could say that could make things any better, or any worse.

'It's not easy for me either,' she said, putting her hand on my arm. 'We can't keep it. You must realize that.'

I felt the tears gushing. I pulled my arm away, choking.

'You bloody can!' I yelled.

She stepped back, a frightened look on her face.

I reached out. 'No, Mel. You know I'd never hurt you.'

'What do you call this?'

I put my hands up. I couldn't say anything, I couldn't stop myself shaking.

'Please, Melissa?' I said, putting my hand on her shoulder.

She shrunk away from me. 'Just go! You'll find someone. You probably have already. That …'

'I swear there's nothing with Jenny. She means as much to me as Jeff did to you. Or so you said.'

'What's that supposed to mean?'

'Nothing,' I muttered.

'Nothing! You're saying you didn't believe me. You call that nothing?'

'Look,' I said.

'No,' she snapped. 'You look. Take a good look at yourself. You flaunt that woman in front of me.'

'I told you …'

'I told *you*, there was nothing between me and Jeff. And all this time, you didn't accept my word. You're pathetic.'

'Melissa?' I pleaded.

'Just go.'

'Melissa, it's you I want to be with. It's you I …'

'Don't say it. All right? Please go.'

She turned away, a hand pressed down on the bench. Now she was shaking, I assumed with the same tension I felt. I reached out to take her hand. She pulled it away and faced me, her eyes blazing. I had never seen her angry. She stared defiantly at me, until I looked away.

I slunk off to the show in a numbed state. I wanted to be with her, I didn't know what I could do to keep our child. Was abortion murder? It was illegal for state as well as church, but was it ever justified morally? If she went ahead with it, was I responsible? God, I had to think of something. It was impossible with this swarm of bees in my head.

All I could hold on to was that she was carrying our child. Would she change her mind? I couldn't take back my stupid remark. I was upset she didn't believe there was nothing between me and Jenny. So I said the dumbest thing I could, doubting her word. I'd give anything to have not blurted that. But I had, and I'd have to live with it.

Perhaps she would calm down and realize I didn't mean it. She must know that it was her I loved, nobody else. If only there was somebody she trusted, somebody I could appeal to. I wished I could confide in somebody, talk through the whole business. Bloody Clair, sponsoring the death of our child from her immoral earnings. No, that wasn't fair. Melissa had asked her for the money. It was good of her.

I did not want to lose our child, I did not want to lose Melissa. I wanted a life with Melissa and our baby. The thought of losing Melissa was incomprehensible. What would I do? I had to go back and try and make up for my madness, beg her forgiveness. Would she stay with me if I agreed she should get rid of our child?

After the curtain fell I was all set to make a quick exit to the dressing room, to hell with all the hugs and kisses, they meant nothing to me. The director asked us to pause a moment. He said the show was a cracker, the whole run was a beauty, a record-breaking season. The cast started cheering but he held up his hand.

'We have made …' Theatrical pause '… £1000 profit towards the new Student Union building.'

Lots of cheers. He had his hand up again for silence. We had all just sung that it was the end of student revelry but, he said with his finger raised, there was one more revel before we went back to our books. To cheers and hip-hoorays he said the booze was on the show at the Little Theatre party. Jenny I noticed was holding hands with the chunky guy she had increasingly shared stage with. I took off for the dressing room.

Maggie was waiting, bright-eyed, bouncing about, saying we were the best she had trained. She gave me a hug and said I had to have a celebratory drink, everybody did. She picked up the bottle off the bench and popped it just as Bosco pranced in, bubbly spraying over him. Randy shrieked with delight.

'Yum yum,' he cooed, clapping his hands. 'Shower me too, please, please, pretty please.'

Not Maggie's style. 'We're not racing drivers,' she said. 'This is for drinking.' There were no cups, so she took a swig and passed the bottle to me. I had a token swallow before Randy grabbed it, shaking it up and inviting Bosco to open wide, spraying him. Then the others entered and Maggie recaptured the bottle, passing it around, male ballet dancers gulping and choking and laughing.

I was applying the cream to get the greasepaint off when the dressing room door was flung open. Several excited young men in velvet gear crowded in, exclaiming how gorgeous we were, eyeing Gull in particular, embracing Randy and Bosco. One of them waved a limp hand at Gull and asked if he was taken.

'Bloody hell,' Morry complained. I got on with rubbing off the grease with tissues.

A tap on the dressing room door was followed by Dad's head appearing. I hadn't seen him in the audience, but then you couldn't see anybody beyond the footlights and the band below stage. I figured he wasn't going to bother with this stupid student revue stuff.

'Come in if you're good looking,' Randy called, to shrieks of amusement from his mates.

'Everybody respectable?'

'Yes, Dad,' I said, moving to accept his handshake.

'Well done, well done. Very enjoyable. You have more visitors.'

Irene came in. 'Darling,' she said, as she embraced her son, unaware of the reason for the nudging, suggestive whispering and tittering from the Randy/Bosco brigade.

'You remember Heather, don't you, Steve?'

I was slow to react. It was a surprise. She was dressed to the nines in a smart dark blue silk jacket and floaty trousers. I could see the line of her bra through the semi-transparent light blue blouse.

'Nice to see you too,' Heather said, arching an eyebrow as she looked me over. I had my cords on, but no shirt and vestiges of the white cream clinging like shaving foam around my jaw and neck. 'Need a hand?'

She plucked a tissue from the box and swiped it across my mouth before kissing me on the lips. I heard Randy gurgle, as I glanced Dad's way. He and Irene were talking to Gull.

'Your father mentioned the show,' she said, as she dabbed her lipstick off me, its slightly sweet taste lingering. 'We were at the same function, he mentioned it was your last night. You don't mind, do you?'

'No,' I said. 'Of course not.'

'Here,' she said. 'I brought you this.'

She had leaned forward to collect her bag, her long straight blonde hair trailing across her blouse. She stood and handed me a bottle of champagne.

'Lanson red,' she said. 'Hope you like it.'

I took it. I said there were no glasses, looking around to prove my point.

'Isn't there an after-match function?'

I admitted there was.

'I'll give you a lift.'

'There's no need, really.'

'Come on,' she said. 'Get that muck off you and a shirt on — if you must. The night is young.'

I looked at Dad. Irene had an arm through his as she patted Gull on the chest.

'He's proud of his son,' Heather said in my ear, and then nipped it. More cause for nudging among the Randy/Bosco team.

'I don't know,' I said to Heather. 'I have to get back.'

'To your little love bunny. Paddy told me about your arrangement. Your daddy know about it?'

'God, Heather,' I said, not wanting the others to hear this, never mind my father.

'You can't manage a few drinks with your cast? You that eager?'

I didn't want this conversation. I told her I'd look in on the party.

'What are we waiting for then?'

She wasn't, stepping over to tell Dad I had asked her to the party and all were invited. Dad cried off, said tomorrow was a big day.

'You go,' he said. 'Enjoy yourselves.'

He shook my hand again and left with Irene hanging on his arm.

'Don't panic,' Heather said. 'I'll drop you back at your love nest.'

The party was in full swing when we arrived at the cleared floor of the theatre. The music was loud and the lights were low. The older folk were clustered to one side, the mostly younger crew were either drinking or dancing or snogging, or all three. The show-offs were on the stage, not surprisingly Randy and Bosco, and among them Jenny flinging herself about and around her leaden-footed partner. Heather propped a hand on my shoulder to remove her high heels, which she slung into a corner. Then she removed her jacket and tossed it on to a chair.

'You going to open that?'

I didn't move fast enough for her satisfaction. She grabbed the bottle and began shaking it, yelling at me to get that duffel off. I did so as the cork exploded and hit the ceiling to cheers and enquiries about passing it around. She upended it and glugged a good slug, then prodded me with it. I'd had a few already, on an empty stomach,

Melissa not cooking before I left, unsurprisingly. I took a swig, feeling the familiar numbing around the forehead. Somebody grabbed the bottle as Heather grabbed my hand.

Up on stage the wrestler was working the record player and microphone: 'Ho! Ho! Ho! Ravers! All you chickies and shagnasties who've had enough of Bali Hai squaresville, here's our own Mister Rock and Roll, Johnny Devlin.' There were whoops and yells and yips as Johnny belted into '*Lawdy, lawdy, lawdy, Miss Clawdy*'.

Heather pulled me to her and we began jiving, her leading as we bopped about. She gripped both my hands and did the bump in to the left, out and in to the right, then corkscrewed on my hand, back to repeat, urging me to get with it like everybody else. It was the last thing I felt like, but she had the moves, twisting our hands above our heads and pivoting our bodies around, flinging herself away on the end of one hand, keeping a tight grip as she pulled us back to the bump routine.

'Come on, Steve,' she urged, reinforcing her message with a tight grip on my upper arms. 'You can do better than that.'

'And now, folks, the one you rock and rollers really dig, Mr Kiss Curl himself.'

The speakers blasted out '*One, two, three o'clock, four o'clock rock*', many calling the rock time along with Bill Haley and his Comets. Now people were really jumping. I found myself jumping too, Heather gyrating opposite me, her mouth open, her hair flying about. As the record crashed to a close, she fell against me, gasping that was more like it.

The wrestler had adopted a familiar pose, his free hand raised, his hip jutting. 'Lazies and Jellymen! I give you, the King!'

'*You ain't nothing butta hound-dog, cryin all the time.*'

I was into to it, posing like the King, Heather matching me, laughing. Then we were away, Heather nodding as I signalled we try the fancy stuff. 'Well I said you was a high class,' I mouthed as I checked for enough space and flung her up in the air above me, bringing her down by her hands and through my legs. It worked and we both laughed. She was looking around and snatched the Lanson back. We polished off the last of it. Then the deejay called *Rave On* and we were. Heather got hold of another bottle of bubbly and that fuelled another bout of wild dancing.

Pretty much everybody was into it by now, those who were staying. Jasper was the surprise package. He had reverted to his stick insect green body stocking and was on the stage dancing up a storm. He did a solo performance to Little Richard's *Long Tall Sally*. This involved him accelerating his *T'ai chi* moves into a spastic jerking and leaping and whirling in every direction. We formed up beneath him, clapping in time as he gave it his demented all. I would never have picked him as such an exhibitionist.

When the track ended he leapt high in the air and flattened himself on the floor, before starting to spin like a dying blowfly, faster and faster. Suddenly he did a backward arch and a forward spring and catapulted himself to his feet, a skill the Phys-Ed jokers could only envy. The deejay called for a round of applause and was drowned out by it, people passing bottles up to him.

Things were getting blurry and I was trying to articulate that I wanted to get going. I got bumped from behind. It was Jenny.

'You get around,' she said, eyeing Heather. 'Come on, swap.'

It was not a good deal for Heather, but I was away with Jenny, who still had astonishing energy. *Red River Rock* was on and she was going for it, using me as her vaulting horse to go up in the air to the vertical, skirt upside down and her knickers on display, then back and under and around, out and in, pumping her pistons and puncturing mine. As Johnny and the Hurricanes finally ran out of steam, so did I, bent in a crippling stitch.

'No,' I pleaded, as the deejay promised all you smoochers the perfect veh-hicle, *Love Potion No 9*. Jenny was trying to pull me upright when Heather intervened, pulling me away. Jenny protested but Heather was determined, and I was being pulled in different directions. Before I was done any serious damage, Jasper fronted Jenny. She let me go and they were away dancing.

Heather decided it was time we went. I had no objection, except when she drove down Salamanca Road.

'Wrong way,' I said, hiccupping, the cold night air tightening around my head.

'I don't think so,' she said, changing down and squealing tyres on to The Terrace. 'You know what time it is? Bit late to turn up in your state?'

I started to object I was not drunk, but I hiccupped again.

'Hold your breath,' she said as she accelerated. It was the side strap I needed to hold as we careered around Bowen Street and hard again on the orange light into Lambton Quay. Just as well there was no traffic cop around, I knew I couldn't walk the white line, but I doubt she could either.

She pulled into the kerb, banging up on to the footpath. 'Whoops,' she laughed, graunching gears, reversing on to the road. She got out, leaving the car on an angle sticking out into the street, tottered to the entrance of the Midland Hotel. She turned and motioned me to join her. I got out, thinking about taking off, I should be sober by the time I walked back to Melissa.

'Come on, Steve. Least you can do is see a girl to her room.'

The door opened. She held out her keys to an elderly man, who exchanged them for a large key.

'Look after the car, would you, Turner.'

'Turnbull, madame,' he corrected. 'Is the gentleman …?'

'Yes,' she said. 'Stephen?'

He held the door open, his eyes straight ahead. I entered the dark foyer. To the left the cut-glass panels in the heavy doors flashed a dull gleam over the reception desk surface. There was a sharp carbolic smell overlaying the gust of beer rising from the thick red carpet. Heather led the way past the desk to the lifts. She waited for me to open it, said top floor as I closed it behind her. I started to say I couldn't stay long, but she placed a finger on my lips.

She missed the keyhole with the first jab. She reached in and switched on the lights, revealing a large room with plush pink velvet couches facing tall dusty pink curtains either side of matching mullioned windows, behind them the gleam of streetlights on the curved wrought-iron railing. She told me to take a seat, she needed to get into something more comfortable. I sank deep into the sofa. A white marble coffee table hosted a dripping metal bucket with a bottle of bubbly in it, sheathed in a white napkin. Beside it was a tray with two tall flutes and plates, the big one hosting club sandwiches and cheeses and crackers under a muslin wrap.

Heather emerged in a long, form-fitting cream satin dressing gown looking not unlike the languid Jean Harlow poster on one wall. She plonked herself down beside me, the gown falling away from her bare legs. She tucked the gown casually back over her thighs.

'Would you do the honours?'

'Not for me,' I said.

'Don't be rude. One drink is sociable. You might care for something to eat.'

I was silent as she reached across, her perfume strong, and pulled out the bottle and napkin halter. 'Oh dear,' she said as water dripped on to her gown. 'Would you?'

I took the bottle, she retained the napkin, pushed back her gown and dabbed at her thighs.

'That's better. Are you going to hold that all night?'

I pressed hard with my thumbs at the sides of the cork and it exploded. I involuntarily followed the path of the cork as it hit the white plaster ceiling with some velocity. Bubbly gushed all over my trousers. Heather laughed as she rubbed the napkin across the strategic staining. I tried to stand, but was unable to get any purchase in the spongy sofa with the bottle held in the air. Rolling sideways only succeeded in crashing the bottle down hard on the marble table. Heather tested the state of the trousers with a firm squeeze.

'You'd better get those off. I'll dry them in front of the heater.'

With a gargantuan effort I managed to stand and then wished I had not, my head spun out of control and took the rest of me back down on the sofa, on top of Heather.

'And here's me thinking,' she spluttered, 'you didn't care.'

I stumbled out to the bathroom, felt around the walls until I found the switch, depressing it on an explosion of light on gleaming white. I shut my eyes and saw black roving galaxies. Eyes open an absolute minimum, I leaned against the huge towel rail and got out of the trousers. I wrapped an enormous thick white towel around my damp underpants and risked opening my eyes. The sight in the middle of the huge, gold-framed mirror was of vampire eyes and a demented person I scarcely recognised. My head was revolving like the glitter ball in the middle of the dance floor, splintering my vision into black dots and blazing bright fragments not far removed from *National Geographic* images of exploding stars.

There was a tap on the door. 'What are you doing? You're not being ill?'

'No,' I croaked, splashing water on my face, scrubbing vigorously with another towel, taking deep breaths, which only increased the turmoil. I gulped several handfuls of water, and emerged.

Heather eyed me with a cock-eyed smile, though that could be due to my eyes not working very well. No question however that she had removed the satin gown and was wearing only black knickers and black frilly bra. I think it was frilly.

'Please, Heather?'

She flicked her hair away from her face. 'Why not get into bed and sleep it off.'

I nodded glumly. I couldn't trust myself to slide open a lift door, let alone walk back to Melissa's.

She held a hand out. 'Come on. I'll tuck you in.'

The black dots were increasing as she led me into the bedroom. I held a hand up to shield the harsh experience of bedside lamps. I could feel myself tilting into the blessed relief of black, my head spinning but the splinters of light subsiding.

'Yes! Yes! Yes!'

I pounded into her and I could feel her meeting me with her own thrusts, and she was urging me to go harder. I was in a frenzy, but I was worried about something.

'Don't stop,' she urged. 'Fuck me hard.'

She held me and howled and bucked, her hand slapping across my face and sealing my mouth.

'Stephen,' she gasped. 'At least one part's in working order.'

Not anymore. Now my head was asserting itself, being pounded internally by a succession of sledgehammer blows. I groaned and rolled off her.

'Sorry,' I said. 'I'm feeling terrible.'

She reared up.

'No,' I managed. 'It's not you. Me.'

'I didn't want you saying her name.'

My headache was apocalyptic, but it didn't suppress reality. I had cheated on Melissa when she needed me. No, she didn't need me, she didn't want me, she didn't want our child.

'Oh God,' I groaned.

'It's okay,' she said. 'I wear a cap.'

I didn't say anything. I couldn't say I was thinking about Melissa. I felt her stiffen.

'You meant her, didn't you?'

'Heather.' I reached out to touch her. She pulled away.

'I know,' she said. 'I dragged you here.'

'I'm sorry. She's pregnant.'

Heather flung the bedclothes off and reared out of bed.

'You okay?'

She had gone into the bathroom. I clutched my head, wishing I was dead, or at least unconscious.

'Here.' She handed me a glass of water and two Aspros. I gulped them down.

She sat on the edge of the bed, facing away. She had her satin wrap back on.

'Bugger.'

I sat up, and wished I had not. I put a hand on the back of her gown.

'You're a beautiful woman.'

She reached behind and felt for my hand, squeezed it. 'Nice of you to lie. I'm not beautiful – not yet. It's okay, this is not about love. Come on, I'll take you back to her place. I'll have a bath first. Order what you like for breakfast, phone's on that little table by the window.'

I lay in bed while she had a long soak. Periodically I heard the tap come back on. Steam seeped out the door. I was paralysed by my behaviour. How could I? I don't know. I wasn't a child, I didn't have to go to the party, drink so much, come back with her knowing what was likely going to happen. Betraying Melissa.

Heather finally emerged, looking as good as she had when she entered the male ballet dressing room a lifetime ago.

'You look great.'

'You look like shit. Better eat something. You want a bath?'

I nodded. She said she would order.

When I came out she was sitting at the small breakfast table, sipping tea. Delicious smells were coming from under tin hats. She pointed to my clothes, folded. They were dry, including my underpants. I thanked her. She removed the hats and we both got stuck in to bacon and eggs, tomatoes and mushrooms, washed down with freshly squeezed orange juice, a rack of toast with marmalade, several cups of tea.

'Better?'

I reached across and took her hand.

'Friends?'

I nodded.

'She's getting rid of it.'

Heather looked at me, lifting her hair away from her wobbly eye. 'Her choice?'

I said it was.

'You got the Catholic thing about abortion?'

'I don't know. Yeah, I suppose. I'm not sure.'

'Your problem. Come on.'

She dropped me at the top of Rimu Road and took off.

There was a white envelope attached to the door of Melissa's flat, my name on it. Nobody home. The note read: 'It's for the best, Stephen. I can't have a child, you can't accept my choice. Our stars did collide, but …Goodbye and have a good life.'

I went home and played *Swan Lake* again and again. My headache faded, my heartache increased. I had thrown away the person I loved. Melissa was my sun and moon and stars. I could not think of life without her, but it was what I deserved. I had betrayed her at her most vulnerable moment, with a woman I did not care one jot for. If I had come home, could I have persuaded her to have our baby? Now I would never know. Better that a millstone had been tied around my neck at birth. The life we made would have no birth. I wished I had never been born.

Alone in bed, I keened for the comfort of her. I was so miserable I thought of reversing the witch lady and the clown. I wished I had a photograph of her. I wished I could paint, I would depict her like the Pre-Raphaelites she introduced me to, the Rossettis I knew as writers not painters, and the magnificent Millais. Melissa is a Millais model, a willowy, rangy lady in a long green dress like the one she wore to Extrav, her red tresses flaring behind her, her pale face at rest on the pillow with her eyes closed, her lips slightly apart as she sleeps beside me. I ached for her, longed to bury my face in her neck and smell the musty, mossy fragrance that conjures the essence of my beloved. If, if, if — if I rubbed a lamp and a genie appeared and gave me three wishes, I would make the same wish three times over, to be with Melissa forever and ever, amen.

Rain teamed down all day Monday. Perfect. *Raining in My Heart* was Buddy Holly's last song last year, the flip side the bigger hit, *I Guess It Doesn't Matter Anymore*. Pluperfect. Buddy was dead and I might as well have been. Nothing mattered anymore. I was a dead loss at Kelburn Model School with Miss Wilkes and 18 kids. It was supposed to be the plum section job, but I was a zombie. At my varsity tutorial I got 40 out of 50 for an essay I wrote on Joyce Carey's *The Horse's Mouth* when I cared about life as much as Mr Carey, another dead subject. Now I was a *derrière du cheval*, a horse's arse. I proved it in the French test.

My life began after varsity, when I went downtown to search for Clair, my only lifeline to Melissa. I had an hour before closing to check the cats' bars. No sign of her in the George and Grand. In the Royal Oak I had progressed through the subdued businessmen's drinking hole into the rough bar where the clamour was like an amplified version of the audience gabble before the opening night of Extrav. If I'd had on my Gear jacket, I would have fitted right in. A duffel did not. A battered young bloke who looked like he'd spent too long under a losing scrum blocked my attempt to get through.

'Before you spend your hard-earned, eh?'

I flinched at the beer and BO pouring off him. I looked away from his unfocused eyes at his hand pressing against my midriff. He was using his other hand to push up the sleeve of his bulky black windcheater, revealing an arm encircled by half a dozen watches.

'Rolex, mate,' he said in a hoarse whisper, as if his voice box had taken a direct stomp from a footy sprig. 'The best. Only seven quid apiece.'

'Sorry,' I said. 'I'm a student.'

'Look at them. Bargains, eh? Tell the time in three places.'

I peered at the dials all featuring second hands flicking like thin threads of ectoplasm, the two smaller dials set inside the face presumably telling the time in two other places.

'No use to me.'

He continued to block me in. 'Student, eh? Special price, four smackeroonies. I don't make anything on it.'

I told him the only thing I'd pay for was information about Clair.

'Wrong place for the fair sex, mate. You don't wanna waste yer parents' hard-earned on a shag. Look at these. You'll never see better.'

'No thanks,' I said, endeavouring to push past him.

'You must want somethink,' he said, his wheezy voice rising a notch. 'Dirty pictures? Funny fags? Come on, what is it, eh?'

'Hey, Jacko. You heard the man. Piss off.'

Jacko jerked as if he had been stabbed. 'Yeah, okay, Gerry. Can't blame me for tryin, eh?'

'Elvis!'

Peters was nursing a jug under his arm, a glass in the other. His tall mate was leaning against the window shelf. I had lost a pest in exchange for a couple of prize pricks I had no desire to spend any time with. I didn't have a choice, I was boxed between them. Peters moved closer. He had more Brylcreem coating his quiff than he sported at the Mardi Gras, and he certainly had applied an excessive amount of cologne.

'Shout you a beer, cock.'

He was better dressed than I remembered, a white shirt with creamy bands fresh out of a Van Heusen clear pack in Vance Vivian's front window. His smirk revealed gaps in his dentures top and bottom. The drink he was offering was his own.

I shook my head.

'Cat got your tongue?'

'Piss off,' I said, stepping to his side. Peters stepped my way at the same time.

'Elvis here's turning down our hospitality, Heff.'

Heffernan, I think. He was giving me a blank appraisal. I gave him one back. He had stayed with bodgie black, but with a country and western flavour, the black shirt knotted at the throat with one of those singing cowboy string ties. It was held in place with a nasty clip suggestive of steer horns.

'I'm not here to drink,' I said. 'I'm looking for somebody.'

'Who might that be?'

'You wouldn't know her.'

'No sheilas in here, chief. Can you see any sheilas in here, Heff?'

Heff looked around, slowly shook his head.

'We can't help you,' Gerry smirked, 'if you don't tell us her name.'

I repeated my request to piss off and stepped right into him, spilling his beer over his fancy shirt. I was through before either could react, or the others I bumped, who swung about to check what the trouble was. I left behind the exchanges, Gerry's voice the most indignant, pushing through the door into the low lights of the carpeted cats' bar. I could make out small groups huddled down in easy chairs. I was about to step up to make enquiries at the small bar when I saw Miranda, flanked by two older men who looked like they should be in the bar I had just vacated.

'Stephen!' Miranda said, beckoning me. 'Come and meet my new friends.'

The two faces either side of her looked anything but friendly. Both had bristle crew cuts and moon faces with flat noses stuck on unevenly.

'Bora. Boris. This is Stephen.'

'Fock off,' Bora growled.

Miranda put down her glass with a slice of lemon on the small table, used a shoulder of each man to prise her splendid bulk upright.

'You boys stay put a mo,' she purred. 'Comprendez-yous?'

Miranda steered me up to the bar, then wheeled round and pointed until Bora and Boris subsided.

'They Frogs?'

'Search me, lover – but later. What brings you into my little parlour?'

I told her I was looking for Clair.

She waved away the woman coming to take our orders.

'Nah, my lovely, not a good idea. Clair is right off you big time, won't say why. You want to tell me why, make it quick.'

I told her I owed Clair £100 and I didn't remember the address of the place where they operated.

'Operated? That's a new word for it.'

She told me the address and suggested I not call before ten, Harold needed his early evening downtime. 'Now scoot.' She used my elbow to spin me and emphasised the message with the kind of pinch she had objected to from that drunken old judge.

I glanced back with my hand on the door. Miranda was patting the upper cheeks of her two new friends, both on their feet and only half her height. The door was pulled open and me with it, into the arms of a large policeman.

'Looks like the very lad we want,' he said heartily, passing me to his colleague.

'Take him to the car, Wilson. I'll check the reported disturbance.'

Wilson was another of those assistant pub patrolmen who looked about my age. He had a grim set to his mouth as he adjusted my arm behind my back and used it to propel me through the public bar, ignoring the jeers from the patrons. Advice to take on some real men instead of baby-bashing added a burst of laughter.

Outside, Peters and Heffernan were enjoying the result of their tip-off, me being hustled across the path of people hurrying to catch trams and buses home. I kept my head down, not wanting to be recognised by anybody who mattered, and was bundled in the back. Wilson took the front passenger seat and waited.

The sergeant came out shaking his head. 'Queer business,' he said as he got in.

'No complaints from any of those, ah, ladies. Well, we've had stranger calls. All we catch is a tiddler.'

He paused with his hand on the ignition button, adjusted the rear-view mirror so our eyes met. 'Surprise us,' he said. 'Show us your driver's licence where it says you were born 21 years ago. Ah, what year would that be, Wilson?'

'1939.'

The sergeant tilted his head towards Wilson.

'1939, sir.'

I said I didn't have a licence and I wasn't in there drinking, so there was no cause to arrest me.

'Date of birth.'

I told him.

'Wilson?'

'Eighteen by my reckoning, sir.'

'Under-age on licensed premises. We have to book you. That's the law.'

The sergeant eased into the traffic. He flicked a glance at me.

'Cheer up, lad. You get a ride in a police car and you shouldn't get more than one night in the cells. So long as you don't catch old Olly Ogilvie tomorrow morning. He's a right bastard, pardon my French, when it comes to students. You'd be a student?'

I nodded.

'Wilson, we have another example of our idle student bludgers, wasting taxpayer's money on illegal indulgence. Don't know the meaning of a decent day's work.'

'No, sir,' Wilson said, staring straight ahead. 'I mean, yes, sir.'

I surreptitiously tried the door handle.

'They don't open,' the sergeant informed me. 'Stop villains doing a bunk. You wouldn't want to bunk on us, would you, ah, what did you say your name was?'

I told him. He glanced my way again, then suddenly pulled left, as if he had changed his mind. The rest of the short journey was made in silence. Wilson escorted me inside the grim granite walls I had observed from behind the Green Parrot window glass opposite without ever expecting to be a guest. I was not required to give my biographical details, my wallet or my belt. The sergeant instead went into conference with the desk sergeant, the latter directing me to the bench in the corner next to a figure slumped inside an army greatcoat, snoring. It was better than the cell I was expecting.

Wilson took up a position alongside me, at attention, eyes front. The desk sergeant rang somebody. A few moments later a side door opened and an older, quite dapper policeman appeared in better quality haircut and tunic. Both sergeants were at attention. He spoke to the desk sergeant and turned to look me up and down. He gave the desk sergeant his instructions and retreated through the door he had entered. The desk sergeant got back on the telephone. I asked Wilson if I could use the toilet.

'Sir?'

Wilson's sergeant took a long-suffering breath but nodded. Wilson directed me downstairs, where the smell was not unlike the public toilets at the junction of Taranaki Street and Courtenay Place. But here were no enormous white porcelain pissing cubicles the size and art deco shape of juke boxes, just a conventional toilet pan and seat. Its door was different from the public ones for not having any holes bored in it at penis height. Wilson told me to leave the door open, but at least he turned around while I did my business.

When I got back, the figure in the greatcoat was gone. I resumed a seat on the hard wood. I asked Wilson what was happening. He said he hadn't the faintest. It was harder for him than me, having to stand there for a good hour. Finally Gull arrived and drove me home.

At the gate he killed the bike and heaved it on its stand. He glared at me, said I was lucky the sergeant recognised the name, one of those that had been circularised during the 'No Maoris, No Tour' protests. I didn't respond.

'What were you doing there?'

I shrugged. I didn't intend to go into any of the sordid fallout from my relationship with Melissa.

'We have to talk about things.'

'We haven't so far.'

'I'll see you first thing.' He jump-started and roared off. I slunk inside.

I picked up Donne off the bedroom floor and idly flicked through the poems. 'I am two fooles,' he writes, 'for loving and for saying so.' I could relate to that.

Further on: 'Our hands were firmly cimented.' I moved on smartly, that was too close to my memories.

*Since she must go, and I must mourn, come Night,*
*Environ me with darkness, whilst I write:*
*Shadow that hell unto me, which alone*
*I am to suffer when my Love is gone.*

I rested the book while I felt sorry for both of us.

'No man is an island, entire of itself ...' Ha! 'Never send to know for whom the bell tolls; it tolls for thee.' I'd found Scotty's quote, the one I attributed to Hemingway. Donne is uncanny. He writes about love lost exactly as it is. Tomorrow I would find Melissa. She can't have gone far. I had to tell her how I really felt, accept any conditions she cared to lay down. I could not live without her.

When I went to catch the bus, Gull was waiting. I'd forgotten about him.

'Is this what you call a stake-out?'

'If you like. Come for a walk.'

'I can't. I'm running late.'

'Indulge me.'

'Sorry, I can't.'

'I know about the pregnancy, Steve. I spoke to Heather as well as Clair.'

I blinked, avoiding his gaze. 'Where's Clair?'

'She doesn't want to see you.'

'Did she say if …?' I cut the question. He might not know about the abortion.

He led away from the bus stop, down Rimu Street to the beach, into the gums of the declining southerly. He was well wrapped up in his flash duffel coat, much the same spot beside the wharf where he had done his freedom gesture with the wool hook. I glanced at the handful of yachts tilted over on the sand and the ledge of marram grass. I wished I had never set foot on that yacht. I could clear off now, leave him contemplating his freedom, chase my own.

'You know Florence May Radcliffe?'

'Should I?'

'She performs backstreet abortions, for a price. You probably know the going rate.'

Bastard.

He thrust his hands deep in his duffel pockets, sighed. 'Time to put the cards on the table, Steve. I can find out where Melissa is. Clair will tell me. But only if you help me out.'

I lost it, lashing out and catching him with my fist on the side of the head. He stumbled and fell over the lip of the grass and sprawled on the sand. He got up slowly, shocked but not exactly stunned, given I was half his bulk and totally unpractised in king hits. He put his hands palms out in a gesture of surrender.

'Calm down, Steve. I have to be blunt.'

'Eh?'

'You're blundering from one bloody thing to another. It's only a matter of time.'

'Hang on,' I said indignantly. 'I was dropped in it with the cops by those bodgie pricks Peters and Heffernan.'

He shook his head. 'The caller did not identify himself, but that's not the point. You got caught. You must realise, Steve, there is a lot at stake. If your father is dragged into this, the bloody papers will have a field day. *Truth* won't be able to resist.'

He was making no sense. 'What's any of this got to do with Dad?'

'Everything. From day one. Why do you think I've been keeping tabs on you?'

'He doesn't want to be embarrassed.'

'You don't know the extent of it. Look, we know about Peters and Heffernan. They're petty crooks, deal cigarettes and watches, and whatever else they can cop off the ships. They are not the problem. You are.'

I looked at him as if he had gone mad. I think he had.

'Sit down,' he said. 'It's not exactly comfortable, but it will do.'

He moved behind one of the yachts. I joined him on the ledge, our feet touching the sand blowing past in spurts. We were in the lee of it, if he knew the term.

'Okay. I'm still on the Force.'

'So it's all bullshit, the law degree and all that freedom crap you came out with.'

He pushed sand around with the toe of his shoe. 'Not at all. I am doing a law degree, and I would welcome more freedom.'

I was going to scoff at that, but there was an undertow of bitterness. I waited for him to continue.

'Yeah, job in hand. It's a simple problem, we're short staffed. I haven't yet worked out how to be in two places at once.'

'Ha ha. Not my problem. I'm sure your various ladies can assist. What are these places you have to be?'

'Okay. Will you tell me next time Jasper is planning something?'

This time I really did laugh. 'Like letting off a packet of Double Happies in the grounds of Government House?'

He stood, picked up a pipi shell and flicked it into the wind. It soared over the wharf, before it stalled and fell into the sea. He turned to face me. 'You don't care about much, do you? Your father's career and his contribution to society, our political structure, social stability, prosperity, none of that matters a toss to you. The only thing that does, is Melissa. You want to find out where she is, tell me what Jasper is up to. I'll be in touch.'

He left me to it. I caught the bus, stewing over what he said, staring mindlessly at the ruffled sea all the way round the harbour until we squealed to a stop below Parliament. As I got off to walk up Lambton Quay to the cable car, passing the coffee gallery where I had talked to Liz and Melissa, I continued to burn. What I cared my father or politics was of no consequence, Dad would think it laughable that I could have any influence on his career or political events. I didn't think Jasper was of any consequence either, with his silly little pranks. Gull was right, I had only one priority, Melissa. I would tell Gull what Jasper was up to, if anything. Did the deal require that Jasper got up to something?

There was no way of finding out until after school. I was at Kelburn Model and I didn't actually know where he was.

It was an interminable day. In the staff room all they talked about was some nine point something earthquake in Chile and a tidal wave coming our way and what they should tell the kids. Diving under your desk was scarcely relevant to an earthquake 3000 miles away and Kelburn was not exactly in danger from any wave that managed to get into the harbour. It was decided to do nothing unless alerted by the authorities. As the Deputy Principal put it, we'll have plenty to worry about when the big Wellington quake strikes, Kelburn is smack on the fault line. If this was supposed to calm teacher nerves, I would say by the look of them it had failed.

When I should have been off at three, the teacher handed me a whistle and told me I was expected to pitch in and take 14 girls for basketball practice. I had no idea what the rules were. Having 14 girls simultaneously shrieking instructions and corrections was the recipe for total chaos. It might have suited Jasper's philosophy.

I hared down to the Symposium and almost cried when I saw Jasper deep in a huddle with Ben and some woman. The woman looked up. It was Jenny, now kitted out in black. She waved me over and suggested I take a seat. Jasper did not look up from his conversation.

'Don't look so surprised,' she said as I sat next to her.

'Am I? Sorry. What's happening?'

'You know Jasp. All steamed about this new Howard Morrison song.'

'*The Battle of the Waikato*? That's not exactly political.'

Jasper looked up, lip curling, giving me his intense blind-mole glare. Jenny pushed his shoulder. 'Relax, Four Eyes.'

Jasper positively beamed at her. Weird.

'So what's the song then?'

'As I was saying,' Ben bored in. 'Popular music can subvert the powers-that-be. Look how worked up they get about rock and roll promoting immorality.'

'Sounds good to me,' Jenny cut in. 'Do tell more.'

Now Ben was looking boiled, like he was not being taken seriously.

Jasper jabbed a finger towards Ben. 'Morrison is four square establishment, man.'

Jenny grabbed his finger and shook it. 'Have you listened to the words?'

Jasper's mouth gaped. 'Yeah. All Blacks, silver ferns, all that crap we protested outside Parliament.'

Jenny pushed her chair back and adopted a haka crouch. That got the attention of the other patrons, chairs scraping, important conversations on hold. She started stamping her foot rhythmically, hands extended and quivering. 'Fi, Fi, Fo, Fum!' she yelled as she slapped her thighs. 'There's no Horis in this scrum!'

'All right!' someone shouted. 'Far out, man,' from somebody else. There was a smattering of applause and then seats and debates resumed.

Ben nudged Jasper. 'Point taken?'

Jasper removed his glasses, drew Jenny to him and kissed her. You could have knocked me down with a fantail feather. I did not picture Jasper as romantic, I thought that would be the ultimate bourgeois sell-out.

'Point taken,' he agreed, replacing his glasses, as if nothing untoward had taken place. Now he was being conciliatory? Not quite. 'If,' he cautioned, finger raised again, 'the hoi polloi get it.'

He smirked as he dodged another finger-grab from Jenny. The bloody leopard had changed his spots. This was not what I needed.

When I got home there was a note from Dad saying he was dining out and he was sorry I would have to make do with the leftovers in the fridge. Fine with me, half a casserole of devilled sausages. I fried an egg as my contribution and went down to the milk bar for dessert, a banana split with three scoops of hokey-pokey ice cream.

Gull rang. An argument over the significance of a Howard Morrison pop song was not the security threat to the country he wanted to hear. He said he had spoken to Clair and she didn't know where Melissa was, but was expecting an address. He wanted to confirm I was going on the Extrav trip to New Plymouth. He couldn't go and this was an example of what he meant about not being in two places at once. I told him I had paid my £2 for the bus and I'd find out if Jasper was going.

 **18**

Jasper was on the bus, down the back with Jenny. My designated seat was next to Ron. I'd not known of his interest in American politics, or indeed any interests he had, but by the time we got to New Plymouth I did. He was all for this Senator John Kennedy to be next president, but he reckoned Tricky Dick Nixon the vice-president would win because he was a master of the black arts. I didn't ask what such arts might be. I told him I couldn't see it made any difference who won, they'd dropped a couple of atom bombs already and they were getting ready to try out the new improved models on Cuba and Russia. Ron told me I was naïve and had no idea of *real politik*. I could only acknowledge he was correct. He said I should do Pol Sci next year and learn what was really going on in the world.

It was a relief when the chorus began singing the finale from Extrav. This led on to more songs from the show and other random efforts like *On Top of Spaghetti*, the interminably silly *Long Strong Black Pudding Up My Aunty's Cat's Pyjamas Twice Nightly* and, from one show-off, *My Old Man's an All Black*. All this jolly singing mercifully denied Ron any chance of furthering my political education.

At New Plymouth Jasper was not the only one denouncing the billeting arrangement which split up girls and boys. The trip organiser, the suave Des Deacon, was not defending the arrangement, merely asking us to grin and bear it.

I nudged Ron. 'Would that be an example of *real politik*?'

'Dickhead,' he growled.

Gull might have reason to be pleased, I was billeted with Jasper. No question Jasper was gravely displeased and putting a belittling face on it. 'Yawnsville,' he said as we watched the bus pull away, leaving us to survey a street of solid brick houses behind mature hedges with glimpses of neat lawns and clipped shrubs.

'It's only for a night,' I said as I opened the wrought-iron gate. The path to the front door was bordered by the severely pruned skeletons of rose bushes. I pressed the buzzer and the Westminster chimes sounded within. Jasper gazed at the opaque etching of a stag at bay covering most of the front door glass.

'Monarch of the fucking glen,' he growled.

The door was flung open.

'Come in, come in,' said a tall, bent slab of a fellow in a thick dark-brown jersey with leather buttons. 'You like my big fella, do ya?'

We must have looked somewhat flummoxed. 'Saw you through the clear bit,' he said, his square black eyebrows semaphoring like alternating flags, his black eyes sparky. 'Yep, he's one of your 20-pointers. Monarch of this glen, eh?'

Jasper darted a glance my way.

'Ernie Meadows the name, shootin was me game.' We shook a hand the size of a small shovel, introduced ourselves. 'Least I was, before me back came back to bite me. Give's yer bags.' His long arms pounced on our kits. 'Follow me, lads.'

He led the way in a canted fashion, down a hall brilliantly lit by two chandeliers, the embossed cream wallpaper setting off three ducks in a row.

'Mallards,' he said, pausing at a door. 'Nearest I get these days. Season's almost over. In here. Our daughters've flown the coop, scuse the fancy stuff. I'll leave yous to clean up. I'll be in with the wife, pouring a beer, eh?'

'Ernest?' a woman's voice called. 'They might prefer sherry.'

Ernie winked at us, I think. 'When you're jake.'

Jasper snorted as he dumped his bag on the bed next to the window. The quilts were a shocking pink, like the walls which featured two studio photographs of plump, smiling lasses, one in a nurse's uniform.

'You mind?' he said, gesturing at the window. 'I need an escape route.'

'He seems okay.'

'Let's get this over with.'

I followed Jasper into the sitting room, where the dumpy mother of the portraits was patting at her blonde layers. She wiped a hand on her spotless daisy-patterned apron and stuck it out. 'Maureen,' she said, and we shook. 'Is there anything you need? Did Ernest ask what you liked to drink? Would you like a bath? Or a sit down before we eat?' I assured her we were fine and a beer would be great.

'Four X,' said Ernie, winking and eyebrow wriggling as he handed us the poured glasses with thick heads. 'Put hairs on yer chest.'

'Ernest,' Maureen chided. 'I'll get rid of the apron and join you. I'll have a sherry, dear.'

Above the fireplace was a huge framed copy of the famous Monarch of the Glen painting.

'He's only a 12-pointer,' Ernie said, moving over to admire it. 'Damned fine painting, whad'ya reckon.'

'Champion,' I said.

'Might haveta sacrifice the possie when this television catches on, eh?'

I didn't look at Jasper, I knew his eyes would be rolling. 'Could be years away,' I suggested.

'Nah,' he said. 'Auckland's got it, rest of us'll get in behind, no worries, you mark my words.'

'It's only just begun, I read.'

'Yeah. Robin Hood the first thing they had on. Can't wait to see the old king's deer shooter in the comfort of me own home, eh? Box of fluffy ducks, mate.'

'Now, dear,' Maureen called out. 'You're not boring them with shooting stuff.'

'No fear!' Ernie yelled. 'We're discussin' this new television caper. Reckon she'll be a goer.'

Maureen entered. 'Really, Ernie, you could have sat them down. Please. I'll get you a table for your drinks.'

We sat where she indicated, either end of the yellow and brown Chesterfield sofa. Maureen unlocked a nest of little tables and set one next to each of us. The room had a massive chandelier in its central rose, with enough bulbs blazing to light an entire street. There was a small mahogany bookcase dedicated to the Encyclopaedia Britannica's many volumes. Above it were two prints of vases of irises, and on the Davenport in the corner rested a slim blue vase with real irises in it.

'You'd be from Pongolia then?' Ernie enquired, standing proud beside his stag.

'Ernest,' Maureen objected as she perched on the edge of a cane-seated easy chair. 'He means Great Britain.'

'England's fine,' Jasper conceded.

'Bottoms up,' Ernie said heartily, eyebrows active, ignoring Maureen's look.

'Did you have a good trip?' she asked.

I thought it best I answer and said it was fine.

'We're looking forward to your production,' she said.

'Oath,' Ernie agreed. 'Not much on around here. Sleepy Hollow.'

'Quiet,' Maureen qualified. 'It's been that way since the girls left home. We like it.'

'Another beer?'

Ernie shuffled out for reinforcements. Maureen looked at both of us, smoothed down the perfectly smooth shiny beige frock, stood and said we could bring our drinks through to the table when we were ready. As she left Jasper gave me an eyes-to-the-ceiling look, his lenses flashing in the excessive light.

We moved through to the dining room, where under another ferociously bright chandelier the table was set with best silver and dinner plates featuring fox-hunting. Jasper leaned close and murmured: 'Pursuit of the uneatable by the unspeakable.'

There was no concern about the edible nature of what Maureen deposited on the big table mats. Firstly a huge platter of roast leg of lamb, then an even bigger platter with every roast vegetable you could think of, the steaming up of Jasper's glasses suggesting he was as ready as I was to attack this nose-ravishing feast. Maureen completed the succulent array with ceramic boats of mint sauce and gravy and a tureen of steaming peas.

'Export grade,' Ernie announced, giving us the wink as he took up his carving position before this splendid sight. 'I'm not a meat inspector for me good looks.'

'Oh, Ernest,' Maureen objected. 'Don't skite.'

We needed little encouragement to have seconds, which Maureen pressed on us whilst insisting we leave space for the pudding. She exited with the bare bones of the beast and returned with dessert proud on a large glass platter, as if she was bringing in the Crown Jewels. In a way she was. It was a spectacular edifice of meringue shaped perhaps like Egmont. Ernie moved across and lifted the cantilevered lid of the polished cabinet containing glasses behind sliding doors, producing a bottle of brandy.

'On top of Old Smokey, whatcha reckon?' he said as he poured the brandy in to a small crater in the top of the meringue mountain which I had figured for a variation of a pavlova. He lit the brandy and flames streamed down the sides of the meringue, carving little rivulets.

'Bravo!' Jasper said, clapping. 'What's it called?'

Ernie proudly announced this was Maureen's first attempt at a *Bombe Taranaki*. 'That's bombe with an "e",' he added. 'As in *Bombe Alaska*, if you know it?'

'Eee, ba boom,' Jasper managed before he exploded with laughter, his glasses falling off as he doubled up. He recovered glasses and composure and then stood, reached for Maureen's hand and planted a kiss on it.

'Oh really,' Maureen giggled. 'You have to try it before you get carried away.'

'I'm sure, madame,' said Jasper gallantly, 'it will be as superb as its cognomen.'

'You're too kind,' she said. 'Let me serve you.'

The inside was amazingly full of ice cream and sponge and was totally fantastic. Maureen beamed as we polished off our portions. She insisted we finish the entire pudding, it wouldn't keep.

'Well done, dearie,' Ernie beamed.

'Best pud I've ever eaten,' Jasper pronounced.

I threw in my penny's worth of praise. No question the ice had finally been broken in a veritable flood of frozen milk product.

'If you don't mine my asking?' Ernie asked. 'Is that by way of a north of England accent? Sort of reminds me of George Formby.'

Jasper started pretend strumming. '*I'm leaning on a lamp post at the corner of the street,*' he sang in a strange, high-pitched warble. '*Watchin a certain little lady go by. Oh me, oh my.*' He stopped his imaginary playing and did a very broad dialect: '*Eee, champion, it's turned out nice again.*' Quite the performer, he resumed his normally thick accent: 'Yes, Mr M, I plead guilty to coming from our George's patch. Wigan, in Lancashire.'

'Mr Porteous?' Maureen began.

'Please, Maureen, my name is Jasper.'

'Yes, Jasper, well, if I may be so bold, how did you come to be out here?'

'You one of them Ten Pound Poms?' Ernie interjected, at Maureen's glance hastily adding, 'No offence.'

'None taken, Ernie. I worked my passage as a galley slave. Saw the ad for teachers. Beats scrubbing pots and pans for a living.'

'Ha, got ya,' Ernie chortled. 'Galley slave. Very good.'

Jasper smirked and after that little burst of bio, the Meadows insisted we had more important things to do than help with the washing up.

'Now we know what to expect,' Maureen said enthusiastically, 'we just can't wait for your show this evening.'

Jasper's smirk was expanding to a nauseating degree. Amazing what a decent feed and a bit of flattery can do to calm down a societal dissident.

Ernie gave us directions to the theatre and we set off. We needed the exercise, not only to work off the somewhat bloated feeling of too much food, but also to counter a chilly wind bombing briskly off the real Egmont.

Jasper was in fine fettle, talking about the Meadows as the salt of the earth, his usual position on boring middle-class values forgotten for now. He even conceded you could not judge a book by its cover, when he'd seen the fox-hunting plates following the Monarch of the Glen, he thought we were in for a right night of hunting, shooting and fishing stories. He made no further comment on the streets of solid, staid brick houses behind their extensive walled gardens. His social dissatisfaction had been dampened by good old Kiwi tucker, the way to an anarchist's heart through his stomach.

That was obviously the problem back in Wigan, not enough to eat. I knew several of Macaskill's Hot 100 were by another Wigan-spawned George, as in Orwell, represented with three titles, *1984*, *Animal Farm* and *The Road to Wigan Pier*. I'd read the first two and knew about 'Four legs good, two legs bad,' and 'Big Brother Is Watching', the latter phrase explaining where Jasper was coming from. I had not read the pier story, which apparently was about the poverty of the area, which could be a clincher I guess for Jasper's dislike of the state. Funny how a few questions from somebody he had never met before and Jasper proved an open book. It wasn't going to help with Gull's view of him.

Jasper had an extra task, replacing Gull on the tummy tomtoms. He took it to a new level of idiocy, managing to add in some strange, sideways skips between stomach extensions. He brought the house and then the curtain down, performing an impromptu tummy encore as the show ended to standing applause. It was a great house, packed to the rafters. They laughed and clapped everything.

After the show, the Meadows came round to the stage door to offer us a lift back.

Jasper continued his goodwill to the provinces mission by inviting them to join the cast for a drink backstage. Jasper and Jenny led the way in a chorus line that included the Meadows singing

*Oh, knees up, Mother Brown,*
*Knees up, Mother Brown.*
*Come along, dearie, let it go,*
*Ee-I-Ee-I-Ee-I-O.*
*It's your blooming birthday,*
*Let's wake up all the town,*
*So, knees up, knees up,*
*Don't get the breeze up,*
*Knees up, Mother Brown.*

Jasper organised the increasingly lusty repetitions and the little guy on the guitar got strumming. The crescent of interlocking arms doing high kicks somehow morphed into a conga line, each person holding the waist of the one in front as we emerged into the auditorium and wound our way down the aisles and across in front of the stage and up the other side and backstage behind the solid fire curtain. After this somebody started *Old MacDonald Had a Farm* and that was a repeat conga line. There was no knowing where it was all going if the lights had not been doused and a grumpy voice announced that some people had to get home for the night.

On the way back in the Humber, Maureen continued singing the lines of *Knees Up*, nodding her blonde rinse this way and that. Dabbing her eyes with a hankie, she said it was the best night out in years.

'You can say that again,' Ernie said, then did so, and laughed so much he got an angry toot from a car as he momentarily veered across the road.

'Glad to be of service,' Jasper said.

Maureen insisted on making us a hot Milo drink to help us sleep, as if we needed that. She came in to turn back the pink quilts, informing us the daughters up and got married within months of each other. She pointed out where the spare blankets were if it turned *parky*, was that the word, Jasper? He assured her it was. She hoped we would not find the beds too small. Jasper planted a goodnight kiss on her cheek.

'Oh,' she giggled, retreating quickly out the door.

I was unpacking my pyjamas, eyeing the huge poster of Fabian on the wall behind the door, when a blast of cold air swept in. Jasper was climbing out of the sash window.

'See you in the morning,' he said, and was gone before I could think of anything to say.

I shut the window and went to bed, pulling the quilt over my head and trying to shut out images of Melissa.

I was woken by a tap on the door. 'Cooeee!' Maureen's voice.

'Hello?'

'We're off to church. You lie in. Breakfast is laid.'

I was awake now. A tapping on the window. I pulled the blind up. Jasper and Jenny.

'Come on,' he said when I lifted the window. 'Church.'

'You're kidding.'

'Would I con a Mickey Doo, Jens?'

'Shift your lazy butt, Steve,' she said, rosy-cheeked to go with her red turtleneck sweater.

'Jens is going to introduce me to your medieval world. Let's go.'

Church bells were chiming from several directions as we walked through the crisp morning. They were hand-in-hand and hardly touching the ground. The transformation of Jasper was incredible. I felt like the wallflower at the school dance, watching the newly crowned dance champions strut their stuff.

Jenny whisked round, catching me in mid-trudge. 'Cheer up, Steve,' she said gaily. 'As you well know, it doesn't usually last more than an hour.'

'Bloody hell,' Jasper complained.

The first set of bells proved to be Presbyterian, but our second try was successful.

'With any luck,' Jasper said, 'they'll be over halfway.'

'Spoilsport,' Jenny said, tugging him inside.

The church was packed, and it was well underway, judging by the priest up in the pulpit bellowing out to a cowed congregation *What doth it profit a man if he gains the whole world and suffers the loss of his own immortal soul?* There was no need for the microphone, it merely distorted his voice and sent it caroming round the high plaster walls. The big inner doors were opened back and an elderly lady in a powder-blue woollen jacket and three strings of pearls was standing by the holy water font, facing us with two green felt-lined wooden plates in her hands and a fraught look on her face.

Jasper stepped up to her. 'May I be of assistance, madame?'

'Um,' she said uncertainly. 'I don't know where Tom and Ed are. We have to take up the collection.'

'Mathew continues,' the priest barked, causing her to cringe, as if her hearing aid was turned up too high. *'For the Son of Man is going to come in the glory of His Father and His Angels, and then will repay every man according to his deeds.* Mark this well, each and every one of you – yes you – and you – and you – will be judged according to your deeds. We are a fortunate community, we do not lack for anything, we have three square meals a day, we do not scrimp and save for a bowl of gruel, we live off the fat of the land, we have been blessed. Do not forget in your blessings those less fortunate. We have our Peter's Pence collection, as you know, sent to the Holy Father in Rome, for dispensation to the poor benighted heathen that they may come to see the light through easing their physical burdens and then addressing their spiritual impoverishment. We ask you to give with double generosity, for the maintenance of our own parish and for the great parish of the dark world overseen by Our Holy Father in Rome.'

The be-pearled lady looked anxiously either side of Jasper. He turned to us. 'What is the problem?'

I told him the collection was supposed to be taking place, but the collectors had slept in or something.

'We'll do it,' he said. 'Sounds like the fund raiser out front wants cash in hand.'

He stepped close to the lady and said he and his friend would be happy to help. He took the plates from the uncertain hands and gave me one, stepping into the church.

'No,' I hissed. 'To the front.'

I led the way up the centre aisle of the nave, feeling somewhat self-conscious, stopping at the first row of pews, passing the plate to the person on the end. Jasper did likewise on his side. The plate came back down the second row and we relieved the holder and passed to the third row. So it went down the church until we moved into the foyer with our plates brimming with coins and notes, some of them £5 designation. Clearly the priest's words were being made manifest.

'*Dominus vobiscum,*' the priest intoned, hands outspread. He had done his pulpit dash and was back at the altar.

'*Et cum spirtu tuo,*' the congregation murmured, rising to their feet as the organ pounded overhead and the choir started the *Credo in unum deum.* The old lady was not to be seen, perhaps having gone inside to join in this profession of faith.

I glanced at Jenny watching Jasper keep going with his plate of money out the main door.

'Jenny?' I hissed, putting my plate of money down on the long table beside the pile of leaflets about the Leper Man missions in the Pacific.

The old lady was alongside, asking me where the other man was. I said I didn't know.

'Oh dear,' she said, a look of shock on her face. 'He hasn't taken it?'

I shook my head. She had a big grey bag in her hands. She looked at the plate of money, pulled the strings apart on the top of the bag.

'Let me help,' I said.

She turned between me and the money.

'He might be still collecting,' I said feebly.

She gave me a quick glance. She returned to her task, tipping the money into the bag and pulling the strings tight. Clasping the money to her bosom, she backed away from me.

'Stay where you are,' she said, moving across the foyer to enter the side aisle.

Jenny had gone. The old lady was coming back with two front row forwards bulging out of their Sunday best. I took off out the door, ignoring the shouts of the two men, the words *remissionem peccatorum* bringing the *Credo* to a conclusion, with the final words about the resurrection of the dead and the life of the world to come. I leapt down the steps like a ballet dancer, Maggie would have been proud of me.

A quick glance over my shoulder indicated the two rugby players were nowhere near so nimble, but were looking angry and determined. I accelerated out of the church grounds and veered right, no sign of Jenny or Jasper. I pinned my ears back and ran for dear life and liberty. The rugby lads had no chance.

My problem was that by the time I had turned and twisted through a dozen streets, I was lost. I slowed to catch my breath. A church was spilling out its congregation, this seemingly the only activity in town on a Sunday. I moved to mingle with them, snatching glimpses to check that my pursuers were not in sight. I asked a lady if she knew which way the bus station was. She told me and I headed into town, figuring it was best to flag my kit, which only contained pyjamas, a spare pair of underpants and Donne's poems.

The bus station was like Good Friday, empty and desolate, not even a cafeteria. I sat down and took stock. The clock was working and said I had an hour to wait. I went for a wander, nothing open. The only activity was the curling white smoke from a huge chimney by the rocky beach. Beside it were ramshackle buildings and piles of white and yellow powder. This could be what it looked like after a nuclear exchange, New Plymouth's version of *On the Beach*.

The bus arrived but the driver kept the door shut, had his feet up reading *Best Bets*. I tapped on the window and he waved me away, pointing at his watch.

I sat down until the cast began to arrive. Among them were Jasper and Jenny. Jasper had my bag and asked where I got to, the Meadows were sorry to miss me. I said I got lost and what happened with his little score. He smiled at Jenny and said that he had acted as an intermediary. 'Doesn't Jesus say to give your worldly possessions to the poor?'

'So who was the lucky poor round here?'

'We woke up this old drunk,' Jenny said.

'We were having a shufti at the gardens,' Jasper explained. 'Found him under a rhododendron bush.'

Jasper gave Jesus-like to a down-and-out drunk, I had not. 'Sooner the bus leaves the better,' I growled.

I was wrong. It was not better being next to Ron again. He wanted to continue educating me.

'Would you buy a used car from this man?' he asked.

I ignored him, relieved the bus was in motion and there were no flashing blue lights overtaking us.

'That's what they say about Nixon.'

'Who's he?'

'You were not listening. He is the Republican front runner.'

I continued not to listen as he volunteered to explain the relative differences between Republicans and Democrats. The singing reprised Extrav songs and, now a firm favourite, *Knees up, Mother Brown*.

As we reached Wellington I pondered telling Gull about Jasper's latest prank. It was hardly going to cause widespread social disruption. It might provoke a few curses and reinforcement of the general status of students as thieves and layabouts in certain Catholic circles. I don't think Gull would disapprove of what Jasper did. I might settle for telling him Jasper had changed since he had fallen in love. It only reminded me of my own miserable condition. I was literally love sick, a condition for which there was no known cure.

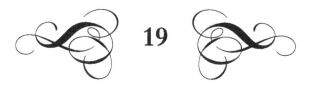

# 19

'Oi! Fuckknuckle!'

I reared off the pile of coiled rope, a sharp pain in my back from the awkward position in which I had fallen asleep.

'Shift your arse!'

I clambered to my feet, rubbing my eyes to get rid of the roaming black dots. The sun itself was blotted out by a huge alien presence swinging overhead. I ducked and lurched away to the side of the coaster, as the huge pallet thunked to the deck fairly close to where I had been asleep on the job.

'You stupid fucker!' the foreman was screaming as he advanced on me. 'You do that again and you can fuck off back to the fucking sandpit you fucking crawled out of. That clear?'

There was nowhere for me to retreat, I was against the railing. I glanced down at the dock 20 feet below. He was up against me, his dirty big forefinger jabbing into my chest. He was front-row forward size, and although a goodly portion had graduated to his gut, there was still a massive amount of upper body bulk behind the jabs. His few remaining strands of sandy hair were flicking about as he quivered with rage, his face volcanic.

'Jesus fucking Christ, boy! You bloody well watch it. Now get to fucking work.'

I joined the other three jokers unloading the crates of cheese.

'Fuck him,' Jack said, hauling off the ropes on one side. 'Sandy's always blowing his stack. Take no notice. He'll be off for a snort now.'

Sandy had roared up and gone like a gorse bush in an incinerator. Jack paused to pull out his tobacco and roller and make himself a durry.

'He'll bust his boiler one day,' he said, squeezing his eyes shut and turning sideways from what little wind there was. He used his lighter, blowing smoke and releasing a contented sigh.

'Come on,' Chas complained. 'If we don't shift this, he'll be back doing his block.'

I worked with Jack, his fag fixed in the corner of his mouth, smoke making him squint. Nohi and Chas were the other team. It took us all of 15 minutes to shift the crates and Jack to fling the ropes over the pallet and signal the crane driver to take it away.

I felt sheepish to be caught out my first day on the job as a non-union worker or seagull. I guess the idea is not to get caught. The other guys had disappeared into the hold to play poker around an upturned apple box. I didn't want to squander any of this soft-earned cash, I needed to get £100 as quickly as possible to pay Clair before I got caught out skiving off from my teaching section. Mrs Watson, my Form Two associate at Karori School, was sympathetic when I explained my problem catching up with the punishing university load, but she reminded me that three days' absence required a doctor's certificate.

It had been my intention to work my ring off to raise the money, especially as Gull claimed Clair did not know where Melissa was and Training College admin would not divulge any details about her sick leave. I figured if I came across with the dough, I had reason to front Clair and she would relent. I wanted to believe she had loaned Melissa the money knowing where to recover it. It was I recognised a slender thread, but it was something I could try. I couldn't bear waiting in the hope that Gull via Clair would put me in touch with Melissa. At least Gull's nickname had made me think of the solution to the funding shortfall, casual work on the wharf. It was the only option with no seasonal work and no Art Unions or TAB punts yielding the necessary.

I turned up at the wharf shed well before 8am last week and watched the jobs being handed out to the motley collection of students and deadbeats. I was not eligible until I got the seagull card, which I had collected this morning. I was detailed to the *Breeze*, where I sat on the deck with Jack and the others for several hours of a union meeting from which us seagulls are excluded. We did a quarter hour of stacking and then it was back to the caff attached to the yard for smoko. The tea was like brown tar, but, with plenty of sugar, was sustaining. Not that we needed it. The other guys disappeared below for poker, until it was time to take off for lunch. The afternoon was a repeat of poker, smoko, poker, and this flurry of stacking.

Not a smidgeon of the draconian toil of the Gear, but also not half the income. I volunteered for overtime and copped really unpleasant work. We toiled in poor light guiding with our hands these huge, swinging bands of pipes into designated piles. No gloves provided and no way the crane operator could see us. When we had the pipes in position we shouted until he heard us, then we clambered out of the way as the pipes were dumped.

The last half-hour was even worse, working in poor light stacking pig iron in rail trucks, the risk of smashed heads a constant threat. That finished at 8.30 and I got a pie on the way to the bus, starving and stuffed. The bus driver had to wake me at the depot and there was the 20 minute shamble home to bed. I was up again at 6.15 to get to the wharf.

Those of us who got jobs reported to the Dry Dock at the bottom of Aotea Quay.

It was the coldest day since I've been in Wellington and we had nowhere to shelter, standing in the raw wind waiting for work. When we finally got on the dock the wind slashed at us like stock whips. I blessed the wharfies smelling rain at three, requiring we all repair to the caff. There we got the news that the All Blacks had been thrashed 13-0 by the Springboks. I could care less. We had to stick around the caff until the boss gave us the all-clear at 4.30. No overtime, not with rain threatening.

No work the next day, so I got to Karori School for a full day, avoiding the need for a doctor's certificate. Me of all people had to take the junior soccer reps down to Macalister Park. It took us ages to find the park and I spent most of my time begging officials to give my four lads, Donald, Eric, Michael and Jamie, a trial. Donald got one, and then was disqualified for being too old.

Back at school I read the kids *Children of the Poor*, a waste of time, they did not relate to delinquent kids in Dunedin at turn of century, the wrong demographic, I guess. It's not easy holding the attention of 40 kids. I had to accept it was only fair I had discipline problems, given the roles were now reversed on me from my days of playing up at the back of the classroom. I was proving neither much of a seagull nor teacher, not much chop as worker or boss.

The longest day's loading into night frozen sides of lamb was the hardest work I've done. The evening shift we were working with wharfies, who would sling the carcasses hard at us, two in the wagon, one to the side. They gave no explanation for the one in three that went to the side.

A weekend was needed to recover, and catch up on study reading. This gave me an idea at Karori School, when I got no wharf work on the Monday. I called in at Training College library on the way, and was able to produce another book for Form Two, to predictable groans from the yahoos at the back of the class. It was called *Our Street,* and I wasn't even sure if it was on the approved school reading list, or if indeed there was a list of banned books such as the Catholic Index, which was alive and well denouncing the likes of James Joyce and even movies like *Duel in the Sun*. I didn't ask, I simply told the class to shut up while I read. The book I knew had been denounced as morally unacceptable for children and banned from libraries, but honestly it was harmless stuff about kids in an Island Bay street playing cricket, chucking crackers into doorways at Guy Fawkes and smoking in their forts and the like. The class loved it and after the lesson, one of the troublemakers at the back asked if he could borrow it. I was happy to, though I warned him I had to have it back.

Next day I got attached to the interisland ferry the *Maori*, which led to big problems. We lounged about all morning, then had a hard afternoon lifting oil cans. By the time we got to the stage of checking cars were properly tied to the hoist, I had lost concentration. The rope caught around my foot, quick as you like, and suddenly I was up 30 feet in the air, dangling beneath the hoist with the car on it, guys screaming out below, the crane driver unable to see me.

This was the time, Batman, for reverse acrobatics. I bent my body like an outdoor Houdini, grabbing the rope above my ankle and pulling it free, still upside down, the side of the huge ferry looming as I gathered momentum on the end of the rope. I risked a glance below, too far to release the rope and land on the hard. The rope was swinging through an increasingly wider and faster arc, with me acting as the pendulum weight opposing the rising hoist above.

In a matter of seconds I was going to smash into the side of the ferry and fall from there like a squashed bug into the water or worse, against the anchor or a bollard. I hauled myself hand over hand in a reverse rappel up the rope, scuttling like a crazy crab, grabbing the side of the wooden platform and pulling myself up beside the car.

Now I had the tied rope to use for leverage. I stood and contemplated the wriggling line of rope that might have been the end of me, flicking this way and that over the small but horrified audience of seagulls and unionists. They were shouting and waving towards the crane operator, who by now had seen me and was lowering the entire hoist back to the asphalt.

As I descended, I flung my hand skywards and dipped my body in a brisk bow. I turned this way and that to acknowledge my audience, popping with the same adrenalin surge I got on the Eastbourne pole.

No applause.

Sandy was first to me. 'You fucking idiot!' he yelled. 'What the fuck you trying to do, get yourself killed?'

Fuck him. 'I think I managed to avoid …'

'Jesus H!' he screamed in my face, likely pumping more adrenalin than me. He was scarlet and lost for words. He swung about, waving his arms. 'All right, everybody out!'

The unionists shook their heads as they headed to the shed. The seagulls gave me filthy looks and sloped off.

I was left on the wharf, wanting to know why there was no sympathy. I chased and grabbed Jack.

'Piss off,' he said. 'You've cost us.'

'You mean that's it?'

Jack removed his durry. 'Yeah. Fine for the fucking union, they get paid regardless. For us, no work, no pay. Get it?'

'I didn't plan this.'

He left me to rue my bad luck alone. I was, as Jack put it at smoko in regard to Walter Nash, about as popular as a pork chop in a synagogue.

It got worse. I was passed over for work the next day.

The following day I did get a job, working on the *Squall* way down at the bottom of the hold, at least 20 feet, which smacked of a punishment detail. I could see two levels or storeys above us. The lumber swung over, rough planks the length of a room, tied loosely with rope about the middle. A worker way above angled each stack so they fitted through the aperture. It was not a big space and as they came down there was little light visible. The planks yawed about, sliding out of alignment, sticks unfolding in different directions like the blades of a Swiss army knife. I was working with this Aussie joker Brian who had been spouting about his sex adventures with a rich girl, until a plank end knocked him against the bulkhead and that took the wind out of his boasting for the rest of the morning.

After lunch Brian didn't reappear, instead it was Gull, who was not best pleased with me. Before I could object to this unwarranted surveillance, he snapped that I seemed determined to sabotage my father's career. No more grinning from the big guy. Did I not realise that the union would now know who I was after the little incident with the ferry rope? I protested I failed to see how this would matter. He said it mattered because there was a lot of paranoia around the wharf at present, with different factions promoting different agendas.

I could only shrug. What did I know of wharf politics? What did I care?

'Look,' he said. 'The big cheese, Fintan Patrick Walsh – I assume you've heard of him?'

'Sure,' I said. My knowledge was little more than a hazy mix of Dad's fulminating against F.P.'s Federation of Labour holding the country to ransom and our Extrav send-up of him as F.P. Hoffa.

'Okay then, there is a faction among the wharfies, seamen and other unionists out to dump Fintan. He might be getting past it but opponents of Fintan have been known to fall overboard and never be seen again, or get washed up somewhere with an indentation in the back of the skull, as in marlin spike.'

He didn't have my full attention. I caught movement far above. The recent shock to my system had put me on red alert, given the lack of any attempt at providing safety standards, especially where seagulls were at work. I lunged at Gull, pushing him aside in time for a loose plank of wood to thump on to the floor of the hold. It wasn't done, springing viciously sideways and clocking me a slap across the side of the face, fortunately not with the blunt end.

I fell to the floor, dazed. I got slowly to my feet, peering through the poor light, wondering where Gull was. I saw him, ascending the second ladder to the deck, I heard him remonstrating.

I sat back well out of the path of any more missiles and waited. Eventually Gull returned, said it appeared to be an accident, some incompetent went to smoko and left the lumber suspended overhead. He sat beside me in the dark hold, sighing.

He banged my arm, thanked me for the push out of harm's way.

'Let me try and explain,' he said. 'No, don't worry, I told them we're not going to make a complaint, you know what happens, no work for us seagulls, unions agitated, further notice taken of you and yours truly. Not good. They already associate me with Bill Dwyer. You might recall he carried a wool hook everywhere he went on the wharf, to protect him from Fintan's mates. Stupid prick, always trying to get motions of no confidence passed in the union. He must have a death wish.'

'Where is he?'

Gull snorted. 'You don't even bother with student politics.'

I waited.

'Dwyer's now trying to pass votes of no confidence in the student executive. He's barking mad, if you ask me.'

'Does that mean he's off your list?'

'Not at all. Nor is friend Jasper. Those japes you got involved in might have been harmless fun. It doesn't mean the next time will be quite so benign. Those fellows are loose cannons with a lot of resentment. I don't trust them anymore than the wharf union trusts Dwyer.'

'I still don't see any connection to me in all this, or Dad.'

Gull took a deep breath. 'A lot of students work on the wharf. The militant wharfies like to know about the politics of those working on their patch. They can add two and two together, like you and me. If it's true Fintan's having secret talks with the National Party movers and shakers, then it's not a good look for him to have National Party associates like us on his premises. Yeah, I know it sounds far-fetched. But that's the job I'm in. I've pretty much shot my bolt on the wharf, unless I want to fall off the end of it one dark night. I can't let you stay here either. Guilt by association, I'm afraid. Come on, let's go.'

'No.'

'Yes. If you don't, I'll make damn sure you get no more work. That's why you're here, yes? It will cost you your teacher training. It's going to see you forcibly removed from Wellington. That means you do not see Clair, you do not find out where Melissa is. Before you try and whack me again …'

'No, I was just wondering whether you really can command all those things?'

'There is still that under-age drinking charge available, plus, let's see — causing a disturbance in a public place, attacking women with intent to cause grievous bodily harm, trespassing on a public thoroughfare, namely Athletic Park, and acting in a disorderly manner, assaulting police in the execution of their lawful duty – shall I go on?'

'Not good for Dad.'

'He'll cope. Your grandparents in Whangarei will take you in, local employment will be arranged.'

'Crikey dick. Am I that important?'

Now I detected a grin, or a grimace. 'Not as such. But you make my life easier if you're out of the picture.'

'I need to earn another fifty quid.'

'No you don't. I've recompensed Clair. You can owe me, okay? No hurry about repayment.'

Gull told me to see out the day and left me to it, somewhat dazed and confused. Was he really threatening me with prosecution and, effectively, deportation up north? Did he think I'd just fold and do his bidding? I was getting mighty fed up with his interference in my life, but on the other hand I didn't want to embarrass Dad. I found it difficult to believe I could, that the newspapers would have the slightest interest in me. Or the wharfies either. Their main agenda seemed to be stop-works to gouge more perks and pay out of the bosses.

The Aussie guy Brian was suggesting daydreaming on this job could cause me serious bodily harm. I didn't get it at first, the same police-speak coming from this dork. The call from above and another swaying load of lumber coming towards us woke my ideas up.

I was signing off at 4.30 back at the shed when Sandy told us we had overtime, a rush job down at the Cheese Store.

'Dinky-di,' Brian said. I didn't object. I had nothing to go home for.

The floodlights outside the cheese store were doused just before nine. We were sweaty from heaving crates and the night chill cut through my zipped jacket like, well, a slaughterman's knife through a sheep's throat. Brian asked me to join him at the pie-cart for a cuppa and a feed, but I declined. I was still churning inside with resentment that Gull could order me about. I was in his debt now. I thought I might visit Harold, see if Clair would relent and talk to me about Melissa. I pulled up the collar of my jacket and walked head-down towards Queen's Wharf and the lights from the big ship in port, vaguely planning to walk around to Oriental Bay and up to Harold's establishment.

I had not seen fog or night mist before in Wellington. It was like a shroud muting the blinking harbour lights. I could smell coal smoke and hear the distant chugging of sturdy marine engines, tugs and scows and coasters about their nocturnal business. The lugubrious honking of a fog horn came from beyond the blurred outlines of the wharf sheds, with only the occasional security light above a door glowing in a halo of vapour.

A searchlight from a small craft cut across between the wharves. The blue lights on its superstructure identified the police launch the *Lady Elizabeth*, coming in to its berth from some night patrol. It was moving slowly, but I could hear the throb of its engines because it was so close. The usual wharf sounds of creaking ropes and distant clangs and the vibrations of distant engines and propellers were blanketed by the conditions.

The big brick stores paradoxically took on a more solid appearance in their shadowed presence as the police searchlight licked across facades, deepening angles and apparently enlarging buildings momentarily. The searchlight's slow and jittery progress suggested a stealthy tracking of a perceived prey.

It was an eerie experience for me, reminiscent of the elongated shadows and looming menace of that remarkable Graham Greene movie *The Third Man*, with its extreme black and white chiaroscuro (a word Melissa taught me) camera pursuit of the penicillin pusher Harry Lime over the wet cobblestones and through the rushing sewers of post-war Vienna. Any moment I was expecting to see the light fall on the patent leather shoes the cat was rubbing against, then the stark, enigmatic Mona Lisa smile of Harry Lime, caught for one frozen white moment, before disappearing like a magician in a puff of smoke.

What I did not expect to see was Gull, his head thrust up at the night sky, his mouth agape, his eyes closed. A figure in a dark jacket crouched at his waist making a small but urgent bobbing motion.

The searchlight had flicked by the deep shadow of the inside of the disused Eastbourne ticket office, that strange building with its midriff removed to allow passengers with tickets to pass through. Now the midriff shadows were too deep to perceive any shapes. I froze, no more than 30 or so feet away. I didn't want to move, to alert them to my presence. It had happened in the twinkling of an eye. I had no doubt what I had seen. Gull was in his duffel. It was definitely him, and there was no question that he was being serviced by another male. My stomach heaved. My flesh crawled with hot, prickling sensation.

Slowly, carefully, I backed away, putting the bulk of the building between us. I turned slowly and moved back towards the big redbrick store on the corner. I was relieved to be round the side of it. I put my head down, crossed to the Railway Station, reversed behind the pie-cart and veered up Stout Street. I wanted to put as many street turns between us as possible.

I was finding it hard to comprehend what I had inadvertently witnessed. This meant those hints from Randy and Bosco were true. Did it mean Gull wanted to have me do the same thing to him? I had travelled on the back of his motorbike, held him tightly. He had got up behind me. Was it because he fancied me? Gull! I could not align this behaviour with him. It was so incredibly rash for a start, not to mention utterly disgusting. He was seeking out anonymous sex on the wharf. It was so shabby and demeaning. Did he engage those penis-height holes in public toilets? God, I was totally flummoxed and revolted. He was Catholic!

What about Clair? What about Miranda saying Clair was gone on Gull? Did Gull like being serviced by her in the same way? Was he one of those bisexuals? Was he an out-an-out queer? Whatever he was, he was finished in the police if he was caught. He was heading for jail, for lewd conduct in a public place. Him threatening me with charges! What a hypocrite! How dare he play this moral high ground police officer crap, when all the while he was leading this double life. What would his mother think?

God, the National Party, Dad, all those upright types, they would be totally scandalised. He was living a lie with his entire life. Trying to get me to help him spy on Jasper and prove the anarchists were some kind of threat to our society, and he was breaking every rule himself as a sworn police officer.

A blinding light in my face caused me to stumble.

'Now, lad, easy does it.'

I put my hand up to shield my eyes. The light mercifully moved off my face, flickering over the rest of me. I peered at the figure of a policeman. How ironic.

'What's your business around here, lad?'

'Nothing,' I mumbled.

'Been drinking, have we?'

I indignantly denied this as I reached into my pants pocket.

'Steady,' he said forcefully, the torch back in my face. 'Keep your hands where I can see them.'

I explained I was getting out my wharf employment card. He told me to go ahead, slowly. I handed over the non-registered waterside worker's card. He took it, the torch scrutinised the little blue piece of cardboard with my name, address, date of birth, signature and Number 18308. He handed it back to me.

'Thank you, Mr Marr,' he said. 'Best not loiter around here.'

I looked up the imposing line of run-down brick warehouses. I knew this one well, the name 'EW Mills' carved across the pediment. I twigged where I was, in Victoria Street. I had not noticed. I had not been aware of any surroundings, only of the internal image replaying incessantly, like a scene from *The Third Man*, the soundtrack a distorted, speeded-up zither. It was a startling relief, like the reel breaking and spooling round and round while the cinema audience groans. The spell cast by my unsolicited observation of Gull breaking the law had been broken by a policeman's torch.

I was back in the land of the living and, as that poet Eliot added, partly living.

Behind the public library nearby I often encountered drunks with brown paper bags camouflaging flagons of port or sherry from John Bull's across Wakefield Street. Depending on the hour, they would be loudly arguing with each other on the public seats, or silently slumped across them or on the asphalt underneath. Their flagons were often lying in broken fragments beside them, the smell enough to put you off the contents for life. Later still on my way across the Harris Street area I had been propositioned by furtive men or women Clair and Miranda no doubt knew.

It was the first time I'd been stopped by a cop. I muttered I was taking a short cut. His torch followed me as I headed up the street, away from his surveillance, left into Mercer Street. He should be directing his torch the other way, might surprise one of his own.

I passed my after-college office, the public library, the town hall opposite, where I sat next to Melissa in raptures at Dave Brubeck's meandering music. I hurried on, swinging around Taranaki Street, past the steamed-up plate glass windows of the Green Parrot, the only restaurant packed with punters at this hour. I headed for Courtenay Place, the public toilets below street level a grubby reminder of Gull's secret preference.

At Courtenay Place there was a further prompt regarding Gull's night life, a group of men lurking by the pohutukawas next to the public jakes. A tram rattled by, heeling and squealing round the iron rails past the now shuttered Embassy Theatre and up Kent Terrace towards the doughty old bronze statue of Queen Victoria. A police car drove past slowly, headlights identifying the group. They turned away. After the police car had gone I saw several scantily clad women in high heels approach the group. Were these more crewmen off the ship, seeking more conventional sex?

I walked round past the all-night diner with a few men sipping hot drinks and flicking looks my way. The Taj Mahal toilets to my left were closed, but there were figures in the shadows of the seating along its side. Either Gull was on my mind or there were a lot more of his persuasion than I realised.

I passed the closed glass doors of the fire station, the huge red engines resting in a row waiting for the next call out. I shambled along Oriental Parade, on my left the Royal Port Nicholson Yacht Club and the old baths, the beach, the rotunda, the crescent of Norfolk pines. Across the harbour the wharf buildings with the safety lights were a smudged painting, too far to see any of the people moving about in the shadows.

I was overcome with weariness as I slowly ascended those two steep streets. I paused, wondering what I thought I was up to. Then I moved down the overgrown pathway and up the steps and pressed the buzzer.

After the usual pause, the eye check, Harold opened the door.

'My dear boy?' A question in his warm warble, and he had not moved out of the doorway.

'Harold. I have to know. Is Gull – Paddy … is Clair here?'

He stiffened. 'I think it best, dear boy, if you left.'

I stuck my foot in the closing door.

'Here's half what I owe Clair.'

He opened the door, my eyes going to the flexible leather sock he was tapping in the palm of his hand. 'No need,' he said, his crinkly laughter lines gone, his face set like cement. 'Patrick took care of that little debt.'

'Is Paddy queer?'

'Stephen,' he beckoned in the lightest whisper, pausing as I craned forward to catch what he was going to say. His eyes narrowed to sharp, vindictive dots. 'If you return, Stephen, I will sic Gus on to you. I take it you recall that somewhat unstable colleague of Patrick's?' Before I had thought of a response, he eased the door back and slammed it. I got my boot clear in time. I saw the slight flicker of the eye-hole.

There was nothing to do but retreat. I slunk home, feeling as if I had been the offender. No question of falling asleep on the bus. I watched out the window as we wound our way round the blurred harbour lights, getting farther and farther from Gull's other life, farther and farther from any chance of finding Melissa. Once again I was plagued by the 'what if' factor? If I had not been asked to do overtime, if I had not turned down Brian's dinner invite, such as it was, if I had not chosen to once again whimsically pursue a meeting that was not going to happen, then I would not have seen Gull in this shameful light. I did not know how I could face him now.

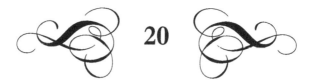

# 20

Gull rang first thing to offer me a lift in to college. I declined. His tone was unruffled as he reminded me I had not said anything about Jasper's plans. I said there was nothing to report, Jasper was about as dangerous to law and order as a sodden Tom Thumb cracker. I told him not to bother ringing me again, I was done with spying on his behalf and the next time he saw me I would have his £100 and then we were square. If he was worried, I could assure him I was not planning to work again on the wharf. I hung up.

Jasper sidled up to me at the end of Assembly and asked if I was free at four tomorrow. I nodded, my face noncommittal. He asked me to meet him opposite the floral clock, I could check the time that way. Jasper being deadpan, I had to assume that was a sort of joke.

'Don't be late,' he said, which was bourgeois of him. I didn't know the half of it.

Given this was Survey Week, I had to put in hours correcting mental tests, about as boring as teacher training gets. We were also required to take Phys-Ed classes, a total drag of a different kind. The Phys-Ed clique showed how it was done on the vaulting horse and the rings and heaving around the medicine ball, unwilling to moderate their power when tossing the ball at the girls. The good thing for me it was a distraction. After college I went down to the library to catch up on study.

Tuesday I was back in the varsity library and almost forgot Jasper. I caught the cable car and jogged to the meeting. If the floral clock was to be trusted to tell the correct time, I was five minutes late. Jasper was standing outside a nondescript door looking anything but in a moss-green tweed suit open to reveal a daisy-patterned waistcoat that could have been an off-cut of Maureen's apron. He had a white carnation in the buttonhole of the jacket and a beam as wide as the face of the floral clock. His large earring was even more prominent due to his hair dragged back and tied in a tight pony tail over the other shoulder. While I gawped at this transformation, he waved me across Wakefield Street.

I asked what was going on. He ignored my question, reminding me I was late as he hustled me inside.

Jenny was there, looking like a million dollars in a cream and gold dress a size too small for her magnificent figure. Alongside her was a petite straw blonde in a pretty yellow frock, a more compact version of Heather, without the eye problem. Jenny introduced Sue Gifford and hugged me, thanking me for agreeing to witness their marriage vows. I apologised for being in my cords, duffel and desert boots, I had not been informed what the occasion was. Jenny gave Jasper a look he ignored, instead beaming as he suggested we get on with it before any bodies changed their minds.

'You,' Jenny objected.

I thought it a perfunctory service, or at least minimalist in the exchange of promises as directed by a fierce woman with steel-rimmed glasses and matching steely-grey hair tied in a bun. She wore a sensible brown jacket and skirt and sensibly reminded Jasper and Jenny that this civil contract carried obligations in law that were not to be entered into lightly. Jenny and Jasper repeated the required phrases, Jasper produced a thin gold ring not much more impressive than the curtain ring in his ear, and didn't wait for the celebrant's permission to engage Jenny in a long kiss. Sue clapped her hands and then burst into tears. Jenny gave her a hug and accepted a kiss from me, Jasper shook my hand. The various documents were signed where the celebrant – hardly the right word for the grim lady — indicated and the business of getting married was concluded.

Nobody had said anything so I asked about relations, did they not want to come? Jenny said it was going to be a surprise when they got to Nelson. I'll bet it would be.

We repaired to the new flat Jasper and Jenny had acquired in Devon Street, the goat track that winds between university and Aro Street. We caught a taxi, Jasper announcing it was on them, though it was Jenny who paid off the driver. He had earned his money, bumping up on to the footpath on the tightest corner.

Jasper lifted Jenny off her feet and carried her up the single step to the front door. He proved how agile he was by continuing to cradle her while he produced a key and opened the door. They entered and we followed.

There was a long hallway of peeling wallpaper bulging in places, a sash window at the end, rooms off to each side. Jasper led the way into the sitting room, except there was no seating. It offered a large wooden floor, a bay window with four sash windows, no curtains. Interior French doors led to the kitchen/dining room, absent a table and chairs but at least sporting new, unpainted gib instead of the tatty wallpaper. Jasper pushed open the doors.

'Voila!' he said, bowing and sweeping his arm in an arc towards the brown chipped Terrazzo bench top, which was host to a tin bucket packed with bottles of bubbly in ice and several plates of sausage rolls, asparagus rolls and club sandwiches. A bowl contained a bunch of grapes, beside it a wedge of cheese on a small plate.

The entire room was tongue and groove, walls and ceiling, painted a bilious green, including the cupboard above the sink Jenny opened. She removed several of those glasses with transfers of native flowers on the side, formerly hosting peanut butter or honey.

'It's all we have, folks.'

Jasper popped a bottle and poured drinks.

'I'll trek over for oysters and chips later,' he said. 'I've rung Alan and teed it up.'

We tapped glasses and toasted the marriage. Jenny invited us to take a look, springing another surprise by saying the dinky bedroom we entered first would be for the littlie. I was the one not aware she was pregnant. I congratulated both of them, feeling a twinge at the thought that I too could have been a father.

Jenny detected something. She asked me where that pale girl was she saw me going off with one night after Extrav. I said she was on sick leave. Jasper observed he had not seen her around college and was it anything serious? I initially did a double take, thinking he meant our relationship, before I said I didn't know and left it at that. He gave a slight frown, but obviously this was not the day to be going into that.

The second bedroom was also empty, the third one on the end opposite the kitchen, bathroom and toilet was huge. This did have a double bed, a home-made quilt over it, massive dark wood ends that matched a wardrobe in the far corner big enough to fit all of us inside its double doors. Each door was inlaid with a full-size mirror with extensive blotching like the liver spots on an elderly person's hands. The view from the gargantuan six-sided bay window was of the entire valley and a glimpse of harbour to the left. Street lights backlit the upper set of small leadlight windows, revealing a gorgeous pattern of grape clusters looping through the six windows in vivid reds, greens and blues of a depth I'd only seen before in church windows.

'Fab, eh?' Jenny said. 'So long as you don't fall out the window.'

We crowded the window seat, looking down what must have been a drop of 40 feet.

'Stilt foundations,' I said.

'You wouldn't want borer in them,' Sue giggled, then burped. 'Pardon me,' she said. 'Bubbly always does this.'

'Speaking of which,' Jasper said, retiring to pop another. We sat along the window seat, it being the only seating in the house. As best man I proposed a toast to the double bed and those who sailed in her. Jenny gave me a nudge with her elbow, Jasper snorted and Sue got the giggles and hiccups and had to go into the bathroom.

Jasper went off to get the oysters and chips, Jenny suggested we explore further. There was no electricity on yet, but Jenny provided a torch to navigate the broken concrete path down the side of the house and underneath, where we forced a rusted bolt and then the stiff door. Sue said there might be those trapdoor spiders. I proved I wasn't scared of creepy crawlies, silently praying there were no wetas, as I pushed my way in. The torch identified a rusty-springed single bed and several very bent bentwood chairs. At Jenny's urging I hauled them out and swiped off the cobwebs the ladies were eyeing dubiously. I gave the items a good shake and brought them up inside the house.

Jenny lit a plain white candle in a milk bottle and put it on the high wooden mantelpiece in the sitting room. She told us both to put our feet up. I protested that pregnant ladies came first in that category.

'Piff,' she said, disappearing into their bedroom. We heard her squeal and went in to see her lift a small wooden step ladder from the huge wardrobe. The ladder looked rather flimsy to me, but she was excited.

'Steve,' she said ingratiatingly, 'would you be a starter?'

She was nodding at the ceiling, in the direction of the hall. I got it. I picked up the ladder and we congregated below the attic aperture.

'No looking up my trouser legs, girls,' I said, Sue spluttering and burping and rushing off again to the bathroom.

'She's my oldest friend,' Jenny said as she steadied the wobbly ladder.

On its top rung I could just reach the trapdoor. I pushed and it hardly moved. I pushed harder, feeling it give. I told Jenny to hold steady and heaved as hard as I could, the door flinging back into the attic and showering me with dust. I turned my head away and sneezed violently, jumping to avoid falling off the ladder. I had a sequence of sneezes, doubled over, my eyes streaming. 'Bless you,' Jenny said, 'but forget it.'

'Not on your nelly,' I said, remembering the last time I said that, to Melissa. Everything reminded me of her. I rubbed my eyes and remounted the ladder, telling Jenny there was no way I was stopping now. I felt around with my hands and got a grip, hauling myself up and into the gap. Trying not to disturb too much dust, I leaned down and asked for the torch. Sue was looking up, asking if there were spiders and rats.

'Thousands of them,' I said. 'Katipos in my hair, the old *rattus norvegicus* streaming out of the rafters — they must think I'm the Pied Piper.'

Sue had another giggling fit, but this time did not have to retreat to the bathroom. The front door was flung open, Jenny startled into knocking over the ladder. Jasper was there with the tucker steaming. I had a quick glance about and said the missing furniture was here, just about anything and everything but the old kitchen sink. I didn't wait for the ladder, lowering myself on hand holds and then dropping to the floor. Sue stopped me toppling over. We congregated around the opened newspaper on the kitchen bench and demolished the oysters and chips, washed down with the third bottle. I asked Jasper was he ready to claim his attic rental inheritance.

'Kin oath,' he said, eyes glinting behind his thick frames.

Just as well we were reasonably fit and not subject to sinus collapsus, we did a lot of sneezing as we manoeuvred bentwoods and easy chairs and a damnably heavy carved wooden chest through the gap. The kitchen table had the advantage of coming apart in segments and having one leg missing, otherwise I doubt it was going to get out of there. The paintings were something else, old Victorian or Edwardian portraits in oils of sombre bearded gents and the kind of wild stag-at-bay landscapes that Ernie would have liked.

The result of our labours was that there was, with the aid of the broken bricks we found under the house and the lip of the pantry, a usable dining table and six wobbly chairs that could be improved with a crescent spanner and some penetrating oil. The three moth-eaten and mustard-coloured easy chairs would need a lot of cushions to avoid being sprung when you sat on them, and the chest could serve as a coffee table. Jenny opened its brass-clasped lid to reveal part of the weight problem, heavy lamps packed in greased fabric. When we assembled them, there was enough kerosene to give us a shadowy amber aura from the two cracked but intact glass shades.

The problem of where to sleep in this fridge of a house was resolved generously by Jasper and Jenny sharing their bed. Its springs were well and truly gone and we were as bent as the chairs and awfully stiff when dawn arrived. I had a bit of a headache and a very prominent erection which Sue was pressed against, but fortunately we had remained clothed. I left her giggling as I staggered to the bathroom. I might have momentarily forgotten Melissa.

Melissa's painting was my lifeline and threatening to be my death-line. I spent too much time staring blankly at the clown. The more I stared gormlessly at the clown, the more paranoid I got. Was Melissa sending me a message here? I was the clown, sprouting a hopelessly romantic flower from my hand. Was my optimism merely asinine? What grounds did I have for it? Wasn't the world about to be blown up? And I was optimistic? The optimism of the insane. I was in denial of reality. Was the cool blue witch so pessimistic? She had a halo of stars round her head, which had to relate to Melissa's astrological beliefs. So I was the clown, she was the elegant seer – or should that be seeress? No question, I was losing it. Meanwhile, my study load piled up.

I knew it was pathetic, meditating at the altar of this fancifully enigmatic painting. It was enough to make me gloomy. I should dump it, or at least put it in a drawer.

I couldn't bring myself to act. I did not even turn the painting up the other way, as a true reflection of my black mood. I was like I was after Mum died, stunned and unable to muster the energy to do anything. I no longer bothered with Elvis, I never played *Swan Lake*, I put the increasingly threatening letters from the World Record Club under my bed.

I thought the controversial *Lady Chatterley's Lover* would be a distraction. It was a solemn and dispassionate lecture on the importance of sex as a necessary nuisance. Like all the allegedly rude books, such as *The Decameron*, it was a fizzer. No, there was one exception, *God's Little Acre*. God and sex and even the King were out of my life at present, and indeed, any and every, joyful possibility. The only relief was wandering the beach, flicking shells that never soared, aimlessly walking to Pencarrow Lighthouse and back.

Dad asked me what was wrong. I grunted that it was just work pressure, something he could relate to. There was nothing I could say to him about how much I missed Melissa, how much I craved her, how I was implicated by my own irresponsible act in the creation and murder of our child. I hardly saw Jasper and Jenny, and when I did I simply felt spurts of envy for what they had, for what I had and lost through my own grievous fault, through my one euphoric, ecstatic spurt. I was unable to stop wallowing in self-pity.

It was becoming increasingly difficult for me to relate to Irene and her experimental cuisine. The final straw was the meal we were having together for once, a Saturday. There was some occasion they were going on to in Dad's new Mercedes, with him apparently enjoying a dispensation from overseas car purchases he kept harping on about Walter Nash denying the country. The occasion did not involve dinner, so they were eating at our place before leaving. They served wine, just a glass Dad said he would allow himself, he could not otherwise do justice to her superb gourmet steak. Unctuous, gooey, oleaginous, eager Dad, into his second adolescence while I was still in my first.

I was looking forward to this apparently normal steak, after some of Irene's shockers, such as the dog's dinner she called moose-arka and I would have called moose excrement. Then there was the truly appalling steak tartare. I'd thought she meant cream of tartar Mum used with meringues. I'd assumed in my clownish innocence that Irene was dressing up a steak with a cream of tartar-flavoured garnish which I could if need be surreptitiously remove. Instead, it was raw mince with an egg yolk in it. I'd seen plenty of raw steaks at the Gear, but I never in my wildest dreams would have imagined people eating one. It seemed totally unhygienic. My stomach was still heaving at the thought of that.

This steak smelled and looked as it should, a fine, fat, nicely braised fillet, no sign of anything suspicious. The odd smell I foolishly attributed to the sauce on the chokos, and I wasn't going near them. I was actually trying to be positive as I cut a portion and stuffed it in my mouth, realising as I did that there was something like snot attached to its innards. It came straight back up, all over the white tablecloth, and I shot straight to the bathroom, Irene whingeing to Dad she thought I liked oysters. Well, yes, but not with flippin steak.

So, the cuisine side was not working for me. The day I blundered into the kitchen and caught them snogging was more of a shock than it should have been. I retreated hastily, telling myself I had no right to object, Dad was entitled to a relationship, it was more than two years since Mum died. Logic and reason are all very well, but the image haunted me. I knew I was being puerile and immature, but it did not stop me feeling this way.

Things were getting to the stage where I thought I was going to explode, and most likely Irene would be the target. I was not literally going to lash out at her, like I had at her son, perish the thought. I found it hard to get my head around Irene getting to Dad's heart through his stomach, an alarming image in and of itself. I found it even harder to reconcile Irene with her son, with his secret other life revealed to me in a snapshot, a seedy and incredibly rash act which seemed to have no impact on his daylight life. Dr Gull and Mr Hyde. He rang every few days. I gave him monosyllabic replies, invariably a negative to his enquiry about whether Jasper was planning anything.

I should have challenged him over this obsession with a totally harmless person – well, a person who was no meaningful threat to law and order. I didn't because I did not want to talk to Gull. Let him think what he liked, put me down as being simply surly and drenched in misery over Melissa's disappearance, which was 100 per cent true. He knew I wanted to know where she was, he had volunteered nothing. It was a Mexican stand-off.

I was stuck in this groove and I could not lift the record out of it. I was continuing to go to Training College, university and section. I had a section at Muritai School, but home base gave me neither pleasure nor pain, I was indifferent. Well, not to the kids. I got them writing their own free verse. The teacher was so pleased she said it was good enough to publish, and indeed she did publish it, cyclostyled and stapled pamphlets with a stick drawing by one of the kids on the cover. Her praise meant nothing to me.

The only positive I got out of the section was the day an old lady called Nelle Scanlan came to talk to the kids. The teacher told me before she arrived that she was a New Zealand novelist who had written four novels about Pencarrow, but nothing to do with the lighthouse. I was only vaguely interested, but she held the kids' attention with her strong and simple advice to carry a notebook everywhere with you and describe what you see and things that interest you. She told them it was a good habit to get into to write every day, whether it was a diary or a notebook, and you got the reward later of reading your notes and remembering what interested you.

I may not have taken the advice if I had not passed the stationer's later and saw these palm-sized little notebooks with a pencil which fitted in the ring-binder. I bought one and began jotting down notes and thoughts and it became quite addictive. I suppose it was a distraction. It didn't of course lift the burden of living at home. If anything, the tension increased because I was at work a few hundred yards away and only got out of Eastbourne when I went in to lectures. The section ended, the tension did not.

Jasper provided the solution. As usual, he sidled up behind me at Assembly, following a mind-numbing lecture on maths by some visiting American. They were off to Nelson on their honeymoon which, he said in his fish-eyed, lugubrious fashion, was a Meet the Parents exercise for him. Would I consider looking after the flat while he did the necessary?

Is the Pope a Catholic?! Too farkin right, mate. I could have kissed him, if I was that way inclined. I was like a rat up an incandescent drainpipe, scrabbling for purchase on this sudden solution to my entrapment. I almost choked on my own words asking him if we could go around to the flat right now.

The flat had been transformed in the few weeks since I had helped clear out its attic. The sitting room was like the Eastbourne classroom during art lessons, each of the walls a different colour, red, blue and green. He said Jenny and Sue had modified the heavy and faded blue velvet curtains he informed me with absurd pride he had scored at the St V de P shop. He had gone to the Sallies for pots and pans and crockery and cutlery. Talk about puffed with his own performance. He had what I would have called, if I wanted to be nasty, a bourgeois strut.

I guess he had reason to, having also acquired basic second-hand tools and nailed into place the missing table leg he located under the house. The loud whirring motor that was periodically shuddering to a stop was one of those old cream fridges with the huge sprung handle that had the heft of a possum trap. As he informed me it came from the Bargain Basement in Newtown, I checked the contents, which were a pound of butter, two bottles of milk and a pack of saveloys.

Next task, he said, was stripping the hall wallpaper, or painting over it. Jasper has surely been bitten by the happy family bug. Jenny was bringing more stuff, he said as he led me across the hall, now hung with the heavily-framed Victorian gents. He wanted me to see the army-issue blankets on their double bed and the single one I rescued from the basement, which he had put in the spare bedroom, not the one designated for their 'littlie'. Next to the collapsed single was a somewhat battered blond chest of drawers, above it a mirror free of the spotting of the wardrobe ones. In the sitting room he flung himself down on the huge old green velvet roll-arm sofa, arms splayed across its back. A cloud of dust and some squeaky springs suggested it was well past its prime.

'Virtually a spare bed,' I suggested.

'All yours for a few weeks,' he said.

I was back for dinner with Jenny and Sue, cooked by the born-again bourgeois

Jasper: crumbed saveloys, fish cakes, chopped cabbage with caraway seeds. Just to prove he was still unconventional, Jasper then served Chinese coconut sweetmeats. Sue said she'd have to come round and cook for me when they were away. I replied without conviction that would be great. She stayed the night, I headed off to the cable car.

When I told Dad about this temporary flat, the relief on his face was palpable. He asked if he could come visit. Why not? He said he could help me move. Naturally I waited three days until Jasper and Jenny were gone before I took Dad up on his offer.

He drove me there with a suitcase containing my meagre supply of clothes and the books I could not live without, like Donne and Yeats and *The Catcher in the Rye*. I don't imagine many less salubrious flats have been moved into from a Mercedes. I thought it best to get him to leave the car at the top of the street.

If he was shocked, he disguised it, saying that it was very handy to college and university. I said it was spartan before he could. He asked me if I'd used the wok, I told him not yet. I didn't say I might never, that it was forever associated in my mind with Melissa. He suggested we could stock up on a few supplies, which we did at the Four Square up the road in the village. Macaroni, rice, cans of Irish stew, baked beans and spaghetti, fruit salad and peaches, a slab of cheese, a loaf of wholemeal, and some fresh fruit and veg from the fruiterer next door. We crossed to the butcher, where I got shoulder chops and steak and half a dozen sausages. I pointed out Alan's fish and chip shop as a vital ingredient.

'Fridays anyway,' he said, as he dipped into his wallet and handed me a fifty pound note.

'Neat,' I said. He had no idea how neat. Now I could clear my debt to Gull and then he could do what he liked, without any required help from me.

The first night was quite strange, my minimalist occupation of a house to myself, alas and alack. The feed of Alan's fish and chips initially cheered me up, but with no beer to wash them down, the meal lay like a grease trap in my stomach.

This was only part of the reason I had trouble sleeping. There were screeching tyres and squealing brakes, Devon Street being a popular shortcut for taxi drivers and students on motorbikes and jalopies the likes of Model A's, Morrie Minors, VWs and Austin A35s. The single bed was another reason I couldn't sleep, its springs were bumping the floor. And then there were the damp and freezing conditions in this big old bungalow with high studs on the wrong side of the hill for much sun. Biggest reason of all, no Melissa.

I got up at some ungodly hour and walked with the blanket draped over my pyjamas around the place, switching on lights and checking the door was latched. I could have lit the single gas fire in the sitting room, but I'd not handled gas before and was not sure if you should leave it on when you left the room. All that peeling wallpaper, the ancient wood floors, the place would go up like a municipal bonfire on Guy Fawkes night. The disapproving eyes of the old gents seemed to follow me down the hall. They would be the first things to go if it was my flat. I put all this down in my notebook.

Next evening I nervously lit a hob and the oven and stepped back from a feared explosion, before proceeding to grill chops and boil spuds on my first foray into gas cooking. It was going okay when there was a tap on the door. It was Sue, holding a bottle of Cresta Doré, a nervous grin on her face, damp and framed in a sheepskin hood sprinkled with drops.

'No phone so I couldn't ring you,' she said. 'Hope you don't mind?'

I assured her she was welcome, wishing the coat did not remind me of Melissa.

'Smells nice,' she said. 'As promised, I was coming round to offer to cook.'

'You can help me eat.'

'If you let me do the next meal,' she said, shrugging off her coat. Underneath a loose blue sack dress with decidedly loose movement beneath it.

The smell alerted us both to my loss of concentration. I wasn't used to the extra speed of gas cooking. We rushed the stove, bumping against each other as we flung the door open and were engulfed in a horizontal eruption of black steaming smoke. Jasper's second-hand tea towel was no real protection as I pulled out the grill tray, dropping it on the floor, burnt chops and hot fat falling where they may. We jumped backwards, me yowling at the pain in my hands.

'Quick,' Sue said, pushing me to the sink. 'Under the cold tap.'

I needed no encouragement.

'Got any Ungvita? No? Hang on.'

She got the butter out of the fridge, retrieved the dropped tea towel, dabbed my palms dry and smoothed butter on them.

'Butter makes better?'

I managed a smile at her ditsy remark, said I hoped so. She directed me to the dining table, told me to stay put while she sorted things. I liked her priority, first opening the wine, which was not easy for her. She was using the only available opener, the nasty combo implement with the vicious little perforating knife likely to slice into the webbing between thumb and forefinger and cause instant paralysis and death before the can was even penetrated. The flimsy wire corkscrew lodged awkwardly inside the metal handle, with the familiar result of her first attempt removing fragments off the top of the cork. I would have offered to do it if my hands were not on fire. Her second effort removed more bits of cork.

'Push it in,' I suggested, just as she did.

'Great minds, eh?' she giggled, pouring two generous measures into the peanut butter glasses. We clinked glass, me slopping some of it on my chin from not having great grip.

'I could get you a straw.'

We both laughed. She checked the grill with her fingers, then picked it up and put it in the dish, replaced the chops and put my burnt offering back in the oven. She checked the temperature, then the shaking aluminium pot of boiling spuds, hastily dropping the lid back.

'Don't want two casualties, eh?' she said as she pushed at the stiff window above the stove. She forced it open, put the arm on the longest notch, held up the tea towel and waved away the lingering smoke. She pretended to tie the tea towel round her head, mock-curtsied, asked me if I thought it fitted the busy little hausfrau.

'Perfect,' I said, sipping the last of my drink.

'You like?'

I said I did, surprised that it was true, given my previous experience with still wine. This was not the kerosene quality of the altar wine, nor as sickly sweet. I accepted another.

I had to answer in the negative in regard to any greens. She said this would be fine, and it was. She mashed the spuds with butter and plenty of salt and pepper. She served up the humble meal on the decidedly humble and mismatched collection of chipped plates, mine yellow with a flower border, hers a venerable white. She asked if I wanted her to cut up the chops.

'Nah,' I said, picking one up by the sides of my hands and hoeing in.

'Like a barbecue, eh?'

I could only nod vigorously, my mouth full of good, plain, burnt meat.

The wine and the main and only course finished at the same time.

'Liquid pudding,' Sue said as she polished off the last of her second glass.

'That was great. Wish I'd brought another. Leave the dishes to me.'

Trust Jasper to have acquired the oldest, least effective of all washing-up materials, one of those wire cages on a wire arm with a yellow slab of Sunlight soap in it. Sue poked in the Zip heater above the sink and it soon whistled. She used the potato pot to pour boiling water into the sink, frothed it up and took care of the dishes. The grill was tricky with a distressed remnant of a pot-scouring pad, but she got the gunk off and declared it fit for use.

'No tea or coffee,' she said, drying her hands on the damp tea towel that had just dried the dishes. 'What do we do for afters?'

'Raid the liquor cabinet?'

I was joking, but she raised an approving finger. Another new furniture edition to the sitting room was what I had assumed was one of those old 78 turntable boxes, a chest-high little chalet of dark, peeling varnish. Sue knew better. She lifted the lid. It may once have been the repository for a turntable, now it was home to a goodly array of bottles.

'Jenny's tiptop on the hospitality,' she said. 'Even if it's now off-limits for her.'

She lifted bottles until she approved a bottle of brandy.

'Just what the doctor ordered for burns,' she said, waggling the half-full bottle, liquid light glinting courtesy of the bare bulb gracing the rose bowl overhead. She rinsed the glassware and poured two stiff drinks.

'Bottoms up,' she giggled.

'God,' I exclaimed, my throat now on fire too.

She grinned. 'Practice makes perfect,' she said, draining her glass. 'Shall we find a more comfortable seat?'

'We can try,' I said, getting up. 'The kero lamps might improve things.'

'Let me,' she said, taking one of the mighty brass monsters from my fumbling hands.

She removed the outer rippled amber bowl and the clear tulip glass, shook the brass bowl to check for kero and raised the wicks. She tested the edges, went to the kitchen for the mega box of Vesta matches, got the lamps underway. She extinguished the overhead bulb and eyed the fireplace, asked me for the torch.

'No fun without a fire, eh?'

It was damp and freezing, I could already vouch for that. I did point out there was the small gas heater.

'Not the same, is it?' she said, heading outside with the torch. I could hear her knocking stuff about in the basement. I thought she was frightened of spiders, so the brandy would have provided Dutch courage. She staggered back in with an armful of what looked like broken floor or wall boards, the tongue and groove stuff. She dumped it by the fireplace and went back for another load. She found old newspapers under the sink and set about lighting the fire.

I sat on the sofa watching. You could see the fireplace had been used recently, presumably by Jasper and Jenny. If possums had been in chimney residence, they would be gone by now. We'd never had open fires, no real call for them in Auckland. Well, not in our St Heliers villa, which had wall-to-wall carpet and central heating.

Sue got the fire going, blowing on the huge pile of paper until it was roaring up the chimney. I prayed silently she had not set fire to it. She didn't seem concerned, sitting cross-legged on the threadbare strip of carpet, feeding in bits of wood. I was glad she was not facing me, given how floaty her dress was.

Satisfied, she spun round to face me. My gaze stayed on her face, which was glowing from the fire. The flickering light from the lamps and the fire highlighted her cheek bones and the heart shape I had not previously noticed.

'Time for a freshen up,' she said, rising in a graceful pivot without needing to use her hands. She poured what was left in the bottle into our glasses.

'May the best of your yesterdays,' she said, sitting on the sofa next to me, tapping my glass, 'be the best of your tomorrows.'

'Where'd that come from?'

'Me dad. He likes his sayings.'

'Know what you mean,' I said, sipping with the glass held by the sides of my hands, asking her if she minded if I noted this down. She didn't, so long as I wasn't putting in names. I promised not to, saying it was going to take me all my time with my fingers to get it down. As I laboriously entered the quote, I asked her where she came from, adding I didn't know a thing about her.

'Fair enough,' she said. She told me she was a local born and bred, the family home was just round the corner in Rawhiti Terrace. She'd seen me to-ing and fro-ing in Glasgow Street and on the cable car. She didn't mention seeing me with Melissa, but she must have. She said her parents were in Sydney at the moment, opening an outlet for their leather goods. One or other of them rang every week.

I asked what the story was with the leather. She said it was the full range you'd find in Kirks, ladies' handbags, wallets, gloves, you name it. All started with her dad practising what was preached by his former boss at Industries and Commerce, Dr Bill Sutch. You know the thing, Switzerland of the South Pacific, need to diversify, added value to our primary produce.

'No shortage of cows and sheep,' I said, the image of Melissa in her sheepskin coat surfacing unbidden.

'Exactly,' she said. 'I'm doing a commerce degree, following in the parental footsteps.'

'Any brothers or sisters?'

'You fishing?'

I protested my innocence, which happened to be true. She gave me a tipped head look. Once someone suspects you of something, proving yourself innocent is tricky.

'Mikey, my older brother, he supposedly holds the fort. Bit of a pain, actually. But he's the arty one, takes after mum. She designs a lot of our lines. He's studying art history. What a con.'

'So how do you know Jenny?'

She looked at me, surprised. 'She didn't tell you she lives with us? Oh, no reason why she should, I s'pose. We were same year at Queen Maggots.'

Now it was my turn to look surprised. 'Queen Margarets? I thought Jenny was

Catholic?'

'Her dad was. But when they split, that was the end of the left-footing. Her stepfather's big in Dalgety's. He wouldn't be big on all this.'

She paused, indicated with her hand the flat was what she meant. She sipped her drink, staring at the fire. 'Jenny doesn't get on with him. Misses her dad.'

'So this is a protest. Jasper, marriage.'

She stared at me. 'No.'

I said I was sorry to pry, I was just interested, which sounded feeble.

'They clicked,' she said.

'Love's old sweet song?'

'Something like that. Well, I'd best leave you to it.'

She was on her feet. 'Make sure the fire's out before you hit the hay,' she said, putting her unfinished drink on the mantelpiece. 'Don't get up, you need to watch those hands.'

She collected her coat and was gone, the door shutting, leaving me looking at the bits of smouldering wood. Not much to worry about there. I wish I could put out the fire inside me. For most of this evening I had. It was nice having Sue here, she was good fun; the problem was, I wasn't. I went to bed and pulled the army blanket over my head, trying to shut out the noise of vehicles, the sound inside my head.

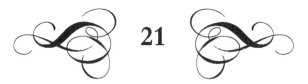

B anging on the door belted me out of a vile, sleepless night bent like a banana by the stuffed springs. I groaned I was on my way and rolled on to my knees, sure I'd slipped several discs. I levered myself upright on one knee and staggered to the door. Sue giggled, said she was not coming in, didn't want to add to my obvious distress. She had clearly slept well, her cheeks were rosy as Cox's orange pippins. She was dancing from one foot to the other, perky as a parrot in a sack of grass seed. I asked her a tad grumpily what time she called this.

'Time you were up and about,' she said gaily, teeth like a toothpaste ad, everything about her fresh and fizzing, everything I was not. She was saying she was sorry she had disappeared abruptly last night, it was just that Mikey had told her to be back for an announcement. As usual, it was no big deal, he was the original drama queen. He was off skiing for a week. The coast was clear so she was cooking at her place, if I could make it by six? It was the least she could do, given the injuries I had incurred. Her left eyebrow was raised. I said fine.

'Must dash.'

And she did. No question she brought a breath of fresh and indeed icy air. I hastily shut the door, endeavoured to slap my arms around my pyjamas to get circulation going and stiffness eased. The shower was on go-slow but at least the trickle of water was hot. I bathed in small increments of back and body, not getting much of a lather out of the other half of the Sunlight soap bar. First purchase today was going to be Knights Castile.

It was a bitterly cold day, so on my new section at Karori I took Phys-Ed in the school hall. Thank God it was not me having to do cartwheels on the mats and dive over half a dozen kneeling pupils. As it was, the overweight lad crashed into the middle group, provoking an all-out fist fight. I was grateful for several things. The separation of the sexes meant it was not girls Pork Barrel burled into and no teacher observer was present to witness my total lack of control. We flagged the vaulting horse, my hands and back were not up to my role of catching the failed vaulters before they crashed off the mat on to the hard wood floor.

The afternoon was easier, getting the kids painting the poem 'Ozymandias'. They could do what they liked with crayon, chalk, pastel, paint, linocuts, dyes and inks. A glorious mess and no rules, the kids loved it, even the tough crew at the back of the class.

Miss Teesdale wanted to talk teaching technique in the staffroom for half an hour after school. I warmed up with Milo and coconut macaroons while she gabbled. I passed on the Lit Club reading of candidates for the end-of-year poetry publication, none of mine up to scratch, and went instead to *Our Man in Havana*, which was hilarious. I caught the cable car and got to Sue's house just after six with several tins of South African guavas, the theory that if she was into experimental main courses, the dessert was guaranteed to please.

It was a massive white stucco house, all the more imposing as you entered below and climbed a winding concrete path lined with hibernating roses, before ascending a broad set of a dozen steps to the colonnaded entrance. The tinkling chimes sounding somewhere behind the massive blond wooden door provoked a flash of Melissa's bangles. The door was opened by Sue in a short and revealing black dress and cute cotton apron with frilled edging, a replica of what Liz wore at the Flynn function. Did this mean another National Party laager?

I told her I was sorry I had not walked her back last night and she looked nice, which was true, her hair had been artfully arranged and reminiscent of the cover of my World Record Club free introductory offer, a graceful ballerina with a swan-feather band around her head. The inward wings of blonde hair emphasised her heart-shaped face. The make-up was the invisible look of a Max Factor ad. Tiny diamond studs in her ears, very understated.

'Thank you, kind sir,' she said, accepting the brown bag I thrust at her. 'I'm a big girl, no need for an escort.' She peeked inside the bag. 'Goody gumdrops. My fave fruit. It'll go with the mousse. Come in before we both catch cold.'

No chance of that, the place was toasty warm and white as the Hollywood idea of heaven, white wallpaper, thick white carpet, several chandeliers maximising white light. As she took my duffel coat and hung it in an annexe behind the door, I looked down the length of a cricket pitch at the huge, gilt-framed mirror redistributing more light. The white wooden stand in front of it hosted a pottery vase the shape of a gigantic rough white coin, toitoi fronds arcing out of it like the makings for a Red Indian headdress.

'Groovy,' I said, following her through the glossy white mullioned set of open French doors into a room the size of the school hall and decidedly more comfortable. The kids wouldn't need rugs to cartwheel across the wall-to-wall merino to the biggest expanse of window I had seen in a house. Allowing for the sides occupied by tall white drapes, there was still most of the city and harbour laid out below. 'Double groovy,' I added.

'Glad you like it,' she said, her black high heels sinking through the thick pile on her way past a dining table the colour of peanut butter and big enough to seat a rugby

team and three reserves. Big as it was, the table was a small part of an open-plan sitting/
dining room as expansive as the view. My attention tracked past the floor-to-ceiling
white bookcase with tidily recessed contents to something I did not know existed, a
white baby grand piano. It occupied the acreage beyond a suite of white linen chairs
and couch and plastic-looking coffee table. A cello resting next to the piano was the
not-white item in the room.

While I pondered superlatives, she breezed through more interior French doors
into a kitchen, where her stiletto heels made staccato taps. She dropped the cans of
guavas with a solid clunk on some kind of white granite bench that ran the length
of the room. Sequences of white cupboards above the bench sported miniature
versions of the mullioned French doors. I was a country cousin in my sweater, cords
and desert boots.

My state was not really helped by the wonderful warmth I sourced to a perfect
array of logs glowing in a pristine grate set in a huge white mantelpiece centred
against the back wall. There was a faint smell of gas. Were the logs artificial? No
doubt the heating amplified the delirious meaty smells emanating from the kitchen.
I was drooling like Pavlov's dogs. I switched to looking at the large exotic landscape
hanging above the fireplace.

'That a Gauguin?' I asked, by way of deflecting my awareness of my uncouth gear.

Sue swivelled with a squeak on the chequerboard of white and black marble
flooring.

'It's a Paul Olds. Isn't he a lecturer at your college?'

I continued to stare at the semi-abstract scene, recognisable I could now see as
New Zealand high country without the painting-by-numbers gloss of the ghastly
Kelliher Art entries. I felt the flush spread from my ears down my neck.

'Ah, yeh,' I managed. 'We call them masters.'

'As in schoolmaster?'

'I s'pose.' There must be another diversion I could muster, one not fraught with
the further adventures of Mr Hick in Blunderland.

She had been busy in the double-door fridge, another first for me. As was the
dining table, a magnificent scalloped structure with a surface that you could see
yourself through the shine, its centrepiece an elaborate silver candelabra sprouting six
tall white candles. There were high-backed dining chairs at either end, the surface in
front of them laid with large wine goblets and heavy silver on painted cork mats that
were too fancy to put hot plates on. The mats featured purple and orange landscapes
which looked like Namatjira paintings, but I wasn't going to risk saying that.

'Reminds me of the dining scene in *Citizen Cane*.'

'The diff being we'll have more to say than they did. You like serious movies?'

I cautiously said I did.

'We could take in the Film Society if you like?'

I said that would be a groove.

'Here we are,' she said, carrying in an oval platter. 'Finger food. Grab a plate and napkin from the sideboard.'

The sideboard was a partner for the table, with a backboard inlaid with an oblong mirror with bevelled edges. She set the bright green and red king plate down on the sideboard. Not a sausage or asparagus roll in sight. There were short celery sticks filled with yellow gunk, tidy little parcels of some green leaf alarmingly reminiscent of turds, desiccated bits of possibly fish on triangles of crustless toast, moist wee mushrooms, big grey-green olives, stuffed green olives, small glistening black olives, toothpick rolls of a meat that might be underdone ham. I asked her what the green things were. She said they were vine leaves stuffed with rice and beef and garlic and such.

'Actually, I'm not sure of all the ingredients,' she said with a giggle. 'I cheated, got most of it from the Dixon Deli. Hoe in. You like white or red wine?'

I told her I enjoyed the last white we had. She said she could do better than that. She returned to the fridge, bringing back a bottle, holding it at an angle for my inspection.

'Pouilly fuissé.'

'You know it?'

'I do French at Vic. Looks grouse.'

It was, a clean and refreshing bite, delicate, oaky, a taste a million grapes removed from the last white, and that had been good. This wine breathed the distilled fragrance of the sweet peas Mum grew every year and the memory of her gooseberry fool.

'Fantabulous,' I said.

'Dad gets cases of it. You going to try the vine leaves?'

I did. Yummy. I had another. She asked if I liked eel. I guessed correctly the smoked fish on toast and polished off a mouthful quickly, then realised how nice it was and had another.

'I'll be full at this rate,' I said, looking around the room at several more large oils very different from that of Master Olds. One featured lots of yellow and green geometric intersections like Matisse, another was a mad-looking red cardinal too modern to be from the Velasquez school, trapped in some kind of cage. I steered away from any more guesswork.

'Your parents like art, obviously.'

She nodded, said it was mostly mum's choices. She suggested I go for a wander while she attended to the main course. With her out of sight I sniffed the celery filling, cheesy. I had one of those and then another. Oh, the bounty of the rich man's table. I tried the ham and gagged on raw meat, gulped wine, coughed to clear the passageways, and in the process I spilled most of the wine over my sweater.

'Fuck,' I said, my voice coming out far louder than intended.

Sue appeared, saw the problem, rubbed her hands on her apron and patted at my wet tummy.

'Still a bit fingers and thumbs,' I said.

'You can't eat in that. Follow me.'

We went back out and down the mirror pitch, right into a bedroom which had posters of masked skiers launching into alpine space and swooping down icy runways, a red Maserati, a nude Brigitte Bardot on her stomach by a clothesline, her bottom prominent. I think she was smiling at the camera, I didn't risk lingering on her as Sue walked past the double bed with black satin sheets in a tangle and slid the mirror door aside. There was row after row of trousers. She slung the door the other way to reveal row after row of mainly dark-coloured shirts. She flipped through them, turned to check me, told me to get the sweater off. She handed me a sage-green corduroy shirt.

'He never wears this,' she said. 'Should be a close enough fit.'

She checked my chest, smiled and took my sweater.

'Bathroom's second on left, if you need it.'

She was gone. The shirt had a small zip and a high neck. I pulled it on, zipped it up, tucked in the ends, belted up and looked in the mirror. Prat. The shirt was an XOS that looked like a cowboy poncho on my weedy frame.

Sue stuck her head round the door. 'Nice.' She moved across, eyeing me in the mirror.

'Turn round.'

She unzipped the top, turned down the collar, swung me back to face myself.

'Better?'

I agreed it looked better unzipped. She said the main course was ready and no need to worry about the wine, she'd opened it.

There was a thick fibrous mat where the candelabra had been, on it a lime yellow casserole, beside it a cream tureen of steaming spuds with butter sliding over them and sprigs of parsley, a Matisse-bright plate with two divisions, one containing shiny fingers of carrot, the other whole green beans speckled with bits of white stuff. Beside all this splendid looking fodder was a bottle of red wine, a change of goblets.

'Would you pour,' she said. 'I'll serve the *boeuf bourguignonne*. Hope you like garlic.' I said I did, not sure if that was true.

Big white plates heaped with plenty of everything, the chunks of meat in rich gravy in which I could see bacon, onions and mushrooms. I followed her lead removing a large white linen napkin from a wooden ring the same colour as the table, saying this looked like the dainty dishes you set before a king.

'Proof in the eating, eh? Chin chin.' She raised her glass, we sipped, me careful not to spill a drop. It was my first taste of Chateaux Margaux.

'Quite an upgrade from my effort,' I said.

'Cheers, Citizen,' she said. 'Get stuck in.'

I said it was the best meal I had eaten.

'You are incredible,' I added for good measure.

'Thank you, sweet sir. There's still the *mousse au chocolat* to come. And your guavas. Helps to have done a cordon bleu course. Dad's wines don't hurt either.'

'Reckon,' I said.

We heard the door open, Sue looked startled.

A man the size of Lofty Blomfield lurched in, his peanut-shaped head too small for his frame. He was having trouble shrugging out of a bulky fire engine-red windcheater. His black tracksuit was speckled with mud, what looked like cricket boots coated in the stuff, his dirty prints all over the carpet as he wove in an increasingly agitated circle. The arms were caught in the classic Diddle Diddle Dumpling bind, except it was not shoes but each sleeve pulled halfway out. He was trapped in a straightjacket of his own making. At which point he noticed me, did a double take.

'Fuck are you?' he slurred. 'Fuck you wearing my shirt?'

Sue was on her feet. 'Calm down, Mikey. This is Steve Marr, a friend.'

His eyes were the colour of gooseberries, and they were protruding, as if they had been injected with fluid. His face was turning the colour of his jacket.

'Take my fuckin shirt off an' take a hike, friend,' he snarled, advancing in lolloping fashion towards me, shaking and pulling at his trapped sleeves. Sue intercepted him, as I stood up. He bumped her aside with his hip and got up close, alcoholic fumes and testosterone-laced spittle spraying over me.

'You fuckin deaf? Friend?'

'Mikey!' she yelled, pushing at him. 'Leave him alone. Get your filthy shoes off and get under a shower. Preferably a cold one.'

He stared at me, blinking to clear his vision but failing to achieve the impact his words sought. He got one hand free as he did a three-point tack to face his sister. 'Gerrim fuckin outta here.' His free arm allowed him to manoeuvre back to me, a fist shaking under my nose. 'You here when I return, I'll sling ya out your arse. Geddit?'

He stomped more mud as he released his other arm, tossed the offending jacket on the floor and left.

Sue took my arm. 'I apologise for my pig brother. Looks like he never got to the Chateau. That's no excuse.'

'He's spoiled your dinner.'

'Not to worry. Might be best if we shot through.'

'You don't have to.'

Sue laughed mirthlessly. 'Yes I do. Let's doggy-bag dessert and get out with the wine. Come on.'

'What about his shirt?'

'Keep it. Your sweater's in the wash.'

Sue put me in charge of the two half-empty bottles sharing space with the guavas. She got two cocktail glasses full of the chocolate pud out of the fridge. She wrapped the glasses in tea towels and placed them in a leather carrier bag the size and not unlike the shape of a seal, adding a large pack of biscuits and several cheeses in greaseproof paper. She grabbed her coat and we left.

This time I descended under the house to dodge spiders and collect more tongue and groove. It was lying in an uneven stack to one side of the damp and smelly dirt floor. I used a foundation as prop, jabbing at the lengths to break them into manageable bits. They were rotten with borer so that was not a problem, though the dust was. The adage about houses surviving by borer holding hands would not apply if this lot had been left *in situ*.

We got a reasonable fire going. With the curtains pulled and the lamps lit, but our coats still on, the place was tolerable, though a far cry from the luxury we had abandoned. The sublime mousse was a warmer in itself. As we crouched over the fire on the two relatively best bentwoods, I spooned in a mouthful, half of it brandy. I told her this was one recipe I had to have.

'Easy as pie,' she laughed. 'Use a *bain-marie* to melt cooking chocolate. Beat in several egg yolks along with a dollop of butter. Whisk the whites and fold them in. Add cognac. Bob's your uncle.'

'Fanny's your aunt,' I said, reaching across the fire to tap together our glasses of claret.

I told her how mighty impressive her home was. She sipped, gave me that perky look over the rim of her glass, another factor in adding to the warming ambience of the flat.

'I'm not fishing,' I protested.

'I will then,' she said. 'You haven't told me much about yourself. What's your dad do?'

I told her he was a banker, adding value to the National Party cause.

'You don't approve?'

I confessed I did not have any interest in politics.

'You and Jasper both?' She had the over-the-rim look again. I asked her what she knew about him. Only what Jenny had told her, and that included our little escapades with poor old Queen Vic, Big Brother America's nuke sub and the All Blacks. It was my turn to ask her if she disapproved. She shook her blonde bob.

'I'm cold,' she said very perkily.

'I'll get some more wood.'

'Bed would be warmer. No?'

'Um,' I said.

'I'm very organised,' she said, standing up, putting her glass on the mantel. She fished in her leather bag and pulled out a packet, waggled it in her fingers. 'Helps having a big brother sometimes.'

I agreed it was cold, my voice perhaps proving it, coming out hoarse and indistinct.

'The single bed?' I said feebly.

'Don't be daft,' she said. 'I warned Jenny we might, if things worked out. Are they?'

I accepted her hand and we were kissing, a faint bell tolling in the back of my head, a bell tolling for Melissa, for my Judas kiss. I closed my eyes and my mind to consequences. I was smothered in her embrace. We moved like some kind of awkward creature, locked in a shuffling embrace sideways by feel into her best friend's marital bed. We soon warmed up. She initiated me in the use of what she called Frenchies.

After the first time, as she lay curled up with her arm across my chest, she started talking about how she had always wanted to put on the kind of dinner party her parents had all the time. They loved entertaining and had all sorts of people, mostly from the Labour and left side of life. This caused a silent start of surprise from me, I thought people who had money voted National.

She didn't appear to notice, wittering on about a lot of the Training College masters among the guests, lecturers at Vic, bureaucrats, politicians, poets, artists, business folk. She grew up with this. Jenny in the last few years got to join the parties. She said there were always one or two guests who had a bit much to drink and made a pass at Jenny.

'You too?'

'Sometimes.'

I told her I was flattered she had only asked the one guest.

'Practice run,' she laughed. 'I've never had the opportunity before. So you'll have to wait for the next time to meet some of your lords and masters, eh?'

I said gallantly I couldn't wait, but hoped her brother would not declare World War Three on me. She promised next time he would be the one to leave, she would make sure there was a quorum of bouncers in the party.

I felt relaxed enough to risk asking her if she knew Heather Anderson at Queen Margarets.

'The legend!' she said. Heather was a few years ahead of them and notorious for getting away with murder. By that she meant that Heather could do no wrong with teachers despite several blatant affairs she had with fathers of other pupils. She had no shame. She had style, a huge appetite for men and the Devil's own gall.

There was a slight stiffening next to me. She asked if I knew Heather. I said she was in the same National Party scene as my father, had called at our place once, but the politics was absolutely of no interest to me.

'What about the lady?'

'None at all,' I lied, keeping my eyes closed. She levered herself up on top of me, insisted I look at her. I did. She gave me a calculating scrutiny, but let it go at that. Soon after she returned to another calculated kind of scrutiny.

Sue was gorgeously energetic through the night and again in the morning, before she slipped out of bed, saying she had to dash and we could catch up later today. I murmured I would love to.

I got up some time later. She had removed the evidence of the night and morning activity. I felt light as a feather and made every effort not to think about whether I had betrayed my feelings for Melissa. I decided in a vague sort of way to play it by ear. Sue was fun and fantastic and totally without any hang-ups.

The pummelling on the door would not be denied. Surely it couldn't be Sue, not unless she had even more energy than I had so far encountered.

It was her brother.

I stepped back hurriedly, but not quick enough to stop his foot in the door. I looked around for something to defend myself, like a bentwood chair. No, that would be matchsticks in milliseconds. I pulled the door open suddenly, the instant plan to dart past his stumbling form and to hell with pyjamas on parade. I bounced back from his brick wall.

'Whoops,' Mikey chuckled. 'G'day.'

I back-pedalled. 'I'll get the shirt.'

'Forget the fucking thing, I never wear it.'

This was no Mexican stand-off, this was Tom trapping Jerry. He was even bigger than I remembered him, probably because he was in a clean tracksuit and in focus.

'Promised Sue I'd drop by and apologise for last night. I'd had a few with the truckie I hitched back with. Farkin Citroens, eh?'

I pretended not to see the hand he held out, it was the size of a softball glove and my hand was in no shape to be redesigned. I asked him to come in, there was a bit of wine left. Bad call, he'd recognise the family product, for sure.

'Nah,' he said, checking one of those watches I'd been offered in the pub, or possibly the real McCoy. 'Gotta do me five miles before lectures. Catch you later.'

I hoped not. Couldn't imagine why he thought we would.

Wrong. Sue was the most organised person I'd met. When I got to school there was a message waiting at reception. We had a date at the Picasso at four.

Over coffee she asked me if I'd seen *Battleship Potemkin*. I hadn't. It was on at the Film Society, in the freezing little room under the public library. There were eight people there. She paid for me as a guest. The seats were better than the bentwoods, but not by much. Sue scraped hers close and snuggled into my duffel, as the lights went down and the film got underway. It was a bad print, flickering and often jerky black and white, no sound, but it was one of the most powerful films I've seen. Even the film breaking with the pram halfway down the Odessa steps didn't spoil it. I told her that I now had an equal favourite film alongside *The Third Man*.

'Grouse,' she said, hugging me. 'You can put that in your notebook. What do you fancy now?'

'You,' I said, hugging her back. 'Let's get f 'n' c, it'll warm us up.'

'It'll do for a start.'

We got fish and chips from Alan and walked back to the flat eating them, our hot breath ballooning into the cold street in front of us like a scene out of the movie. We were passing Rimu Street, a place whose memories I had to suppress, before I even noticed we were taking the long way to the flat.

'Can't use all their wood, eh?' Sue said. 'It's warmer at my place.'

I'd told her about Mikey turning up to apologise. She said with any luck he'd be gone on the night train, to pick up his car at Taumarunui, or the wreckers at Horopito. I said he'd mentioned a Citroen, he had not said it was old. Not so much the age, she said, as the wear and tear it was subjected to.

He was gone, no message. We enjoyed the enormous green-tiled bath and champers, very decadent. I could get used to these mod cons on a regular basis, and I was already used to her non-stop chatter. We adjourned with the bubbly to her bedroom, where framed movie posters took up a lot of wall space. I recognised Audrey Hepburn, Charlie Chaplin, Humphrey Bogart and Ingrid Bergman in *Casablanca* and Marilyn Monroe, whom I was studying leaning sideways in *Bus Stop*.

'Come on,' she said, turning back the pink quilt. 'Drag yourself away from her before you disgrace yourself.'

I presume she meant the naked condition I had in the past envisaged sharing with Marilyn. I assured Sue it was nothing to do with images behind glass. She said the proof was in the pudding, giggling.

When we were sitting up a bit later, I asked her about some of the more arresting movie images. The scowling Japanese warrior ferociously leaping out of his poster with a curved sword raised was, she said, Toshiro Mifune, who was in all Kurosawa's films and they were all masterpieces. I didn't know him or the tormented old man in a film by Bergman called *Wild Strawberries*, but at least I was able to contribute a few remarks about the amazing Bergman masterpiece *The Seventh Seal*, Max Von Sydow as the medieval knight playing chess with Death.

I was able to translate *Les Vacances de M. Hulot*, but that was as far as my knowledge went of this very tall, skinny, peculiar looking chap with a pipe. She said Jacques Tati was a comic genius. I'd not known the French had comics, let alone genius level, but of course I kept that thought to myself. Instead I said the most intriguing image was the couple in the fountain, the lady in the evening dress like an Amazonian Marilyn.

'Dad's just got that for me,' she said, snuggling close. 'Can't wait to see Marcello, he is so scrumptious. It's from his latest, *La Dolce Vita*.'

'The guy looks like Gregory Peck.'

'I know who you're looking at,' she said, prodding me where it would previously have hurt. 'He is my total favourite.'

'You wouldn't be thinking of him?' I countered, given what she was up to under the quilt.

Later again we did our Top Ten movies, both including *Some Like It Hot* and *On the Beach*. She said *The Third Man* was a boy's movie. She talked about the arty films from Russia, France, Italy and India at the Film Society. I hardly felt *Miracle in Milan* warranted me mentioning the one Italian movie I'd seen. We both wanted to see *Sons and Lovers* and she was keen but I was not sure about *The Nun's Story*, even though I loved Audrey Hepburn. I told her Miss Hepburn reminded me of her.

'Flattery will get you everywhere,' she said. 'But it would mean dyeing my hair.'

'Don't change a thing,' I said. 'You're perfect the way you are.'

'That's just the bubbly talking,' she objected. 'Unless you can show you're not all mouth and trousers.'

No question we ended the evening a lot warmer than we started, and not entirely because of the central heating.

 **22**

We were sitting at the breakfast table at the end of the kitchen drinking Sue's drip coffee, the southerly shaking the picture window, when she let out a shriek and rushed from the room. I assumed she was reacting to the good-looking couple getting out of the taxi. The woman was trying to balance several hat boxes and hold on to her beret, her long brown leather coat flapping like a loose sail. He was lifting suitcases over the gutter, glancing up as Sue hurtled down the steps. He dropped the suitcases to catch her.

I hovered like a job applicant by the opening front door. As the mother dropped the hat boxes in the hall and slipped off jacket and watery green silk scarf, Sue peppered her with questions about how the trip was, why they were back early, were they in for dinner, where she got the gorgeous hair-do. The hair was what I was staring at, pure platinum slicked against her head like a chic bathing cup Hollywood's swim queen Esther Williams might have worn, from which a tantalising fringe of stray hairs had escaped at the sides and neck. Cécile Gifford could have been her daughter's film star older sister.

'Ah, Sue-Sue, thees is your young man. Allo, Ste-phan. I am Cécile.'

I was looking at these large violet eyes rimmed in black and before I knew it, she was kissing me on both cheeks. She stepped back to assess me, then advanced again to dab at my cheeks with her thin, lemon-coloured leather gloves.

'Maman,' Sue laughed. 'You've got lipstick on your gloves.'

'Any chance of getting inside?'

'*Mon pauvre* Pe-ter!' Cécile exclaimed, easing me to one side, while Sue hefted one of the suitcases. Cécile's perfume was light and elusive, like you might get from brushing against a lemon tree in flower. 'Leave the boring bag-gage,' she said, waving her arm. 'We must 'ave a drink. Oh, you would not believe, Suzanne, the flight is 'orrendous.'

'Apart from that,' Peter said, consuming my hand in a mercifully soft grip, 'nice to meet you. Stephen, yes? Peter. Drink's not a silly idea, the flight in was a bit dodgy. Come through and let's see what we can rustle up.'

I followed him into the sitting room. He'd shed the thick fawn overcoat, was in a light green suit with brown flecks, one of those check Viyella shirts and a woollen tie that matched his tan Oxfords. He must have been twice his wife's size, the couth original of his son.

It was my first elevenses, my first gin and tonic. We sat on the easy chairs, Cécile bringing out a tray of olives, cheese, crackers and a bowl of mixed nuts, roasted and salted. Peter fixed the drinks and we clinked glasses.

'*Santé,*' Cécile said, her shoes off, sitting with her legs at an elegant angle, as if modelling the sheer stockings and/or her thick turquoise jacket with big green buttons, wide lapels and a high belt and skirt of the same material.

'*A la vôtre,*' I replied.

'*Très bien,*' she said. '*Parlez vous Francais?*'

'*Un petit peu,*' I said, holding my forefinger and thumb close together.

'Steve does French at varsity,' Sue explained.

'You should too, darling,' she said, patting her husband's cheek. '*Non, peut-être.* You 'ave the *oreille d'étain,* the ear of tin, *n'est-ce pas?*'

'When in New Zealand, my sweetness and light,' Peter said sternly, 'we speak New Zild. Don't we, Sue?'

'Boxabirds, daddy-oh.'

'Ooof, you Kiwis. Why did I ever agree to come to thees *place invicillisé?*'

'I can answer that,' Peter said. 'This digger swept you off your pretty Parisian feet.'

Cécile shaped her bright red lips into a moue. '*Oui, cher* Pe-ter. You were so, what we call *jolie laide.*'

Peter turned to Sue. 'What does that mean in Kiwi speak?'

Sue laughed. 'You are beaut looking.'

'Too bloody right, mate,' Cécile said in a terrible effort at our accent, all of us laughing.

Peter offered us a freshen-up, but there were no takers. Cécile wanted to soak away the flight in a very long lavender bath. Sue said we had lectures and, speaking for herself, she needed a clear head.

'Probably for the best,' her father agreed. 'I might end up on my tin ear.'

The three of them went into a quick catch-up, neither parent seemingly surprised at Mikey away on the ski slopes. Cécile exclaimed at the news about Jenny, wanting to know why she would not wait, was it a matter of necessity, where were they living, when could she visit, what did they need? Peter was also trying to get in a few questions edgeways. Sue said they were not back from visiting her family and she would tell them all about it this evening.

We were in the hall when Cécile called out that of course I was coming for dinner. Sue answered in the affirmative, escorting me to the door.

On the way to varsity Sue told me not to worry, her parents were relaxed about me being there. So long as, her mother insisted, she took precautions.

'Those Frenchies,' I said, dodging her swinging fist. I asked her what *jolie laide* meant. She said it was a compliment and left it at that. The words were in the dictionaries I looked up as separate entries, but not together. I asked Frances after French class. She gave me a calculated look. 'Ugly pretty,' she said, just like the dictionaries. I didn't pass this on to Sue, it sounded like half a compliment, half an insult.

It had been a perfect three weeks alone playing house together, before her parents got back. Jenny had sent a postcard from Collingwood, saying that they were honeymooning up large and could we keep an eye on the flat for another few weeks. This we scarcely did, spending all our spare time at her place or the movies, including *The Nun's Story*, which was too worthily Catholic for me to enjoy, saved by Miss Hepburn, and *North by Northwest*, which to my surprise Sue enjoyed as much as I did. After the latter we went to the Embassy Restaurant for fried oysters, proving to myself I actually did like them, exorcising the memory of Irene's oyster ambush in the guise of a good steak.

I rang Dad from Sue's place, telling him the minimum about flat-sitting, saying I had no need of further funds. Mikey rang Sue late one night to say he was busy getting hands-on experience at a Parnell fashion house and hoped all was well. Sue's conclusion was the hands had gone on initially *après* the ski slopes.

My musical education progressed, courtesy of the amazing hi-fi system they had in their library, after I had done a tour of its contents. The novels were French authors such as Balzac, Zola, Voltaire, Jean-Paul Sartre, Albert Camus. There was a slim volume of poems by Baudelaire. The English tomes were non-fiction subjects, history, warfare, economics, *The Hidden Persuaders*, *Seven Years in Tibet*, A.J. Cronin, H.V. Morton, Winston Churchill, Paul Brickhill's *Reach for the Sky*, Russell Braddon's *The Naked Island*.

We spread out on the white leather couches, one apiece, bathed in the glorious sound of the Romantic piano concertos Sue was addicted to as much as I was to Elvis – the past tense these days in regard to my relationship with the King. It didn't mean Sue was not into rock 'n' roll. We went to the Beatnik dance at Training College and the flaring white skirt she wore attracted a lot of vulgar interest from the Phys-Ed mob. This dance was probably when I put away my Elvis fixation, like St Paul says about putting away the things of a child when you become a man. At least I put away the look, Sue persuading me to get a Brutus cut from Rodney Roché, the James Smith men's hair stylist.

Rodney chattered away throughout the styling, jabbering about the previous evening he spent in the Royal Oak cats' bar, where his friend Miranda's friend Clair came in with the most gorgeous hunk. I didn't say I knew the hunk, the last thing I wanted was this clockwork orange going into orbit about Gull and no doubt wanting to know how I knew him, with Sue only feet away. A few weeks later I ditched the dorky comb-forward with curly bits after a few cracks from the Phys-Ed crowd, but I did not revert to the greasy quiff. I didn't want to look bodgie around the Giffords.

Back at Sue's place we listened to piano works by the Three Big Bs, Beethoven, Bach and Brahms, but also lots of Mozart, Tchaikovsky, Chopin. When she put on Khachaturian, I suppressed an image of Melissa whirling and undulating to the 'Sabre Dance'. Composers new to me included Scandinavians Sibelius, Nielsen and Grieg. I liked the Mozart K414 and Grieg's concerto so much, I went into World Record Club and purchased them, and barely in time to avoid being in breach of the contract I had signed.

Teaching and varsity were background noise. There was a tournament between our college and 140 from Auckland, mostly basketball and debates, which I dodged. I had given up on writing poetry but read enough of it to get a pass mark when we had to identify 130 poems. I was only aware that the All Blacks lost the fourth test and the series from passing headlines.

My reading was spasmodic, notable for another new local writer Maurice Shadbolt and his excellent short stories *The New Zealanders*. Sylvia Ashton-Warner's *Spinster* was a dire warning of the sole-charge teaching positions we heard graduates getting assigned. She was inspiring on children's play, but I didn't need to read a book to know that, I loved the classroom observations we did at Karori, Eastbourne and Newtown. The Newtown class was a mini-United Nations of 19 different nationalities, and none had English as a first language. Playtime was notable for the smell of garlic in the sandwiches.

The good times accelerated, to my surprise and delight, with the return of Sue's parents. They were so welcoming, treating me not only as one of the family, but as an adult.

Cécile needless to say concocted the most incredible meals. It might be a chop, a steak or fish, potatoes and French beans, *naturellement*. It was the way she arranged them on the plate, the chops stacked and garnished with an amazing green mint jelly, the steak running red through a dark, intense juice, the cod in a sauce to die for, the potatoes as straw chips or croquettes or *pomes frites*. There was always some extra, like fried fingers of courgette, a caper sauce, shaved Roquefort cheese or slices of heated brie, of course the French beans in garlic, always garlic. Her desserts were divine. Not simply the mousse, which Sue did almost as well, but things I had had only approximations of, custard that was in a different league when she made *crème caramel*, the dark, almost burnt sauce, or baby meringues with cherries soaked in brandy.

Wine with every meal. I had forgotten I ever objected to it. Mostly they served French, occasionally Australian, once Hungarian wine they called 'Bull's Blood' with good reason, it was like imbibing liquid black pudding.

Every meal was an occasion. It was preceded by drinks, gin and tonics, cocktails with olives on toothpicks, the amazing whisky sour. We sat at the table with a white cloth, silver, always candles. Afterwards we repaired to the comfy seats for cognac and black coffee in tiny cups Cécile called *demitasse*. It was all done at a leisurely pace, there was no gulping of huge quantities of booze, bottles were not always finished.

My favourite period was after the meal, when Cécile played piano and sang French songs in a husky, heartfelt voice, like *Sur Les Ponts de Paris* and *Non, Je Ne Regrette Rien*. The most astonishing was one she had only just heard called *Milord*, which she built to an astonishing climax that sent shivers up and down my spine. I took notes on these songs, figuring to check whether the World Record Club stocked such stuff.

Sue joined her on piano sometimes for fun duets. We men were the audience, my ear as tinny as Peter's. At Cécile's urging, Sue would reluctantly accompany her on cello. Cécile would announce the composer, usually French, like Debussy, Fauré or Saint-Saens, all rather wispy and gloomy to my mind. I was asked to turn the pages of Sue's music stand, from which position I watched her in concentrated repose sawing at this huge instrument. It was then that I felt most drawn to her. She hated it, only playing to please Maman.

Peter leaned to confide that Sydney was a shot in the arm for Cécile, especially after they met a champagne distributor and his wife. Cécile was able to talk French till the cows come home.

'I 'eard that,' Cécile said. 'You be'ave yourself, Pe-ter, or I drag you along to *Le Club Français*.'

'*Sacré bleu!*' Peter mangled, making us all laugh.

What surprised me most was that her parents liked to be in our company. We went to the Monde Marie, where they knew many of the performers and the woman who ran it, Mary Seddon, Cécile kissing her on both cheeks and she returning the favour with Peter. They took us to this fancy restaurant Orsinis one night, spending much of the evening talking to the owners about their silverware collection. They came with us to the Brecht play *Mother Courage* at the Concert Chamber, lots of us from Training College there to see Jack Shallcrass in one of the big parts. It was a powerful satire on the Church and war. After it Peter and Cécile chatted to Jack and the lead actress Anne Flannery.

I had told Peter about Jack's encyclopaedic knowledge of current affairs. After the play, on our way back in the taxi, Peter said Jack told him how he stayed current by getting up early each morning and spending an hour or so speed-reading overseas papers and journals, like *The Manchester Guardian*, the *New Statesman*, the *Paris Review* and the *New York Times*.

Peter can talk to anybody about anything, with the notable exception of sport. When I asked him what he thought of the other Peter winning the 800, he asked me to remind him what that was. I have no great interest in longer-distance running, but I would have thought it hard to find a New Zealander who didn't know Snell won the 800 metres gold medal at the Olympic Games last week.

'Oh, of course,' he said when I told him. 'The Olympics. That chap with the gammy arm won something too, didn't he?'

Blimey. Yes, Murray Halberg won the 5000 metres about 30 minutes after Peter Snell's amazing gold. Of course I didn't say anything, though I would have thought even left-wing Kiwis might have been proud of this uncontroversial sporting achievement. They struck me as like the poets and jazz aficionados at the Mung, totally wrapped up in their world, looking down on the philistine majority of Kiwis who obsessed about rugby, racing and beer. Arguably it went both ways.

Cécile had her own office at home, where she drew her designs in pencil or charcoal on large sheets of paper clipped on to a tilted board. She usually spent mornings at work, but often had her afternoons free. She was interested in the cafes we frequented. I had told her about the Mung Café where the Lit Club often adjourned to read poems. She asked if she could come along.

It was, to use her language, like *déjà vu* when I took her there one afternoon, Sue busy in the varsity library swotting for an exam. Cécile entered with her hand tucked in my arm, Frank nudging Don, who looked up myopically as Frank stood to offer Cécile his seat.

'*Merci,*' she said, accepting the chair and Don's outstretched hand. He leaned over the coffee cups and smouldering fags to kiss her hand. '*Oh là là,*' she said. '*Très gallant.*'

Frank was still admiring her snappy yellow check outfit. She swivelled round to protest that she had taken his seat, it was not fair. Frank grinned in his evil fashion, winked at me and said with his hand on his heart, *Pour l'amour.* Cécile gave a splendid shrug, her shrugs speak volumes. Frank hauled a chair from another table next to her, telling me that my taste in women was getting better and better, but there was no need for me to hang about.

Cécile's eyes widened. Don told her to ignore Frank, he couldn't help his affliction, he was not himself when pretty women turned up. But how did she know this callow lad? She wiggled her hands side to side, another of her gestures that are so enigmatically eloquent, looking up at me.

'*Peut-être,* Ste-phan?'

I did the introductions, then took orders. When I got back, they were listening intently to Cécile quoting French with the gesticulations she made when she was animated, which was most of the time. They nodded as she finished, Don saying he had read Baudelaire, but only, alas – giving a huge Gallic shrug – in translation. She might be able to offer some tuition in the original, *oui*? She laughed and said Ste-phan was available. Nobody looked convinced, least of all me. Frank asked her if she knew more Baudelaire. Cécile obliged, her audience transfixed.

When she finished the poem, she checked her wristwatch and said she must leave, or her husband would be eating alone. There were protests, but Frank did rise and hold her chair. '*Merci beaucoup*,' she said, rising on her toes to kiss him on the cheek. Frank looked excessively pleased, except when she kissed Don on both cheeks. He and Don together said she must come again. Don added he would love her to help him understand the nuances of *Les Fleurs du Mal*. She said he had made a good start with the title. As she took my arm, Frank said he expected a full report from me later.

On our way back Cécile said it was *magnifique*, these young Kiwi men interested in Baudelaire, but she wanted to see my poetry. I told her I had run out of ideas. She told me, squeezing my arm, I must not let this writer's block win, I should fight eet, *oui*? I said yes, I would fight eet. She pushed me away, said in mock hurt tone it was not *civil* to make fun of an older woman with not so good English. I asked her who this older woman was. She laughed and took my arm and said I was good for Suzanne, she was more 'appy. I said that made two of us, four counting her generous parents. I got a kiss on the mouth for that.

Later we were sitting on the side of her bed when I told Sue about the visit and how Cécile reckoned I should get back into writing poems. She said I had not taken her to the poets' café. I said I thought she wasn't interested, I wasn't really myself since I'd met her.

'No need to give up things for me,' she said in a resentful tone.

'I want to be with you. Poetry doesn't mean that much to me.'

'So why are you talking about writing again?'

I shrugged, not exactly eloquently.

'My mother,' she said, turning away. 'She always interferes.'

'I don't think she meant any harm.'

'You don't know her.'

I went to put my arm around her. She pulled away.

'I'm sorry,' I said. 'We can go to the café.'

'It's not that,' she said in a quiet voice. 'Let's forget it, okay?'

She got into bed, her back to me. I didn't know what to do. Did she want me to go? It seemed so stupid. I don't think we were quarrelling, but she had withdrawn.

'Switch the light off,' she said.

I did, and then she was in my arms.

'I'm the one should be saying sorry,' she sniffled. 'So I am.'

We laughed at that, and the tension was gone. Kissing and making up is potent, but it is also poignant. Nothing more was said about her mother.

Cécile was most excited by Jenny's marriage and the flat. Sue and I took her round one afternoon to look at it. She was full of exclamations and gestures, both delighted by things like the three colours on the walls, appalled by the *conditions*. She said there was much they did not need that she would give Jenny and Jasper.

When Sue told her she had to think of three, Cécile at first thought she meant me, giving me the raised shoulders by way of enquiry. Sue told her it was the baby, which sent Cécile into orbit, hugging her as if Sue was pregnant, laughing and wiping away a tear, saying this was *encroyable*! She said it made her a *grandmaman manqué*. There was Suzanne's own bassinet, they must borrow it. Oh, she was *trop excite*, at which her French got the better of her and she raved too fast to follow.

When she calmed, Sue said we should wait to see when they got back what they would accept. Cécile hugged her, said she was like her papa, the sensible one. She understood, we would collect, but not deliver. She spent the next week rummaging around in the basement, summoning Sue to assess rugs and curtains, baby clothes, the harness Sue spent time in as a toddler swinging from the ceiling, which Sue said she had no recollection of.

On our way out I blurted 'What's your mother going to be like when you …?' I didn't finish the sentence.

'Get pregnant?'

She had a bright-eyed look.

'Um,' I said, looking away.

We only knew the newly-weds were back when Jenny turned up at the Giffords and I answered the door. She was momentarily surprised, but then smiled.

'I wondered where you'd got to. You two an item?'

I said we were.

'You be nice to her.'

I assured her I would. I said I was the only one there, just back from a lecture. I asked her if she wanted to come in. She said Jasper was unpacking, she'd better get back. I offered to come with her.

'I didn't mean to imply anything,' she said as we strolled down Glasgow Street. 'Sue comes across more confident than she is.'

I said I thought I knew what she was saying, Sue had confided she felt there were expectations on her. I stopped.

'Cécile?'

This was the time for an enigmatic Gallic shrug. I said I was not sure, I was not used to a parent so full-on.

'Same here,' Jenny said. 'We only stayed two days. He was so indignant, and mum said nothing. None of his business what I do.'

'Sorry to hear that. How'd the honeymoon go?'

'Super! Once we got out of Nelson. I know I shouldn't go on about it, I know my mother is in a cleft stick — if she sides with me, he gets his nose out of joint, if she sides with him, then I get hissy. I know there are always issues with the new person in a parent's life. Knowing sucks. It doesn't help. I did psychology because I thought I'd get some insights. Whoops, sorry about the rave. Psych encourages the verbals.'

'I might need to consult you,' I said. 'My father is getting with this woman I can't stand. Nothing she does, you know? I get in an insane rage about her, and I have no justification.'

'We both need counselling, I guess. Sue as well, she finds her mum a handful.'

I warned her that Cécile had assembled clothes and furniture, bedding, a spare double bed, and was itching to descend with them. Jenny sighed, said they had already received a pile of manuka and several sacks of coal, stacked under the house, and guessed it was Cécile's doing. Jasper had rung the landlords. They knew nothing of these deliveries, but said it was what the house needed, the gas fire did not warm the bones of the house. He was okay about it, said it was one gift horse they were not going to look in the mouth.

The proof was about to be demonstrated as we entered the sitting room, Jasper crouched in front of the fireplace with a newspaper spread across its aperture. There was a whoosh and the paper turned red and then burst into flames. Jasper looked up with a devilish grin.

'Brings out the anarchist in me,' he said. 'How's Sue?'

I said Sue was champion, and he'd see for himself any time now.

We were having a cup of tea when Cécile and Sue arrived, Cécile charging in to embrace both of them, full of indignant and delighted gestures and exclamations in her inimitable version of franglais. Cécile insisted they come and choose what they needed, which involved mostly Jasper and myself lugging the bed and chairs between houses, Sue and Jenny staggering behind with bedding and clothes, Cécile moving between us like a corporal directing a platoon.

We returned the back-bending bed to its spider hole, Jasper put in place the old fireguard he had found under the house, and we repaired to the Gifford residence for much talk, laughter, drinks and another of Cécile's instant gourmet meals. Sue chose to come back with us, Cécile accepted it with a deep shrug.

Jenny and Sue disappeared. Jasper removed the fireguard and stoked up the manuka logs, getting the fire up to speed. He crouched in his Lotus position beside it. I grabbed a cushion, not being up to the Kama Sutra contortions, and joined him. We stared at the flames in that mindless, cosy fashion that open fires seem to inspire.

I had to go and spoil the mood by idly observing manuka was good to establish the fire, but coal generated more heat. Jasper grunted, said he wouldn't care if he never saw another lump of coal in his life.

'I know it stinks,' I said unhelpfully.

Wigan, he said dourly, had 1000 coal mines. Some folk had their own coal mines in their backyards. His dad didn't, he had been a coal miner until his lungs finished him. Jasper looked accusingly at me, or so it seemed, it is hard to tell when the flickering firelight transformed his glasses into the blank orbs of a mutant post-nuclear ant.

'Get an education and get out,' he said sourly. 'That was my father's advice. I was able to take it, my sisters not. They've married into misery.'

Infected by his sombre mood, I said that from what little I knew of *The Road to Wigan Pier*, I thought it was the cotton mills that had all the child labour misery, the dark satanic mills kind of thing. Jasper grunted, stirred the logs with the poker, said you could take your pick, coal or cotton.

'At least you had a pier,' I said, thinking it might provoke some happier memories.

Jasper just about choked on his own laughter, and it wasn't the happy variety. 'It's fucking inland, mate,' he said when he had more or less recovered. 'The pier is where they tied up on the ruddy canal, shipping out the coal. George Formby said it led to t'sands on stilts up in the air. For sands think the slag heaps they left behind, they were so fucking huge we called them the Wigan Alps.'

I asked him a little desperately what they did for fun. He said the Empire Ballroom was where he learned to trip the light fantastic, but there was two-thirds of five-eighths of fuck all to do until he got to Liverpool and a job. Soon as he could he shipped out of that shower. He hadn't eaten a pie since.

The hint was there, so I asked why not.

'Wigan folk are called pie-eaters. Northern humour. There were no pies to eat. During the 1926 general strike, the miners were starved until they went back to work. No do-gooders visible in government and the churches. They forced the poor bastards back to work, forced them to eat humble pie. That's the way it always was for our lot. The Lowland Clearances enticed my ancestors out of Scotland, the only work slave labour for the lords and masters.' Another pause to give me the giant ant look. 'They were permitted free coal. So? Let them eat coal.'

'My ancestors didn't even have spuds to eat.'

'Which country would that be?'

I figured he was pulling my pud. 'The potato famine?'

Jasper did the mutant stare.

'Is this more Northern humour?'

'The Scottish Highlands potato famine was no joke.'

'Sorry,' I mumbled. 'I didn't know.'

'You know where you come from?'

'Yeah. Ireland. Well, Mum's family. Dad's Scottish, I think.'

I got the stare. He could be very tiresome. 'My great-grandparents emigrated. To Tasmania. I think. I'm not really sure. My grans never talk about it.'

'So you don't know where you come from.'

'Not specifically,' I said defensively. 'Anyway, like my father says, the future is what counts.'

'Brave new world, eh?'

Thank God Sue and Jenny emerged before Jasper delivered any more of his mordant Northern humour. Sue was in high spirits, and brought them to bed.

Our biggest problem next morning was abandoning the excellent French invention of the duvet and, in my case, rushing without breakfast to catch the bus to Karori. Jasper was going in the opposite direction, to his new section at Clyde Quay school. I almost asked him if he knew it was like Wigan, land-locked, but that might have been a facetious remark too far. Jenny and Sue were off for croissants and coffee with Maman, the lucky pigs. Now that I had tasted croissants, the idea of a slab of wholemeal toast with Vegemite seemed almost, as the Latin has it, *infra dig*. At least the girls promised to have dinner on the table for us hard-working boys.

Dinner was a casserole, the same lime green, one of the Le Creuset range, Sue informed me tightly in response to my question. Maman had delivered it, and it contained something I had not had since staying with my grandparents, venison. Its gaminess was pretty well disguised by an astonishing amount of garlic, plus bay leaves, red wine, and a number of flavours I was not familiar with. It was spectacularly good.

The following nights were not so splendid, but entirely acceptable offerings from the fair hands of our ladies. Jenny did a mixed grill and potatoes in their jackets in sour cream, which drew loud praise from Jasper and endorsements from the other two. Next night Sue's steak and kidney pie drew loud praise from me, pleasant praise from Jenny, and muted praise from Jasper.

Jasper did a grand wok-up on Thursday, everything but the kitchen sink, carrots, onions, celery, leeks, tinned asparagus, broccoli, beans, peas, all in sweet and sour pork courtesy of a tin of pineapple, vinegar, sugar and Uncle Tom Cobley and all. Oh yes, and brown rice. Crash hot.

Friday I went to Alan and returned with his unsurpassed f'n'c. There was no time for prep, Sue and I were off to the Museum this time, to see *The Cabinet of Dr Caligari*.

We had only won Cécile's approval to cook for ourselves by agreeing to come to her Saturday dinner with friends. Sue was not looking forward to it, but it would be churlish to object when Jenny was pleased and Jasper had Cécile's approval to bring along the headmaster he was sectioned with, whom he got on with like a house on fire.

Saturday morning Jasper and myself watched an organised competitive sport, namely hockey, somewhere in deepest Hataitai. The reason we did was that Sue and Jenny played, although this was probably the last game Jenny would for awhile, after throwing up in the dressing room several times. She still played a doughty goalie, I think, my eyes were on Sue, a forward with a ruthless path to goal that won her two goals, the second the winner. She looked stunning in her hockey outfit, and I did go on about it. Finally she suggested I was some kind of fetishist. I confessed myself guilty.

It put her in a sunny mood. The sun set, the flat dropped temperature like a stone, and so did Sue's mood. Off we walked, to the dinner party.

 **23**

W e arrived to a sitting room packed with an eclectic and rowdy group drinking shorts or wine, a fug of cigarette and pipe smoke hovering above them like early morning mist over the harbour. Head and shoulders above everybody were two magnificent men. The swart, bespectacled, big-headed fellow in a dark suit, close to Don Clarke in both height and girth, had a bass boom that might well be what was making the picture window vibrate. He was relating a joke to James Robertson Justice, or near as dammit, a Falstaffian fellow with sandy hair and red-streaked spade beard and the spreading girth of an ex-wrestler, wrapped in a splendid blue and green kilt with sporran. His laughter was more baritone, but equally penetrating. Beside them Pat Mascaskill adopted the familiar quizzical tilt to his head, no doubt waiting for a pause in the performance to intrude an outrageous pun.

Counterpoint came from the high-pitched and heavily accented voice of Albert Einstein's tweedy younger brother, his protuberant eyes as startling as his electrified pepper-and-salt hair. A younger man with a square, pallid face and heavy black spectacles was benignly puffing a pipe, the smoke a filter for Einstein spraying opinions directly into his face. I had to stand on tiptoe to make out the other recipient of this rant-fest, a small, dark-featured man in a loose cream silk shirt.

The women were a stylish cluster in off-the-shoulder gowns and jewellery ranging from classical diamonds to the pottery necklace on a frizzy-haired lady with excessive amounts of purple eye make-up and matching lipstick talking French to Cécile. Beside these women were a demure, dark-haired beauty and a fresh-faced lady with long, stringy blonde hair and an uncanny resemblance to the Frances Hodgkins painting of the girl with flaxen hair – a momentary reminder of Melissa. *En masse* the ladies abandoned their conversations to descend on Jenny and Sue for much embracing and exclamations of delight.

Jasper drifted around them to hail the Scotsman, who bellowed out a greeting and introduced him to his companions. Knowing how indifferent Jasper was to such bourgeois practice as including me in the introductions, I stood uncertainly surveying the room.

'You must be Steve,' the dark-featured man said. 'I think you have met my mother several times. I'm Harry Seresin.'

'Roy Parsons, right?'

'He has the bookshop beneath my gallery.'

'Oh. But how did you know me?'

'Mama pointed you out as the shaking – her word — young man with the pretty ladies. I gather she had to sort out that daft old district court lecher. He tries it on with all the damsels.'

'Not successfully, I hope.'

'No. Pat tells me you are one of his stars.'

'Eh? Oh, you mean Pat Macaskill. Yeah, he's great.'

'Can't have you talking about me behind my back.' Pat had his cheeky grin. 'Thou shalt not take the name of thy lord and master in vain. Isn't that what your Bible says?'

'I dunno,' I said. 'Catholics don't teach the Bible much.'

'Sign of a misspent youth. Somerset Maugham read the Bible every day, and he was no believer. He read it for the literary quality.'

'It's not on your Top 100 list.'

'An oversight. Perhaps it is a sign of my misspent age. Now, Harry, how's Jackie's exhibition?'

'Most of them sold. Which makes a change. Are you free to come up to Grass Street next Saturday? Maurice is down from Auckland, Lou and Alistair are bringing him. The Adcocks will be there.'

'It's the Ad-hens I'm interested in. Yes?'

'I'm pretty sure both lovely ladies are coming. I'll check with my prettier half.'

At which point the warbling music ceased and Cécile clapped her hands.

'*Attention, s'il vois plaît?*. Would you take your seats, where your names are, *merci*.'

I was at the window end, Jenny on my left, the Scotsman on my right, the other giant opposite, Peter at the head of the table. Sue was down the other end, between Pat and Harry, her mother presumably occupying the space at that end facing her husband. Peter introduced Ikar Lissienko to Jenny and myself, and Ikar introduced Calum McLeod, the Scotsman who had been teaching in the States and Jasper was on section with. Ikar I learned was a pharmaceutical salesman who obviously, it soon became apparent, belonged to the same compulsive joke-telling club as Calum.

'I heard a new one this week,' he said, eyes dancing as he leaned over the soup towards Calum. 'A man walks into the doctor's office. Doctor asks him what is the problem? The man replies he has five penises. Blimey, the doc says. How do your trousers fit? Like, the man says, a glove.'

Calum exploded with laughter, Peter steadying his soup before it spilled. 'Man with a strawberry stuck up his bum goes to the doctor. The doctor says, I'll give you some cream for it.'

The merriment attracted interest from the other end of the table. 'Two Eskimos in a kayak,' Pat piped up. A pause while he gets the table's attention. 'The Eskimos are chilly.'

'Unlikely,' Peter murmured.

'So,' Pat continued, 'they light a fire in the craft. Not surprisingly it sank. Which proves once again – you can't have your kayak and heat it too.'

Universal groans. I made a mental note to copy these jokes down the moment I got the chance, and not to drink too much to fuzz my memory.

'Eat your vichyssoise,' Cécile advised.

'Before it gets warm?' Pat proposed.

'Clown,' snorted the heavy-set man next to him.

'Vich reminds me,' Einstein chortled. 'Two cannibals are eating zis clown. One says to the other: Does this taste funny to you?'

'*Assez!*' Cecile commanded. '*Mange. Mange.*'

The soup was potato and leek and it was fantastic. Peter asked Calum what he thought of the education system in the States. Calum asked him how much time he had to spare, then launched into a description of the deficiencies in basic readers. The small man with a keen, owl-like appearance behind big glasses opposite and to my left said he had plans to do something about that. The thick-set man said he reckoned we're overdue to take Sylvia Ashton-Warner to the world. The frizzy-haired woman said we must not forget our artists while we're at it, they're as good as anything coming out of the States or Europe.

'Exactly,' said Pat. 'Doreen Blumhardt came out of Europe and now her pots are on the way back.'

'We need to start our own theatre,' Harry added. 'Bruce Mason is a one-man band.'

'What's wrong with a one-man band?' Ikar enquired.

'Vy don't you start a theatre, Harry?' Einstein challenged. 'You haf every poet and writer in Wellington in your coffee bar.'

'You're on, Erich. You can perform next Friday. Anything but *Eskimo Nell*.'

'I like *Eskimo Nell*.'

Sue and Cécile collected the soup plates, Cécile telling Jenny not to get up. I asked Peter who were the small man and the thick-set fellow with the cowlick. Hugh Price was the small man, he ran Modern Books in Manners Street, Con Bollinger was the trade union writer.

'Author of *Grog's Own Country*,' Calum said. 'Larraps the liquor industry. Hugh's firm published it.'

'Price Milburn,' I said. The penny had dropped. I told him I'd read their publication *Our Street* to the kids.

'They lap it up,' he said. 'We need more local content. You hear that, Hugh?'

Hugh said the sequel was coming out next year, called *Smitty Does a Bunk*.

Calum said he'd order the first box of them. He said I could come along and read them to his class. I said I'd love to.

Peter was moving round the table with a choice of white or red wine, to go with the *coq au vin*. Pat turned round to tell him that chickens were the only animal we eat before they are born and after they are dead.

'Yuk!' Jenny said.

Calum beckoned Ikar forward. 'Best chicken joke ever. The chicken and egg are in bed, the chicken smoking a fag, looking satisfied. Egg is pissed off, grabs the sheet, rolls over, says: I guess we finally answered THAT question.'

'Clever,' Peter observed as he filled their glasses.

Cécile and Sue silenced further silly jokes carrying in the real thing, two huge casseroles with the lids off, the steaming contents attracting approving remarks from round the table. Distribution of the delicious chicken and vegetable dishes of glazed carrots, broccoli and potatoes was the priority, then the eating thereof.

I asked Jenny if they got to the end of the sand bar that stretches on the map in a crooked finger around Golden Bay. She told me about the fun they had in an old Combi van that just made it, Jasper celebrating by doing cartwheels at its edge. Then he didn't want her doing the same thing, which she ignored. The van stuck in the sand and the six of them pushed and dug like Jack Russells under its tyres and used floor mats for traction to get it going.

I could hear fragments of animated conversations. Peter, Calum and Ikar were gloomy about the likely change of government. Calum said what a buffoon Holyoake was. Peter claimed there had been more coverage of this young Kennedy's chances as a Catholic in the American presidential elections than our own ones, indicating how apathetic we were. Ikar growled that the Commie-baiting Nixon would probably win and we were no different, Nash not helping his chances with a trip to Moscow. Kiwis he reckoned were almost as paranoid as the Yanks and Aussies about the Commie threat. Calum said the impression he got in the States was that the Pope was considered an equally satanic threat.

'You familiar with Norman Vincent Peale?'

'Of course,' Peter said. 'Author of *The Power of Positive Thinking*.'

'That's the one,' Calum acknowledged. 'He led this congregation – if that's the word – of well over 100 Presbyterian ministers in a Catholic-bashing exercise. They reckoned electing Kennedy would mean America was going to dance to the Vatican's tune.'

Ikar: 'The Pope has the best tunes?'

'Sounds more like a KKK convention,' Peter grumbled. 'I don't even know if the Vatican has a foreign policy, let alone one it could impose on the States. Typical fundamentalist scaremongering.'

'Looks to me,' Ikar said, 'like Kennedy's caught between the Commie devil and the Papist conspiracy.'

'And we know what Stalin said,' Peter added. 'How many divisions does the Pope have?'

'So what're the odds?' Calum asked. 'Two to one on Nixon?'

'Five to one,' Peter countered. 'Five Protestants for every Doolan.'

From the other side of Jenny, Jasper and Con were having a robust disagreement about whether left-wing governments were any better than conservatives. Jasper, I knew, poured scorn on all state power. Opposite them I heard Harry ask the elegantly horsey woman if she read Jock McEwen in the paper saying in a generation all New Zealanders would have some Polynesian blood. It was the only word I heard from her all night, a murmured negative. I think Harry said, as he leaned confidentially close, that the sooner the better, then the All Blacks would be all a bit black and it would be the end of playing the appalling Boers. I suppose I was paying more attention to the woman than the words. Her long face and grey, heavy-lidded eyes were framed by coils of rich chestnut hair, which toned in perfectly with the toffee red leather jacket and skirt. I wondered if she was a model for a line of the Giffords' merchandise.

Because of the thickness of his accent rather than any reduction of the full volume, I was not clear what Erich was on about as he harangued the woman next to him with high-pitched indignation. The gist of it was a doom-and-gloom view of Thor Heyerdahl's Kon-Tiki experiences cleaning his teeth in an oil-polluted ocean. Between Erich's stertorous pauses, I could hear a woman saying the All Blacks got what they deserved.

I switched in to Pat and Hugh talking about the insidious softening of the nation's brain by ubiquitous promotion of popular culture. Pat quoted somebody called Dwight Macdonald on whether a roller-skating horse was elevated by being depicted opposite a Rembrandt, or whether Rembrandt was sullied by such crass contact. The rapid-fire French from Cécile and the frizzy-haired lady reduced the conversation at the far end to a Tower of Babble.

The table came back together in universal praise of the food. Cécile thanked everybody but said there was one more experience. She disappeared into the kitchen and Peter began filling small glasses like little champagne flutes with a wine that was thick, yellow and potent. It was a perfect complement to the sharp lemon tart and this curious stuff like congealed sour milk, which Jenny informed me was yoghurt. It was *spectaculaire*!

Again the table acclaimed as one the meal. Peter said in that case we could sing for our supper. If we repaired to the sitting room, port and cognac would be served, cigars available, and of course the bourbon Calum brought back with him from the States.

First everybody pitched in with the clearing of the table, crowding into the kitchen to do the dishes, ignoring Cécile's protests it was not *necessaire*. It was Con, drying plates as Sue lifted them out of the suds, who began the round of limericks:

*There was a pert lass from Madras…*

'*Mon dieu!*' Cécile exclaimed as she took control of the dried plates. 'Not more of your dirty jokes.'

The kitchen crowd all looked at Con, who smiled benignly. 'Not at all, madame. This is merely a necessary *divertissement* from the mundane business at hand. If I promise it is not naughty, will you permit me to continue?' I edged up against the far end next to the pantry and took the opportunity to write down the jokes I could remember.

Cécile managed a shrug whilst retaining control of a dozen plates. '*Mais, moi aussi*. I am next.'

Con bowed and offered to cede the floor to Cécile. She declined, urging him to go on.

*Who had a remarkable ass.*

'Conrad!'

'Let him finish,' somebody said. Cécile gave a moue of indifference.

*Not rounded and pink*

Con paused, enjoying the murmurs of alarm.

*As you probably think.*

*It was gray, had long ears, and ate grass.*

A chorus of groans and chuckles, while I recorded the limerick.

'*Attention!*'

We all stopped. Cécile put down the plates on the bench and faced her guests:

*While Titian was mixing rose madder*

*His model was posed on a ladder.*

*Her position to Titian*

*Suggested fruition*

*So he mounted the ladder and 'adder.*

I got it down on paper amidst laughter, clapping, cries of 'Bravo' and good-natured protests that it was she who promised to keep it clean.

'I won't,' Erich growled. 'Now listen:

*A niece of the late Queen of Sheba*

*Was promiscuous with an amoeba.*

Protests from Cécile and others were ignored, his voice rising:

*This queer blob of jelly*

*Would lie on her belly*
*And quivering murmur: Ich liebe!*

Laughter and acclamation, me scribbling. Pat raised his hand, delivering a rapid-fire limerick too quick for my informal university shorthand about a woman called Gail who had her behind tattooed in Braille. Ikar charged through the laughter with one about swans and dons. Calum was just clearing his throat when Jasper darted in with a ditty I missed all of except the man protesting his name was Simpson, not Samson. Calum was not to be denied, but most probably wished he had been with the reaction to his Aussie in the outback making a zizi of his hat.

When the groans died down, Calum asked Cécile if he got her language of love right. 'Not that kind of love,' Cécile objected.

'If,' Erich said, tea towel in one hand, a finger raised, 'the cunt fits, say it.'

'*Assez!*' Cécile declared. '*Chansons.* Leave the dishes. *Allons-y.*' She waved us all out of the kitchen, pushing and prodding those of us too slow for her liking.

Con declared that as he started all this nonsense, he would seek to make amends by singing the first song. Cécile inclined her head in acceptance. We joined Peter arranging chairs in the sitting room and breaking out the port, brandy and cigars and promised bourbon.

Cécile took up position at the piano, Con standing beside her and the rest of us settled down in a semi-circle round the piano. Cigars and pipes were being lit, scenting the room with curling wreaths and spirals of seductive smoke. I thought of smoke signals and realised not all of us were there, Sue and Jenny had disappeared. I assumed Jenny was not well and Sue was looking after her. I confirmed this with Jasper.

Con announced that this was one of the new songs he collected at Curious Cove, whatever that was. The song was a variation on *The Twelve Days of Christmas*, and he invited us to sing along. As it happened, he had cyclostyled copies, if we wished to participate. He handed a sheaf of crackly Gestetner paper to Ikar and hummed the song to Cécile, who nodded and struck up. 'Marxmas' was substituted for 'Christmas' and we wobbled our way through verses about a picture of Trotsky, two Das Capitals, three bayonets, Fourth International and so on, the pick of them 'Eleven Lenins Leaping'.

Cécile began pounding out the tune *He's Got the Whole World In His Hands,* and we sang the familiar lines. She looked up for the next song. *To ev'ry season*, Peter croaked, and was quickly picked up by Ikar's magnificent voice and Calum and then all of us belting out the biblical *Turn! Turn! Turn!*

Con swung us back to the left with *We Shall Overcome*, the anthem of the 'Ban the Bomb' marches. Calum stepped up to do another favourite, *This Land Is Your Land*. Hugh did an alternative version of *Onward, Christian Soldiers*, his voice not strong but the anti-war words were, especially:

*Atom-bomb the babies, burn the mothers too*
*Hoist the cross of Calvary to hallow all you do.*
*Flatten every city, poison every well,*
*God decrees your enemies must all go straight to hell.*

There was a lull, then Ikar set the Volga Boat Song to a daft ditty about bomsk in Tomsk, which no doubt triggered Jasper's send-up of anarchists to the tune of *Sister Jenny*. I got down one verse:

*In an anarchist garret, so meagre and mean,*
*Smell the pungent odour of nitroglycerine.*
*They're busy making fuses, and filling kegs with nails,*
*And little Slavic children give out these mourning wails.*

Cécile did a remarkable change of pace, singing a powerful song called *House of the Rising Sun*, about a brothel in New Orleans. It won a storm of applause and demands for more. She did the song she had just learned, *Milord*, and that won even more rapturous applause and demands for yet more.

She asked if there were any requests. I piped up *Lili Marlene*. She snapped she did not play that song. In the long silence my ears turned scarlet and I prayed to the saint of disappearing tricks that I be swallowed up by the floor.

Finally Peter suggested *Mack the Knife*, which Cécile played with a much more snarling edge than last year's hit version by Bobby Darin. She got up from the piano to thunderous applause, saying she needed a coffee and went into the kitchen.

Erich was announcing that he would now deliver the much anticipated *Eskimo Nell*, but was shouted down. Peter guided me aside to say I wasn't to know and mustn't worry, she associated the song with the Germans marching into Paris. I was even more mortified and said I had to apologise. He squeezed my arm, said she would have forgotten it already, best leave her be. I said I would see if Sue was okay, but again he counselled me to leave it, both her and Jenny were not well and had gone up to bed.

Cécile did not reappear and Peter began shepherding guests out the door, saying that his wife had had an exhausting time of it. Most agreed it was getting late, some were saying that they had to get back, their wives were coping with kids down with the flu. The women kissed Peter goodnight, hoping Cécile would recover, Peter assuring them she had overdone it again and would be fine after a rest. Jasper suggested we return to the flat.

Erich was clearly feeling contrary about being deprived of his turn, for he blocked the door arguing with Con and Hugh about the nature of laughter, asserting loudly that humour was the release of psychic energy caused by repressed sexual and hostile feelings. Hugh dismissed this as Freudian bunkum, humour was a recognition of silly antics and self-deprecating behaviour. At the most basic level, you had the

Three Stooges. Con was having none of that, asking what was self-deprecating about finding a cricket ball in your fridge, yet it might readily provoke laughter because of its incongruity. 'The power,' he said, 'of metaphor and surprise provokes laughter. Read Thurber and Benchley.'

'Bullshit,' Erich scoffed. 'Laughter is satanic. I quote Baudelaire. It is how we release repression and assert ourselves, by defiance.'

Despite the best efforts of the women to herd them away, the argument continued down to the street and beside their cars. Jasper and I were walking on when there was a sudden soft explosion and eruption of light behind us. We wheeled round as shouts of alarm and indignation were accompanied by the sound of running feet.

'Stop him!' somebody yelled.

Jasper took off towards the group. I could make out figures running past the streetlight, there was another poof and blinding white light. I realised it was the bulb of a flash camera. It caused some mayhem, as Jasper crashed into the person in front of him. Erich was cursing to get after them, which Jasper did, well ahead of the stumbling Erich.

I asked what was going on as the men were ushering women into passenger seats.

'The usual,' Hugh said sardonically. 'The twilight branches of the state like their little games.'

'Caught in the act,' Ikar laughed. 'A den of lefties.'

'Than whom,' Con said in a deep, mocking tone, 'there is none more dangerous to the welfare of our glorious welfare state.'

Pat smiled at me. 'Catholics aren't the only brand of left-footers.'

'Downright sinister, eh?' Calum chortled. 'I wonder if I attracted the State Department in the States?'

'No doubt their lackeys, doing their bidding,' Con said dryly.

'It could be any or all of us,' Hugh said. 'The old Special Branch had me down as a Commie because I sold books from behind the Iron Curtain.'

'Is everybody okay?' Peter asked anxiously from his gate. 'Nobody hurt? What was that bright light?'

'Night shoot,' Calum said.

'I am not okay,' Erich wheezed. 'Bugger's got away.'

'Well, nothing we can do,' Hugh said. 'Not much point complaining to the authorities.'

'Come on, Hugh,' Calum challenged. 'It's not yet a police state.'

'What about Jasper?' I asked.

At which point he appeared, looking the worse for wear.

'I almost had him,' he gasped, checking his spectacles. 'Then somebody tripped me.'

Peter was apologising for this abominable behaviour and he was going to ring the police. A chorus of objections caused him to shrug.

'I suppose no harm done,' he conceded. 'Would you all like to come back up for a nightcap?'

Nobody did, not least impatient voices through the open passenger doors of cars urging the men to come on, it was too late to be standing around inviting colds. Several of the men still had to assert themselves, vowing they were going to lay complaints with the Security Service. Hugh added a warning note that it could well be one of the other branches of our dear Big Brother. Con agreed, said there was going to be some jockeying for grace and favour when the Nats got their grubby hands back on the reins of power.

'Bloody Nash,' Erich growled. 'He probably pisses in the dark to save power.'

'Left or right bias?' Calum enquired.

'That reminds me,' Ikar said, 'of the rabbi ...'

Another chorus of objections, most prominently from the cars, and assertive calls of goodnight.

Jasper and I made our way back to the cold flat, Jasper rabbiting on about a stimulating evening with some decent arguments and some real songs and an excellent conclusion, the functionaries of the state where they belonged lurking all night in the shrubbery. I asked him if he was okay. Athletic Park, he said, was much worse, this time he didn't have to replace his glasses.

'You know,' he mused, 'I was tripped just as I was lunging at the little twerp with the camera. My specs went flying as well as me, and I couldn't see much. What I could see I would reckon was your mate Paddy the prancing policeman.'

I said he was no mate of mine. Jasper said it was no surprise to him, Paddy seemed to be inordinately interested in his comings and goings from the moment he came into the male ballet. I said I'd not noticed. 'Hardly surprising,' he said scornfully. 'You only had eyes for your hippy dippy chicky.'

For my information, he added with utter indifference to my agitation about this dismissive description of Melissa, he reckoned the interest hadn't stopped since. He had seen Pad the Plod several times at the Symposium, with that tart for cover. I could hardly be bothered responding to speculation about what Gull was up to. I said he was a law student, so he would know he was within his legal rights going into public places with whomever he chose.

'Like us?' Jasper reminded me.

'Whatever,' I said. I was feeling as flat as possum on a train tunnel wall, a truly incongruous metaphor that did not make me laugh. My main preoccupation was that once again I'd put my foot in it, and ruined the evening, as far as I was concerned. I found no humour or even interest in the possibility of Gull spying on this harmless bunch of opinionated left-wingers. I had never been to a party like it, I'd collected some great jokes and limericks and had loved every minute of it, right up until my massive clanger. To use the perfect French phrase, I had made an almighty *faux pas*.

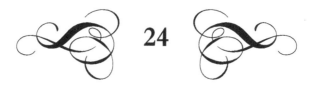

# 24

The morning after the dinner party, Sue and Jenny turned up at the flat earlier than either of us would have liked. They separately reconciled us to any inconvenience we might have felt, showered and then brought us fully alive with bacon, eggs and tomatoes, wholemeal toast and ground coffee. This didn't mean they were in a great mood about the previous evening. Both said they'd had enough of parties that degenerated into endless dirty jokes.

'I wouldn't have minded hearing *Eskimo Nell*,' I said.

'Dirty and boring,' Sue said, as she lifted the boiling pot of coffee off the gas.

'I thought Noel Coward wrote it.'

'So?'

So nothing, I had merely expressed an opinion. I didn't say anything. Sue did, going on about how embarrassing it was her mother competing with the men. Jenny added, giving Jasper a meaningful glance, it hadn't helped bringing along another compulsive/ obsessive joke-teller. Once the jokes started, conversation ended. She didn't care what Freud allegedly had to say about jokes, when it came down to humour, he was just another male egotist flaunting his id at the expense of his superego. Psych students I have noticed like to lecture the rest of us about our hidden motives and tend to treat us like the white rats they direct through mazes and subject to treadmills, as if we are all dominated by mechanistic determinism.

'There's more to Calum than jokes,' Jasper mildly objected. Nothing Jenny says ever moves him out of mild, so I guess his superego is pretty stable.

'We never noticed,' Sue said. 'We'd both had enough.'

'Male pack behaviour,' Jenny said dismissively.

I wasn't going to risk teasing Jenny, never mind Sue, by saying it sounded like a classic example of penis envy. It seemed a pity to be bickering when the sun was out and we should be too. I suggested we go for a stroll in the gardens, smell the daffodils. Sue said she'd love to see the blossom festival next weekend, she'd heard it was a riot.

Jasper and I glanced at each other, then told them there was a college bus hired for the occasion, if they wanted to go. They did. Sue said she needed a break from home and she'd missed the New Plymouth trip, which sounded fun.

'Fun,' said Jasper, 'is the name of the game.'

Wrong. Well, the singing on the bus ride to Hastings was fun, for some, for it was also fairly dirty. A fellow known only as Punch, a huge, hairy oaf, regaled us with a song new to me. I recorded only a verse and a bit, it not being easy in a rattling old bus with a companion who does not approve of such nonsense. It was to the tune of *Colonel Bogey's March*:

> *Up jumped the Colonel's daughter*
> *Something in her arse went bang.*
> *They found her left foot in Oriental Bay,*
> *They found her right foot 10,000 miles away.*
> *And over her left kidney*
> *Was a bird's eye view of Sydney*
> *And on her back was a Union Jack –*
> *Well could you ask for more?*
> *They found her right tit up the Ngauranga,*
> *But her left tit has yet to be found.*

The mostly male occupants of the bus joined in making brass band noises for the chorus of the march.

No way did I risk recording the *mickydidi* chant. By then we were at Dannevirke, where we had a comfort stop. For Sue it had been discomfort personified on this travelling dirty ditty road show. It took a little persuading to get her back aboard, Jenny pointing out that there was no transport for hours and things had to improve.

Things did not. The rain at Dannevirke heralded a stinker of a day in the Hawkes Bay, grey, wet, cold, the parade of blossom floats cancelled. We joined the pub tour, there was absolutely nothing else to do. Sue groused that if we'd come up on the train like everybody else, we could go and relax in a carriage.

We went to the Albert Hotel, where it was generally agreed later the trouble began. At first people were happy to be knocking back the beer. The only incident I encountered was Gerry Peters when I went for a piss. He was coming out of a booth along with a couple of bodgies, stuffing a roll of notes in his pocket. He smirked as one of them bumped my shoulder pushing past. 'Looking for action, Elvis? I got bennies, reefers, give you a good price. Clair tells me you're into happy time.' I just looked at him until he turned his hands palms up. 'Your loss, sucker.' It was later I wondered about his Clair remark.

We didn't see any particularly provocative incident. That was hardly surprising, the place was standing-room only and the tumult of thirsty young people guzzling and shouting drowned out the detail. We did hear glasses smashed and the full range of four-letter words being tossed about. Sue wanted out and nobody objected.

We left as the police arrived, announcing the bar was closed, somebody objecting they had no right to do so until six o'clock. Whatever confrontation followed, it was a mere aperitif. Things moved from frying pan to fire brigade.

When we got outside a crowd was forming a chanting ring around a Maori and a pakeha having a fist fight. Soon several more fights broke out. Policemen waded into the thick of it, becoming part of the street mêlée, with beer jugs and glasses being hurled about.

The first siren announced a standard black police car, its occupants finding it difficult to get out of the vehicle as its sides and chrome grille were kicked. One lout deflated a tyre, another got busy bending the aerial and when it snapped, he took off with his trophy. A cop who had finally emerged gave chase. Despite being shoved and pushed and jeered at, the cop forced his way through after the police aerial thief.

The next siren was advance warning of the Black Maria, the target for bottles and bricks. One well-aimed bottle starred the rear window. It was mayhem and pandemonium, and there was no escape through a mob more excited than anything I saw at the All Black trials. Jasper, I would have to say, appeared as animated as anybody. It was all I could do to hold on to Sue's hand.

Police were, if I may be pardoned the pun, copping it, helmets being knocked off. One cop went down and I saw a boot go into his ankle, before somebody pulled the attacker away. Another cop had blood streaming from a cut on his face, from either flying glass or a bottling.

A more robust parping siren introduced the extraordinary sight of a fire engine driving into the crowd. Firemen in full gear, walking in front of it with their hatchets at the ready, brass helmets as unlikely as Prussian piked helmets from World War One. Sue cringed against me, making a plea I couldn't hear.

Jasper was pointing at the ladder extending over the front of the engine. Two firemen scaled it, lugging a hose, which began writhing like a giant eel, before a thick jet of water exploded out of the nozzle. The firemen directed the stream back and forth over the crowd. The water landed heavily, like a wave you don't see coming, people crying out in alarm and indignation. After the hose swept away from us, we were left shivering and shocked.

Jasper was one of many yelling obscenities at the firemen. The hose action had the opposite effect from what must have been intended. The crowd was incensed, and the firemen were targets for bottles, jugs, bricks and whatever other missiles people could find. A group of youths rushed at the fire truck, hurling what they had.

The behemoth kept coming straight at them, hose directed point blank, the youths peeling away. The hose-wielders did not restrict their action to the attacking youths, they were intent on watering as many of us as they could. The engine moved slowly like a cumbersome medieval war engine through the scrambling people past the Corner House with its sign advertising 'The Home of Coffee', Peter Pan, Wright's

Tailors and Dry-Cleaners.

Behind the engine a civilian was engaged in a fight with two youths in stovepipe trousers and winklepickers. The siren nearby was a traffic cop's car driving too fast along the street. People were falling over trying to get out of the way of this lunatic, who should have been arrested for endangering life and limb. Jasper thought so, directing his obscenities and a bottle at the car, Jenny tugging him away from attracting nearby cops.

We saw several kids dragged off by the cops, including a young widgie in a tight pink skirt who had been systematically snapping car aerials. A bunch of youths followed the police, yelling at them to let her go. The police kept shouting through loud hailers to disperse or we would be arrested, which was ridiculous, you couldn't arrest 5000 people for being in the street. It was the bodgie element who took most exception and aimed to arrest the loud hailers, provoking more tussles with the police.

Youths sporting 'Eagle Clan' on the back of their black leather jackets cracked the heads off quart bottles of beer on the edge of the gutter and went for the cops. Others picked up stones and threw them. The police formed up in groups and charged at stone-throwers and bottle-wielders, and lost helmets and had coats ripped. We tried to move away, but the crowds made it difficult. It was for a long time a milling, cursing, shouting, denouncing, ugly and incoherent mob. The streams of water played over the crowd only fuelled the anger.

Several cars were taken to by groups of youths and rocked from side to side. Nobody was in charge of the mayhem, but I saw two cars tipped on their side. Police were booed as they tackled the car-attackers and dragged them off. By now there was a lot of hysterical screaming and sobbing from youths, young women most obviously, hurt in one or other fashion from fists and boots, bottles and stones. The Zambucks had a busy time tending to the gashes, cut lips and black eyes.

Pulling by Sue and Jenny got us inside the Mayfair, where anarchy, if Jasper will forgive me, ruled. I saw a young woman on a bar with her skirt hiked and bare legs apart, inviting all comers. Youths struggled to get at her.

We left that bar and went upstairs, on to a balcony. From there we could see the futile and stupid hosing, the fire engine marooned along with police in a seething group of thousands of hostile people. It was difficult to tell onlookers from participants, but the only planned participation I saw came from the periodic police group ganging up on one or two unfortunates.

The crowd only quietened down when the fire engine disappeared. Whoever in the police hierarchy brought it in should be broken back to constable and put on cell latrine duties.

We tried all the pubs that stayed open, but failed to find anybody even willing to talk about accommodation. We made calls from the public phone boxes that were operating and had intact phone books to those private hotels and residences offering accommodation. Lines were engaged or off the hook. The few answers we got were negatives. We eventually accepted the reality that the bus was our bed for the night. On the way we passed a pipe band foolishly marching through the crowd playing *Colonel Bogey's March*. If they'd been singing the rude version I had recorded on the bus, it might have worked. Instead, the 'Eagle Clan' took time off destroying shop decorations to start pursuing the musicians, demanding rock 'n' roll. The pipe band members disbanded.

We were approaching the bus when we saw a woman across the road in what looked like a wedding dress encased in plastic, an umbrella for further protection.

'Not the best day to get hitched,' I said.

'Drongo,' Sue laughed. 'She's the Blossom Queen.'

'Lost her blossom,' I suggested, dodging a slap from Sue, who was looking happier. Jenny remained in sombre mood, remarking that crowd instincts are a fight for survival, and we were lucky things had not got totally out of control. Jasper said Harry Seresin had been talking at the dinner party about that very thing, mob rule. He was in Vienna when the Nazis 'liberated' the city. He said he was the only one of a million people not raising his hand in the 'Heil Hitler' to the conquerors.

'He was lucky he didn't get lynched,' Jenny said. 'Mob rule by its very nature turns ugly. Elias Canetti wrote about all that.'

'Harry,' Jasper said, 'took his father's advice to get as far from the fascists as he could. New Zealand.'

'And don't forget silly old Erich,' Jenny added. 'He's another Viennese Jew.'

'They came to the right place,' Sue said. 'It couldn't happen here.'

'You sure?' Jasper asked. 'This looked like a pretty good start today. And what about the ambush outside your dinner party?'

'Dad said there was some stupid photographer. Probably from that gutter rag *Truth*. They see Reds under every bed.'

'Watch what happens when the Nats get in,' Jasper warned.

'Holyoake's no Hitler,' Jenny objected.

'Not many are,' Jasper said dryly. 'There are some nasties in his party. You get them in any party, the party is a cloak in which they conceal their daggers. All the politicians need are the right conditions.'

'Like a cancelled blossom festival?' I suggested.

'Wait and see,' he said.

Jenny began talking to Sue about that girl in the pub, whether she was safe.

Jasper asked me if I saw my mate Paddy the Plod. I told him I had not, and frankly

I could not care less. He couldn't believe I missed him, he was next to the trigger-happy photographer busy with a telescopic lens, right below us on the roof next to the pub. I shrugged, said he might have been brought back on duty. The police would have planned for those trainloads from the Hutt Valley, kids coming up here looking for trouble. Gull might have been after Peters and no doubt his watchdog Heffernan pushing drugs around the pubs. I did wonder if Jasper was getting paranoid, seeing Gull everywhere, probably in his sleep.

If he got any sleep. Buses are the least satisfactory place for slumber, especially when you don't have blankets or pillows. There was no sign of the driver and it was a morose night for everybody. Well, not entirely. There were other reasons for not sleeping. We weren't the only couple huddled under duffel coats trying to make up in discreet fashion for the fun we had missed out on with the dud festival. The giggles and gasps and sudden movements suggested others were at it too, in one way or another.

The driver turned up at six the next morning, as bleary-eyed as all of us huddled and sorry humps of humanity. He closed the door, started the engine and took off without saying anything. There was no singing on the way back.

Sue and Jenny retreated to the Gifford house for hot baths, we made do with the shower. The radio news claimed there was rioting in the streets of Hastings and the police under attack from hooligans. Jasper scoffed the most prominent hooligans were the police. I said the comments reminded me of a Stendhal story of the soldier meandering among occasional fragments of action, wondering where the Battle of Waterloo really was, later discovering he had been in the middle of it. Do battles and riots only become so when they have been written up later?

I had taken notes of the Blossom Festival rumble. Little of what I recorded was not sodden, along with us, but it didn't square with the subsequent hysterical newspaper articles claiming a full-scale riot was instigated by rebellious young people. *The Dominion* said it was mob hysteria. It reported the extremes, like the police forming a cordon outside the Hastings police station to repel youths demanding the release of the widgie who broke aerials; the cop knocked unconscious by a rock; beer bottles smashed against the court house; the tablet stolen at Pakipaki station five miles from Hastings and the tablet arm smashed, delaying trains for 20 minutes; a Hutt Valley gang later that night killing two ewes at Pakowai Bridge four miles from Hastings. The most accurate thing I read was the open sex taking place in a bar, something I witnessed the prelude to.

The papers took a vindictive approach. *The Evening Post* proposed the 'Rock College' where those arrested got the convict-era punishment of breaking stones. 'Must the Hooligans Take Control?' the editorial asked. It wrote of shameful scenes of mob violence, an orgy of disorderliness and destruction by riff-raff deliberately intent on wrecking the festival. It attributed the problem to these louts receiving kid-glove treatment for too long and there needed to be a crack down, send them to the Rock College and The Citadel. *Truth* identified Karamu and Heretaunga streets as the battlefield for a full-scale riot and noted that the Pakowai incident also involved the decapitation of a sheep.

Jasper claimed the press coverage propped up the establishment and was as usual one-sided. History, he said, is invariably written by the victors. Those in charge told their story, those under their control did not get heard. The heavy-handed handling of the mostly harmless crowd, especially the fire engine hosing and the lunatic traffic cop, had provoked most of the trouble. Before that he reckoned it was no more than scuffles, isolated actions of drunken idiots, often exuberantly dealt with by pugnacious police. If there were no confrontational police and firemen, he questioned there would have been such intemperate headlines and pontificating editorials.

I figured I could tell the story from my notebooks, a crowd's eye view. I was starting to think I could be getting political, anarchic even. I'd start writing again for the college paper. It was after all called 'Stud-Op'. I might just pen an opinion or two. I asked Jasper if he was writing anything. He showed me his revolutionary essay. It was an eye-opener.

Marriage had not moderated his incendiary opinions. He called the majority of us Training College students politically naïve and apathetic. He advocated extending protest against the use of nuclear weapons and pakeha-only All Blacks to strikes that break the government — whether of the left or right — to the people's will. He wrote that the recent tour to South Africa based on racial discrimination proved New Zealand was not the racially harmonious society it claimed to be.

He argued that New Zealand was one of the most governed countries in the world, its citizens obedient conformists, soulless, heartless, virtually cultureless, where bureaucracy reigns supreme and the average bloke is a cog in a mean-spirited machine. The dull, organised, welfare state should be replaced by workers controlling the state, and the only way to achieve that was to take to the barricades and bring down government by direct action.

His solution was to form cooperatives to run education, agriculture and housing. There would be no authority and privilege, wealth would be shared by all regardless of occupation, society would be one big mutual aid union free of wage differentiation and any factors that created inequities and exploitation. Nobody would rule over anybody else. All these so-called delinquent youths were rebelling against the authoritarian values of their parents. It was time for youth and rank and file to take back control from the politicians and union leaders and the beer barons. He advocated abolishing six-o'clock closing tomorrow, making booze available whenever people wanted it.

Jasper didn't just want to get rid of Labour or National, he wanted to see the rank and file immediately pass votes of no confidence in union leaders. He denounced the left as much as the right, rejecting the Labour Party and even the Communist Party. The left was as unacceptably puritanical as the right was for entrenched privilege, and the proof was in the Presbyterian Minister and Minister of Finance Nordmeyer incensing the ordinary bloke with his Black Budget taxes on cigarettes, alcohol and tobacco. Jasper wanted to abolish the wage system, get rid of royalty – the Queen was a bludger – cancel parliamentary elections. Basically he was declaring a pox on all political and institutional controls.

I told him he sounded like a modern version of Samson in the Bible, pushing over the pillars on both sides and collapsing the building. But what did he put in its place? He smirked and said he would worry about that when he'd got rid of the pompous pollies and bog-trotting bureaucrats with their snouts in the public trough. People were so frightened of a vacuum, when really, to quote Karl Marx, they had nothing to lose but their chains. Embrace a truly democratic society, where people think and act for themselves in their immediate community. The state is coercive and aggressive, people if permitted can cooperate for their own welfare.

All folk need to do, he reckoned, is start being defiant. Not futile vandalism like the bored Hutt Valley kids in Hastings, with the state authorities waiting to sort them out. Before democracy could be available to those kids, the state controllers had to be neutralised. Those whom you wish to knock over, you first make fun of. Disruption, he said, was the name of the game, the way we had already cocked a snook at the American nuclear sub, the statue symbolising the British Empire, the sacred footy turf of Athletic Park.

When I asked what other targets he had in mind, he suggested my next trip to the movies, refusing to stand when they played *God Save the Queen* at the end of the film. I was silly enough to do so when Sue and I went to see *Sons and Lovers*. She hissed at me to get up, but I stayed in the seat and got clouted on the head by a woman behind me with an umbrella. Sue reckoned I deserved it for a really stupid protest that achieved nothing.

However, Jasper's essay was exhilarating. I wanted to contribute. I had three notebooks to draw on for inspiration, but I was only too aware of how strong Jasper's opinions were. The Hastings notebook would have offered some ammunition. If you think pencil doesn't run, think again. Those passages undamaged were largely those I took on the way up, the efforts to record the street activity were illegible, I guess from scribbling on the run, in toilets. Later it was a waste of time trying to record on wet paper on a shaky bus in poor light. There had to be a lesson here to protect one's sources. In any case, what I could recall from the notes and memory would not survive Jasper's steely assessment. I had been wantonly apolitical, I lacked the confidence to write a version of the 'riot' which challenged the newspaper accounts.

I settled for the trivia of the first two notebooks, which were dominated by jokes, with no connecting thread. I recalled the humour discussion Erich provoked outside the Gifford house and thought I'd write about humour. I read what I could find in the public library and sat at the desk upstairs enduring my first experience of writer's block. I told Sue and she suggested I should write about something I knew, like the Peter Sellers movies I was always going on about.

I did, claiming his three parts in *The Mouse that Roared* proved him as versatile as Alec Guinness in his seven parts in *Kind Hearts and Coronets*. I wished I had paid more attention to the arguments for different kinds of humour from Erich, Con and Hugh. I settled for claiming that Sellers achieved his laughs by maintaining a blank righteousness, whether he was leading the protest or darning socks in *I'm All Right Jack*, refusing to betray his principles for Sophia Loren in *The Millionairess*, which is more than I would have, resisting change in *The Battle of the Sexes*, a meek murderer in *The Ladykillers*. Understatement, I concluded, was what made Sellers memorable, just like Guinness and the other English comics before him. It was not exactly revolutionary, like Jasper's inflammatory essay, but we saw our efforts in print.

Don approached me to contribute to the college poetry publication. I said I had dried up on poems. He proposed they put in my Dead Cat poem, if I had no objections. I was flattered and agreed to share a publication with the mighty James K. Baxter and the budding Katherine Mansfields of Training College.

I should have known there was a catch. I was roped in to selling the slim volume. Jasper offered to help, and several post-pub Friday nights we set up on a corner of Cuba Street just up from the Royal Oak. The Commie guy was trying to push his rag on the opposite corner, and the Sallies were handing out the *People's Voice* and accepting donations. With all these half-cut and beer-happy folk reeling out of the pubs, it was a good time to sell, and it was Jasper's idea to mention it was a student publication. We sold out and left before punters realised it was not like *Cappicade*, full of rude jokes and cartoons. Jasper noticed the photographer snapping us from across the street. I asked him how he knew it was of us, it could be old Vic the Commie nearby.

Selling the publication was actually fun, and we covered half the print bill from two Friday night stints. All this time the study was piling up at Training College and the varsity exams were imminent. Let the cramming begin. I put my head down in the varsity and public libraries, getting through the history essay for Shallcrass on New Zealand history as mainly a grab for land, the Junior Education essay on myths and folk stories, cribbing from Edmund Wilson for Yeats and James Joyce, working on Latin and French. I'd no sooner handed in the history essay than Shallcrass was after another one on the subjection of the individual to the society and whether we should conform. I toyed with Jasper's approach to suggest society could and should change to liberate the individual.

Sue was flat stick on her bookkeeping and stats swotting, but we took time off to see the powerful *On the Waterfront*. I thought it ironic that here was the anarchist anti-hero standing out against the powerful wharfies' union, and then we all stand at the end for *God Save the Queen*. Jasper is right, we must rebel. For the sake of Sue's peace of mind, I did stand. We went back and swotted together, spooning orange yoghurt into each other, then lay down together. I had brought in my turntable from Eastbourne and we listened to my new World Record Club acquisition, Beethoven's 'Emperor' concerto.

The French exam went okay, the Latin was a breeze. Jasper went around the flat waving *The Dominion* and denouncing the trivial nature of the current parliamentary debate on whether pakeha should have a capital 'P' like Maori and whether it was a vulgar expression. His view was that they were a parliament of vulgarians. Jenny was more interested in the report that the Minister of Justice had denied a woman the right to sit on a jury. I noticed a report on lawn tennis losing its grip, but I said nothing, there was no need to reinforce Jasper's view of me as a lightweight. It took me all my energy to study Yeats, and I loved him, and after him Shelley and Auden proved to be plain hard yakker.

The poetry exam was a joke. I answered both the 'either' and the 'or' questions and wrote a load of rubbish about Shelley. Afterwards Sue took me to my first opera, *Don Pasquale*. Interesting to be on the other side of the stage. It was apparently meant to be funny, or at least buffoonish, but struck me as a lot of shouting and warbling by an overweight man and ladies in satin costumes. Sue enjoyed it.

The study became incessant. Macaskill wanted an essay from me on 'The Cinema Tomorrow'. Blimey! And I had to give a talk for Shallcrass on whether the Maori wars were inevitable. How the hell should I know? I said they were, but I knew it was a feeble effort.

Kennedy beat Nixon, and Jasper confessed he had been a Catholic for a brief period, proving yet again he is full of surprises.

We had the end-of-year Training College ball at the Majestic Cabaret. Scotty warned us in Assembly that liquor was forbidden under pain of expulsion. We smuggled in beer, gin, rum, vodka, and danced the night away.

Jasper and I had managed three hours sleep before we struggled out of bed, Sue reminding me to behave myself. We were to join Pat Macaskill and our Kowhai Road group on the DC3 to Nelson and on to the cabins at Tahuna Beach motor camp.

The first few days were like a social studies-cum-scouts jamboree. The group visited the Nelson brewery, cordial factory, art gallery. Those who wanted to played golf and tennis. Jasper and I hitched to the hop research place and looked at hop plants. The next day there was a trip to Waimea College and the intermediate school. In the evenings we had barbecues on the beach, singalongs, walks which led to some pairing off. Jasper and I behaved ourselves.

Macaskill proposed an optional visit to the Riverside Community. Jasper said he had visited it with Jenny when they were on their honeymoon and found it quite interesting, if you wanted to practise organic farming. Pat said it was much more than that, it was a Christian Pacifist lifestyle offering an alternative way of life to our competitive society by promoting a culture of peace through cooperative and sustainable living. Not a pun on offer. He urged us all to experience this radically different way of living.

When I said I was a starter, Jasper pulled me to one side and told me he had seen Melissa there. Jenny didn't know her and was looking at the dairy herd when he bumped into her. Melissa asked him not to mention that he had seen her.

At first I was angry with him, but I accepted he had respected her request. I said I was interested in seeing the community and there was no reason to worry about Melissa, I was involved with Sue now. I might even have believed myself. Most of the group went, Jasper did not.

The bus was old and the roads not great, and it must have taken the best part of an hour to rattle around the coast and inland from Moutere. It could have been shorter, I was feeling impatient as well as apprehensive. There was nothing that stood out as the bus circled the little village of a dozen or so modest houses tucked away among trees and farms on the side of the rolling hills.

We pulled up outside a large building, waiting to welcome us a snowy-haired couple. The man gave us a run-down on what they aspired to, fostering learning and mutual understanding in innovative ways that celebrated life free of the pressures of normal society. It was their belief that a competitive society inevitably led to wars. Here everything was owned by everybody and everybody shared equally, the adults achieving management by consensus. We were free to wander about and lunch would be served in the communal hall behind them in an hour.

Pat stayed chatting to them and the rest of us wandered. It was certainly a peaceful setting, cows munching contentedly, bees buzzing about among the rows of ripening apples. I took the loop road around to where the houses were clustered on the lower side of the hill, my pace accelerating.

'Greetings.' The young man who had hailed me was coming from behind a hedge, holding two metal buckets and surrounded by clucking hens. He was in khaki overalls and gumboots, a wide-brimmed straw hat shielding his freckled face from the warm sun. He had a wide grin on his face, gesturing with one of the buckets. 'The chooks think buckets mean grub. They'd be right. You from the teacher group?'

I acknowledged this and told him I had known one of the community, Melissa Davies, at Teachers College.

His grin widened. 'Not anymore.'

'Pardon?'

'She's Melissa Bridges now. I'm Bob, the other half.'

He put the buckets down, creating an unseemly scramble and furious clucking among the competitive chooks, holding out his hand. I accepted a rough clasp.

'You okay?'

'I didn't know she'd got hitched.'

'Come around the back and meet Mrs Bridges. She's taken up spinning big time, she's dyeing today.

I said I'd best not, we were due back for lunch. He squinted at the sun, said there was a good half hour before we broke fast, and anyway we would hear the bell. I was saying I didn't want to disturb her work when she came round the corner of the house, a large apron stained with blue splotches over her overalls, her hair pulled back under a green handkerchief and tied behind. No earrings, no bangles, no rings. She'd never bothered with make-up. She didn't need to. She looked more beautiful than ever. My gaze was drawn to the apron bulging out over her spreading stomach.

'Hello, Stephen.'

'Your teaching past come back to haunt you, Lissy?'

'Stephen was also in the literary club.'

'Eh?' I said. 'Oh, yes.'

I looked up from her midriff, into her eyes. She wasn't smiling.

'Lissy. I'm going to clean up before lunch. Catch you at our community meal, Stephen.'

He casually squeezed her hand on his way past her. I noticed her return squeeze, and then he was gone around the side of the house. Her eyes were still on me, calm and steady.

'It's not yours, Stephen.'

'Yeh,' I mumbled, looking away. 'Just wanted to say hello. Sorry. Ah, best get back, eh.'

I blundered away, my pulse racing and my stomach turned to water. I felt such a fool. I hadn't expected to be affected like this. I had no precedent for how to handle her being married and pregnant. No way was I going to lunch. I couldn't face her, them, the pregnancy.

I stumbled out of the village and kept going, and going. I wanted the clamour inside my head to ease, my stomach to settle, my heart to decelerate. I felt I had to lie down. I pushed into the long grass beside the gravel road, advancing until I was shielded from sight, lay down with my face to the sun, and passed out.

It might have been the sun going behind a cloud that woke me. I was weak and shivery, and I could feel my face burning.

I began walking, my thumb out. A farm truck pulled up. The window wound down on the passenger side, a woman shouting I was welcome to share the tray with the dog as far as Richmond, if that was any help. I said it was and climbed on the back, just in time as the truck took off in a cloud of dust and spraying gravel. The collie took my arrival as an invitation to lick my face vigorously, before slumping against me.

The truck bucked to a stop, the driver saying he was turning here for Hope, I should get a lift, no problem. I didn't, it was a long walk, but I didn't care, I had nothing to get back to. When eventually I did, I shrugged away questions, said I just felt like a walk. Jasper said nothing.

 **25**

The sitting room looked like the front window of the Dixon Deli, with hot pastry smells wafting about. There was a long trestle table covered in a white cloth, hosting plates of provender under a muslin wrap. I could see sliced meats and fancy sausages, from little wieners to big Polish, cold chicken pieces, green and black olives, vine leaves, cheeses from bright orange to pale white and every yellow in between, lumps of pickled vegetables from tiny carrots to baby beetroot to white onions and indeterminate pale objects. There were baskets full of long French loaves and little buns covered in caraway or sesame seeds. A second, smaller table had dozens of bottles of beer and some wine.

Sue and Jenny stood proudly between the tables in bright floral party dresses. Both stepped forward as one. 'Dah-daah,' they said, hands directed at the display. Jasper and I looked at each other.

'Have we forgotten somebody's birthday?' I asked.

Sue had her head up for a kiss. 'We all passed,' she said excitedly, handing me an envelope. 'Take a look. We couldn't wait.'

I opened up and saw I had scored 78 for Latin, 68 for French, a fluke, and 60 and 50 for English.

'You don't look exactly overjoyed,' she said.

'No,' I protested. 'It's just a surprise. I cocked up the poetry one. The *Bleak House* was okay.'

'We invited all of varsity,' Jenny said. 'And we put it on your college noticeboard. It's flat-closing as well, so we thought the more the merrier.'

'Excellent,' Jasper said. 'Would you step this way, dear lady.'

They disappeared into their bedroom. I said it seemed a bit sudden. Sue shrugged, said Jenny and Jasper were off next month to the Nelson commune, Jasper must have told me. I said he had mentioned he was interested, I didn't know it was confirmed. She suggested I take a shower before the party got underway.

I was in our bedroom with towel round my waist when she came in, a smile on her face. 'We've got time for a rest,' she said, reaching for the towel, when there was a sharp rapping on the front door. She told me not to go anywhere and went to answer it.

Cécile's voice, and Sue remonstrating. I got into my sweater and jeans and was doing up my boots when Sue returned.

'Great start,' she said sardonically. 'I told mum we'd handle it.'

'She bring something?'

'Hors d'oeuvres. She has to interfere. Anyway, as you're dressed, I might as well see to the savouries.'

She left before I could think of anything meaningful to say. When I emerged, she was downing a glass of white wine. She reached for the bottle, asked me if I wanted one. I accepted. She poured herself another.

'Here's to the party,' I said, touching glasses.

'So how was Nelson?'

'Quiet,' I said.

We both stood there, side-on. Another tap on the door stopped the silence getting to the embarrassing stage. I said I'd answer it.

Stump, with a crate of beer dangling from one hand. This was quite an achievement, given it was almost as big as him.

'Not too early?' he asked, swinging the crate at me. I took it and told him to come on in, somebody had to be first.

'Grouse looking tucker,' he said.

I told him to help himself, as Sue shut our bedroom door behind her. He went for the hors d'oeuvres, popped a pastry and then almost choked. He swallowed bravely and reached for two bottles, levering off one cap with the other, and guzzling half the bottle. 'Farkin hell,' he said, looking around. 'That your new sheila I saw doing the old disappearing trick? Shy one, is she?'

'Sue,' I said.

'Champion,' he said, demolishing the rest of the bottle. He burped loudly. 'Scuse I?'

Tentative taps on the front glass excused me. I opened on to several of the Lit Club ladies clutching covered plates. They craned round me, one anxiously asking if they were the first. I was able to tell them this was not so and please come in. Our contributions, they said, loading me up but not advancing far, for Stump had followed me and was giving them the once-over. They hesitated until thcy saw Jasper advancing past Stump, his hands out, looking magnificent in the dry-cleaned Sherlock Holmes outfit, minus cape and hat but with the addition of a bold red polka-dot bow tie.

'Welcome, welcome, thrice welcome, dear ladies.' He gave each a peck on the cheek and ushered them in. Stump followed like a neglected pet. I went past him into our bedroom, colliding in the doorway with Sue.

'I need another drink,' she said, without stopping. I got my turntable and set it up in the sitting room, Sue having joined the Lit Club ladies and Jasper and Jenny. I put on *Jailhouse Rock* and went to answer the door. It was Ron and Peter. 'No Bosco and Randy?' I asked. They laughed, Peter offered an LP. It's the Martin Denny one, he informed me, with the hit *Quiet Village*. Probably best for later, he added. Ron asked if I had anything else but Elvis. I said *Swan Lake*, which caused both of them to groan.

As they went through I welcomed Jeff and some of the other Phys-Ed guys, and then Stump was barging past me and offering Red Band.

'Nun's piss,' Jeff scoffed. 'That the best you can do?'

Stump said he hadn't checked. Jeff pushed past him to do his own checking.

The arrivals were accelerating, a bunch of the guys I had been to Nelson with, bringing more beer for Jeff to assess. A group of girls I did not know told me they were friends of Jenny. I repeated her mantra, 'the more the merrier'. And indeed there were several stranger students behind them, and some girls I recognised from Ngaio Road.

The place was teeming with folk, spilling out of the sitting room and kitchen into the hall. It was looking increasingly like we had half the student population coming in for freebies. It was beyond my control so I left people to it, knowing that once the booze was cut, they'd leave. I worked my way into the kitchen to check the stove. I opened the oven and was engulfed in black smoke from singed sausage rolls. The coughing and spluttering around me was punctuated by somebody wanting to know who the idiot was who opened the oven door. I leaned across the oven to force the window, then abandoned the kitchen.

Sue and Jenny and Jasper were talking to a weedy guy with excessive sideburns and a curled pipe which really belonged with Jasper's outfit. I noticed my bedroom door was ajar and the light off. I went to check, switching on the light to find Jeff and a girl I didn't know on my bed.

'She invited me in,' he said blandly, nodding at the clown/witch painting by Melissa. 'Wanted me to check this weirdo creation.'

'In the dark?'

'Uh huh,' he said as the girl ducked under my arm. He stood and walked out. 'Like your new grommet,' he drawled as he passed me.

Sue was still in the kitchen, knocking back the wine. More people were coming in the front door. I heard Elvis get the screeching stop and pushed through to check. Ron was bending over the turntable putting on the Denny LP. He was wasting his time, the Kowhai Road crew had decided to do the favourite Tahuna Beach barbecue song about the fox going out on the chase one night.

Soon most were joining in, singing rowdily. At least it was harmless, merely about a fox slaughtering ducks and a grey goose. No filth in that, no sucking clean with the ease of a vacuum cleaner, to quote a line from *Eskimo Nell* Jasper had quoted to me as a good example of the Noel Coward lyrics. Sue could not take umbrage at this, at me or anybody else, the way she was drinking. I started to head through the crowd, thinking I might have to take Jenny aside and suggest she take her home. The way the party was going, it might be a good idea for Jenny to stay with her.

Jenny beat me to it, tugging my arm and leaning close to say she hoped I didn't mind she was taking Sue home, she was getting a bit overwrought. I said that was a good idea, resisting the desire to comment that overwrought was a new name for it. Jasper assisted a protesting Sue to the door. I figured it best to stay out of it.

As they exited, in came the wrestler type from Extrav and a bunch of his mates, all bearing full flagons. There were cheers and a mass move from the Phys-Ed group towards the replenishments. *My Old Man's An All Black* was begun by a group in the sitting room, but petered out as words failed them. The Extrav crew started up their version of *Seventy-Six Trombones,* the song that closed the show, and they had that to themselves.

The Phys-Ed guys had collared a few flagons and were employing empty quart bottles in a hall competition to see who could stretch over a mark etched into the wallpaper, below it a dribbled beer line across the wooden floor. The stretcher had to place a bottle upright as far as he could without touching wall or floor, and get back behind the line without any support. The Extrav guys joined in and it became a contest between Jeff and the wrestler, the latter winning after Jeff fell over the line. The Phys-Ed jokers demanded a rematch and made accusations of cheating. This led to some pushing and abuse, but they were distracted by a recitation of *Eskimo Nell* by a duffel-coated streak of weasel piss wobbling about on top of the drinks table. His memory soon deserted him and so did his balance, as he crashed on to the floor amidst derisive laughter.

Then the gate-crashers arrived. We heard the yells of alarm and pain from the hall, just before a bunch of rough jokers charged into the sitting room. They had on the dark blue or black worker jackets like my Gear one, they were roaring obscenities and threats to 'do fucking student wankers', and they had spanners and broken bottles which would make the job easy.

Jasper was at my side, shouting to get the women behind sofas and chairs. He went straight at the leader of the pack, leaping and grabbing his crescent spanner and starting a wrestling match to claim it. The wrestler let out a shout of sheer glee and launched himself at the next in line, warding off a spanner and slamming a fist into his face with a squishy sound akin to a sledgehammer sinking into a pumpkin.

There were ten or so of these intruders, and they made a concerted effort to push their way into the sitting room and kitchen. It was as if they were acting on a plan. Despite the piercing howls and shrieks of alarm and grief, the fact that there were so many in the confined space limited the amount of actual damage that could be inflicted. The broken bottles were what worried me.

A stocky little chap came at me with the jagged end jabbing towards my face. I fell back and fell over, which saved me, and I used the wall to brace myself as I kicked out and caught him in the ankle. It knocked his feet from under him and he fell on his own bottle, screaming with pain and surprise that a student wanker had hit back.

The invasion had cleared the hall and I was getting warily to my feet when I saw Peters dart inside, glancing in the direction of the bedrooms.

'Elvis!' he said. 'Can't keep outta trouble, can ya?'

'Piss off back where you crawled from,' I growled, annoyed he persisted with the Elvis dig long after I'd ditched the wannabe look.

Instead of taking my advice, he moved towards me and pulled out a knife, flicking open the blade.

'Your flatmate's room, Elvis? Tell me and you don't get pricked.'

I ignored the shouting and screaming behind me, concentrating on the knife waving across my vision. 'What the hell do you want?'

'I told you, fuck. You get out of my way while I sort it. Or you're dead fucking pork. I've had a little cutting practice already tonight.'

Somebody was coming through the door behind him. It was Gull, with a face like thunder. I nodded at him, suggested to Peters he had company. He laughed. 'Pull the other tit.'

Gull had the wool hook raised as he strode at Peters, who sensed at the last second and ran at and past me, wheeling as Gull advanced.

'Get away,' Gull spat at me, his voice thick. Peters retreated down the hall towards the back window.

'What's your problem?' he said in a fearful voice. 'I was doing what you wanted.'

'You slashed Clair.' Gull's voice was a flat hiss.

'That whore. She owed me for drugs, man. Got lippy.'

'You ruined her face, you fucking maggot.'

'Hey, man, there're penalties, y'know?'

'You got that right,' Gull snarled, charging at Peters, who retreated, eyes wild, the knife held out in front of him. Gull kept coming. Peters took another step backwards, bumping against the end of the hall. He waved his free hand behind him to steady himself, cringing as Gull swung the wool hook at his head.

Peters groped in space, trying to get purchase. Somebody had opened the window, possibly to clear the air of the oven smoke. He was wobbling backwards as the wool hook caught in the collar of his leather jacket. He cried out, pulling away, ripping the wool hook free. There was a desperate, obscene dance as his feet scrabbled, his eyes wide, his mouth open, like some kind of silent movie melodrama. He disappeared without a sound, toppling head first into the void.

Gull turned on me, his eyes demented. He was hissing, but I couldn't understand him. I could hear the screams and curses and clanking of toppled bottles, but at a muted level, as if I was coming down Ngauranga Gorge too fast on the back of his motorbike. My ears popped.

'You're coming with me!'

I couldn't help glancing at the sharp tip of the wool hook.

'Jesus!' he swore, stuffing the hook inside his duffel, grabbing my arm. People were tumbling out into the hall, spanners and bottles flashing, some kind of counterattack with chairs and broken bottles employed by a group led by Jeff, Stump and the wrestler. Gull grabbed me round the neck and tightened his grip, choking me.

He wrenched me towards the door. I threw a hand out, slapping into the stained glass panel, sliding across its surface, fearing the glass would break and slice my hand. I caught my fingers on the ridged corner of the architrave, attempting resistance, wanting to say something about Peters, I wasn't sure what.

I heard Jasper's shout as if from miles away, my breath shutting down, I could not get air into my lungs. Dizzy and panicky, I kicked at Gull, making contact and having no effect. He let go of me and I fell in the porch, gasping for air, watching helpless as he grabbed Jasper by his pony tail, swung him round and threw him into the struggling group.

I put my hands up, in vain. He brushed them aside, rammed my arm behind me in a painful arm lock. He lifted me off the porch and frogmarched me into the street, my boots dragging against glass, the dull streetlight catching shards of a broken flagon and a dark stain running into the gutter. I dragged air into my lungs, and along with it the stench of spilled beer. Gull tightened his grip and accelerated both of us away from the sirens and flashing lights of the police cars pulling up outside our flat.

'What about Peters?' I croaked. 'You have to tell them.'

Gull ignored my protest, propelling me away from the yelling and screams and a strange grunting chant as police piled in to the party. He pulled me round the steep horseshoe into Fairlie Terrace, where he dragged me to the passenger door of an A35. He shoved me inside, told me to stay put, slamming the door.

A moment later he was back, wrenching open the door, clamping a handcuff on my wrist, locking the other end round the steering wheel.

'No need,' I objected, as he slammed the door on me.

I sat shivering for a long time, during which I heard more sirens. I stared at the light rain streaking the windscreen, unable to think past the appalling violence of Gull raging at Peters, the wool hook raised, slashing into his jacket, Peters falling out the window. There was no way he would survive that sort of drop, unless he hit trees and his fall was cushioned by all that undergrowth. I prayed Gull had gone back to check. By now he had to have calmed down. It was his sworn duty to serve and protect, though the behaviour of the police at Hastings did not exactly support that perception.

When he returned he climbed in, grunted that Peters was being taken to hospital as he undid the cuffs.

'So he's alive?'

'For now.'

'How badly is he hurt?'

'Dunno.'

'What about Jasper?'

'Yeah,' he scoffed, and swung the car up Fairlie Terrace, down Kelburn Parade past the dark hulk of Easterfield and the old Hunter building. He swung round past the tennis courts and left at The Terrace. I asked where we were going. He did not respond.

He took us hard right past Parliament and the marble pedestal I'd contemplated in the company of that drunk a long time ago. We skidded right across the tram tracks into Lambton Quay, left into Waring Taylor Street and inside the Central Police Station.

Gull greeted the cop at reception as he took me through and up the stairs, along a corridor and into a small, brightly lit room. There was a large oak public service desk with lots of drawers and cupboards, its surface empty of anything but a large blotter set in a blue leather sachet. There was a swivel chair with a high, curved back behind the desk, several more modest curved chairs our side. There were framed photos of policemen in uniforms on the walls, a bookcase spilling bulky folders and leather-bound volumes. It was a working police office, obviously, as opposed to the cell I had anticipated.

'No questions,' Gull said, pointing to a chair. 'Pull that up. I want you to look at these photographs.'

From behind the desk he removed a dark grey East-Light box file, dumped it on the desk. He opened its lid, removed a sheaf of closely typed foolscap pages held by a bull clip, put them aside and took out a pile of large glossy black and white photographs. He spread the images on the desk. They covered the entire desk top. He invited me to take a look, starting at the top far left.

The first photograph was a murky, late-night shot of water and wharf sheds, a shadowy figure of a man with his back to the camera. I peered closer. He was holding a wool hook at his side. The next shots were side-on of the man, the hook visible, talking to another man. There was enough reflected light in the second shot to identify Bill Dwyer with his hook talking to Ben. Now inside the Symposium, a group of three men crouched over coffees: Bill Dwyer, Ben, Jasper. Another group apparently unaware of the camera: Jasper, Jenny, Ben, me.

'You took these?'

'Go on.'

Long shots of figures on a roof and flaring vapour trails above them. I knew it was Jasper and me, and the close-ups proved it, both of us peering over the parapet to check the progress of the rockets.

'The Americans helped out here,' he said. 'Keep going.'

We were captured abseiling and running away. The next sequence was much closer, a long shot as Jasper climbed up on me, a middle-range image of him flinging the paint at the statue, a closer one of him jumping off my back, closer still of both of us looking at the camera, a final one of us ducking behind the plinth.

'The tram,' I murmured. 'You were on the tram.'

'Surprised you didn't notice.' He motioned for me to continue.

Athletic Park crowd, Jasper and myself visible, us joining the protesters advancing on to the pitch, clustered in the middle, Jasper grabbing one end of the protest flag and running off, me running the other way straight at the camera.

The protests outside Parliament, us in close-up and long shots among the protesters. No surprise to see the dinner guests leaving the Giffords, Jasper looking demented in full chase after the cameraman. Finally, us in the Albert Hotel ruckus and the Hastings street crowds, Jasper prominent waving his fist at the camera, gesticulating at the fire engine.

'So what's all this prove?'

Gull sighed. 'Taken in conjunction with the signed records of surveillance and conversations overheard, there is more than enough to deport those bastards. Porteous may try and appeal because of his marriage.'

'And baby.'

'Eh?'

'Something your spying didn't pick up?'

He glared at me, proceeded to gather up the photos and put them back in the file.

'Any photos of your attack on Peters?'

He put the file away and sat at the desk facing me.

'Okay. Here's the problem. I have spent a lot of time trying to keep you out of the firing line. You have persisted in your larking about and close association with a known agitator. He has published, as you know, an essay promoting civil strife that aims to destroy the legal institutions of our democracy. This is serious.'

'So is Peters. What was he doing for you?'

Gull looked away. 'Yes. Well, it didn't work out.'

'Planting drugs?'

He shrugged. 'It would have helped.'

'But I know about it. Do I get the high dive treatment like Peters?'

'Christ,' Gull said, putting his hands over his face, making scrubbing motions. He looked at me, clearly distressed. 'I never wanted anything but to protect you. That was my job. I wanted to do it. Do you understand that?'

There was a tap on the door and a senior policeman entered. Gull stood up, the policeman waving him back. The cop gave me a searching look, but stayed in the doorway. I recognised him from my brief sojourn at Taranaki Street police station. He had already given me the once-over.

'Can I help, sir?'

The side of his mouth twitched. 'Lock him up until the election. I'll see you later, Flynn.'

As the door closed, I asked Gull if that was his boss. He nodded. I asked if he was behind all this carry-on, or did it go much higher?

'I can't tell you that. I can tell you that the flat is now off-limits as a crime scene. Will you go home? Please?'

I stood up. 'And forget about Jasper? His wife? Sue? You have to be joking!'

'Sit down.'

'Fuck you. Arrest me, or let me go.'

'I can't.'

'Not if I tell them about your late-night activities on the wharf?'

He looked stunned.

'I saw you.'

'Jesus,' he said. 'Look, Steve.'

'Steve now, is it? You fucking hypocrite.'

He was ashen. 'Please don't say that. I have never ...'

'Laid a hand on me?'

'I wouldn't ...'

'What about Peters?'

'Okay, confession time,' he said heavily. 'If you'll just sit still, I'll tell you why I'm a policeman.'

'Not interested.'

'You're going to hear it anyway. I'm not going to say anything about what you claim to have witnessed on the wharf. That is none of your business. I will say I've no regrets about what I did to Peters. I watched my mother put up with years of physical abuse. Okay?'

I nodded.

'Never mind what he did to me, those were just hidings. The drunken pig, every night he came home with half a bottle of Jamesons in him. Every night he began with the taunts, the verbal attacks. He kept on drinking, and every night he ended up attacking her. It got so bad she was hospitalised with a shattered eye socket and a broken arm, the arm she used to shield me.'

He paused, staring at me, his eyes baleful. 'That night I waited until he flaked and then I took to him with my cricket bat. No, I didn't kill him. I took the Old Testament approach, an eye for an eye, an arm for an arm. But I told him if we ever saw him again, I would kill him. The police knew enough about his activities to get me off with provocation. He has never been spotted since. But there are other women who need protecting. You understand?'

'But you can't take the law into your own hands.'

'Why not? You're Catholic. If you accept what they say, I'm going to hell anyway for my Sodom and Gomorrah perversions. So what have I got to lose? I'll see Peters when I get there. I have not one iota of regret for assisting his descent.'

'That's vigilante stuff. Lynch mob kind of thing. It's wrong.'

'Is it? Who else was protecting Clair? Except I didn't ...'

He stopped speaking, swung his swivel chair towards the window. He coughed, cleared his throat. 'There's nothing to hold Porteous on in regard to the party, but he's not allowed back to the flat. I don't know where he is.'

'Am I free to go?'

He waved me away.

'What about Peters?'

'He's dead.'

'Do you care?'

'No.'

'What about his mate? Heffernan.'

'What about him? He'll have shot through.'

I left the office, walked out of the station, nobody said anything. I had to find out about Jasper. I walked through town, hardly noticing the drizzle, tracking back the way we had driven, up The Terrace and parade, down to Devon Street. There was tape across the front and a cop car outside.

I turned around and walked to Rawhiti Terrace. I rang the bell. Peter answered the door in a thick red woollen dressing gown. I asked if I could come in. He said it was best if I didn't tonight, Sue and Jenny had taken sleeping tablets, upset after Jasper rang to say he was helping the police with their enquiries about a tragic accident at the party. He was not under arrest and had assurances he would be free once the investigation was concluded. He had not been able to get any idea when that would be. He said it would be some time in the morning, and not to wait up.

Peter shrugged, said he was sorry, but Sue had asked to be left alone for now. He offered me the key to his office, where there was a bed I could kip in. I told him there was no need. I did what Gull advised and caught the last bus home.

On the bus I picked up an abandoned paper and idly read before the bus pulled out. A special investigation was underway into the damage done by stilettos. Sue wore stilettos, and so did Clair. Heather? I couldn't remember.

Another item reported Mrs Peter Harcourt compering the Queen Margaret's Old Girls Association summer fashion parade, Kirkcaldies supplied the frocks. Not to be outdone by its adjacent department store rival, the DIC supplied the Khandallah Junior National Party fashion and coffee parade. Heather and/or Liz might have been at the former, even the latter, for all I knew. It seemed such a long time ago. At least the items, and the thoughts they provoked, kept me awake, not that there was anything to look forward to at home.

# 26

Cécile answered the door in a peach-coloured satin wrap, patting redundantly at her platinum hair. She surprised me by holding her arms out, stepping down and embracing me.

'*Mon pauvre Ste-phan*, it must 'ave been a big shock to you. This boy dying at the party, *oui*? It is *un scandale!*'

When she released me, I asked her if Sue was in. She took a step away, looking at me intently. She said Suzanne and Peter had gone to stay for a few days with his parents in Masterton. And Jasper and Jenny were with the landlord and police. She took my arms, still staring intently, said I must come in, have a tisane, it was good I called, she wanted to have a talk with me.

She let go, shivering as the sun went behind a cloud, her robe lifting in the cold breeze. She pulled it across her body, her nipples obvious under the thin fabric before she turned and entered the house. I followed her into the kitchen. She took my duffel and pointed me to a high chair beside the extended white granite bench.

The white Venetian blinds were raised and sun flicked off the harbour straight into my eyes. I looked away. She was running water into the kettle, switching on. She stood on the tiptoes of her cream leather slippers, her calf and buttock muscles tightened beneath her robe as she opened a cupboard and lifted out a packet.

'Erb tea,' she said, pirouetting and holding up the floral-patterned packet. 'Anise, chamomile and lime blossom. *N'est-ce pas?*'

I said that was fine. She spooned the tea into a creamy china pot and poured water in. She placed the pot on a white tray, got out two tall, thin glasses set in wire holders, two liqueur glasses and a small bottle of something like brandy. She saw me looking. 'Armagnac. You look as if you need a pick-me-up.' She filled the tulip-shaped glasses to the brim, handing me one.

'*Santé.*'

I returned her good health and followed her lead, draining the glass. 'Whew!' I gasped. 'That is strong.'

She smiled, joining me on the other high chair, tucking her wrap over her knees. 'Ste-phan? Do you love Suzanne?'

'Um,' I said, my swallowing function again arrested. 'Ah, yes. I think so.'

She raised a perfectly arced line of eyebrow. 'People usually know if *amour est ici*,' she said, gesturing to her heart.

I looked down at the empty liqueur glass, anywhere but at those challenging eyes. When I sneaked a look from under my eyebrows, she was pouring tea through a small strainer. She passed one to me. I had missed her refilling my liqueur glass, but not hers. She motioned for me to drink. I took the tea. It burned my lips, and tasted like it smelled, of old flowers.

'Suzanne is upset. Did something 'appen in Nelson. You met somebody?'

'No,' I said, flushing. 'Not really.'

Her eyebrow lifted, but she said nothing.

'I saw an old friend from college. She's married now. They're having a baby.'

'So soon?'

I nodded dumbly, flushing even more.

'Ste-phan, tell me what 'appened? You are so, how should I say, shifty? Have another Armagnac, it will help.'

I sipped the fiery liqueur. It did help. It irradiated my chest like a benign electric current. I could see dancing red lines flickering around my heart, a graphic parody of the exposed Sacred Heart of Jesus. I blinked. Crikey, surely Armagnac wasn't an hallucinogen?

'So why are you upset? What 'appened with this lady? Did you want a child *aussi*?'

I went into a coughing fit. She was patting my back, taking my arm, telling me it was best to come and relax. She led me down the white carpeted corridor, left and down another, past Sue's room, the other spare bedroom where Jenny was staying. We entered an enclosed sun porch with white linen drapes shutting out most of the fitful morning sun dimpling patches of white wall.

'Lie down,' she insisted, easing me on to my stomach over a wide, white linen *chaise longue*. She removed my boots and socks and then I felt her hands probing my neck muscles and reared up. She pressed her hands on my back, telling me to be still, my muscles were so tight, like *un chien sauvage*.

She began kneading my back muscles, from the neck down both sides. It was wonderful. She moved down my spine, then back up.

'This is no good,' she said, sliding her long, cool fingers under my sweater. '*Levez!*'

I lifted and she pulled it over my head, tossing it on the floor. She went up and down my back in the same sequence, then turned her hands side-on and began drumming down one side of my back. I gasped as she climbed over me, nudging me to the edge of the form and repeating the tattoo down the other side. She swung one leg over and straddled my back, leaning close and digging her fingers into my neck muscles. I was almost fainting with the exquisite agony and ecstasy of her relentless pressure.

She straddled my body as she went to work with more energetic kneading, moving lower and working on my buttocks. I felt her fingers sliding under my jeans.

'*Levez!*'

I lifted and she undid the belt and slid my trousers off, taking my underpants with them. I heard the flutter of cloth and her garment joined the jeans on the floor. I could hardly breathe.

'Relax,' she whispered as she began kneading hard into my buttocks. She moved down my legs, squeezing my calf muscles, gripping my feet between her hands, working on one toe at a time. It was unbelievably delicious. But not the sudden slap on my buttocks.

'*Tournez!*

'No,' I gasped. 'I can't.'

She laughed as she rolled me over, her strength amazing me. I was exposed, my erection painfully close to erupting.

'*Oh là là!*' she exclaimed, and I closed my eyes as her mouth encompassed my penis and I was erupting into her.

I heard her gurgle with enjoyment as she eased her body on to my face.

'Eet is my turn, *oui?*'

I buried my mouth in her, abandoning thought of my behaviour, of her daughter, of her husband, of anything. I could feel her writhing and murmuring encouragement to use my tongue, deeper, deeper, *là, là, plus fort, plus fort, oui, oui, oui*! Her mouth was again over my cock and I was becoming erect, with more murmuring and cooing, and we were bucking about and I lost all reason and surrendered myself to her.

Some time later we lay side by side, her hand idly massaging my limp member. It started to stiffen.

'*Oui, oui,*' she said, pulling me on to the floor. She was kneeling, facing away, pressing her buttocks against me. I entered her and we truly made the beast with two backs.

This time we both collapsed laughing on the white carpet, staring at the white ceiling.

'I should 'ave mirrors up there,' she laughed, mercifully releasing my exhausted member to point. 'That would be *intéressant!*' She rolled over on top of me. '*Voila!*' I massaged her beautiful bottom and we dozed for a time. I could feel her heat and sweat against my stomach, but she lifted and I felt the chill as she got to her feet, looking down at me.

'*Maintenant*, we know, *n'est-ce pas?* Join me in the shower if you wish.'

I did know exactly what she meant, that I had effectively answered her question about whether I loved her daughter. I was too engorged with her to resist poodling after her into the shower, where she soaped me all over with fragrant soap, and then began vigorously soaping the one part of me that would not relax. She laughed, splashing water over it, then descending once more upon its head, until it exploded and subsided for the final time.

We got dressed and she led me to the door. 'Pe-ter understands,' she said, her eyes large and unflinching. 'You see, before the *Libération* I was useful to a German officer. *Comprennez-vous*? It left me with, how shall I say – Freud writes of *obsessions et phobies* — compulsions, *oui*? Off you go. Don't try and see Suzanne again. *Moi, peut-être.*'

Her large eyes filled with tears but remained fixed on me as she felt for and closed each toggle on my duffel coat. She eased me out the door and shut it softly.

I stumbled down the steps, my coat a welcome protection from the gusting northerly. Even so, I shivered like Cécile had when she opened the door and welcomed me inside to an experience I could not have imagined. Now it was over so abruptly, and I was cast out and feeling as raw as the weather. Clouds scudded overhead, the pewter harbour ruffled like the rough scales on the back of a restless sea monster. I pulled up the hood and headed downtown to catch a bus or tram to the hospital in Newtown.

The severe nurse at reception had no record of anybody by the name of Clair de Lune, nor did the hospital have any record of a woman admitted with knife wounds.

'Where did you say the wounds were?'

I shook my head, told her I thought they were on her face. She asked me where the incident took place. I said I was not sure, but did that matter? Her face tightened. The victim, she said, could have been taken to Porirua or Hutt hospitals, or – she paused — a private clinic. I apologised for not thinking of any of that.

She wanted to know if I had been in touch with the police about the incident. I confessed I had not. She looked dubiously at me, suggested it was best if I took a seat, she would make enquiries. She held the phone above the high counter, gesturing with it for me to move across the bleak tiled foyer to the unappealing row of chairs against the sickly green plaster wall; the hospital actually had the legendary hospital-green walls. Only one chair was occupied, by a woman cradling one arm against her body, the other shielding a frightened child in faded pyjamas and bare feet.

I turned back to the receptionist, said I'd leave it. Her face cinched a tad tighter. Best if I wait to speak to the police, she said, starting to dial. Best, I countered, if she tended to the woman and child. I walked out.

With my hood up I crossed the road and jumped the tram downtown. At Courtenay Place I set off around Oriental Bay, up to Harold's brothel.

There was a long pause between me pressing the buzzer and the eye-hole scrutiny, before he opened the door. His dressing gown was a more elaborate red brocade than I had encountered earlier, with gold piping. There was no welcome in his face. At least he did not have his lead sock in his hand. In fact, he had his hands sunk in the large pockets sporting an 'H' monogrammed in gold piping. His eyes were red-rimmed and pouched, his face puffy, his white hair wispy and dishevelled, not the usual smooth, brilliantined middle parting. He looked at me with the doleful gaze of a chastised puppy.

I said I'd come to enquire about Clair, I'd heard she had been attacked with a knife. He nodded, murmured that he appreciated my concern, Clair was in the best care money could buy. I asked if I could see her. His face aped the rigour of the hospital nurse. He said Clair was where nobody would find her. If I wanted some free advice, I should also find a place where I was safe.

'Who from?' I said, incredulous.

'Peters has a nasty associate. Heffernan. He blames you as well as Patrick for his friend's demise.'

'That's ridiculous.'

His face reverted to the sad puppy state. 'He was here earlier, waving the newspaper, raving about getting even. Said he knew Peters shouldn't have gone there, it was a set-up. Was it?'

'Was what? He came in with his knife. He threatened me.'

'If I was you, I'd make myself scarce. I'll pass on your concern to dear Clair.' He closed the door, leaving me more bewildered than concerned.

I mooched back to town, headed up to the Symposium looking for signs of Jasper. It was closed. I went to the Mung, ordered coffee. Nobody I knew there. It was probably the least satisfactory place to read the paper, but I tried, eventually finding the report, a few paragraphs on page four referring to a tragic death at an unruly party in Devon Street. The police had been called there after receiving complaints and discovered that a young man had fallen out of a back window and been found deceased in the shrubbery.

Police were still interviewing those who attended the student hooley. They had no comment to make other than that it appeared to be an unfortunate accident which should serve to remind young people of the dangers of indulging in excessive quantities of alcohol and illegal substances. The man's name was not being given out until his relatives had been informed.

I put the paper aside, feeling depressed. The headlines assuring readers National were going to win in a landslide reminded me that Assembly today was being addressed by the amazingly named Olive Smuts-Kennedy for Labour, plus some anonymous Social Credit candidate and a Communist with the almost anonymous name of Smith. Why they wanted to address us was beyond me, very few of us had a vote. No surprise there was no National candidate appearing in this liberal enclave, no need to chase unlikely votes, National was going to hose in.

The rest of the schedule was folk dancing and gymnastics, of which I felt I had had more than enough. Nobody was going to miss me failing to appear. There had been signs on the noticeboard appealing for candidates for editor of 'Stud-Op', but that, as Pat Macaskill would pun, lacked appeal.

I felt totally apolitical about college and national politics, and indeed apathetic about life. I saw no prospects. I had lost another girlfriend. I had committed adultery with her mother. I had been a passive participant in the murder of my baby. I had nowhere to live but home, where my admittedly improved relationship with my father was predicated on him not discovering my extracurricular activities. Apart from the brief grief hug at Mum's funeral, I experienced the first genuine hug of adult times.

Even the obvious relief in it was understandable. He had been so nervous when I suddenly turned up, as if I had caught him out in something solitary. It proved the very opposite. His shifty behaviour — to use Cécile's word for me – was about his changed circumstances. He rather formally asked me to be seated, offered me a beer. It was a bit late, but I didn't want to come across contrary, so I accepted.

There followed an excessive number of enquiries about my teaching studies. He already knew about my university passes and had sent me a postal order for £100. This had come in handy for Penguin editions of more of Macaskill's Hot 100 and a slew of World Record Club purchases that brought me relief from their reminders for the foreseeable future. I had bought Sue a rather sentimental present, a heart-shaped locket inset with the only serious shot among those little photos we had taken of us at the railway station instant camera booth, me pulling faces in the other ones. In retrospect, this was not a great gift. I hoped I did better with the overdue wedding present for Jasper and Jenny, a boxed paperback set of Freud's works from Modern Books.

Dad questioned me about the Training College exams coming up, the schools where I had been on section, the activities at Training College, avoiding any comment on the liberal masters. When he had exhausted such questions, he turned systematically to what films I had seen, books I had read, music I had listened to. When I told him I had, to my own surprise, bought the World Record Club complete set of *The Messiah,* he was fulsome in his praise of the purchase and wanted me to bring it out so we could play it through one night. I assured him I would, without revealing that all my stuff that survived the party would be coming back here as soon as I was allowed to access it. About then he stalled.

I asked him how things were now he was days away from the big change. He looked startled as well as guilty, but then his face cleared.

'The election, yes,' he said, standing and offering me a refill. 'Ah, Steve, I have some more personal news.'

First we had to mop up the beer he had spilled all over the mahogany side table and the coaster depicting Queen Elizabeth I had not seen before. He laughed nervously when I said he needed to get help with his pouring hand.

'Irene and I,' he began slowly, but blurted, 'we're engaged. I hope you don't mind. I mean, it's only just happened. If I could have rung. Are you okay about …?'

'Dad,' I said, offering him my hand, 'I'm delighted. What about the Catholic thing?'

'She's divorced. He wasn't Catholic, so …'

I nodded, told him I was sorry about any attitude I'd had. Really, I said, it was neat.

He beamed like I had not seen him do in years. He was almost cravenly grateful, saying he was so worried it would upset me. He felt that it was the right time, he hoped I could join them for a celebration.

I told him I'd be happy to, but perhaps we could delay things until after his celebration of the election. He agreed it was the judicious thing to do. He could not stop smiling. He hoped I might come to see that it was good news, the country getting back on course to the prosperity it richly deserved, and he looked forward to putting his nose to the grindstone to assist in his own small way in fulfilling the promise Labour had briefly frustrated.

He stopped, realising he was back in party political broadcast mode. I held my hands up, said I had no regard for the mingy Nash government. I resisted joining Jasper in saying a pox on both your houses. Instead, I said I had some junior education reading to do for the exams. He said he was pleased I was doing so well. He approached awkwardly and grabbed me in a strong embrace, which I reciprocated.

'I love you, son,' he said. I reciprocated that too, and he turned away, saying he would probably listen to a bit of music before turning in. Fair enough, I said, I would join him if I didn't have the study. He promised to keep it low.

I retreated to my old room, opened the window, lay down with my arms behind my head, arms that had just embraced Dad, before that had embraced Cécile with treacherous and comprehensive lust. It was like a purging, a guilty and total release, something neither of us should have done, but we had. Dad had a second chance with Irene, and I was pleased for both of them. I had to credit Gull with making it possible, even if his methods were from the dark ages. There was no justification for me treating Irene coldly now that I knew her circumstances. This did not mean I wanted to share their politics.

I couldn't. Dad had left a file in the sitting room he had collected on the Hastings Blossom Festival 'riot'. It included the local papers and also the *New Zealand Herald* and the *Hawkes Bay Herald-Tribune*. The underlinings indicated what he thought important, such as the open letter from 20 incensed but anonymous Hastings 'concerned citizens', which was published in all the newspapers. It seemed to me it was a letter calculated to spread alarm and vengefulness, going on about 1000 youths attacking the police and courthouse with sticks, stones and bottles. There seemed prurient interest with reports of a drunken, bare-breasted girl carried by youths, a girl dressed only in a singlet chased down Oak Street, and sex in a lounge bar and in a doorway, while of course denouncing this licentiousness as typical of the breakdown of morals. The most indignant remarks were saved for the youth who jostled an old man in the street and launched a foul-mouthed attack, telling the old man he didn't let anybody push him around.

Jasper claimed this letter was a National Party ploy to get solid citizens frightened of this orgy of wanton violence and sex to vote for National, the party strongest on law and order. Indeed its leader Holyoake was calling for a military-style detention camp and claiming that people from North Cape to Bluff were indignant and incensed at the Hastings riot. Like Calum said at the dinner party, Holyoake was a buffoon. National wanted offenders in the 'Glass Houses' the army employed. There was a lot of squawking about judges handing down paltry fines of the order of seven pounds, when these youths needed discipline. It was depressing that National would be the next government, bringing back the hanging, flogging approach. I didn't want to be around to hear Dad defending that, Irene quite likely approving. I literally had to move on.

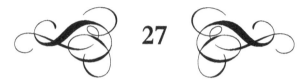

# 27

I looked at the clown with the flower, the upside-down witch/madonna, and felt sharp pangs of regret and loss. I had acted in the worst, most irresponsible manner to Melissa, I had condemned her to the physical wrench of an abortion, and I had condemned myself to mental and religious torment.

I had not come to terms with the loss of our baby, the manner in which it was procured. I scarcely thought about the absolute rules of the religion I was brought up in until this testing moment. I grieved for the child we never had, I felt the psychological loss as a severe stomach wound.

My thoughts turned to poor Clair. I had no sympathy for Peters. Yet Gull had exacted more than the Biblical eye for an eye, a face for a face. My mind relived the unfolding of the celebratory party from Sue and Jenny greeting us through the crowded jolliness to the gate-crashers and the appearance of Peters with a knife, Gull charging in, Peters retreat and fall and death. I felt more guilty than sorry about him, and the guilt was tangled up with what I should do about it.

I had been on the verge of saying something to Dad, but could not face the unravelling that would follow, the exposure of my own complicity, the disappointment I could picture on his face when he heard of my associations and behaviour. I could see no way in which he would not be deeply hurt and disappointed in me. If he knew I was part of the 'riot', that would be another blow to him. I know he regretted the abolition of Compulsory Military Training, its reintroduction one of the Old Testament-style stands of the National Party.

I could not see myself changing my viewpoint. I was not quite in Jasper's camp, more still my Labour Mum, never my National Dad and prospective National Stepmother. However, I was concerned for Jasper. Irene's own son had adopted abominable methods to entrap somebody who had done nothing to deserve his pathetic persecution. I suppose there was a measure of redemption in Gull attacking Peters, abandoning the fit-up of Jasper, even if it was triggered by his protective feelings towards the unfortunate Clair.

It was not fair that Jasper should be hounded when he had opted out of his rather frivolous and amusing anarchist sabotage of the society Dad believed in. Now it seemed Jasper would not be allowed to opt out. I didn't know what Gull intended to do with the file on the three Pommie anarchists, but he would get no assistance from me in any moves against them. I had no idea what he intended to do about me and frankly I could not care less.

I drifted off to sleep, momentarily interrupted by the ghastly whistling of the Devil in Dad's favourite opera. I thought it a strange way to celebrate a resolution of his relationship with his son, as if he somehow suspected it was only temporary. I fell asleep without formulating any solution or plan.

The next day I pondered my options in regard to Sue, Clair and Gull. I felt my first duty was not to run, as I would once have, but to face my fears. The result of facing her mother, the hospital and Harold, had left me with nowhere to turn.

What I wanted was a shoulder to cry on. There was none. I had nobody to confide in. I so wished my mother was here. But I couldn't have told her about the abortion. Or about my sexual activities. Or Gull killing Peters. I could not tell anybody about that. Who would believe me?

I needed to talk to somebody, not to seek guidance, there was none I could accept. I wanted to unburden myself. There was only one place where I could do so, without fear of any consequences. I would go to confession. I would confess my mortal sins of adultery and fornication and drunkenness and murder, the murder of an unborn child, the accessory to murder of Peters. Gull may not have meant to execute him, but was that an excuse? I was culpable for remaining a silent witness to his murderous attack.

With confession I could remain as anonymous as the Social Credit candidate or the communist Mr Smith. The priest could not reveal anything said in the confessional. I could unburden myself without consequences. I could not think past this point, beyond the possessing conviction that I would be shriven. I decided to seek out the most anonymous confessional I knew of, St Mary of the Angels.

'Bless me, father, for I have sinned. I want to confess to two murders.'

There was a grunt from behind the wire mesh grille. A low-key shriek made me cringe with the *déjà vu* connection to Mephistopheles whistling at the end of that lung-busting opera. I could hear rustling of a heavy garment and awkward movement.

'How long since your last confession?

'Ah, it is about …'

'Speak up, speak up.'

'A few years. Three, I think.' Jesus God, does it matter?

'Go on.'

I want to confess, father, to … murder.'

'You did say murder?'

The shriek returned. I lurched away from it, an involuntary movement that caused my right knee to slip off the kneeler. I flung out my right hand for balance and it cracked into the hard wood panelling. I tried to ignore the pain of barked knuckles, wanting to recover, feeling clumsy as I pushed against the smooth varnish of the grooved panels with the finger ends of one hand, my other tentatively feeling the edge of the grille. I eased myself back on to the pad, the silhouette of the priest darting about like interlocking finger shadows spooling through a dysfunctional projector. I felt claustrophobic in this dark, confined space, wishing I hadn't come, at the same time desperate to unburden myself.

There was hasty scratching that could have been taken for a trapped rodent. I sucked several breaths, not easy when I was steaming inside my duffel coat. I should have taken it off before entering the confessional. The scratching I realised was the priest tapping the grille.

'Lean forward, lad. You'll have to speak up. I haven't mastered this contraption. What was that about murder?'

I was not prepared to get any closer. His lack of mastery probably had something to do with the fumes pouring through the grille, like being downwind when the DB Brewery was pumping. Yes, I managed, my voice mimicking his hearing aid into a higher, choked register, before petering out.

'Take your time.'

'Yes, father,' I said hoarsely. I swallowed painfully, the saliva transferred by some mysterious osmosis to a prickling wet heat all over my body. I sipped in what air there was in the stifling oblong box. I might as well be inside a coffin. Buried, the way St Peter was crucified. I could hardly breathe. I thought an asthma attack was coming, something I hadn't had since I was a kid.

Where to start? I couldn't bring myself to get straight on to the abortion, and then there were the adultery, fornication, lust, concupiscence — to use a popular priestly term — drunkenness, deceit, probably pride, the whole panoply of cardinal sins, mortal sins, venial sins, you name it, I did it. God knows how he would react. My last confession four years ago – God, I'd just lied about when my last confession was, another sin. Well, back then, there was only the one significant sin, and the priest habitually conferred a lengthy lecture on the solitary activity of the miserable Onan, immortalised for spilling his seed. I had graduated to mortal sin in spades.

Start with the monty among my sins, the one against the Sixth Commandment, Thou Shalt Not Kill. Peters, the lesser of the two murders, wasn't planned, the moral culpability came in the aftermath. Like the backstreet abortion, it was later that it all came crashing in on me.

'Yes,' I whispered. 'I was a witness.'

'Speak clearly,' he said impatiently, adjusting his bulk. I could see the outline of his ear pressed against the grille. A huge ear, hosting the hearing aid like some grotesque tumour. It was disgusting, as if the ear existed by itself, evolved the better for its secretive purpose, a prop from one of those way-out Cocteau movies always screening at the Film Society. The ear twitched. 'You were a witness?'

'A friend. He used his wool hook. Um, he jabbed this joker … Gerry.'

I stopped. I shouldn't mention names. I wasn't sure what precisely I should tell the priest. I needed absolution, I had to have it, to free me from the nightmares of my own making. If I had paused for an instant, thought about the implications with Melissa, confessed to the authorities at the time I witnessed the demise of Gerry Peters. But I hadn't. I had damned myself. I was in my own hell. The simple act of kneeling in a confessional brought back a swarming sense of guilt. I blinked to clear my vision. Hair filaments embraced the hearing aid like the tendrils of a sea anemone absorbing its unwary prey. What was I saying?

Rat's feet again.

'Spit it out, lad. You were mumbling something about a wool hook?'

'Eh?'

'Have you been drinking?'

Huh! He could talk, him four sheets to the wind.

'What was that?'

'It's difficult.'

I heard him heaving about. 'Listen, laddie,' he said harshly. 'If you know anything about a crime, you must go to the police.'

'I can't.'

'You will. That is your duty. There is no absolution for your sins until you do.'

'But, father …' He had to give me absolution. That was his job. Especially for the abortion. I couldn't rationalise what had happened in the Karori house. I had not protested to the authorities on behalf of the unborn child, and nor had I borne witness to Gull's attack. On the third count, I had not resisted adultery, I had committed the mortal sin against the Seventh Commandment.

There might as well have been a cock crowing three times, for I had been, like St Peter, a coward. I turned my back on a religion I had scarcely fronted. I was a lamb at the unborn child's slaughter. I should have been a father. I should not have condoned Gull's attack. I should not have engaged in a treacherous, disloyal, deceitful lust. I had committed grievous mortal sins of omission and commission. I had to have absolution. The priest was growling something.

'What?'

'Listen to me. Go over to the Blessed Virgin and pray for help.'

'What?'

'You do know the statue of Our Lady? On the other side of the main altar. Go over there, light a votive candle. Pray for guidance. Then come back. Yes, yes, I'll be here. Now go on, collect your thoughts and return and I will hear your confession. Is that clear?'

'Yes, father.'

I looked across the dark, gleaming pews, the massive columns and ribbed ceiling of the nave, doomy as the monstrous shadows shrouding *The Cabinet of Dr Caligari*. The other side of the elaborate white Gothic castellations of the marble main altar were the flickering brass tub and its population of tiny, fluttering flames from the votive candles, silhouetting the beseeching plaster arms of the blue and white lady.

I passed by it when I stumbled in the side door, intent on confession, barely aware of the statue adjacent to the kneeler below the long marble altar rail. I knew you dropped a coin in the box and lit a candle and knelt. The priest's instruction brought back those years of pulpit ranting about obedience and the crucified Christ dying for our sins. The few feeble candles expiring in the sand of the brass tub did not inspire confidence, but I had to be shriven. I had to say the words: *Mea culpa, mea culpa, mea maxima culpa.*

I made my way across the carpet runner below the main altar. A figure was kneeling at the end of the railing, motionless, hands clutching his head. I could see drops of moisture dance in the reflected candlelight across the shoulders of his dark duffel.

Gull looked up as I approached across the carpet below the altar rail. He stood and came towards me.

'Heffernan's around somewhere. We have to get out of here. Okay?'

I glanced back at the confessional, back down the dark length of the nave, into the shadows and dim light of the heavily varnished inner doors.

'He's not going to do anything here.'

'Don't be a fool. I spoke to Harold. Heffernan is out of his tiny mind. And he blames us.'

'Yeah, Harold told me that. So?'

'I know he was in the George earlier. For my peace of mind, will you come with me? I can organise protection until we locate him.'

It was as unreal or surreal an exchange as that with the stonkered old priest. '*Murder in the Cathedral*?'

He looked puzzled. I said it was a play about the king ordering villains to murder Thomas à Becket in his cathedral.

'I'm not joking,' he said. 'If I have to, I'll take you forcibly into custody.'

'Bad for the election?'

'Come on,' he said, grabbing my arm.

'Okay, okay.'

He steered me out the side door, then pulled me violently back behind him as I heard the shout of rage and saw the figure of Heffernan lunge at him. There was a horrible grunt, Gull swung his foot and connected, Heffernan yelled an obscenity. I was on my feet and outside as Heffernan stumbled away through the gate. Gull was bent over in a strange posture, his hand tucked against him, Richard Crookback.

'Should've had the wool hook, eh?' he gasped. I saw the blood dripping and the handle of the knife stuck through his hand.

'Only way to stop him,' he gasped. 'Get an ambulance.'

He slumped against the rough concrete wall. He was looking at me, his eyes wide with shock. I checked the street and then raced back inside, across the nave, flinging open the door of the priest's booth. The old coot gazed up bleary-eyed, a small flat bottle of booze in his hand.

'Your phone! Where's your phone?'

He looked blankly at me. I reached in and grabbed the front of his soutane, got a grip and shook him. He hiccupped. 'Thish … is a house of God.'

'Fuck that! Your fucking phone?'

He waved the bottle feebly. I thought he was fending me off, then I realised he was pointing towards the side of the altar. 'Shack-risty,' he managed.

I let him go and he slumped against the grille. I ran past the altar and into the sacristy. There was a wide wooden bench with a large white linen garment draped over it, beyond it a black phone. I dialled the emergency number.

# Aftermath

Dad and Irene joined me in a long and mostly silent wait until we were allowed in to see Gull in a room to himself. He was asleep, his big face still and white, but we could see the even rise of his chest. The swathed hand was supported on a sequence of pulleys and held rigid beside him in a contraption made of metal pegs. A nurse stood nearby and the solemn doctor with bushy black eyebrows adjusted his white jacket and told us the operation to remove the knife had gone well. Mr Flynn would be kept in for several days while his blood was monitored.

'Poisoning?' Dad asked. The doctor delivered a grave nod. Irene asked if she could approach, the doctor stood aside and she leaned over and kissed his forehead. She turned with tears in her eyes, and a slight twitch of a smile.

'Thank you,' she said, offering her hand to the doctor.

He briefed us on when he expected the patient would be awake. Irene asked him what they could bring and got assurances that Mr Flynn would be no doubt ready to eat a horse come morning. Irene looked startled until he smiled and again adjusted his coat, saying that Nurse Mathews would answer any further questions they might have. He left with Irene thanking him again, me thinking that the only other Mathews I knew had been incompetent at communicating the facts of life.

The next day I visited in the afternoon. Gull was sitting up, surrounded by huge vases of every flower in the hospital florist shop, bowls of grapes and boxes of chocolates.

'All my Christmases, eh?' he said. 'Sorry I can't shake your hand, but thanks.'

I laid my mediocre bunch of daffodils on the bed and reached for his left hand. 'Left-footer and left-hander too,' I said, clasping his hand. 'It's me owes you, mate. For my life.'

'Nah,' he said. 'That drongo couldn't poke a sharp stick up a dead dog's arsehole.'

'Glad you can laugh about it. How you feeling?'

'Thirsty. I could murder a beer. Pass me that hospital piss.'

While he sucked up the dubious yellow fluid, I asked him if he'd had any visitors apart from Irene and Dad. He handed me the drink bottle, waved his good hand at the extravagant bunches of yellow roses and the riot of sunflowers, chrysanthemums, Shasta daisies, strange lilies with red stamens and gypsophila.

'Don't tell me,' I said. 'Miranda supplied the rainbow range.'

'You got it. Harold brought the weird lilies. Yeah, my boss dropped by – my ex-boss, I should say.'

'Eh?'

Gull asked me to move the bedside table hosting some of the vases of flowers and pull a chair up. The nurse appeared and he nodded at her, said he would appreciate a few minutes. She left, shutting the door.

'It's the end of the operation,' he said.

'On your hand?'

'Nah,' he laughed. 'The end of surveillance of our Pommie anarchists. I've resigned.'

He said there was no choice, he had Heffernan to thank, the tendons were irreparably damaged. He put up a hand to silence my sympathy and a half-formed remark about carrying his own stigmata. He said he was ready to chuck in the Force. He had not liked the assignment, thought it was carrying the security of the realm beyond the pale. Anyway, it was all about internal empire building, and that was done and dusted. Special Branch still had its nose out of joint after the Security Intelligence Service took over from them a few years back. His boss …

He paused, said this was telling tales out of school, but then again, he had never been a good pupil. The Superintendent told him he was still bound by the Official Secrets Act. He dismissed this with his left hand. 'Like the dire predictions of the church about hellfire and damnation, eh? All piss and wind.'

'You showing your anarchist side here,' I teased him.

'Bullshit!' he growled. 'It's the fucking rules, mate, I can't stomach, like nobody trusts you to do your job without threats.'

'Methinks he doth protest too much.' He didn't look comfortable at the suggestion of anarchy in his nature, or he was just physically uncomfortable. He wriggled about in the bed. I helped by lifting the pillow behind his back, and he continued with his explanation:

His boss was trialling a new division to demonstrate there should be a parallel security branch alongside the SIS. Gull was the guinea pig. His boss had the theory that nobody was keeping tabs on foreign agitators who had legally entered the country. The SIS was embassy-driven, chasing Reds under diplomatic beds, but nobody was infiltrating the aggrieved and extreme proponents of alternatives to communism as well as capitalism. Like our three prize anarchists.

'Bloody whingeing Poms,' he complained. 'Importing their class struggles into New Zealand.'

'I thought Dwyer was Irish.'

'They're all tarred with the same stuck-up brush. I wouldn't piss down their throats if their guts were on fire.'

'I can't speak for the others,' I objected. 'I know Jasper is dedicated to getting rid of class and privilege. That's why he emigrated here.'

'He's a troublemaker. He was dragging you into his stupid pranks.'

That was the point, I argued. They were only pranks. Did he really ever think any of them a threat?

He frowned, said he did, if they went past big-noting and put words into action. He was satisfied Dwyer and that other guy were all hair oil and no socks, but my friend Porteous was the most likely to translate waffle into action. I didn't disagree, Jasper could be hairy. I settled for saying I thought hair oil was more Peters and Heffernan than the rumpled anarchist bunch.

'A villain's a villain,' Gull scowled. 'Whatever the cut of his jib.'

'Who decides? You? Your boss? His boss? Who thought it appropriate to frame Jasper?'

Gull didn't look too proud of himself. 'Things like that go up and down the chain. Hard to say where that originated.'

'You, wasn't it?'

He shook his head, whether in denial or frustration, I'm not sure. 'Once a decision is made, there is a lot of pressure to deliver. The system decides. Everything goes upstairs for approval, okay?'

I switched tack, asking him for his expert legal opinion on whether the stalking of the Gifford dinner party guests was an infringement of their civil liberties? Didn't he believe in freedom of association? We were supposed to be living in a democracy, not a secret police state like the Russkies his lot got so fired up about. I couldn't resist the sarcasm. It seemed to me that the police and/or their political masters had made an *a priori* decision that these articulate left-wingers were subversives, and then set out to prove it.

'Huh,' he grunted. 'I can't deny there was already a watching brief on those jokers. My boss proposed and I disposed. Mine not to question why.'

'Yours just to do and die?'

There was a hint of a grin at the corner of his now clean-shaven face. 'Not quite, eh? I'm not komaty yet,' he said, flexing the two small fingers of his injured hand, the only two not swathed. 'Not unless I get an infection from that prick's knife, which wouldn't be any surprise.'

He frowned. 'Y'know, I never told you at the time. We both could have been killed by that falling lumber.'

'You said it was an accident.'

'Yeah, well, when I got up top there was nobody about. The crew were returning from smoko. They were pissed off at me asking if they'd accidentally left a stack dangling over the hold. It's only a theory, but I reckon Heffernan or Peters for it.'

'Hang on. At that time they'd nothing against us. Had they?'

'I wasn't just on the wharf to watch your back. I was supposed to be identifying anarchy, and while I was at it, nab any other criminal activity. That included Peters and Heffernan. I knew those two had graduated to pushing reefer. I suspect they knew I knew. So they were another reason to get us both off the wharf. That way, no harm done. At least, not to us. So, I guess we're quits, you saved me, and I got Peters to back off with his knife.'

I didn't want to pursue that situation. He could have disabled Peters without swinging at his head with his wool hook. No question Gull was in a murderous rage. Possibly he didn't notice the window was open; after all, Peters hadn't. But Gull showed no desire at first to bother about whether Peters was alive after the fall. Heather said about the abortion that it was my problem, and the same applied here, this was for Gull and his conscience. I asked him what happened now with the spying on the three anarchists.

'Nothing substantive came of it,' he said. 'It's a dead duck. That shit-show's no longer a concern. Special Branch is out of it. It's not just me off the case, the surveillance is kaput. My boss got his marching orders from above, told to can it.'

I asked him what he would do. He said his mum was keen on him going into the real estate business. He'd wait and see. First he had to cope with a few journos and ruddy photos. I said he would know all about the latter. He said I could piss off, and not to worry about Heffernan, he'd be picked up any minute, there was no escape.

This time I gave him the thumbs-up and said he should be perfect for real estate with his acting skills. I got out as he was reaching with his left hand for a vase, presumably to chuck at my cheeky head.

The newspapers carried photo stories on the police hero sitting up in bed, also giving the thumb-up, with his left hand. There were editorials employing the usual clichés huffing about the dangers of the job for the thin blue last line of defence, the protectors of society, who put their lives at risk confronting the increasingly vicious class of criminal spawned by the permissive modern society.

The election swept away such pontificating, the papers luxuriating in their party returning to its rightful position of power. Dad had all the facts on the record turnout of 89.8 per cent of registered 1,310,742 voters, Labour falling five per cent to 34 seats and 43.4 per cent of the vote, National up to 46 seats and 47.6 per cent of the vote. The anonymous Social Creditors did not disturb Parliament's two-party system, garnering 8.6 per cent of the vote. Heather was correct about Robert Muldoon getting in. Keith Holyoake assured his almost half of the voters that he would deliver honest government.

I shared a glass of bubbly with Dad and Irene. They wanted to congratulate me on becoming editor of 'Stud-Op' for the following year. I didn't tell them it was a set-up, Pat Macaskill putting me forward for a job nobody else wanted. Pat told me I was second choice, Jasper would have been superb.

I didn't disagree. He had got top marks in the Training College exams. I had achieved a full house: two 1s for English, a 2 for Art and Craft, 3 for Phys-Ed, History and Senior Education, 4 for Junior Education, a failure for Music. My bongo drumming had clearly not been up to scratch. Now if I had been examined on Elvis, or even *Swan Lake*, I fancied myself for the top mark.

Speaking of Elvis, there were newspaper reports he was wooing Brigitte Bardot. I could see why when I furtively crept in to see *And God Created Woman*, the audience mostly lonely men like me. I stumbled out when I saw Brigitte lying naked on her stomach. All I could think of was Cécile.

Training College had split up, suddenly I had gone from too much going on to nothing. I started reading *Clochemerle* but gave up, it reminded me of my all too brief experience of French frolics. I couldn't face Elvis in *G.I. Blues*. I had all the time in the world to get to know the two hours plus of *The Messiah*.

During his recovery period, Gull and I resumed the walks I had favoured at the beginning of this turbulent year. He coached me in the choice of the best pipi shell for aerodynamic performance, heavy along the hypotenuse for creating the correct angle-to-weight ratio to achieve lift-off. The coaching to master the critical flick of the pipi shell was a mix of the subtle and the persistent, probably akin to the wrist-spinning my father once practised but never chose to share with me.

My father was part of the era when there was not only a social division of the sexes, but a division of the age groups. At least our gap was narrowing as we shared sitting room sessions of classical music, if not of his absurdly melodramatic operas. At the start of the year I would have rated the chances of this as likely as Elvis giving up rock 'n' roll for the priesthood.

A year of shake-ups had brought some measure of closeness, but I was still my mother's left-leaning son. I fancy at the same time Gull might well have edged an anarchic step or two away from the politics his mother and my father shared, along with anticipation of the same bed. Certainly there were subjects Gull would never discuss with his mother, nor me with my father.

As for ourselves, Gull and I talked through everything, and I suppose we ended up with an unspoken pact to let the Peters incident lie in the subconscious regions of our consciences. We looked to the future, the pipi shells symbolic of flight from our earth-bound demons.

The first time I got the pipi flick, the little oval white wing lifting and lifting high into the sky until I lost sight of it, was a moment of minutely exquisite joy.

I had not fundamentally resolved or should I say absolved my moral dilemma. It helped me that initially Gull and I picked and prodded at everything we had experienced through 1960. Some of the chat was tricky. He brought up the subject of his sexual preferences, said he hated the undercover (ha ha) way he expressed his homosexual urges. He hadn't asked to have them, but they were there.

He sensed my discomfort, laughed and said he had most certainly been attracted to me the first time he saw me, on top of the pole at the Mardi Gras. It was not long after he was briefed to keep an eye on me, following the background checks into my father. I suggested he had not really obeyed his orders to rein me in.

'You amazed me,' he said. 'That slide down the guy rope. Crazy, man. I know I should have taken you home, not for a ride on the motorbike. I'm sorry if you felt disgusted or whatever when you knew about me. I want you to know I'd never have done anything without your consent. I'm a poofter, not a predator.'

Speaking of motorbikes, he reckoned the least he could do was gift me the damn thing, now he could no longer handle it. He arranged with the local traffic cop to give me an easy ride for the licence. It proved a godsend, for I was off after Christmas on it, up to Hastings.

It had been Stump's idea. He had come up to me at the last Assembly and enthused about the piss-up and stoush I provided. I said I was happy to oblige. We agreed it was terrible the gate-crasher falling to his death. I didn't say it was poetic justice, Stump was not into literary references.

We had found common ground, apparently, in the party scene. He told me about the Hastings house a bunch of the guys had rented, plenty of room with half on day shift at Wattie's and half on nights, room for one more if I was interested. He reckoned the party never had to end, there'd always been one crew available to sink a few. Find some local grommet, eh? Napier for New Year, everybody's going there.

I didn't comment on the chances of a second riot in the Bay. Rather, I was thinking that the alternative of returning to the fellmongery at the Gear did not bear thinking about. Packing peas couldn't be any worse.

'I'm a starter, Kev,' I said, extending my hand. 'Sounds grouse.'

'Extra grouse, Steve,' he said, shaking.

I needed to get active and earning and out of Wellington for awhile, away from the reminders of my disastrous love life.

Gull was also planning to get out of town. He was taking Clair, when she recovered, up to her relatives in Northland.

Meantime, we had our walks. Gull confessed one day he had been happiest in the police putting away obvious villains like Peters and Heffernan, the problems for him came with the secret stuff, surveillance of suspected saboteurs, not real police work. He insisted he had no regrets about taking the wool hook to Peters, it meant there was one less abuser out there. I repeated my suggestion at his hospital bed that there was a touch of the righteous anarchist in his make-up.

'Fuck off,' he said. 'Most of the time I did what I was told.'

'Like the German excuse they were only obeying orders?'

'Yeah, when you're in the system, you obey.'

I let it go, I wasn't going to point the finger at him. Let he who is without sin cast the first stone. I was not my brother's conscience keeper, Peters was his problem, and I would do nothing about bearing witness to Caesar's court, as that drunken priest insisted.

We agreed it was time for a fresh start. I did not go back to complete the confession, but I kept the clown with the flower facing up. It is a perpetual reminder of my cardinal sin of carelessly destroying a burgeoning love and the life of our child. It is my penance for granting myself absolution.

This is fictional autobiography inspired by Daniel Defoe's *Moll Flanders* and J.D. Salinger's *The Catcher in the Rye*. The story is based on my 1960 diary. None of the incidents and interactions happened to any living or previously living person, least of all me. In the course of researching the story, I am grateful to ex-policemen Sherwood Young and the late Bill Brien; the late Gerry Evans for insights into wharfie politics; Roger Boshier for student politics of the time; Rex Benson for anarchist history; Helen Mulgan and the Eastbourne Historical Society for Mardi Gras memorabilia; Bill Sheat for his brilliant 1960 Extrav script and related answers.

**Other titles available from Silver Owl Press:**
Visit **www.davidmcgill.co.nz** for discounts on all titles.